MARIA V. SNYDER

THE CITY OF ZIRDAI

T0363215

YOUNG
ADULT

First Published 2021
First Australian Paperback Edition 2021
ISBN 9781489252821

THE CITY OF ZIRDAI
© 2021 by Maria V. Snyder
Australian Copyright 2021
New Zealand Copyright 2021

Published by
HQ Young Adult
An imprint of Harlequin Enterprises (Australia) Pty Limited (ABN 47 001 180 918), a subsidiary of HarperCollins Publishers Australia Pty Limited (ABN 36 009 913 517)
Level 13, 201 Elizabeth St
SYDNEY NSW 2000
AUSTRALIA

° and TM (apart from those relating to FSC°) are trademarks of Harlequin Enterprises (Australia) Pty Limited or its corporate affiliates. Trademarks indicated with ° are registered in Australia, New Zealand and in other countries.

A catalogue record for this book is available from the National Library of Australia www.librariesaustralia.nla.gov.au

Printed and bound in Australia by McPherson's Printing Group

MIX
Paper from
responsible sources
FSC® C001695
www.fsc.org

About Maria V. Snyder

When Maria V. Snyder was younger, she aspired to be a storm chaser in the American Midwest so she attended Pennsylvania State University and earned a Bachelor of Science degree in Meteorology. Much to her chagrin, forecasting the weather wasn't in her skill set so she spent a number of years as an environmental meteorologist, which is not exciting ... at all. Bored at work and needing a creative outlet, she started writing fantasy and science fiction stories. Over a dozen novels and numerous short stories later, Maria's learned a thing or three about writing. She's been on the *New York Times* bestseller list, won a half-dozen awards, and has earned her Masters of Arts degree in Writing from Seton Hill University, where she is now a faculty member.

Her favorite color is red. She loves dogs, but is allergic, instead she has a big black tom cat named ... Kitty (apparently naming cats isn't in her skill set either). Maria also has a husband and two children who are an inspiration for her writing when they aren't being a distraction. Note that she mentions her cat before her family. When she's not writing she's either playing volleyball, traveling, or taking pictures. Being a writer, though, is a ton of fun. When else can you take fencing lessons, learn how to ride a horse, study martial arts, learn how to pick a lock, take glass blowing classes and attend Astronomy Camp and call it research? Maria will be the first one to tell you it's not working as a meteorologist. Readers are welcome to check out her website for book excerpts, free short stories, maps, blog, and her schedule at MariaVSnyder.com.

Also by Maria V. Snyder

Archives of the Invisible Sword series

The Eyes of Tamburah
The City of Zirdai

Sentinels of the Galaxy series

Navigating the Stars
Chasing the Shadows
Defending the Galaxy

Study series

Poison Study
Magic Study
Fire Study
Shadow Study
Night Study
Dawn Study
Ice Study (available as an ebook)

Glass series

Storm Glass
Sea Glass
Spy Glass

Healer series

Touch of Power
Scent of Magic
Taste of Darkness

Inside series

Inside Out
Outside In

This is for my husband, daughter, son, parents, sister, brothers-in-law, sisters-in-law, nieces, nephews, aunts, uncles, cousins…the entire crazy clan! And to my family who are actually reading this, I'm not worried I offended you. After all, who has the craziest imagination? Hint: It's not Uncle Joe. Speaking of uncles, I also wish to dedicate this to my Uncle Bill, a kind, loving, and funny man who will be missed.

CHAPTER

1

Sand.

It was everywhere, in everything, and unending. Shyla moved yet another heavy shovelful of the reddish-orange stuff and glared at the pile as if her censure would keep the annoying grains from returning. Of course, they would blow right on back, invariably blocking one of the many critical air vents of their new headquarters. No wonder the underground cities of Koraha had entire crews of people whose sole job was sand removal. Yet another aspect of life that Shyla had taken for granted when she lived in the city of Zirdai.

She paused to wipe the sweat from her brow. The sun was a few angles above the horizon. Its jump had just started, casting long shadows across the desert. The light breeze cooled her body. This was her favorite time of a sun jump.

Taking in the scenery, Shyla noted the distant clumps of vegetation, the rolling red dunes, the pink sky, and Rendor's muscular arms flexing as he worked. Streaks of sweat ran down the sides of his dark face and stained his sleeveless tunic. He'd taken off his sun cloak, its protective fibers not needed at this time. During the early angles, the sun warmed the land, but as it continued its jump over the sky, the heat would increase until anyone trapped on the surface would be cooked alive.

Rendor caught her looking at him. He smiled. A strange flutter brushed her heart. She ducked her head before she could grin back at him like some lovestruck ninny. After all, she was the leader of the Invisible Sword, a magical organization determined to save Zirdai from the corrupt and power-hungry Water Prince and Heliacal Priestess. Both of whom had no qualms torturing and killing innocent people.

"That sand's not going to move itself, Your Highness," Gurice called. She paused with a full bucket of it in her hands. Her job was to spread out the sand that arrived via a pulley from the deeper levels.

"It will once you teach me how," Shyla countered, ignoring the good-natured jab. She'd been called worse. With her blond hair, eyebrows, and eyelashes, she was sun-kissed and therefore an oddity among the people of Koraha.

"That would be a waste of your energy."

And exhausting herself each sun jump clearing sand was not a waste? Shyla swallowed that comment.

Everyone had been working hard to make the Temple of Arinna—their new headquarters—livable. Like all the ancient surface buildings on Koraha, the sand had eventually buried it.

And while they were happy for it to remain underground—the location was a secret after all—they still needed an entrance, escape tunnels in case of a cave-in, and vents for air shafts. Plus many of the twelve levels were filled with sand, which needed to be dug out and evenly distributed on the surface. The good news had been the inner core of the temple remained sand-free and they were able to occupy it and stay safe during the killing heat and freezing darkness.

Shyla still couldn't help being frustrated. She had so much to learn about magic, The Eyes, and the Invisible Sword. But their survival came first. They had to leave the monastery before the prince and priestess forced the monks to hand over the surviving Invisible Swords.

Instead of acquiring knowledge on her powerful new eyes, she was learning how much food and water thirty people needed each sun jump, how many collection stations were required, and how often they should be cleaned out. Not that she was complaining; it was better than being hung upside down in one of the prince's special rooms or being forced to confess her sins by the priestess's deacons. She shuddered.

The Monks of Parzival had given them some supplies along with a few more recruits…well, the acolytes had decided to join them instead of the monks. But the provisions were dwindling. A point made clear when Shyla and her team of nine retreated underground ten angles before the sun reached the danger zone at angle eighty. The temperature cooled significantly as they descended to level eight, which was deep enough to be safe from the heat. The yellow light from the druk lanterns was weak in comparison to the sun and they slowed, allowing their eyes to adjust to the dimness.

Jayden and Ximen waited for her in the common room. It was a large open area with a handful of benches, low stone tables, and cushions scattered around. A few of their members had gathered in small clumps, eating rolls of velbloud jerky. Unfortunately, jerky was the only food they were able to acquire at this time. Some groups conversed in low tones, while others played dice or other games. The entire organization had divided into three teams of ten to distribute the workload. One team slept while another rested and the third worked. Then they'd rotate.

The two men pulled Shyla aside as the others in her team filled their empty water skins and joined those not on duty for second meal. Rendor frowned, but didn't follow them. Probably due to Jayden's glare.

"We're running out of water," Jayden said to her. He was one of her seconds-in-command for three reasons: his magic was the second most powerful, he knew the city of Zirdai better than anyone, and he had a network of vagrants who provided information and resources.

"How long do we have?" she asked.

"Three, maybe five sun jumps at most."

Alarmed, she asked, "Why didn't you tell me sooner?"

Jayden tilted his head at the glass jugs lined along the wall. "Two of the new jugs are poisoned."

Back before getting involved with the Invisible Sword, she would have been shocked, but, after witnessing the Water Prince's cruelty, she wasn't surprised. If a citizen didn't pay taxes to the prince, then they didn't get clean water. Vagrants who couldn't afford the price or those who chose not to support the prince found other sources of water and took the chance it might be poisoned by the prince's guards. The vagrants had learned to give a sample of the water to sand rats before drinking it.

"Can we get more?" she asked.

"The vagrants are stretched thin," Jayden said. He exchanged a glance with Ximen, her other second-in-command, who'd remained quiet until now.

"We know where there's plenty," Ximen said.

And she wasn't going to like it. Otherwise, Jayden would have told her. He probably didn't want to spark yet another argument between them. Despite waking the power of The Eyes, Shyla hadn't earned Jayden's trust. He also hated Rendor and was used to making all the decisions. The Vagrant Prince she called him. His loyalty was split between the vagrants and the Invisible Sword. But she needed him.

"Don't keep me in suspense, Ximen."

"At our old headquarters. We have heaps of supplies that we left behind, including water."

"Left behind for a very good reason." The Arch Deacons had ambushed them, killing a number of Invisible Swords and capturing over a dozen. Only eleven escaped. And her friend Banqui was still missing. "It's probably all been confiscated by now."

"The supplies were well hidden," Ximen said.

"Doesn't matter. I'm sure someone is watching for us to return."

"We're the *Invisible* Sword, Shyla. We can bypass a few watchers long enough to confirm the supplies are there." Jayden ran a hand through his golden-brown hair—a sign he was losing his patience. "You need to remember that."

"I'm well aware," she snapped. "And you need to *remember* that the Heliacal Priestess has a dozen platinum torques that block our magic, Jayden."

They glared at each other. At one hundred and eighty-two centimeters, he was about twelve centimeters taller than Shyla. He had a thin wiry build and light sienna-colored skin.

"We can send a couple scouts to locate any watchers and check if they're protected by those torques first," Ximen said. "It's worth the risk. We're running out of food, too."

"I need to talk to Rendor first," she said.

"What for?" Jayden demanded. "He's not in charge. *We* are."

"No. *I* am. And I don't have to explain my reasons to you." She strode away.

Jayden was infuriating. He claimed he wasn't in the upper echelons of the Invisible Sword's leadership, but he certainly acted like he'd been in charge and was used to getting his own way. Good-looking and charming when he wished to be, Jayden just had to flutter those long eyelashes that framed his amber eyes and supposedly women melted.

Shyla filled her water skin halfway and grabbed a roll of jerky. She scanned the room. Rendor sat alone in a far corner. No surprise there. The others still avoided him and it would take a long time for them to forgive him. He'd earned his ruthless reputation when he was the captain of the Water Prince's guards. During those circuits, the vagrants and Invisible Swords all feared him with good reason. But he was no longer that man. Shyla had read his soul with The Eyes and had assured them he was trustworthy. Her word was the only reason they tolerated Rendor's presence among them.

She joined him, plopping on the cushion next to him. Gnawing on the end of the jerky, Shyla missed the hot savory gamelu stew and fresh vegetables served in the dining caverns. The Heliacal Priestess's deacons tended about half the flocks of velbloud and herds of gamelu on the surface and they worked in the growing caverns on level six. She could sneak in during one of the meals, but, for those who didn't pay their tithe, it would be stealing. And she decided the Invisible Swords would not steal from the priestess or the prince. Right now, they used Rendor's savings to purchase supplies. He'd been well paid as a captain and had donated them. However, he wouldn't let her tell anyone. Everyone believed the monks had given the osmiums to them. Just what she didn't need—another infuriating man.

"What's wrong?" Rendor asked.

She glanced at him.

"And don't say nothing because you're attacking that jerky like a sand demon ripping apart a fresh kill."

Shyla stopped eating. The roll did appear to be rather mangled.

"Another argument with Jayden?" he asked.

"Not really." She turned her attention to Rendor. Concern filled his dark brown eyes, the golden flecks barely visible in the dull light. "Do you remember when you said you were close to discovering the Invisible Sword's hideout?"

He stilled. Rendor didn't like talking about his time as the captain. "Yes."

"How close?"

"We determined there had to be entrances to it on levels twenty-three to twenty-five. Suspected members were spotted most frequently on those levels. But we didn't know the exact location of their headquarters."

Yet the priestess had. Someone had betrayed the Invisible Swords. Jayden suspected Banqui, her friend who disappeared after the ambush. He'd said everyone else was trustworthy. "Would the priestess tell the prince where it was?"

"No."

"Why not?"

"They hate each other and she wouldn't want the prince to have a chance to recover The Eyes, even if it's a small one."

At least they only had to worry about the Arch Deacons ambushing them.

Rendor scowled. "You're not thinking of going back there, are you? Her deacons will no doubt be watching the place."

Normally she admired Rendor's sharp intellect. This time, she braced for his arguments as she told him what she'd discussed with Jayden.

"It's not worth the risk," he said.

"We're running out of food and water."

"Still not worth it. But if you're determined, pay a couple vagrants to check it out."

She wasn't sure she could trust them. Plus the deacons would be suspicious. No, they'd have to send someone who knew the location, someone who was good at staying hidden, and someone who had powerful magic. Jayden, Mojag, and her.

Rendor clasped her hand. "It's suicide, Shyla. The Heliacal Priestess and Water Prince don't care about *any* of the Invisible Swords. Except you. You're the prize they both want."

"I can't hide here when my people are in danger. That's not how this is going to work."

"I know. But you can't blame me for trying."

She squeezed his fingers. Her golden-brown skin was a few shades lighter than his. He blended in well with the shadows. But with his powerful frame and oversized shoulders, he stood out among the citizens of Zirdai. About eight centimeters taller than Jayden, he loomed over all the Invisible Swords, unintentionally intimidating them. At one point in time, he intimidated her. But she'd grown immune to his scowls, glares, and imposing body language. Well, mostly.

Rendor tilted his head in Jayden's direction. "I'm guessing you'll take him."

"Yes, but we're just going to do a little reconnaissance."

"I can help."

"I know."

"Are you sure you do? I can do more than shovel sand," he grumped.

"I'm sure. But let's face it, you look mighty fine when you shovel sand."

He leaned closer. "Sunbeam, I'd be happy to give you a private show anytime." His voice rasped low and husky.

She swallowed. Was the room always this warm?

He laughed at her expression. Annoyed, she swatted his arm with her free hand. It was like slapping marble. Rendor laughed harder.

* * *

Before they left for their mission, Jayden insisted on teaching her how to cover their tracks in the sand. Jayden, Ximen, and Shyla stood in the desert near the temple at angle one-sixty. Waves of heat rose from the dunes as the sun neared the end of its jump. They'd planned to enter the city at angle one-eighty when all the other citizens were returning home before darkness.

"The monks taught me—"

"How to walk without leaving footprints behind," Jayden finished for her. "This is different and doesn't require special wide-soled boots. It requires magic."

In that case, Shyla was more motivated to learn.

"Remember when the Invisible Sword ambushed you and Rendor?"

Hard to forget. Twelve of them had sprung from the dune, grabbed her and skewered Rendor with two swords. "Are you going to teach me how to travel through sand?" Finally!

"No."

"But—"

"Baby steps, Shyla," Ximen said. "Moving grains of sand is like rolling marbles. If you try to roll too many at once, you'll lose control. Only with practice can you roll large quantities."

"Magic is the real reason we're called the Invisible Sword," Jayden said.

"Really? I thought it was because we can use it to make people think we're invisible, and because we stay out of sight."

"That's a part of it as well, but magic is invisible and it's a weapon that we wield like a sword. Hence, an invisible sword. We call people who can use the magic wielders. When the organization first formed, only wielders were members of the Invisible Sword. However, in the five hundred thousand sun jumps since, there have been fewer and fewer people born with the potential to wield magic." Jayden swept a hand out. "Sand responds to our magic like people do. We push our will at someone and suggest a person falls asleep. You start with one person but eventually you can work up to putting many people to sleep." Jayden turned around, gazing at their three sets of boot prints that trailed back to the temple. "I'm going to concentrate on a patch of sand and suggest it cover one of the prints."

Shyla stared at their tracks. The movement was subtle, as if a slight breeze blew over just that narrow patch. The boot print slowly filled in and disappeared, leaving behind smooth, untouched sand. Impressive.

"Why does the sand respond?" she asked. "It's not alive. It doesn't have a consciousness like a person."

Jayden bent over, scooped up a handful, and held it close to her. Piled in his palm, the mound of individual grains reflected various hues of pink, red, orange, tan, and purple.

"Our ancestors are part of this sand," Jayden said. "As it slowly and inexorably buried their cities and forests, as it filled their lakes and oceans, the sand consumed them as well. Over many circuits the sand is blown away, exposing the skeletons to the abrasive wind. Over time, the bones are reduced to the size of sand grains. This sand remembers who it used to be."

Not sure she believed that was the real reason, Shyla had to admit the sand followed orders. "What command did you use to move it?" she asked him.

"Cover."

"I use smooth," Ximen said. He swept his hand out with his palm facing down. Two boot prints faded away.

"It doesn't really matter what word you use. It's your *intention* behind the command," Jayden said. "Now you try it."

Shyla considered. When she stepped in the sand, the grains compressed under her boots and were pushed out to the sides. She focused on one of her prints, gathered her will and thought, *Return*.

The print started to lose its sharp edges, then it stopped.

"You need more force," Jayden said. "Try again."

It took her multiple tries to erase one print. Each time the print softened, but she couldn't get it to disappear

13

with one command like Jayden had. It took her three or four times.

"Try harder," Jayden snapped, losing patience.

She added her annoyance at him to her magical suggestion. *Return!* Six prints vanished at once.

"Look at that," Ximen said. "You should have made her mad sooner, Jay."

Jayden gave him a sour look.

Ximen ignored him. "It'll get easier with practice and eventually, as you walk through the sand, you'll be able to erase your tracks as you go almost without thinking about it." He demonstrated by striding away. As each of his feet lifted, the sand flowed right back to erase his print. Turning, he grinned at her. "Creepy, isn't it? Another reason we're called the Invisible Sword."

* * *

Shyla crouched in a shadow, watching for ambushers. This mission was dangerous but necessary. Jayden and Mojag waited nearby. The tunnels leading to the Invisible Sword's last hideout were narrow and dark. No druk light shone from them. The fact that Tamburah's temple connected to Zirdai and no one except the Invisible Sword had known about it for five hundred thousand sun jumps still amazed her. She wondered what other discoveries lurked within the labyrinthine depths of Zirdai. The city had ninety-nine underground levels, if she included the level with the prison and the special torture rooms, and the very bottom level where the black river flowed.

"I don't see anyone," Jayden whispered.

Neither did she. And that wasn't comforting. It could mean the watchers were well hidden. It was angle two-twenty. Not many people were out and about at this time, but there were enough that the three of them didn't draw unwanted attention.

"Mojag, do you remember the route?" she asked.

He huffed. "Of course. I've done this lots of times."

"No you haven't," Jayden said. "You've only been there once and that was right before we were attacked."

"That *you* know of." Mojag smirked at him.

"Did Gurice take—"

"Nah. Followed you."

"How—"

"You can discuss this later," Shyla said.

Mojag opened his druk. Orange-tinted light spilled out, indicating they were somewhere between levels thirteen and twenty-four. Druk light changed color with depth—a vital tool for those who were easily lost.

Mojag headed into the tunnel. He was dressed in a green tunic and flared striped pants woven from gamelu fibers. The clothes were shabby but clean and warm. Jayden and Shyla also wore similar clothing except she had her wrap to cover her hair. Most of Zirdai remained at a constant ten degrees Celsius. Only the upper five levels fluctuated, going from zero during darkness to sixty degrees during the kill zone. Shyla had lived on level three. She enjoyed access to sunlight via a mirrored pipe to the surface, but she had to descend to level six every sun jump to survive the heat.

They were currently on level twenty-two. The people who lived here had enough coins to pay their taxes and tithe, but not much extra. Mojag fit in without calling attention to himself. Tall for thirteen circuits old, he was all gangly arms and legs.

Shyla clasped her hands together when he disappeared. If anything happened to him, she'd never forgive herself. A surprise, since at one point she would have happily killed the little sand rat.

If Mojag ran into an ambush, he'd claim he was lost. Neither the deacons nor the guards should recognize him. While his older sister, Gurice, had been an Invisible Sword for circuits, Mojag hadn't been old enough to be invited and tested for magic. No longer. Desperate times called for desperate measures and they needed him. Once things settled down, he would be tested.

Waiting for the boy to return was almost torture. Shyla stood up half a dozen times with the intention of running to Mojag's rescue, but, each time, Jayden tugged her back down.

"Relax. He's been a vagrant since birth, he knows what he's doing," Jayden whispered.

It wasn't Mojag's skills she was worried about. The Invisible Swords had been murdered by the Arch Deacons without mercy. And those same deacons might be lying in wait. They might not even bother to question Mojag before killing him. Shyla turned to voice her concerns but stopped. Tension rolled off Jayden's shoulders. He and Mojag were like brothers. Jayden already understood the risks. No need for her to remind him. Instead she concentrated on keeping still.

When Mojag returned, Shyla relaxed.

"Well?" Jayden asked.

"There's two Arch Deacons watching the entrance into twenty-two, but I slipped around and checked the hidden one on twenty-four and there's nobody there," Mojag said.

"Did they see you?"

"Nah. Smelled them before I even got close. I covered the druk and crept up on them. Not that they would have heard me over their conversation. They're bored out of their skulls."

It had been twenty-five sun jumps since the massacre. How much longer would the priestess keep them here? "How do you know they're Arch Deacons?" Shyla asked. "By their clothes?" Deacons wore oversized green robes, but Arch Deacons wore green tunics and pants. They were the priestess's elite fighting unit.

"Nah, they're waiting in the pitch dark. By their stench." Mojag seemed to think that was all the explanation required.

"Arch Deacons attend a special blessing ceremony every sun jump," Jayden said. "The Heliacal Priestess lights an incense that smells like burnt hair."

"It's awful," Mojag added.

"Then let's avoid them and go another way to twenty-four," Jayden said, leading them toward a different tunnel.

They followed Jayden through a series of tunnels, up a set of stairs, and down a spiraling ramp.

"Is all this necessary?" she asked. Shyla remembered when he took her to the Invisible Sword's headquarters the first time. She'd suspected he tried to get her lost so she wouldn't be able to find the place again.

"Yes. All the routes to reach the hidden entrances are complex. We couldn't be invisible if anyone could accidentally find it." He glared at Mojag, no doubt remembering Mojag's earlier comment.

The boy ignored him. Shyla considered. If Mojag was able to follow Jayden without alerting him, did that mean Mojag blocked magic like those torques? No. Shyla had been able to read Mojag's surface emotions. There must be another reason. Perhaps Jayden put too much faith in the confusing tunnels and wasn't as vigilant as he should have been. Too bad Shyla had promised not to read Jayden's soul. Not without a good reason.

Eventually they arrived at a dead end. Or rather what appeared to be a solid wall. Jayden ran his fingertips along an almost invisible seam until he reached a slight depression in the stone which he pressed with the pad of his thumb. Strange that Shyla noticed it now when the last time she'd been at one of these not-doors, the opening mechanism wasn't visible. Was it due to the power of The Eyes? It could be she wasn't as distracted. Back then she had just determined the Invisible Sword had tricked her into helping them, which had ruined her prior—trouble-free—life.

The not-door swung open. A musty scent mixed with an acrid odor wafted out. No burnt hair smell or the putrid stink of decomposition. Yet. Shyla worried that the priestess hadn't taken proper care of the bodies. When someone died, the body was wrapped in cloth and taken to level one to shrivel. Once baked until no moisture remained, it was buried in a massive sand graveyard. If not dried prior to burial, surface predators like the sand demons would dig up the body for a snack.

Jayden ushered them inside and closed the door. They paused to listen. Silence filled the tunnel. She hoped that was a good sign that no one waited to ambush them. Once again Jayden took the lead. He'd covered almost all of the druk; its weakened light stretched only a meter in front of them. Soon they reached the living area. Dark red stains were soaked into the floor. Jayden's expression hardened as he stepped around them.

"The storeroom's this way," he whispered.

Shyla and Mojag stayed close behind him. Jayden shone the light in the various rooms as they passed. All of them had been ransacked. They entered a large open area that appeared to have been a common room. The stone tables had been knocked over and broken. Jayden wove through the destruction, heading toward a tunnel on the opposite side. After a series of turns, he stopped at a T-intersection where another hidden door blended in.

"This is it." He set the druk on the ground then pulled his knife from his belt.

Mojag yanked his free as well. Shyla didn't carry a weapon. Instead, she slid her feet into a fighting stance and raised her arms so her hands could protect her face and chest from an attack. Trained by the monks in the Ways of the Yarin, Shyla had learned defensive techniques that were very effective against swords and knives. Rendor had offered to teach her how to use a sword so she could handle multiple opponents. Deciding that was a good idea, she planned to take him up on it once they had some time. Unfortunately, that was in as short supply as food and water.

Jayden found the latch and opened the door. The three of them braced for an attack.

They weren't disappointed.

CHAPTER

2

Two Arch Deacons rushed from the storeroom. Their knives glinted in the weak light.

"Left," Jayden called, pushing Mojag behind him. The boy was handy with a blade, but not trained to go toe to toe with an Arch Deacon.

That meant the guy on the right was Shyla's. He lunged, aiming the tip of his long skinny knife at her chest. Surprised, she shuffled back. He pressed forward, stabbing out again. Seven hells, the big man was fast. Unease swirled around her heart. Perhaps the theory that the priestess wanted her alive wasn't accurate. Shyla met his gray-eyed gaze long enough to know he wore a protective torque.

Twisting sideways, she knocked his next thrust wide and grabbed his wrist with both her hands. He jerked his knife arm, pulling her toward him and slightly off balance. The man was as strong as Rendor. She let go, but not quick enough. His punch missed her jaw, but the knuckles on his fist slammed into her shoulder. Pain exploded as the rest of her arm went numb.

Shyla retreated, backing down a tunnel. The good news—the narrow area limited him to a straight-on attack with no chance of getting behind her. The downside was the fading light. The darkness increased with each step.

"Oh no you don't," he said, picking up his pace. "You don't get to disappear again."

Out of options, she blocked his lunge and clasped his arm again. But this time when he yanked his wrist, she used his momentum to shuffle close, kicking him hard in the stomach. She followed him as he stumbled back, staying right up against his chest. One advantage to being smaller than your opponent was the ability to tuck inside. Before he could recover, Shyla cracked his jaw with a well-placed uppercut.

Instead of disengaging, the Arch Deacon cursed and wrapped his arm around her, holding her tight. His knife stabbed toward her side so she twisted and kneed him in the groin. The blade cut across her lower back instead as he bent in half with a groan. A distant part of her mind registered the burning pain. The rest of her struggled to break his hold. The son of a sand demon was a brute.

Then the Arch Deacon yelled. He released her and spun around to face Mojag. Grinning, the boy held a bloody knife. A wet stain spread on the back of the brute's tunic. When he advanced on Mojag, Shyla kicked him hard, aiming for his injury. The Arch Deacon dropped his weapon and staggered to the ground.

Before she could draw a full breath, Mojag had his knife on the man's neck.

"Stop," she ordered, putting magic into the words and stopping his hand.

Mojag looked up. "Why? He was going to kill you."

"We don't kill unless we have absolutely no other choice."

"But he'll just come after us again."

"Probably, but he's just following orders."

"So?"

"So we need to stop the one who is issuing those orders."

"Yeah, but he's going to go back and say we're soft. They'll think they have the advantage."

"Maybe. Or perhaps he'll remember we showed him mercy. And he might start to think that we're not the villains the Heliacal Priestess claims we are."

Unconvinced, Mojag huffed. Just then Jayden strode into view. Blood dripped from a small cut on his cheek. His rumpled clothing and mussed hair indicated he'd had a difficult fight as well.

"Are you all right?" she asked.

"Fine." Then he smirked. "That Arch Deacon is going to have a hell of a headache when he wakes up, though." He glanced down at the man on the ground.

Shyla's opponent's gaze remained on Mojag whose blade still rested on his throat.

"Mojag, remove his torque, please," Shyla said, releasing the boy from her magical hold.

He wrenched the necklace off the man, leaving behind scratches that welled with blood. The man touched his throat but didn't move. Both Jayden and Mojag loomed over him with their knives in hand.

Shyla, though, crouched down and met his gaze, reading his soul. In pain, his emotions flipped between fear, confusion, and hope he might live through this and not bleed to death.

"Tell me how many torques the priestess has," she ordered.

There had been a dozen—nine now if they took his and Yarb's, but he wasn't telling this sun-kissed anything.

"How about the food and water in the storeroom? Is it safe to eat and drink?" she asked.

Of course not. The priestess was smart enough to poison it just in case he and Yarb failed. "Yes," he said.

Shyla suppressed a sigh over his lie. He either didn't believe what The Eyes could do or didn't know the extent of their power. Good news for her. "Does the priestess know where we are?"

Until this encounter, the Blessed One worried the Invisible Swords had moved to another city. Learning they were still here and might eat the poisoned provisions would help him remain in her favor after this fiasco. "Yes."

"How?"

He scrambled to come up with a convincing lie. "She has prayed to the Sun Goddess who has told her your location." Hopefully the heathens would panic and leave their current hideout, making them easier to find.

Turning to Jayden, Shyla said, "You were right. We better leave the city."

Jayden played along. "I'm always right."

The Arch Deacon couldn't understand how these fools lasted this long without being caught and killed.

Shyla kept her expression neutral even though she wanted to punch the man. "Last question. What are the priestess's orders regarding me?"

This one was easy. "She wants you dead or alive. It doesn't matter as long as your stolen eyes are intact."

She laughed. As if The Eyes could be stolen. The Eyes of Tamburah had been in the Invisible Sword's possession since they assassinated Tamburah nearly fourteen hundred circuits ago. They were crafted from priceless gemstones—sapphires, black diamonds, rubies, and pure white topaz—and resembled real eyes in both size and shape. They contained powerful magic but required a leap of faith and a sacrifice to use them.

If The Eyes stirred in a person's hands, that meant they had the potential to wield them—though there were no guarantees. The sacrifice was exchanging their real eyes for the gemstones. Shyla had taken that leap and Rendor had cut her eyeballs from their sockets. The Eyes had woken, healing her injuries and allowing her to peer into others' souls along with other abilities that she was still learning.

The Eyes were rightfully hers. Plus she doubted the prince or the priestess had the courage to make that sacrifice.

"Thank you for the information," Shyla said to the Arch Deacon. She gathered her will and directed it toward him. "You will forget that you fought with me. Instead you will remember fighting with an Invisible Sword member. You will forget this conversation. Sleep," she ordered.

The man's body relaxed.

Jayden peered at her. "I didn't know you learned how to erase memories. Are you sure it worked?"

"Why wouldn't it work? You taught me yourself. Don't you remember?" Now it was her turn to smirk. Better that than snapping at him in annoyance for doubting her.

"Me? When? Did you…"

She laughed at his panicked expression. "Relax, Jayden. I didn't erase your memories."

"Then how did you learn to do that?"

Gesturing to the prone Arch Deacon, she said, "When I'm reading a person's soul, he's mine. His thoughts and emotions are like patterns in the sand and I can smooth some out, redraw others, and add my own. It's instinctual and rather easy." And so very tempting to smooth out Jayden's lingering suspicions and doubts. But she wasn't Tamburah and she wouldn't abuse her power. And if she did, Rendor promised to remove The Eyes.

"You know he was lying, right?" Jayden asked.

"Of course. Did you get the torque from your opponent?"

"Of course."

"He didn't tell us anything useful," Mojag whined.

"Oh, he told me quite a bit. He just doesn't know he did." She put her hands on her hips. "You both know what The Eyes can do, right? Or are you like this man, who refuses to believe?"

Mojag ducked his head. "All I know is that they gave you power."

Jayden had the decency to appear abashed. Before he could respond, she turned to Mojag. "I'll explain later. For now, can you take us to those two Arch Deacons on level twenty-two?"

"Yeah."

Jayden glanced at her. "You want to take their torques?"

"Might as well. After this, the priestess will know for sure that we're aware of their protective properties. Then she'll ensure the Arch Deacons travel in bigger packs."

They returned for the druk and Mojag led them to the tunnel with the waiting ambush near the entrance on level twenty-two. As she walked, her tunic rubbed against the cut on her lower back, increasing the burning pain. When she woke the power of The Eyes, they had healed all her wounds and erased all her scars. But unfortunately it was a one-time occurrence.

When they neared the Arch Deacons, the boy wrinkled his nose and stopped. He must have a good sense of smell because Shyla couldn't detect the scent of burnt hair here or when she had fought the other man. No sounds of a conversation reached her, either. Did he have sensitive hearing as well or had the Arch Deacons been alerted to their presence?

"This is how it's going down," Jayden whispered. "We'll snuff the druk, creep up on them, then Mojag will uncover the druk right before Shyla and I jump the Arch Deacons. Mojag, you can distract them while we fight. Got it?" he asked.

She nodded. It was a solid plan. Yet it annoyed her he'd taken charge. And it annoyed her that she was being petty about it.

"Good. Mojag, you go first. When we get close, open the druk and dodge to the other side of the tunnel."

Mojag stood next to the wall with the druk. Jayden was right behind him and Shyla last. Jayden put his left hand on the boy's shoulder and his other on the wall. Mimicking Jayden, Shyla clasped his shoulder and placed her fingertips on the cold stone. This way they had contact with each other and hopefully wouldn't stumble in the complete darkness. A nervous tremble traveled through her legs at the thought of being in the dark.

"Now," Jayden said.

Mojag snuffed the light. She gripped Jayden's shoulder. Hard. Her fingernails dug into his flesh.

"What's wrong?" he hissed.

"I can't see." The panic in her voice was unmistakable.

"Hold up, Mojag." He pried her hand off and his boots scuffed on the floor. "That's the point. What's really wrong?"

"I'm…very uncomfortable being in the dark."

"And you're just figuring this out now?" Jayden's tone was incredulous.

"I haven't been in the dark before now." In fact, the thought of being in the dark scared her more than fighting Arch Deacons.

"Don't you sleep?"

She really didn't want to have this conversation now, but Jayden needed to know. "I always have a druk on low when I sleep. I can't…ever since I was locked in the dark for twelve sun jumps, I can't…I don't…I avoid being in the dark."

"So our fearless leader is afraid of the dark? Heck of a time to tell us."

She'd never claimed to be fearless. In fact, her fears increased with all her new responsibilities. "Can we talk about it later?" she snapped. "I don't know how long I can…tolerate it."

"How about a quick magic lesson?"

"What? Now?"

"Yes. Your magic can sense others nearby. It's a handy skill and helps us avoid encountering people. It's similar to gathering your will and directing it at a person. Instead, you send it out in a wide arc to seek. And if anyone's within five or six meters, you'll know. Not who they are or what they're doing, but you do get a vague sense if they're coming toward you or heading away."

"That is handy." She thought about it. "How does this help me now?"

"You can use that to *see* me and Mojag. You won't truly be blind."

"Oh."

"Try it." Amusement colored his voice.

She followed his instructions, sending her magic forward. Two…bumps rippled her magic, and if she focused, she picked up Mojag's surface thoughts. It appeared that once she'd read a person, she could link to their thoughts even in the dark.

"Did it work?" Jayden asked.

"Yes. Thank you." Her breathing calmed and the blackness wasn't so…menacing.

"You catch on quick. Must be because of The Eyes. Just remember it won't work if the Arch Deacons are wearing torques like the two hiding in the storeroom. That's why Mojag's in the lead," Jayden said. "Okay, let's try this again."

They resumed their creep. Shyla was glad for the soft soles of her dillo leather boots. Eventually, the scent of burnt hair—Mojag was right, it was vile—filled her nose. Jayden stopped and touched her fingers on his shoulder—a signal to let go and get ready. She released her hold and prepared to attack.

"Now," Jayden ordered.

Mojag opened the druk. Orange light spilled out, revealing the two Arch Deacons. Being caught completely off guard, the two didn't stand a chance. Between her, Jayden, and Mojag, it took a fraction of an angle to knock them unconscious. She put their torques into her pack.

"You're bleeding," Mojag said behind her.

She tried to downplay it. "It's just a scratch from the other fight."

"Scratches don't soak your tunic," Jayden said. "Keep still. Let me see." He lifted the material.

Cool air caressed her skin, sending a shiver up her spine.

"It's deep. We need to get you to Zhek."

"We need to get back before the Arch Deacons wake up or the next shift arrives," she said, yanking down her shirt.

"Don't be stupid. You could get sick if it gets infected. Zhek's at Orla's commune on level thirty-nine. It's not far."

"How do you know where he is?" she asked a bit petulantly.

"I'm the Vagrant Prince. I know where all my people are."

Mojag chuckled.

When she didn't follow Jayden right away, he grabbed her wrist and tugged her along. "They're your people, too, Shyla. The Invisible Sword was formed to protect the people of Zirdai from tyrants. *All* the people."

"I'm well aware, Jayden. Except that's a tall order at this time. We only have thirty of us. We need to secure the means to our survival first and then we can right the very long list of wrongs."

For once Jayden didn't argue. Shyla almost fainted from the shock. Instead she followed him as he navigated the twists, turns, ups, and downs that she had come to realize was required to travel through Zirdai without encountering anyone.

The druk light turned red when they entered level twenty-five and stayed red until they reached level thirty-six where it changed to green. A fluttering in her stomach started about then. The last time she went to Orla's commune, she had to cross a thin plank over a deep vertical air shaft. It hadn't been the best time to learn that she was uncomfortable with heights. However, on the way back, Adair had pushed her off and she fell twelve levels until she hit a net, which saved her life. The man hadn't warned her, nor did he tell her about the lifesaving device. Jayden had theorized Adair was probably angry because she'd found their well-hidden commune.

Despite the fact she survived, Shyla wasn't in any hurry to cross that plank ever again. She'd happily avoid it for the rest of her life.

And perhaps Jayden sensed her unease. They entered the edges of the commune from a different direction. The guards hidden in the shadows nodded at Jayden as they passed.

Orla was in charge of the largest vagrant community in Zirdai. She had plenty of room since technically the levels they occupied were outside of the city's limits, which were loosely defined by the major vertical air shafts. Zirdai was roughly bowl shaped with the deeper levels narrower than the upper levels.

"Do all the communes have multiple entrances?" she asked him.

"Yes. There's always the danger of a raid. Even though this one is well hidden, they still have at least five different exits."

That was three more than their hideout. Shyla considered how to add at least another. Then she remembered the old headquarters had been under Tamburah's temple, which was three kilometers away from the city, but Jayden hadn't taken them to the surface to reach it. Had the Invisible Sword built tunnels to connect the two or were they already there? She'd have to ask Jayden later.

A dozen druk lights shone from the heart of the multi-level commune. Shyla blinked in the brightness. Shouldn't everyone be asleep? She checked the sand clock. It was angle three-forty. "Why all the light?" she asked Jayden.

"Vagrants don't follow the standard sleep schedule of the rest of Zirdai," he explained. "Most raids come during darkness and moving around the city is easier in the late angles of a sun jump."

They entered the main area. Ladders stretched between levels, curtains covered doorways, and colorful cushions and furniture decorated common areas. The pleasant aroma of incense and cleanser floated on the air. A few kids spotted Jayden and Mojag and dashed over to ask them questions in a breathless rush. Adults worked at various tasks, crafting goods to sell at the market. Others bustled about. It was a bubble of peace. They didn't need the Water Prince's guards or the Heliacal Priestess's deacons here. Yes, they had to find their own food and water, but they policed themselves and prayed to the Sun Goddess on their own terms.

Of course this wouldn't work on a larger scale. There was a reason for guards and organized religion helped a number of people. Unfortunately for Zirdai's citizens, those in charge had been corrupted by the power. She hoped that wouldn't happen to her.

Orla spotted them and hurried over. Gray streaked her black hair, and although older, she moved with the same energy as a child only a few circuits old. Her gray-eyed gaze met Shyla's. The woman's curiosity blasted Shyla and was followed by wonder and awe. Surprised by Orla's intensity, Shyla strengthened her mental shield. It'd been easy to block Mojag's rambling thoughts and, since she hadn't read Jayden's soul, she didn't pick up his thoughts and emotions.

"Your eyes," Orla said, stepping closer. "They've changed color."

Oops. Shyla glanced at Jayden.

"Orla helps the Invisible Sword from time to time," Jayden said. "Who do you think has been supplying us with water these last six sun jumps?"

"Thank you," Shyla said.

Instead of answering, Orla cupped Shyla's cheeks. Her bony fingers were cold. "I knew you had greatness in you. Even shunned as a sun-kissed, you persisted, and look at how the Sun Goddess has rewarded you."

More like ordered her, but Shyla wasn't going to correct the woman. She'd only told Hanif about her... encounter with the Sun Goddess that may or may not have been a heat-induced delusion. *I do not enjoy seeing my people suffer,* the goddess/delusion had said to her. *Make it stop.*

Orla released her. "I'm sorry I don't have any extra jugs of water for you." She gestured to the others nearby. "The last batch we received was all poisoned. We are rationing what we have until another source can be found."

"That's terrible. We're not here for that. You've done more than enough," she said.

"Where's Zhek?" Jayden asked. "Shyla's injured."

"It's minor," she rushed to assure Orla while frowning at Jayden.

"He's checking on Darma. Her baby is due soon. I'll let him know you're here. In the meantime, please help yourself to some refreshments."

As the woman hurried off, Shyla wandered around. She wasn't going to drink any of their limited water. Jayden and Mojag went to talk with who she presumed were friends or maybe family members. It occurred to her that, other than Mojag's sister, Gurice, she didn't know anything about Jayden or Mojag's family. There just hadn't been time to learn. Maybe if she understood Jayden's life better, they wouldn't argue so much. She added it to her list of tasks.

First on that long tally was getting clean water. She needed to understand how the black market for water worked. Then she had to secure a supply they could trust, which meant paying more coins per jug. And that led to earning coins. Shyla imagined setting up a market stall, hawking soul readings for two osmiums. Ah, no. What else could she do?

Shyla almost laughed out loud at her next thought. She could sell sweets to the treasure hunters. That had been how she survived when she'd first arrived in Zirdai, locating valuable artifacts for the hunters. However, she had switched to working with legitimate clients. And the thought of those treasures being sold to black-market dealers and collectors didn't sit well with her.

She doubted the Water Prince's new archeologist would hire her to find temples and castles that had been buried by the sand. Who else would? The history professors? Well…not the ones in Zirdai. Perhaps in another city but— The answer popped into her mind. Aphra! A treasure hunter who sold her sweets to professors in other cities. It was a compromise Shyla could live with. Her good mood lasted until Zhek arrived.

"Ten sun jumps," Zhek said instead of a greeting.

"Excuse me?"

"You managed to stay healthy for ten whole sun jumps." His grumpy tone implied it was unacceptable.

"I've missed you too, Zhek."

His bushy white eyebrows shot up into his mess of white hair in surprise. "Well, er…" He cleared his throat. "Where are you injured?"

She turned and showed him the cut on her lower back. Zhek tsked, hustled her into an examination room, and instructed her to lie down on a table on her stomach. Once the numbing paste soothed the pain, she ceased listening to his admonishments as he stitched the skin closed.

Shyla fell asleep soon after Zhek finished, but she didn't rest for long. Jayden woke her at angle three-fifty-five. Only five more angles before the sun started its jump.

"We need to go if we're going to get out of the city without attracting attention."

She suppressed a groan. He was right. Angle zero was the perfect time to slip out with all the others who went to the surface: the velbloud caretakers, the deacons who joined the Heliacal Priestess for her early angle worship service, archeologists with their diggers in tow, and various others.

However, since she was already in the city, she needed to do a few more things. "Send Mojag back to headquarters to tell everyone we're going to stay another sun jump," she said.

His shoulders tightened. "Did you forget about the Arch Deacons we attacked already?" His tone implied she was an idiot.

Instead of snapping back—something she'd done in all their prior arguments—she kept her voice even. "No. In fact, they're one of the reasons I want to stay. By now, they've reported to the priestess that the Invisible Sword is still around and deacons will be stationed at all the city's exits." She held up a hand to stop his retort. "I know we can use our magic to slip by them, but I've a couple other tasks and need your help."

The tension eased from him. Shyla refrained from celebrating. While Jayden went to find Mojag, Shyla changed into a clean tunic. She folded the stained one. The blood had dried, stiffening the fabric and making it difficult to stuff into her pack. The four torques clinked together. They needed to be hidden somewhere very safe. The Monks of Parzival had kept The Eyes of Tamburah safe for close to half a million sun jumps. Perhaps she should give them to Hanif to put in the Fourth Room of Knowledge. Not many monks had permission to access that room.

While growing up in the monastery, and even after she left, Shyla was allowed in the First Room of Knowledge. She earned the right to enter the Second Room of Knowledge when she retrieved a vial of "water" from the black river for Hanif—it had ended up being a rivulet of blood. She hoped to be able to earn admittance to them all—it would be a first for someone who was not a monk.

"Mojag isn't happy to miss all the fun. His words, not mine," Jayden said when he returned. "But he's gone to tell the others we'll be delayed. What do you want to do?"

"First, can you tell me how the vagrants get water?"

"There are water dealers in the black market. We make arrangements with one of them, but when we get poisoned jugs, that understanding is voided and we have to find someone else."

"Do you know where they get the water?"

"No. Not many do. It's one of those closely guarded secrets. We really don't care if they steal it or bribe the guards or have another source as long as it's clean. Do you want me to arrange a deal with one of them? I've done it for my commune on level sixty-two many times."

His comment about bribing the guards made her pause. Rendor should know about how the Water Prince's guards collected and distributed the water. "Not yet."

"Why not? We're going to run out of water soon."

Again she resisted snapping at him. "How much would it cost?"

"Quite a lot. Thirty-six osees for the first shipment of a dozen jugs. And if it's poisoned that's just bad luck, you don't get a single coin back."

Wow. She'd figured it would be expensive, but not that pricey. "What's to keep them from just giving everyone poisoned water?"

"Once a dealer's jugs are discovered to be poisoned, he's out of business. No one would buy from him again. The problem is that person just hides behind another to keep selling until the guards figure him out again and lace his jugs."

"So the guards eventually find the dealers?"

"Some of them. The ones who have stayed hidden the longest charge forty-eight osees a dozen. But they're picky about who they sell to. We'd be too big a risk for them. Besides, we can't afford it."

Not yet. She hoped her talk with Aphra would be profitable. "What about food? Are there food dealers as well?"

"Jerky is always easy to get. There's not much supervision in the smoke caverns on level four and the workers steal rolls and sell them. That's where we've been getting our supply. Fresh meat, eggs, and vegetables are harder to obtain. You can't get into the growing caverns, but the delivery people and kitchen workers can be bribed."

She considered. "Is that how the Invisible Swords acquired food before?"

"No. Truthfully, there were only a handful of people who had to remain truly invisible and they all had magic so they slipped in the dining caverns and helped themselves without anyone the wiser. The other members either were legitimate citizens or vagrants and had their own sources of food and water."

He didn't say it, but Shyla sensed his impatience over her decree that they not steal. Technically, obtaining food and water illegally was stealing, but at least someone was getting paid for taking the risk.

Then there was the problem of transporting food and water to their headquarters. "Can we connect our headquarters with the city? Maybe dig an underground tunnel?"

If he was thrown by the change in subject, he didn't react. He frowned in thought, gazing over her shoulder. "Our headquarters is further than Tamburah's temple. It'll take time and plenty of manpower. Plus we'd have to dig a bunch of fake tunnels to confuse anyone following us. The maze to our old hideout was the result of thousands of sun jumps' work over the last thirteen hundred circuits." He scrubbed a hand through his hair. "Having just one tunnel would be a start and I think needed since traveling topside is becoming increasingly risky."

"Can you scout out a location in Zirdai we could connect to?"

"Yes. We'd need to link to a place down some long-forgotten tunnel that's not too deep. Somewhere between levels six and twelve." He straightened. "I'll take a look. What are you going to do?"

"I'm going to talk to a treasure hunter about earning us some coins."

"Do you know how to get back here?" he asked.

"Only by crossing the plank." She crinkled her nose, remembering the strength of the air blowing up from the depths, threatening to knock her off. Just the thought of standing on the edge conjured up the scent of gamelu meat mixed with damp sand that had been seared into her senses.

"Then pay attention on the way out."

"All right." Shyla pulled her wrap from her pack and arranged it to cover her short blond hair. Though it no longer stood up like bristles on a brush, her hair still had a long way to go to return to the length it had been before the deacon cut it off. One benefit to its current state was that it was easier to cover and keep clean.

She grabbed a druk as they crossed the common area. The vagrants had gathered to share first meal together. Her stomach grumbled when she smelled the velbloud eggs, but she continued past the tables.

Jayden grabbed her arm, stopping her. "We should eat first."

"No. We're not taking food from them. They—"

"Are happy to share. They know we're trying to make their lives better. They want to support us in the ways they can. This is one way."

And Jayden knew them best. But she only filled her water skin halfway before joining them. Their conversation reminded her of the meals she had growing up in the monastery. It was a similar exchange of their plans for the sun jump, a bit of gossip, a bit of teasing, some good-natured grumbling about work shifts, and arguments over stupid things like who cooked the best eggs. She'd missed that connection, that sense of family. The Invisible Swords hadn't gotten there yet.

Once the meal finished, Jayden led her out to a familiar part of the city. They parted. She pulled her wrap lower, putting her face in shadow. Dressed like one of the citizens, she was practically invisible. No magic needed. She kept to the edges to avoid encountering them. But, of all the people she did pass, not many even glanced at her, and those who did didn't really see her.

It struck her that all these people were just trying to survive, earning enough coin to pay for food and water for themselves and their families. And to avoid being noticed by the guards or deacons. The air hummed with a current of fear. People struggled to breathe in this toxic atmosphere.

But would their lives change once the Invisible Sword defeated the Water Prince and Heliacal Priestess? Taxes and tithes would still be needed to grow food and distribute water. Yet there would be no harsh punishments for minor crimes, no threat of torture just because a deacon decided someone didn't show the proper devotion, and no more fear simmering in the air. It was going to take a great deal of time, coin, and effort, but she was determined to bring laughter back to the city of Zirdai.

Shyla reached the dining cavern on level nineteen. It was angle thirty—the end of first meal. Almost everyone had gone, but a few lingered inside. The deacons in charge of making sure those who entered had paid their tithes rolled up their scrolls of names, preparing to settle in for the boring angles between meals. Citizens could stop in for water at any time, but most filled their water skins during the three meal times.

Gathering her will, she used her magic on the deacons. *Look away,* she commanded them.

Look away.

Both men turned to glance in the opposite direction and she slipped by them. Her magic worked differently than the power of The Eyes. She could influence a person's perceptions or give them simple commands like *sleep* or *look away* without the need for eye contact. However, The Eyes made her magical commands stronger.

Only a few people sat at the tables scattered around the cavern. Since all the dining areas spanned two levels, the ceiling arched high above. The sounds of the workers cleaning up the serving line bounced off the hard stone walls as the lingering spicy scent of roasted gamelu meat perfumed the air. She breathed in deep. It'd been so long since she had a hot juicy meal that she just about drooled.

Pulling her focus back to her task, Shyla scanned the diners. When not recovering artifacts, the treasure hunters gathered here each sun jump to swap stories, dig for information, and to team up if a job was too big for one of them to handle. Except this jump. No one lingered, which meant they must all be working.

Most of the hunters worked as freelancers for Fadey. He arranged jobs and hooked up hunters with buyers.

For a fee, of course. When she'd first arrived in Zirdai, she had worked for Fadey, finding the location of hidden treasure for his hunters. It had been a temporary arrangement until she'd set up her legitimate business.

Shyla headed to Fadey's rooms. He lived on level seventeen despite having enough coins to afford a deeper place. Hunters stayed close to the surface for easier access to the buried ancient ruins, temples, and palaces full of artifacts.

As she walked through the tunnel leading to his door, Shyla slowed. The…bumps of hidden watchers reached her. She sensed two people lurking in the shadows. Guards or hunters or maybe a rival's men? Perhaps a couple of Fadey's minions, protecting their boss's home. When she neared his door, she had to make a decision— keep walking or stop and knock.

She needed to find Aphra. Deciding to stick to her original plan, she knocked on his thick colored-glass door. The last time she visited, one of his minions wouldn't let her in without a bribe. Shyla dug into her pack, finding her pouch of coins.

The door slid open without anyone demanding that she state her business. Fadey stood on the other side. His mouth hung open as he stared at her in shock. She was equally surprised as his clothes were rumpled and stained. His curly black beard was straggly and unkempt. She'd never seen him so disheveled.

"Fadey, what—"

"Come inside, quick." He grabbed her wrist and yanked her into the room, shutting the door right behind him.

"What happened? What's going on?"

"You've returned from the dead. I can ask you the same thing."

"I asked first."

"And it would take me angles to tell you everything. Unfortunately, we don't have the time. You need to leave before the guards arrest you."

CHAPTER

3

That explained the two shadows outside his door. "Do you have another exit?" she asked.

"Of course," Fadey said, gesturing to his back rooms. "But they're being watched by the prince's dogs as well."

She thought quickly. "All right. I'll be back."

"No. Run away and don't come back!"

"Don't worry, Fadey. I've a plan. They won't know I returned."

He pulled on his beard. The long strands of curly hair straightened. "I can't help you if you're arrested." Fadey released his hold and the beard bounced back into place.

"I know. Keep your door unlocked so I can slip inside." She left his rooms and glanced to each side as if nervous, clutching her wrap tighter.

The guards stepped from the shadows to her left, but she pretended that she didn't notice them. Instead, she turned and hurried down the tunnel. They followed her. Shyla led them further away from Fadey's rooms and snagged a druk lantern before going into the abandoned tunnels. Unlike Jayden, she wasn't as knowledgeable about all the back ways, shortcuts, and hidden areas of Zirdai, but she'd explored many of the upper levels, including level seventeen.

She looped around a few times, hoping to get the guards lost. They didn't grab a druk. No doubt to stay hidden in the darkness beyond the reach of her orange-tinted light. When she entered the next intersection, she turned right and closed the druk, plunging them all in complete blackness.

A muffled cry of dismay sounded. The men hustled around the corner. She didn't linger. With a hand on the wall, she raced ahead of them. When she reached the next intersection, she turned left and then right at the following one. Once satisfied she'd lost them, she opened the druk and returned to Fadey's.

This time no one lurked nearby and she entered his rooms without any problems. Fadey stuck his curly head out the door to check that no one waited to arrest her.

"Scorching hells, Shyla. What did you do?" he asked, closing and locking the door.

"I led them on a merry chase and lost them. By the time they figure out how to return, I'll be long gone. Now, let's sit down and catch up."

He grumbled but led her to his sitting room. The opulent touches—lava stones, a hand-woven rug, and oversized cushions—were all gone. A few battered thin cushions remained and Fadey plopped onto one while Shyla sat on another, facing him.

"What's going on?" she asked.

"The Water Prince sent his dogs to round up all the treasure hunters," he said in a defeated tone.

"Round up? Are they—"

"They've been arrested. They're either rotting in one of his black cells or have been tortured to death."

Horrified, she pressed her hands to her chest. "Do you know what happened to Banqui?"

"Dekel spotted him creeping around the city, looking skeletal. It was about twenty to twenty-five sun jumps ago. Then one of my hunters reported seeing him about two or three sun jumps after that with a deacon escort. And I've heard nothing since."

Captured or collaborating? Either way it wasn't good news.

"Sorry, I know you are friends. I'd look into his whereabouts, but I've my own problems to deal with."

She focused on Fadey. "Why is the prince arresting the hunters now?" The prince had mostly ignored them and the black-market merchants.

"Those blasted Eyes. You stole them from him and he's determined that no more artifacts shall be taken. Rohana, his new archeologist, is the only person authorized to dig." Fadey leaned forward. "If you still have them, you need to give them back!"

It was a good thing Fadey's powers of observation tended toward ancient artifacts or else he would have noticed the change in her eye color by now. "The Eyes don't belong to him."

"But we're *all* suffering."

"Do you really think if he had The Eyes he would release the hunters?" Guilt and sadness twisted around her heart. At least Fadey wasn't locked in a cell. A beat later—why not? "Why didn't he arrest you?"

"He did. I was…questioned and forced to give him the names of treasure hunters." He hung his head in shame.

"Did he interrogate you in one of his special rooms?"

A nod, but he wouldn't meet her gaze.

"Fadey, no one is going to blame you for cracking. You survived a terrible experience."

"No one else thinks that way. They all say I'm a coward. Then to rub it in, the prince assigned me to be Rohana's assistant and if I don't locate artifacts for her, she threatens to send me back to the prince." He shuddered then hooked a thumb behind him. "Those dogs outside my door are looking for the hunters who got away."

A spark of hope. "Some escaped?"

"A few. Fortunately, I don't know all the hunters in Zirdai so couldn't name them, and they're smart enough to stay far away from me. No one has visited me except you, and now he'll know you're alive."

"No, he'll learn someone came to visit you. They didn't recognize me."

Looking miserable, he put his head in his hands. "They'll *ask* me, Shyla. And I'm not strong enough to keep it secret."

"Don't worry about it."

He glanced at her. "Are you that confident you can avoid being arrested?"

"No, but I'm learning how to stay hidden, probably like the hunters who escaped. Or do you think they left Zirdai?"

"I don't know where they are. If they're smart, they're long gone."

"Do you know who escaped?"

"Someone tipped off Dekel and he told his crew. They scattered right before the guards arrived."

"Is Aphra part of Dekel's crew?"

"Yeah."

Shyla was glad the woman escaped. Aphra had treated her like a normal person.

"I answered your questions, now it's my turn. What happened to you?" Fadey asked. "The deacons said you went topside during the killing heat and died. We spent an entire service thanking the Sun Goddess for taking you home."

She found it interesting that the priestess hadn't informed her flock that the evil sun-kissed had returned. That would be quite the embarrassment. It also might prove to be to Shyla's benefit.

"They lectured us about reporting sun-kisseds as soon as they are born. Sorry." He ducked his head.

Everyone believed Shyla had been left on the sands to die when she was a newborn, including her until eighteen sun jumps ago when she'd learned she was born in the monastery and Hanif was her father. "Why are you sorry? You haven't sacrificed any sun-kissed babies, have you?"

He stared at her in horror. "No!" Then he recovered. "They want us to report *all* sun-kisseds."

"Does this mean you're going to report me?"

"Of course not. But why would the deacons lie about you?"

"They didn't. I did go topside right before the killing heat."

"How did you survive? No one has before."

Shyla leaned closer to the man. "Fadey, look at me, please." She lowered her shield as he met her gaze.

Finally noticing her new eye color, he jerked in surprise. "Your eyes—"

"Fadey, you will forget my visit and our conversation. Shyla Sun-Kissed is dead. When the guards ask who came to see you, tell them it was a merchant look-ing for treasures to sell on the black market. Tell them you turned her away and lay down for a nap."

Sleep.

He slumped over. Shyla lifted his head and tucked a cushion underneath. Even though it would save him from getting into trouble, erasing his memories sat heavily on her heart. She wondered if she would reach a point where altering memories no longer caused her concern. Would she be ruthless in order to win? Shyla hoped not, but it worried her.

As she navigated the tunnels down to level thirty-nine, she considered her next move. Even if Aphra remained in Zirdai, would the woman still be able to sell treasures for Shyla? The hunter had mentioned working with someone at the university in Catronia—the closest city to Zirdai—so perhaps Aphra's network hadn't been shut down by the prince's sweep. But how would she find the woman? Maybe Jayden had some ideas.

She arrived at the commune before Jayden. Zhek waylaid her almost immediately, demanding to check her injury. With her history of ripping stitches, there was no way he'd trust her word that it was fine. She grinned at the surprised tone in his voice when he declared it "healing nicely."

Then she found Orla writing on a scroll at a low table. The leader was alone so Shyla approached and asked her if she wouldn't mind answering some questions.

"What type of questions?" Orla asked.

"Boring ones about how you take care of everyone."

"Ah. Ilan," she called to a group of children.

A boy around ten circuits old skidded to a stop. "Yes, Grandmother?"

"Fetch us some tea, please."

"Yes, ma'am." He raced off.

Orla smiled fondly at him before turning to Shyla. "One of the things you need to instill in everybody is that *everyone* is equally important to the group's survival. No one is more important than anyone else. From the youngest to the oldest, we rely on each other and we all have important jobs. If you can walk, you can help."

Ilan returned with a teapot in one hand and two cups in the other.

"Take Ilan here," Orla said as the boy set the items down on the stone table. "He's our best sand rat catcher, and he takes good care of them."

Ilan beamed. "They like me. And do you know they have an excellent sense of smell?" He didn't wait for a reply. "Big Bad and his offspring can sniff out the poison in the water. If they smell it, they'll refuse to drink it. Isn't that amazing?"

"It is," Shyla agreed, suppressing a grin over the boy's enthusiasm about *sand rats* of all things.

"And they're really loving creatures. Smart, too."

Interesting. "Can they be trained?"

"Oh yeah. I've taught Black Tail to retrieve items. And I've a bunch that I've taught how to play hide and seek—they can find anyone, anywhere, but my friends say using the rats while playing the game is cheating." He shrugged. "And..." He lowered his voice. "I sent Cat Toy to sneak into my sister's room. You should have heard her scream." He laughed.

"Shyla probably did," Orla said dryly. "Along with everyone else in Zirdai."

"Is that what triggered the level twenty cave-in?" Shyla asked, playing along.

"No, that was Ilan's mother yelling at him for scaring his sister."

"Worth it," Ilan said before dashing off.

Shyla laughed.

Orla poured them tea. "If you're buying water from the black market, you'll need sand rats as well. Ilan will sell you a few of his."

Good to know and a reminder for her to get back on track. She asked Orla about acquiring resources. Gesturing to the people around them, she asked, "How do you find enough clothing for them all?"

"We own a herd of gamelu. We shear them and make our own fabric."

Completely shocked, Shyla stared at the woman. "You own a herd? How is that possible?"

Orla sipped her tea. "We're vagrants by choice. Some of us are even upstanding citizens who pay taxes, tithe to the church, and own herds. Once we supply our people, we sell the rest. We also own a herd of velbloud. Our sun cloaks are highly sought after," she said with pride.

Recovering, Shyla asked, "Is that how you got the eggs and meat for first meal?"

"Yes, but the herds don't provide enough to feed everyone so we have to find supplemental sources." Orla brightened. "We're saving to buy two more herds."

Astounding. "What other ways do you earn coin?"

"Ah. We sell a variety of goods, including information. Our scouts keep an eye on the guards and deacons and will pick up gossip. The Invisible Sword paid us for any news that could compromise their organization." Orla set her cup down. "The hardest thing to manage is the waste from the collection bins. We're too deep to schlep it up to the surface to dry out."

Shyla remembered having to cross through the worst stink she'd ever smelled when she had visited the commune on level sixteen. "What do you do with it?"

"We carry the bins to various collection stations in Zirdai and swap them for clean ones."

"And the deacons don't notice the extra...er...waste?"

"It's an unpleasant job given to those who have sinned in some way. I doubt they think in depth about what they're doing as they cart it up to the growing caverns to be turned into fertilizer."

True. Right now the Invisible Swords dumped it on the surface and covered it with a layer of sand. Except she worried the smell might attract sand demons. Too bad they couldn't turn it into something useful. Shyla straightened. Why not? They could clear out level six, install mirror pipes, and grow their own vegetables. They had plenty of fertilizer and "water." The biggest hurdle would be getting plants.

She chatted with Orla for a while. The woman was a great source of information on how to handle the daily tasks of living.

When Shyla covered a yawn for a second time, Orla touched her forearm. "Here's the most important thing to remember as a leader… You have to delegate. You can't do everything or you'll wear yourself out trying." She squeezed once and let go. "Now go get some sleep."

"I will."

Orla gave her a skeptical look.

"Once Jayden returns." His name triggered another question for Orla. "Are all the communes separate organizations with their own leaders?"

"Mostly. The vagrants used to be one group with one leader. We had to live in separate areas of Zirdai because it's harder for the guards to find a smaller commune than one big one. However, over time, we grew into our own individual units. Jayden acts as our liaison and we help each other when needed."

Seemed her nickname for him was more accurate than she'd realized. "How did he get that job?"

"When Ezra, his father, died, Jayden assumed his duties." Orla lowered her voice. "Ezra was one of the leaders of the Invisible Sword as well. Many of the vagrant leaders took care of their people and helped the Invisible Sword."

Shyla couldn't resist asking, "Was that why Ezra died? Did the Water Prince find out about him?"

"No. Cave-in. He was in the wrong place at the wrong time." She sighed. "Jayden was only sixteen circuits old and he took it hard. Not only did his father die, but he suddenly had a great deal of responsibility on his shoulders." Orla peered at her intently. "Much like you."

True. And she still had so much to learn. "Do you mind if I take a closer look around?"

"Go ahead. My lot will tell you if you're in the way."

The other times she'd been here, she'd noticed the cushions, curtains, and furniture, but now she picked up on the little details: where their food and water was stored, where people slept and worked, the areas designated for relaxation, and where Ilan housed his sand rats—he'd carved a complex mini-city for them into one of the walls of a tunnel, complete with warrens, rat-sized passages, and velbloud fibers for bedding (they had a nicer home than she did).

It was all very overwhelming. So much to do, to learn, to organize, and to keep it all hidden…it was a massive undertaking. Orla's advice of delegating would help and perhaps Shyla needed to focus on the immediate needs of the Invisible Swords instead of trying to figure it all out. Their biggest needs were coins, water, and food.

Jayden caught up to her as she watched a man weave six colored threads into a fabric with a complex pattern. His fingers moved with such deft precision there was no doubt he'd spent thousands of angles perfecting his craft.

"Thinking of starting a new career?" Jayden asked, joking.

"What I'm thinking is that if I had that job, I'd end up with a very colorful knot." Then she mulled it over. "Actually, our jobs are rather similar."

"How do you figure?"

"There are so many threads we need to weave together in order to set up our headquarters."

"True. And it's going to take us a while to get settled."

Meanwhile, the Invisible Swords and the treasure hunters locked in the black cells continued to suffer. But if they rescued them now, they'd need a place to hide them and she wouldn't endanger the vagrant communes or the monks.

"Did you locate a place we could connect to?" she asked.

"Yes. It's on level ten back in the northwest quadrant. There was a cave-in there about six or seven circuits ago. A bunch of people died so no one wants to live there now. In fact there's still rubble, which we can use to our advantage."

"Great."

He smiled, but it was half-hearted. "That was the easy part. Digging a tunnel is going to be the hard part." Jayden's shoulders drooped with fatigue.

"Go get some sleep."

"I will after I visit my commune."

"Do you have family living there?" she asked in a neutral tone.

"Yeah. I haven't seen my mother since I was captured by the Arch Deacons."

She paused as his comment hit her. Even though she didn't have traditional parents, even she knew mothers tended to get upset when their children didn't visit. Did that mean Jayden and his mother didn't have a good relationship? "You could have visited—"

"I know. Do you need anything else before I go?"

Ah, his mother was a touchy subject. "How would you find someone who is hiding from the prince's guards?"

"Who do you want to find?"

She explained about the treasure hunters. "I think Aphra might still be in Zirdai, but I don't know how to find her."

"I can ask the vagrants to keep an eye out for her. They're usually in the same places as those wishing to remain hidden," Jayden said. "What does she look like?"

Shyla described the young woman. "She usually wears her long brown hair in an intricate knot."

"All right, I'll tell the network to be on the lookout for her." Jayden strode away.

"Jayden, wait," she called after him.

He paused and glanced back.

"Can you have them look out for Banqui as well?"

If a frown could be wielded like a weapon, he just stabbed her with his. "Do you really think that's necessary? He's either gone or living in the wealthy levels where the vagrants don't go."

Where Banqui was spending his blood coins, Shyla finished his unspoken thought. Actually she was surprised he hadn't said it. "Just ask them to, please."

"Okay."

Too tired to think anymore, Shyla found an empty room. During her explorations, she learned the commune had a number of guest rooms for visitors and this was one. Orla had ordered her to sleep and she was more than happy to obey.

* * *

At angle zero the next sun jump, Shyla and Jayden left the city with the others. They all wore sun cloaks. The white, slightly hairy fabric crafted from velbloud hair protected them from the sun's harsh rays. A few deacons in their long green robes milled around the exit, studying faces. Shyla kept her hood pulled low, but both she and Jayden used the *look away* command for extra protection.

They headed in the wrong direction just in case anyone followed them. When they were confident that no one had paid them any attention, they angled toward the temple. Jayden erased their tracks as they walked. Shyla still hadn't mastered the technique of "moving and smoothing," according to Ximen.

The cool air smelled fresh and clean after the musty city odors underground. They passed a flock of velbloud. The fuzzy white creatures converged on the caretaker as he set out buckets of feed for them. Their long tethers striped the sand, making a pinwheel pattern. Shyla wondered how they managed to avoid getting them all twisted together.

She held a special fondness for the animals since they'd saved her life. Caught topside during the killing heat, she'd been desperate enough to wrap two tethers around her body as the velblouds floated into the sky. They had lifted her above the dangerous hotness. After the velblouds had reeled in their tethers and descended, the monks had found her lying almost dead among the creatures. If Zhek hadn't been at the monastery, she'd have never survived.

"Shyla?" Jayden asked from a couple meters away.

She'd paused to watch the flock without any conscious decision to do so. Her thoughts about the monks reminded her of another concern. "Do we need to keep the torques to protect our people?"

He moved closer. "What do you mean?"

"Are there others in Zirdai who can wield magic? People we need to shield ourselves against?"

"Oh." He considered. "No."

Thinking of Mojag, she asked, "How can you be so sure? How many people have magic?"

Jayden pulled up his hood against the strengthening sunlight. "From what I've learned, only a small number of people have the potential to wield magic. But, of those, not everyone can tap into it."

"Is that why the Invisible Sword doesn't test everyone, only those who show potential?"

"That's right."

"How do you know who has the potential?"

"One way is bloodlines. Certain families have the skill and they pass it down. Gurice inherited hers from her grandmother. In my family, my grandfather and my father could wield magic. My sister was tested but failed."

Questions about his sister pushed up her throat, but the scowl that arrived when he mentioned her warned Shyla to keep quiet.

Jayden continued. "Those that seek out the monks tend to have the ability. Hanif has sent us a few candidates."

"What does he see in them?"

"An open mind, being flexible in their thinking and not set in their ways. Confidence. Intelligence. Resourcefulness."

All great qualities. "But not everyone you test taps into their power, right?"

"Right."

Memories of being chained in the dark threatened to overwhelm her. "Why do you have to test them? Why can't you explain about the magic and teach them how to do it?"

Jayden huffed in amusement. "Even though the candidates are open-minded, all of them would think we're insane. I believe a certain sun-kissed didn't believe in magic even after she witnessed it and successfully wielded it. Then again, she wasn't that open-minded to begin with."

She refrained from punching him. "Then why did you test me?" she shot back.

"You have all the other qualities. And you fought back when Payatt took you through the sands."

Still. There had to be a better way to wake a person's magic. "Isn't there another way?"

"Yes, there are plenty of ways, but they're cruel. Stress and fear are the triggers. When people are pushed to the breaking point, they tap into that inner spark of survival. Our way allows the person time to experiment and then we're there to teach them."

Not many people were in those dire situations. "The people in the prince's special rooms are terrorized."

"And some of them do access their magic. But, unfortunately, they don't know how to use it and no one survives the torture."

"What about the deacons' confession rooms? Those people live through it and are forced to become deacons. Do some of them have magic?"

"It's possible," Jayden said slowly. "Although we haven't heard any rumors."

"Might be why the Heliacal Priestess started having her Arch Deacons wear those torques."

"An interesting theory. We don't know when she stole them, or even if she did. It could have been one of her predecessors who passed them along. Or Banqui could have discovered their location and sold them to her." He frowned.

Jayden suspected Banqui had betrayed the Invisible Sword by telling the priestess's Arch Deacons where to find their hideout, but he had no proof. Shyla's new information from Fadey would support his suspicions. However, she just wasn't convinced it'd been him so she didn't share it with Jayden. Not yet. Instead, she asked, "Who had the torques before they were stolen?"

Jayden gazed at the rolling sand dunes. "The Invisible Sword leaders."

Good thing they didn't have The Eyes as well. Shyla debated whether she should press him for more information about the old leaders. Instead, she considered his comments about magic. "What about Mojag?"

"What about him?"

"I think he's using magic, but he hasn't been through the test." Nor would he or anyone since the "testing cavern" was part of the old hideout and off-limits.

"That's ridiculous. Mojag hasn't shown any potential."

Really? She'd thought he'd be an ideal candidate. "Then explain how he followed you to the Invisible Swords' hideout. Explain how he's so good at avoiding people and getting around without being seen."

"I've been training him. Most vagrants are adept at hiding from the guards and deacons. It doesn't mean they have magic."

She wasn't convinced, but she didn't want to fight about it. They'd been having a perfectly civil conversation. It was nice.

"We should go. The velbloud caretaker has noticed us standing here," Jayden said.

"You go on to headquarters. I'm heading to the monastery."

He frowned. Shyla waited for him to figure it out.

"You're giving them the torques."

"For now. It's the safest place. If we think the priestess is using magic, we'll get them back."

"That's a good idea," he said.

Was that an actual compliment? Shyla didn't let it go to her head. They walked together for a bit before Shyla headed south. Without Jayden, she had to stop every ten meters, turn around, and erase her boot prints. It wasn't ideal, but it worked.

When she was within a kilometer of the monastery, she slowed. At least a dozen monks would be on the surface, blending in with the desert and keeping watch for any visitors. Not many people could spot them, but since she'd grown up with them and had taken her turn as sentry too many times to count, she noticed them.

This time she wondered if she could slip past them unseen. Plus she needed the practice. The *look away* command would work, but she'd have to smooth out her tracks with every step. *Sleep* might work, but when the monks woke, they'd be alarmed. *Gone* required more energy and they had to see her first, which would ruin the fun.

Reaching out, she sensed the hidden monks in the distance. Before she crested the next dune, she pushed her will forward.

Look away.

Then she pushed it back to her tracks.

Return.

When she reached the top she spied a number of monks.

Look away.

Return.

Then she went down into the shallow valley and up another dune.

Look away.

Return.

And repeat.

It was slow going. After two more dunes, she spotted the single-story structure that marked the entrance to the monastery. Unlike Zirdai's colorful surface buildings, it was unremarkable, blending in with the surrounding desert. Only its straight lines gave it away as unnatural and man-made.

Four monks were stationed around the entrance and one was on duty inside. Shyla thrust her will toward all five and they suddenly found various other areas of the desert very fascinating.

The pace was brutal, draining her energy with every step. But she was determined. By the time she entered the building, she dripped with sweat. The rectangular space contained only one bench. Large windows had been carved into the walls. Velbloud curtains hung limply, covering them. Sitting cross-legged on the bench was a monk, the official greeter to those seeking solace or shelter or directions—it was easy to get lost in the desert. Like all the monks, she wore a tunic, pants, and dillo leather boots. Everything matched the color of the sand. The monks stationed in the desert also wore turbans and veils to protect their skin from the sun.

Shyla didn't recognize the monk, but that wasn't a surprise. The children raised in the monastery didn't spend much time with the majority of the monks. Not until they turned eighteen circuits old and took the oath, pledging their loyalty to Parzival and the King of Koraha. Even after all this time, Shyla still wasn't sure who exactly Parzival was. The monks worshipped the Sun Goddess, but Parzival must be the founder of the order. There were other monasteries throughout their world and all within a few kilometers of a major city. Not to teach or aid the people—what a radical concept—but to keep an eye on them as the King's spies.

Slipping past the greeter, Shyla descended the stairs into cool semi-darkness. She relaxed, releasing all those monks from her magical hold. When she reached the monastery's receiving room on level two, she sat on the floor, taking a few angles to recover. Unless she spent the rest of the sun jump here, she wouldn't have enough energy to sneak past the monks on her way out. Guess they'd just be surprised to see her.

The monks embraced the sunlight and they'd installed long mirror pipes throughout the monastery to bring the light from the surface to the depths. Warm golden light shone in the area set aside for visitors. It appeared they weren't expecting visitors this sun jump, as normally a couple monks stood guard in here, ensuring no one wandered into private areas or tried to enter one of the four Rooms of Knowledge. They protected knowledge like a miser hoarding coins. Shyla never understood why. Everyone should have equal access, but you had to be a monk to enter those rooms—with one exception. She was allowed to enter two.

Once she regained some of her strength, she headed down to Hanif's office on level eleven. She used the *look away* command on the few people she encountered. Influencing one person seemed easy compared to the twelve on the surface.

Hanif's door was ajar. She'd never seen it closed. Voices drifted from the opening. The conversation went from an undecipherable murmur to clear speech as she neared. She stopped outside, debating whether she should wait here or retreat to give her father some privacy. As she backed away, she caught a snippet of the discussion.

"…Water Prince is not pleased," said a familiar male voice.

She froze and tried to place the voice. Its deep timbre stirred fear in her heart.

"It's not my concern if the Water Prince is pleased or not," Hanif said.

"It should be. Especially if he decides to withhold your water rations."

"The *King* would not be *pleased* by your threat, Captain."

Clamping a hand over her mouth, Shyla blocked her gasp. Captain Yates! The man who had replaced Rendor as the prince's captain of the guard. What was he doing here?

"By the time the King learns of your hardship, it will be too late," Yates said. "Just tell us where the sun-kissed is and we'll stop bothering you."

"For the fifth time, Captain, I do *not* know where she is."

"I do *not* believe you," Yates said.

An irritated sigh. "You're welcome to search the monastery. If you find her, we will not interfere."

71

CHAPTER

4

What colossally bad timing. Shyla needed to leave the monastery right away. Except she didn't have a great deal of energy. Avoiding the captain as he searched shouldn't be too difficult, but she needed to stay hidden from everyone so they didn't have to lie about knowing her location.

"You'll allow us to search the Rooms of Knowledge?" Yates asked.

"No. They are off-limits, but you can look everywhere else," Hanif replied.

"That's ridiculous. She could be hiding in one of them."

"She isn't."

"I can't take your word for it."

They continued to argue, but Shyla tuned them out. Maybe she could wait until Yates left and then hide in Hanif's office, where no one would think to look for her. Then it hit her. She'd been thinking like a sun-kissed, hiding and scurrying away. Not like Shyla Sun-Kissed, leader of the Invisible Sword.

Making a bold—stupid?—decision, Shyla strode into Hanif's office as if she did it every sun jump.

"Hello, Captain Yates. I hear you're looking for me," she said.

Poor Hanif's face drained of all color while his mouth dropped open. Yates jumped from his seat and brandished his sword in an impressive display of speed.

Yates aimed the tip of his blade at Shyla's throat. "You're under arrest."

Not as tall as Rendor, but just as muscular with thick arms and broad shoulders, Yates radiated menace. She met his gaze and read his soul.

Excitement sizzled through him. He had finally caught the cursed sun-kissed. After all the failures, the prince would be very pleased. Yates just knew she was hiding in the monastery despite the prince's claims she wouldn't be that stupid.

Shyla pressed her lips together. Not stupid enough to hide here, but idiotic enough to come visit the same sun jump as the captain.

"Care to explain this?" Yates asked Hanif.

"I…" Hanif shot her a panicked glance. "What are you doing here?"

"Come on, don't try that nonsense," Yates said.

"I wanted to surprise you," she said to her father.

"Mission accomplished."

She smiled then concentrated on the captain, pushing her magic at him. "Captain Yates, you searched the monastery and didn't find me."

"What are you talking about? You're standing right here."

Perhaps she shouldn't have been so confident. She glanced at his neck; he wasn't wearing a torque. Increasing her efforts, she tried again. "You searched and didn't find me."

"I did?" he asked with a hint of confusion, fighting to remember. The tip of his sword dipped down. It snapped back. "No. You're here."

Son of a sand demon, the man was fighting back. Perhaps she could recruit him. And perhaps she could fly. Both scenarios were equally likely at this point.

Gathering all her strength, she gazed right into his dark brown eyes. "You searched. You found nothing. The monks are not lying to you."

"I...searched."

"Yes."

"No sign of the sun-kissed?"

She pressed, driving the command home with all her might. "Yes. She's not here. Say goodbye to Hanif, thank him for his time, and leave."

Yates sheathed his sword, turned to Hanif, thanked him for his time, and left.

Hanif stared at Shyla with a combination of awe and horror. "That was truly impressive."

She tried to respond, but the floor underneath her feet dropped away like the edge of a sand dune. Darkness rushed up and buried her.

* * *

Warm and comfortable under the fur, Shyla snuggled in deeper. It'd been ages since she'd slept on a decent cushion. Plus every muscle in her body ached as if she'd been shoveling sand in the hot sun. Her heavy limbs required too much effort to move. All were excellent reasons to go back to sleep. So she did.

Voices woke her the second time. She instantly recognized the deep unhappy rumble. Just how long had she slept? Prying an eye open, she spotted Rendor interrogating the poor monk who'd been assigned to watch over her. Rendor still wore his sun cloak. The hot anise scent of the desert wafted from him. Sweat dampened the hair around his forehead. He must have just arrived. The sand clock read angle twenty. That explained his glower. Shyla had slept for an entire sun jump.

"I'm okay, Rendor," she said. Her voice rasped as if sand coated her tongue.

When Rendor turned his attention to her, the young monk just about swayed with relief. "I'll go inform Hanif that you're awake." The man bolted.

"What happened?" Rendor asked, striding over to her.

She struggled to sit up. He helped, steadying her. His large hand warmed her shoulder. Glancing around, she searched for her pack. It was on the floor next to the cushion. Understanding, Rendor swept it up and handed it to her. She fumbled for her water skin. Empty. Shyla wilted.

Rendor grunted, pulled his from his belt, and gave it to her. The warm water quenched the fire in her throat. Ah.

"Now are you ready to tell me what happened?" he asked.

She stabbed a finger at him. "Stop looming. I'm fine." When he didn't move, she snapped, "Sit down and I'll tell you."

The aggrieved sigh he released said he didn't spend the entire darkness worrying about her just to be scolded for being concerned. That was quite a bit of information for a sigh. Shyla strengthened her mental shield. No need to read Rendor's thoughts when it was clear he was upset. Instead of arguing with her, he shrugged off his cloak and settled next to her.

"I'm sorry," she said, taking his hand in hers.

The tension eased from his shoulders.

"I'm just mad at myself for being stupid. No, don't bother protesting," she said even though he hadn't. But that earned her a small smile. "I exhausted myself and almost got caught." She told him about wanting to practice using her magic on the monks and then confronting Captain Yates. "He's strong-willed and I just managed to convince him."

"That's good you convinced him," Rendor said. "Yates is stubborn, persistent, and capable, which is why the Water Prince chose him to replace me. He would have harassed the monks until they proved to him you weren't here."

"Which begs the question, why are you here?" Hanif asked from the doorway. He wore a loose tan tunic and pants. The light-colored fabric contrasted nicely against his golden-brown skin—the same shade as Shyla's. A wide dillo leather belt was cinched around his waist. Gray eyes glinted with curiosity.

"Is anyone with you?" she asked.

"No."

"Then come in and shut the door. Please," she added when he scowled. This was his monastery after all. Then she dug in her pack and removed the four torques. "I hid the other one in the Second Room of Knowledge after we rescued Jayden, but I think all five of these should be stored in the Fourth Room." She gave them to Hanif.

"What do they do?" he asked.

"It's better if you don't know."

"Are they dangerous?"

"Not to you. It's extremely important that no one knows they're here."

Hanif quirked an eyebrow. "That sounds ominous."

She remembered when Yates threatened to cut off the monks' water supply. "If you'd rather not hide them, I understand."

"No. They'll be safe here. After all, we hid The Eyes for thousands of circuits."

"What if the Water Prince stops sending you water? Or the priestess refuses to give you food?" she asked.

Hanif gave her a sly smile. "You don't really think we're *that* dependent on them, do you?"

"But Yates said…" Her tired brain churned through his comment. "The King supplies you, too?"

"Not quite."

"They have their own sources for food and water," Rendor said.

Hanif's gaze snapped to him. "Does the Water Prince know?"

"No. But I lived here long enough to figure it out."

"Wait. You've lived here for what…forty-odd sun jumps, but I grew up here. I lived here for eighteen circuits. Why didn't I know?" Was she that obtuse?

"You were a child for most of your time here," Rendor said. "I'm an adult and trained to investigate when things don't add up. I can put the clues together."

Shyla liked to believe she was capable of the same thing. She had earned a living these last two circuits uncovering lost ruins, ancient temples, and artifacts. Yet she missed it. "Why didn't you tell me?" she asked Hanif.

"Because you never swore the oath and became a monk."

That was his go-to excuse for everything.

"And…uh…can't you just…" He tapped a finger on his temple.

"I can read your mind. But I respect your privacy. Unless you're saying I shouldn't?" She leaned forward.

Hanif stepped back, holding up his hands. "No, no. That's an admirable policy."

Score one for her. But she still couldn't help feeling like an idiot because, once she actually thought about it, the clues were always there. "You have your own growing cavern."

"We do. It's small, but it will provide enough for the monastery if the Heliacal Priestess ever decides to cut us off."

Excited now, she asked, "Can you show me?"

Hanif hesitated. "I suppose. Why do you want to see it?"

"I'm curious." She told him about her plan to start one in their headquarters, which wasn't as original of an idea as she'd thought.

"All right. We can grab that other torque and swing by the Fourth Room of Knowledge on our way."

"*After* she eats," Rendor said. Then to her, "You've been asleep for an entire sun jump."

Now that he mentioned it, her stomach growled with hunger. Although she was quite capable of standing up, she let Rendor pull her to her feet. He frowned when she wobbled.

"Didn't Jayden tell you where I was going?" she asked him.

"No. Only that you'd be back soon. I woke him up when you failed to return by darkness." He crossed his massive arms.

Boys. To say the two of them didn't get along was being kind. Jayden considered Rendor to be a low man in the Invisible Sword's hierarchy. Rendor was used to giving orders, not taking them.

There was nothing she could do about it at the moment. The three of them stopped in the empty dining cavern for a meal. Since they were alone, she asked Hanif about the water. "Do you have your own well, too?"

"No." He squirmed then sighed. "We exaggerate our numbers to the Water Prince so he sends us more water than we need. We stockpile the rest just in case. If he cut us off, we have enough to last until we can get word to the King of Koraha."

That explained why he could spare a few jugs when the Invisible Sword moved to their new location. "Smart."

"Not if the prince figures it out," Hanif said, glancing at Rendor.

"The prince doesn't keep track of things like that," Rendor said. "The water accountant does. As long as you're not being greedy, he probably won't pick up on it."

"That's good to know."

"I wonder if the Heliacal Priestess does it as well," Shyla said. "She can't be happy relying on the prince for water." The two of them were supposed to share equal power in the ruling of Zirdai, but the prince held a slight advantage since people couldn't last more than three sun jumps without water. He also lived one level deeper than the priestess—another sticking point.

"I suspect the priestess has tapped into the aquifer," Rendor said.

"Can we tap into it as well?" she asked. Being able to access the underground cavern filled with water would solve one of their many problems.

"No, *we* can not." Amused, he leaned back as if waiting.

Had he been expecting her to ask about the prince's water supply by now? Why wouldn't he volunteer the information when she mentioned they were running out? She suspected it was due to his pride. If they treated him like a grunt only capable of shoveling sand, then he would act the part. "The aquifer is not within the city," she guessed.

"It's kilometers away, and the exact location and depth is kept secret."

Of course. "But the location of the pipes that transport the water to Zirdai are not."

"Correct. There are the ones that go into the prince's rooms, but there are others that are used to fill the jugs and skins."

"And they're guarded."

"All sun jump, three hundred and sixty jumps a circuit."

"That means the water dealers must bribe the guards."

"Some do. Although the guards are only assigned the duty for short periods of time to limit that. Some dealers find other sources."

Shyla resisted asking the obvious question—what other sources. Instead, she asked, "How would you obtain water for us?"

Rendor smiled and, damn, the man had a melt-your-insides smile. She almost forgot what they'd been discussing.

"I'd tap into the outflow pipes," he said.

A strange word. "Outflow?"

"There's plenty of water that flows through the prince's level. A prime example is the fountains. You've seen those."

More like gawked at them—a very decadent waste of precious resources. "Yes."

"That water is collected and piped out of the city to eventually flow into another city's aquifer," Rendor continued. "There's an entire network of aquifers and underground rivers throughout Koraha. But the key thing is that outflow water is still drinkable and, as far as I can tell, no one knows about it."

"How do you know about it?" Hanif asked.

Rendor gazed at Hanif for a moment as if deciding whether the question was accusatory or asked out of mere curiosity. Back when he'd stayed in the monastery, Hanif had clearly disliked and distrusted him. Shyla laid her hand on Rendor's forearm and squeezed, reassuring him. Then she clamped down on her mental shield again. Even after sleeping so long, her energy was already flagging.

"When I was working my way up the ranks in the prince's guard, I had some free time," Rendor said. "I used that time to explore and learn everything I could about the prince's organization so I would become an invaluable resource."

"Can you tell us where the outflow pipes are?" she asked.

"No, but I can show you."

Ah, tricky, but understandable. Rendor was part of the Invisible Sword. It was time for everyone to accept it. "All right."

Another smile, this one equally dangerous to her insides.

Hanif cleared his throat. "Well then, let's keep moving." He led them to the Second Room of Knowledge on level eleven.

Shyla ducked inside and retrieved the torque she'd hidden, then rejoined Hanif and Rendor. In case of a cave-in, each room was in a different section of the monastery. The Fourth Room had been built in the southeast corner on level seventeen.

"How deep does the monastery go?" she asked Hanif. She'd explored as much as possible when she was a child, but had always been stopped from going further than level twelve.

"I can't tell you all our secrets, Shyla."

"At least twenty-five levels," Rendor said.

Hanif skidded to a stop and rounded on him. "How... When... There are guards."

"Yes, there are. And I may have led you to believe it took longer for me to heal than it did."

"I should have put a tail on you sooner," Hanif muttered.

"Do you think it would have made a difference?"

"Let's keep going," Shyla said before Hanif could respond. "I'll feel safer once the torques are secure."

Hanif didn't take long to hide the torques in the Fourth Room and soon they were climbing up to level six. The cool air disappeared, replaced by dry hotness. Level six was deep enough to be safe during the killing heat and, unlike the upper levels, which cooled quickly, it held the warmth during the darkness. With mirror pipes installed in the ceiling, level six was the perfect level for growing plants.

Like Hanif had said, the cavern was small compared to the ones in Zirdai. Rows of green plants lined the long narrow space. The ceiling arched high overhead with the ends of at least a dozen mirror pipes poking through, piping sunlight down from the surface. As they followed the caretaker's path through the greenery, Shyla noted there was quite a variety of vegetables, with short bushy plants growing next to ones with tall stalks and thin leaves. Moisture thickened the air. It smelled unlike anything she'd encountered before—a heavy vibrant odor.

The amount of work needed to build and maintain something on this scale was beyond their small organization. Plus they'd need someone who was knowledgeable. "I don't suppose any of your caretakers want to become an Invisible Sword?" she asked Hanif.

"They're all sworn monks, but if you decide to build a growing cavern, let me know and we can work something out."

"Work something out? As in…?"

"Your people have certain skills that mine lack. There might be a future situation where I need you to do something in exchange for me loaning you one of our gardeners."

That was fair. After all, the monks had supplied the Invisible Swords with food, water, and shelter without charging a single coin. And she couldn't expect to keep getting everything for free. "It will depend on what you need us to do—I'm not risking my people unnecessarily—but I'm certainly open to working with you in the future."

"Diplomatic," Rendor said.

They retraced their steps through the plants. Shyla yawned twice and caught Rendor yawning as well. Poor guy had stayed up all darkness worrying about her. They had enough time to return to their headquarters before the danger zone, but she wouldn't be strong enough to erase their tracks. Best to nap first.

A monk entered the cavern. She carried a basket but stopped in surprise when she spotted them. Shyla also halted. The monk's blond hair shone in the sunlight. Another sun-kissed. While there was a handful of them living in the monastery, Shyla hadn't interacted with any of the adult sun-kisseds while growing up, unless she had been out on patrol with them in the desert. Everyone wore turbans and veils, so it had been difficult to tell one monk from another.

The woman recovered and walked toward them. Shyla studied her, noting her rich bronzed skin and elegant oval face. Fine wrinkles creased her forehead. She was probably around Hanif's age, which Shyla guessed to be around forty-five circuits. Long blond eyelashes framed her light green eyes. Something about the woman seemed familiar.

Shyla met the monk's gaze. Her heart lurched, recognizing the woman before Shyla's brain caught up. The monk was her mother.

CHAPTER

5

Hanif's gaze darted to Shyla before he recovered his manners. "This is Kaveri, one of our gardeners. Kaveri, this is Shyla and Rendor."

"Pleased to meet you both. Although, I do remember when you were found, Shyla. Such a sweet baby."

Interesting that Hanif hadn't told Kaveri that Shyla knew the truth about her origins. She wondered if Kaveri even knew that she had figured out Hanif was her father and that he wouldn't tell her the identity of her mother, claiming it was the woman's decision.

Shyla smiled at her mother. "That's nice to hear." She shot Hanif a sour look. "Much better than being told how difficult and stubborn I was all the time."

"You?" Rendor feigned surprise. "Difficult and stubborn?"

Shyla elbowed him in the ribs. Hard. He had the audacity to chuckle!

Kaveri laughed, a charming light sound. "Hanif can't show his true feelings to the children or else they'll never listen to him. He enjoys teaching them too much."

"Enjoys? He could have fooled us," Shyla said, giving him a mock glare.

"Yes, well...we'll let you get back to work, Kaveri." Hanif herded them toward the exit. Fast.

But Shyla paused and turned around before leaving. "Can I ask you something?" she asked Kaveri. All the air in the cavern seemed to disappear.

"About the plants?" the woman asked, hopeful.

"No, about you."

Hanif tensed.

"What do you want to know?" A slight wariness crept into her gaze.

"Were you abandoned outside Zirdai like I was?" Shyla would wait until Kaveri was ready to claim the relationship between them. And if she never did...then Shyla would accept it.

Kaveri's tight grip on her basket relaxed. "No. I was found near Tarim."

That was over a hundred sun jumps away. "How did you end up here?"

"Some monks travel to other monasteries as part of their spiritual journey. The people living here soothed my soul so I stayed."

"That's lovely," Shyla said, trying not to grit her teeth. When they'd left the cavern, she rounded on Hanif. "Why didn't you tell me monks can travel?"

"You didn't ask."

Her fingers curled with the desire to strangle her father. "You knew one of the reasons I didn't want to become a monk was because I wished to visit the other cities of Koraha."

"You had many reasons, Shyla. A person who takes the oath must be completely at peace with their decision."

"But how is a person to make an informed decision when vital information is being kept from them?" She held up a hand. "And don't say they needed to have faith."

Hanif stopped and faced her. "You decided you weren't staying when you were ten circuits old. From that point on, you turned a blind eye to everything going on around you."

She opened her mouth to argue, but no words escaped her lips. He had a point.

"You had faith when it was needed, Shyla," Hanif said in a softer tone. "Besides, you wouldn't have been happy as a monk."

"No, but I missed all of you." It had been a lonely and difficult two circuits.

He wrapped an arm around her shoulders. "That was the point. You needed to be on your own to figure out what you truly desired."

She leaned into him for a moment, taking comfort from his steady presence, drinking in the knowledge that she was no longer on her own. However, along with her newfound family, she also had accepted a great deal of responsibility. A bone-deep fatigue pulsed, reminding her of Orla's good advice not to wear herself out, which she'd promptly ignored.

"I don't have the energy to return to our hideout. Can I stay a little longer?" she asked.

"Of course, you're always welcome here." Hanif released her, then added with a glint in his eyes, "But not when you have guards or deacons chasing you."

"When? Thanks for the confidence."

"Anytime."

Shyla and Rendor headed back to her room. By the time they arrived, her legs had turned into mush. After kicking off her boots, she just about crawled under the fur. Rendor hesitated, glancing at the door.

She skootched over and patted the cushion. "You look as exhausted as I feel."

He gave her a tired smile and joined her. Resting her head on his shoulder, she draped an arm over his broad chest. They hadn't had any time alone since moving to the new headquarters. Too bad they were both exhausted.

"I'm glad you didn't become a monk," Rendor said, tucking her closer.

"You do know that celibacy is not part of the oath, right?" she teased, then sobered. It was another fact about life in the monastery she'd only recently learned. A blind eye indeed.

"Oh yes. I got that when I noticed the resemblance between you and Hanif. And…"

She waited, but he remained quiet. Because Rendor was observant and smart, she could finish his sentence. "And between me and Kaveri."

"Yes. It was striking." A pause. "Do you plan on acknowledging the relationship?"

"No. Not unless she does. It's an odd way to raise a child, but, if I think about it, it's better than growing up a vagrant and worrying about raids, having enough water, and your next meal." She huffed. "Like we're living now. If I became a monk, I never would have ruined your life."

Rendor moved so quickly, Shyla didn't have time to react. He sat up, pulling her with him so she faced him.

"You did *not* ruin my life." His intense gaze seared her. "I thank the Sun Goddess every sun jump that you came into my life."

Even though she had read his soul when she'd first awoken the power of The Eyes and knew he spoke the truth, she still struggled to believe it. "But you went from captain of the guard to a grunt who shovels sand."

"Someone told me I look 'mighty fine' when I shovel." He smirked.

Figured he'd remember that. "You know what I mean."

91

"I do. And I'd rather shovel sand than torture people for the Water Prince."

And just like that, he put it all in perspective. "Sorry. I know. It's just…"

"Your heart is still not sure about me." Rendor cupped her cheek.

Actually, it was thumping its approval quite loudly. But she'd told him of her confusion before she read his soul. She hadn't yet revealed that she knew his commitment and love were genuine because she wanted him to see just what he'd gotten himself into. He might change his mind. Plus the rest of the Invisible Swords needed to witness his efforts to become a better person.

He dropped his hand. "Don't worry, Shyla. I'm willing to prove myself so you'll jump into my arms."

She smiled. "You're not going to let me forget that, are you?"

"Not for one degree." He lay back, bringing her down with him, once again tucking her close. "Now sleep."

"You're rather bossy for a grunt."

"In *this* case, I'm in charge."

"Of what?"

"Of making sure you take care of yourself by getting enough sleep and eating well."

"How'd you get that job?" she asked.

"No one else wanted it," he teased.

* * *

Shyla smoothed out her and Rendor's tracks as they returned to their headquarters. The sun hung just above the horizon. They had woken at angle one-sixty. And while she was refreshed, the effort to erase their boot prints was quickly draining the energy she'd regained. It was a good thing Rendor had insisted on carrying the two jugs of water Hanif had insisted on giving them. She'd vowed to pay him back.

Jayden and Ximen waited for her near the main entrance.

"What's wrong?" she asked, noting their tight postures.

"Nothing now that you're here," Ximen said. "We heard Captain Yates was at the monastery. Did you see him?"

"Yes." She explained what had happened.

"That's exactly why we haven't been teaching you more about your magic," Jayden said. "You don't know your limits."

Oh no, he didn't get to pull that on her. "Knowledge is *never* a bad thing. If I knew more about my magic, I wouldn't exhaust myself experimenting."

They glared at each other.

"Perhaps a compromise?" Ximen suggested.

"I'm listening," Shyla said.

"We'll teach you, but we determine the pace. And you have to promise not to overextend yourself again. Agreed?"

That was an easy question to answer. "Yes. When do we start?"

Ximen glanced at Jayden.

"How are you feeling now?" Jayden asked.

She straightened. "I'm fine."

"She's still recovering," Rendor said. "You promised not to exhaust yourself," he added when she frowned at him.

"All right, then we'll start at angle zero of the next sun jump. We can meet here on the surface," Jayden said. "Unless you need more time to recuperate?"

Mindful of Rendor, she chose her words with care. "I should be sufficiently revived by then. If I'm not, I'll let you know."

Jayden just shook his head. He gestured at the water jugs. "That'll help, but we need to address the water situation before we run out."

Remembering Orla's advice about delegating, she said, "Rendor has a good idea about getting water." She turned to Rendor. "Time is critical so put together a team to restock our supplies. No one is off-limits. Let us know if you need anything."

Rendor nodded, keeping his expression neutral, but appreciation sparked in his eyes.

Jayden drew in a breath but wisely kept quiet in front of Rendor. She suspected he'd corner her later. Too tired to care, she retreated to her room on level nine. As they cleared more and more space inside the temple, the others insisted she have her own spot instead of sharing. Even though only a worn curtain served as her door, it was a nice gesture and gave her the illusion of privacy.

Eventually, they would open up all the dorms. And she hoped she could move up to level six and install a mirror pipe. When she lived in Zirdai, her room had been on level three and she missed being close to the sun.

At about three meters by two meters, the space was… cozy. The thin mat kept her off the cold floor and she used her sun cloak as a blanket. There was no need for a heavy fur this deep as the temperature remained at ten degrees Celsius no matter what the angle. A long table stretched along the wall on the other side of the room. She set her pack down on it. A couple bedraggled sitting cushions were beside it. Two druks kept the darkness at bay, although she wondered if she'd still need them while she slept now that she had the ability to sense people nearby. It'd been embarrassing to admit she was afraid of the dark.

A pile of clothing occupied one corner, and a pyramid of scrolls sat in another. Borrowed from the monks, one of the scrolls showed the layout of the Temple of Arinna, their current home. Another contained information about The Eyes.

She closed one druk and turned the other low before lying down. But her thoughts whirled with all the tasks she needed to do and sleep refused to come. After a few angles, she gave up and unrolled the velbloud skin with the guidance on using the power of The Eyes.

The problem was the information was written in an archaic language and rather cryptic. She'd learned how to read it as that had been her specialty—transcribing old tablets and scrolls—but it took extra time to translate.

So far, Shyla had learned how to block others' thoughts and emotions, which helped keep her sanity. And she was getting so good at lowering and raising her mental shield that it almost didn't require a conscious effort. The Eyes also increased her magical power. Before she woke them, she could only influence one person, but afterwards she had persuaded twenty-five people that she'd disappeared. And now she could also alter a person's memory. She wondered if that was the real reason for Jayden's reluctance to teach her. Perhaps he was scared of her powers and didn't want to give her even more abilities. She didn't blame him; if she thought about it too much, it frightened her as well.

Shyla worked on translating a section of the scroll until the pain in her head forced her to return to her sleeping mat where she proceeded to toss and turn, unable to find a comfortable position. Perhaps some hot tea… No, she wouldn't waste water. Besides, they didn't have any lava stones or fuel to heat the water. And tepid tea was…well, tepid. She added lava stones to her wish list along with decent sleeping cushions and extra furs and blankets and fresh meat and vegetables. Perhaps she could buy some from the monks.

Lying on her back, she was staring at the ceiling when she sensed Rendor outside her room—that really was a handy skill! Shyla lowered her shield. He'd brought her a water skin and a couple rolls of jerky since she'd missed second and third meal. Not wishing to disturb her rest, Rendor debated whether to leave them next to her door or to set them inside on the table.

"Come in, Rendor. I'm awake," she said, raising her mental barrier again.

He swept the curtain aside. "Did I—"

"No, you didn't wake me." She sat up. "Thanks for bringing food and water, but I don't need it."

"Yes, you do," he said, stepping into her room. "You haven't been eating or drinking as much as you should. How can you function properly without sustenance? People are relying on you."

He'd noticed. "I don't—"

"Have a headache? Aren't hungry?"

Now that he mentioned it, the dull ache flared to a sharp pounding, and her stomach rumbled. Loudly. At least he didn't gloat. "How did you know?"

"I'm observant and can count." He handed her the skin.

She took a couple sips of water, but it tasted bitter.

Rendor crouched down beside her. "I know you think you're helping the others by not taking your full share,

97

but you're not. You're making all the decisions. Important ones that shouldn't be made when you're weak and dehydrated."

The desire to grump at him pushed up her throat. But he was right and she had been skipping meals. So she gulped down a few more mouthfuls of water and chewed on the dried jerky.

When he stood to leave, she suddenly didn't want to be alone. "What time is it?" she asked between bites.

"Around angle three hundred."

"Have you gotten any sleep?"

He hesitated. "Not yet. I wanted to talk to Jaft and Elek about joining my team before their shift."

The two men had been acolytes when they'd volunteered to help Shyla rescue Banqui and then they joined the Invisible Sword after she'd woken the power of The Eyes. "Good choices."

"I need strong men. Water is heavy."

"Are you taking the cart?"

"No. That's too difficult to conceal and the water jugs are too awkward to carry. I've another idea."

"What is it?"

He smiled. "I need to figure out if I can get the right materials first. If not, then I'll have to think of something else."

In other words, he would tell her only when he was ready. "Let me know if you need anything."

"I will." He left.

She hugged her arms to her chest as a sudden chill raced up her spine. The room seemed colder without him. Shyla resisted calling him back. She'd slept so much better with him beside her. However, many of the Invisible Swords didn't like or trust him despite her repeated assurances that he was sincere. And they wouldn't be happy about him staying in her room even if all they did was sleep.

The Invisible Swords believed in the power of The Eyes, yet she was learning that they needed to experience certain things for themselves like Rendor. Which shouldn't have been a surprise as she'd been the same way. Hanif had warned her that the citizens of Zirdai wouldn't welcome a sun-kissed, but she left the monastery anyway, determined to change everyone's mind. It took her two circuits to admit he was right.

Eventually, she slept. In her dreams, a sand storm chased her. She tried to run away from it, but her feet sank into the soft surface, slowing her down. Soon the storm caught up to her and she was lost in a dense fog of sand that obscured everything and cut her off from everyone—the worst part, until the airborne grains filled her nose and blocked her throat. Unable to breathe, she woke with a strangled cry, clawing at her neck, convinced she was suffocating.

Hands grabbed her wrists and pulled her fingers away from her skin.

"Easy there," Jayden said. "It's just a dream."

She stilled and focused on him as her heart slowed to normal. He knelt next to her mat. When she no longer gasped for breath, she said, "Thanks."

Jayden released her and sat back on his heels. "I came to check on you. It's angle ten."

"Oh. Sorry. I'm—"

"Still recovering?"

"I don't think so. I couldn't sleep, but when I did, it wasn't restful." Far from it. She wondered if her bad dream was a symptom of using too much magic. Jayden stood and brushed the sand off his knees. "Do you want another sun jump to rest?"

"No." Remembering Rendor's comment about taking care of herself, she said, "Just give me five angles and I'll meet you."

Shyla hurried to change and eat. When she reached the surface, she paused to drink in the sunlight. It warmed her even though the air around her was still cool from the darkness. A breeze blew the sand, the ribbons flowing over the surface like translucent snakes. She breathed in the familiar scent of ginger mixed with anise.

Nearby, the first crew cleared sand. Rendor was among them. She wondered if he'd gotten any sleep. As if feeling her gaze on him, he glanced up and smiled at her. She returned it. What a sap.

Jayden was helping to smooth out the piles of sand that had been brought up from the temple. He used his magic to move the grains, making it appear to be undisturbed—a small dune in a series of equally unimposing dunes.

She joined him. "Is that the same as erasing tracks?"

"Yes, except you have to control more of the sand so it takes more concentration. And you need to envision the end result." He swept a hand out to the miniature dunes. "As we clear the sand from the temple, I'm building these just like if they were etched by the wind. Slowly, gradually, angled perpendicular to the dominant wind direction. So if anyone noticed this patch of the desert over time, the dunes would not appear suddenly from one sun jump to the next."

Gurice trudged over with another bucket and dumped it onto a new pile. "Must be nice to stand around doing nothing, enjoying the view," she snarked.

"Yes. It's lovely." Jayden didn't rise to the bait.

"You know I can make dunes while you schlep heavy buckets," Gurice said.

"I know." He turned to Shyla. "Gurice can make dunes as well, but, while I created four small dunes in a few angles without much effort, it would take her longer and sap all her strength."

"Yeah, well, moving sand grains isn't my forte," she grumped.

"Can you erase your tracks?" Shyla asked.

"Yeah, but it's harder than making a person see what I want them to see." Her green eyes glowed with mischief. "That's my specialty."

"But, again, she can only do a few people at a time, while I can influence a dozen."

"Rub it in." Gurice strode away, muttering.

"She's a little sensitive," Jayden said.

"Does everyone have a specialty like Gurice?" Shyla asked.

"Yes. Everyone can do one thing better than the other skills. A few can only do one or two things. The weaker the magic, the more limited the person."

"What's your specialty?"

"I'm rare in that I can do all things equally well."

"How rare?"

"Before the ambush, there were four of us. After…" He stared into the distance. "It's just me and Ximen now." Grief thickened his words and dragged them through the air.

"How many people could wield magic before?"

"Twenty total."

She stared at him in shock. "That's it? I thought the Invisible Sword had—"

"We don't. While there were dozens of people in the different levels of our organization, we didn't have many that could wield magic."

And there were only eleven of them left. Twelve if she counted Zhek. His ability to heal had to be magical. Then there was Mojag and his sensitive nose. Which made her wonder… "What are the 'things' you keep mentioning?"

"Magical skills. There are three of them—influence, manipulation, and movement. You already know about influencing a person's perceptions, making them see or not see what you want them to, making them smell an odor, fall asleep, or sit down, things like that. Influence also allows us to 'sense' a person like we did when we were at our old headquarters.

"Manipulation is more advanced as it goes into a person's thoughts and emotions, changing their memories, causing fear or happiness. Movement is what we do with the sand." Jayden smoothed out Gurice's small pile. "Reverting the sand to its undisturbed state is a lifesaving skill. You already know how to erase tracks in the sand, but there are a few other skills that are essential. Remember when we ambushed you and Rendor on that dune?"

"Hard to forget." Her tone held an edge. Rendor had almost died.

Jayden ignored it. "When you crested the dune, the sand was undisturbed. But just under the surface were twelve Invisible Swords."

She perked up. Was he going to teach her how to travel through the sand?

"This is how we did it." Jayden stepped a couple meters away. He pulled the hood of his sun cloak over his head and down so it covered his face as well. He gestured. A thick cloud of sand rose up in front of him, leaving behind a shallow depression. Shyla moved back, instinctively covering her nose and mouth. But the grains remained near Jayden.

Then he stretched out in the dip in the sand on his stomach. Resting on his elbows, he held out the edge of the hood. It resembled a tent around his head. The sand cloud settled over him and dissipated.

She stared at the sand. It was smooth, pristine. Jayden had disappeared. Nothing happened for an angle, then the sand exploded into the air, obscuring her view. When the sand settled, Jayden stood there. The spot around him was once again undisturbed.

"That was impressive," Shyla said. "How long can you stay under the sand?"

"It depends on how deep you are. I was pretty close to the surface and you saw that I trapped a pocket of air with my hood. I could have stayed under for about ten angles. Once you go deeper, you have less air and less time."

Fascinated, she asked, "How deep can you go?"

"Only as deep as the loose sand. Once you hit the hard stone, that's it."

That didn't add up. "But when they captured me, we traveled through the ground."

Jayden gave her a wry smile. "That's what you were supposed to think. It was a bit of a show."

"A show?" She tried and failed to keep the outrage from her voice.

"Remember fear and desperation trigger magic. Come on." Jayden strode away, heading for a large dune.

She followed. They climbed to the top.

Jayden faced her. "When I disappear, look over the side." He pointed. Then he pulled his hood down. A cloud of grains spiraled into the air. It wasn't thick enough to block the sight of Jayden sinking into the sand.

Even though she'd seen it before, it still startled her and she had to stifle the desire to rush over and grab his arms. When any other person sank, it meant the poor soul had stumbled into a patch of unstable sluff sand, which, if he was alone, meant he would soon suffocate and die.

Once Jayden vanished, the cloud settled and the sand rushed to fill the hole, leaving behind no sign he'd been there at all. Shyla hurried to the dune's edge and peered over. After a couple heart-pounding moments, sand poured from the side as if the dune was bleeding. Then a man-sized slit opened and Jayden sauntered out. The grains reversed direction, plugging the gap.

He turned toward her and held his arms out wide. "Ta da!"

Show-off. But she had to admit it was impressive. She slid down the side of the dune until she reached him. "Why did the sand run out of the dune before you exited?"

"My body took up space inside the dune. The sand will compress to a certain point, but the rest has to go somewhere. When I sank, the sand moved to give me room. Some of it went into the air so I could cover my passage, and the rest went out the side."

"So, after the ambush, I was taken through the dune?"

"Yes. Payatt took you with him, then he erased your memories of the trip to the testing chamber."

A nice name for what it really was—a prison—but she kept quiet. Instead she focused on the fact Payatt had erased her memories. It was strange to think she had an experience that she no longer remembered. Unease grew, knotting her stomach. "Was that the only time my memory was altered?"

He hesitated and a longing to read his soul gripped her. She studied him, searching for any indication he was about to lie.

"I think so," he finally said.

"Think?"

"I wasn't with you the entire time. Plus you moped in your room those three sun jumps after we rescued Banqui. Someone could have visited you to find out how much you knew about our organization."

Shyla recalled the events after Banqui's rescue, but something nagged at her. A detail that…didn't quite fit. It clicked.

"Why didn't you erase my memories?" she asked him. "You can do manipulation as well as the other two skills. But you told me it wasn't your specialty."

"I lied. I was furious at you for that stunt you pulled with the Water Prince. If I'd accessed your memories, there was a very good chance I would have wiped everything." He swiped his hand through the air in one harsh chop. "Clean slate. Baby fresh."

Stunned, she grappled with his admission. So much there... She'd known he was angry, but this was on an entirely different level. Also the fact that a person's mind could be obliterated back to infancy... Scary.

She regained some of her composure. "I don't regret that *stunt*. It saved us all."

"So you say."

Yes, she did. The Water Prince had been wearing armor under his tunic. But she hadn't woken The Eyes yet, so Jayden hadn't believed her. Obviously, he was still upset. It explained why he argued with her on everything. And why he didn't fully trust her. It occurred to her that Jayden was the only one who hadn't witnessed her sacrifice for The Eyes. Hanif had been right to invite the Invisible Swords to watch. It'd made a difference in how they treated her.

"Do you think The Eyes made a mistake choosing me?" she asked.

"I think The Eyes don't choose. I think they'll work for anyone who is brave and conceited enough to allow another person to cut out their eyeballs."

CHAPTER
6

Shyla thought she'd been astounded before. This was so far beyond it she didn't have a word to describe it.

"I'm being honest," he said into the silence.

Recovering slightly, she said, "I got that. But what about all the warnings that The Eyes might fail to work and leave a person blind?"

"That's where the brave part comes in. That supposed risk kept so many people from trying. From even touching them." He shook his head. "And it put doubts into their heads so even if The Eyes stirred to their touch, they still wouldn't go through with it."

"And the conceit? Where does that come in?"

"Believing that you're so special that there is no doubt they'll work for you. Having the conceit to actually go through with it."

It hadn't been like that for her. She'd had lots of doubts about whether they would wake, but she went through with the sacrifice despite them. Unlike now when she doubted Jayden would believe her even if she tried to enlighten him. His bitterness explained so much.

"You wanted to wake The Eyes," she said.

"Yes. It should have been me." He flicked his fingers. Sand burst into the air. "I've spent my entire life working to make the people of Zirdai's lives better."

There was nothing she could say that would ease his anger. Best to keep quiet and let him get it out. The grains formed the shape of an arrow and zipped around them. One part of her wanted to ask him to teach her how to do that, and the other wanted to duck and cover.

"The Invisible Sword leaders thought I was too young. Too inexperienced. They wouldn't even let me touch them." The arrow swooped close to the surface, sucking up more sand. It grew larger. "And then you came along. No experience. Younger than me. You couldn't care less about people's lives. Just your own agenda." He laughed, but it was a humorless sound. "After all that, you really did steal The Eyes of Tamburah." The arrow slammed into the dune. Sand sprayed out in all directions, leaving behind a sunburst pattern.

"Why didn't you say something sooner?" she asked.

He rounded on her. "What could I say? You did it to *rescue* me. I'd come off as an ungrateful jerk." Scrubbing a hand through his hair, Jayden glanced around as if searching for a reason for his outburst. "I can't believe I'm saying all this now."

She touched his arm. "You needed to say it."

"Yeah, well, it's not like it's going to change anything."

It already had for her and she suspected for him as well. "Rescuing you was only one of the reasons I sacrificed my eyes. Dyani, the little girl who was poisoned, was another. And I realized I not only wanted to help the vagrants and the Invisible Swords, but that I could. Huh. I guess that was conceited."

"See?" He gave her a wan smile.

"You're right, bravery and conceit." And, according to Rendor, insanity. "I never felt I was special, though."

"But you're sun-kissed."

"That makes me an outcast, unwanted, and, if you believe the Heliacal Priestess, cursed. Not special." She thought about why he'd think that. "Do I act like I am?" That would be terrible.

"No."

One positive. Probably not enough for Jayden. "If you leave, I'll understand."

"Why would I leave?"

"You think I stole The Eyes from you."

"You did."

"My point exactly."

"I'm upset but not stupid. We're stronger together. Besides, who's going to teach you how to move sand? Gurice? Ximen? I think not."

"But you said Ximen can do all three magical techniques equally well."

"He can, but I'm twice as strong as him."

"Now who's conceited?"

"Shut up," he said with a grin. "And if you're finished distracting me, let's get back to the lesson. Smoothing out a boot print is on a small scale, but to be able to bury your body in sand, you have to command a larger area. You have to extend your focus and concentrate on what you want the sand to do."

"What do I want it to do?" she asked.

"You want the sand to lift up, creating a body-sized hollow. Let's start with a small area," he said. "Think of using your will to scoop up a shovelful of sand."

Shyla considered. Using *return* wouldn't work in this case. Fly? Up? "How do you target a certain size when there's an entire desert full of sand?" At least a boot print had edges.

Jayden bent down and drew a circle in the sand with his finger. "Sorry, it's been a while since I learned. This will help you visualize. Eventually, you won't need it."

Concentrating on the circle, Shyla imagined digging down about two centimeters.

Lift.

The circle heaved, but only a few grains flew into the air.

Adding more energy, she tried again.

Lift.

Same result.

"Did I say it was easy?" Jayden asked.

She huffed. "You make it look easy."

"I've eighteen circuits of practice. My father kept a bucket full of sand next to my sleeping cushion just so I could practice every sun jump."

Eighteen? That meant— "You started using magic when you were six circuits old?"

"Yes."

"They tested you that young?" She couldn't keep the horror from her voice. Chaining a young boy in complete darkness was beyond cruel.

"I wasn't tested in the chamber. My father didn't have the patience. Try to move the sand again, but this time put some energy into it."

What did his father do to cause a young Jayden to be scared and desperate enough to invoke his magic? It had to be equally terrible. She channeled her outrage into the command.

Lift.

Sand exploded, shooting into the air before raining back down.

"Better. Do it again," Jayden said.

She did it another thousand times. Okay, it was more like a hundred, but at least her control improved with each repetition. When Jayden was satisfied, he taught her how to keep the sand in the air. He demonstrated, lifting a section. The cloud hovered above the surface, remaining in place. "Your turn."

Shyla needed another order. Stay? Hold? Focusing on her circle, she gathered her will.

Lift.

Before she could issue the second one, the grains fell. She glanced at Jayden, but he remained quiet. Obviously using two commands wasn't going to work. She needed one to do both.

It took her longer to figure out a command than she'd like to admit. Once again, she aimed her will at the circle. She imagined the velbloud flocks.

Float.

The sand rose in the air and stayed.

"Not bad," Jayden said. "Now put it back so it appears undisturbed."

Visualizing the smooth rippled pattern of the surrounding sand, Shyla sent her magic to the cloud.

Settle.

The grains drifted to the surface and flowed, matching the pattern.

"Nice. Do it again."

This time the repetition included lifting sand from a bigger and bigger circle. Each lift used more of her energy. The increasing heat didn't help either as the sun jumped higher. Eventually, the hot air wicked the sweat from her face and the desert's scent now held a burnt aroma. Time to retreat underground.

The crew clearing sand had already quit. Except Rendor. He waited for her by the temple's entrance, which was a meter-wide hole with a ladder that ended on the first level. There were ramps and steps between the other deeper levels.

"Did you think she needed to be rescued again?" Jayden asked Rendor before climbing down.

Rendor ignored his snide tone and sour look. Or so it appeared. Shyla noticed the slight stiffening of his shoulders. Otherwise, the big man's expression remained neutral—a skill that was unfortunately needed as he endured many cutting comments and nasty glares. Rendor was smart enough not to snap back, but it had to be difficult.

Once Jayden disappeared, she asked, "How are your preparations going?"

"Gurice and Mojag have agreed to go into the city at darkness to purchase the supplies. I'm having…difficulties recruiting people for the rest of my team."

Surprised, she asked, "Jaft and Elek said no?"

"They agreed, but that's all. I need four more at least or it's not worth the effort."

Scorching hells. "Who else did you ask?"

Rendor stilled. "I'm not giving you names."

Figured. Although she understood why. The temperature rose and the intensity of the sunlight burned on her head and shoulders. Without further comment, they descended and joined the others in the common room on level eight. Technically it was too early for second meal, but it was a natural break as all three crews were awake and together.

As she filled her skin, she noted the low water level. Then she checked their supplies. Only one full jug remained. She glanced around the room. Not everyone was here so she sent a few runners to gather the rest.

Once all twenty-nine of them were in the common room, Shyla stood on a table and raised her voice above the murmur of conversation. "I'm sure you've noticed we're low on water."

Quiet descended. Everyone turned to her. Good.

"Rendor came up with a plan to supply us with clean water. Yes, it's from his knowledge from working as a guard. And yes, I'm aware of the terrible things he has done."

"Are you sure you are aware?" asked Ajay, one of the Invisible Sword survivors. "Safe in the monastery, you didn't deal with the constant fear of being caught by him or his guards. You never had anyone you loved taken, tortured, and murdered by *him*."

The others rumbled their agreement. She'd known there was animosity toward him, but not to this degree. Rendor sat alone in the back corner, appearing as if he'd turned to stone.

Shyla swallowed. "Yes, I *am* aware. I've seen the Water Prince's special rooms and witnessed the torture.

I've also witnessed Rendor coming to our aid when we rescued Jayden from the Heliacal Priestess."

"He only came to our aid after he almost died. If he returned to the Water Prince, the next guard in line for captain would have challenged him and won. Killers like him don't get second chances."

Seven hells. This wasn't how this was supposed to go. "Everyone deserves a second chance. Everyone can change. Yes, I grew up sheltered in the monastery and then was blind to the people's pain and suffering when I lived in Zirdai. I changed and am working just as hard as all of you to help the citizens. Rendor has changed, too, and is making amends."

"Yeah, by biding his time until he can report to the Water Prince," Titus, another Invisible Sword survivor, said.

"He's trustworthy," she said.

"You only think that because you're in love with him," a male voice called from somewhere in the back of the group.

Titters and gasps followed. Scorching sand rats. That explained why her word wasn't good enough for them. They thought she was biased due to her emotions.

Projecting her voice over the rising din, she said, "It is *because* I read his soul. You all witnessed what I've gone through in order to do just that." She went up onto her tiptoes, making a show of searching for someone in the back. "Does the person who doubts me wish for me to read his soul?" Some uncomfortable shuffling. She let them sweat for half an angle. "No? I've respected everyone's privacy. And you have accepted my leadership. I assigned Rendor to lead this mission. He needs volunteers." In other words, she could order them to do it. "We. Need. Water."

Shyla stepped off the table, grabbed two rolls of jerky, and left. Only when she was alone in her room did she relax. How... Why did they think she was in love with Rendor? He'd made his feelings for her clear, along with his desire to atone, but she thought she'd been treating him like everyone else. She wondered if Jayden had been spreading rumors in order to undermine her authority. Or perhaps their fear and hatred of him were too strong to overcome. Too bad leadership skills hadn't been included with her new eyes. Did she just make it worse?

Her exertions caught up to her. She plopped onto her mat and chewed the dried jerky.

Gurice visited her first. After a quick knock, she entered Shyla's room. "Nice speech. I'm gonna need coins to purchase the air bladders for Rendor."

Why would he—oh, to carry the water. Velblouds had four air bladders inside of them. Just before the start of the killing heat, the animals filled their bladders with hot air and floated, escaping the deadly temperatures on the surface. The bladders weren't the best water containers for long-term storage, but, in the short term, they were lighter than leather and would be easier to carry.

"How many osees do you need?" she asked, digging into her pack. Shyla had hidden the bulk of the coins but always kept a few with her.

"Four or five."

She handed six to Gurice. "Just in case."

"Thanks."

"No, thank you for going on this mission."

Gurice cocked a hip. "Did you know Rendor caught Mojag once?"

"No. He doesn't like to talk about what he did when working for the prince." Not like they had any time to talk.

"This was before you came to Zirdai. Before Rendor was the captain. He could have arrested Mojag and tortured him for information on the location of the vagrant communes. Mojag was only nine circuits old. But he didn't. Instead, he showed my brother a shortcut to avoid an area where there were lots of guards, and then let him go. Mojag didn't even know the guard was Rendor until he was promoted to captain."

Shyla wasn't sure where Gurice was going with the story so she waited.

"What I'm trying to say is, working as the captain for the prince drained his soul. Or so we all thought. I'm glad he still has some left."

Nice of Gurice to share her thoughts.

"And, scorching hells, girl. He's a fine-looking specimen. Hope you're taking full advantage." She winked.

Not so nice now. "Don't you have buckets of sand to dump?"

Gurice laughed, waggled her fingers in goodbye, and left.

Her room was too quiet without Gurice. Shyla debated. She should rest, but she was…restless, which didn't make any sense. Her thoughts kept circling around in her head, but she refused to analyze them. Or rather, overanalyze. Instead, she decided to help clear sand from the dorm level.

Leaving her room, she walked straight into Rendor. Hitting a wall would have been softer. He grabbed her elbow to steady her even though he scowled at her. It didn't take the power of The Eyes to sense she was in trouble.

She glanced down the hallway. At least no one lurked nearby to overhear their forthcoming argument. Suppressing a sigh, she returned to her room. Rendor followed.

He didn't even wait until the curtain swung back into place. "I've my team. Ximen, Balin, Lamar, Daksh, and Nard volunteered after your speech."

Except Lamar, they were all strong men. Balin, Daksh, and Nard were ex-acolytes. Hanif had grumped over losing them, claiming they were top level fighters— a high compliment from him. Lamar was one of the eleven Invisible Swords who had survived the ambush. With Gurice, Mojag, Jaft, and Elek, Rendor's team had nine people. So why the scowl?

"That's good. Is everyone entering the city this darkness?"

"Yes. Gurice and Mojag assured me they could obtain the supplies without delay."

"Will everyone be able to leave at angle zero?"

"That is my plan. If we run into anything unexpected, we might have to stay another sun jump."

Her stomach twisted with just the thought of waiting that long for news. "Do you need another magic wielder?"

"No."

Short and to the point. Was he afraid she'd order Jayden to tag along? Or that she'd join them and take over his mission? She'd told everyone she trusted him. So she kept those thoughts quiet. "All right. What else do you need. Osees?"

"No. Nothing else. But I want to know something."

Oh boy. Shyla laced her fingers together to keep from cringing at the rumble of anger in his tone. "Go ahead, ask."

"When were you planning on telling *me* you read my soul?"

"I didn't—"

"So you lied to everyone?"

"No. I… When I first woke The Eyes, your and Hanif's thoughts inundated me. I didn't know how to block either of you. At that time, I picked up on your sincerity, your desire to atone, and your emotions. It was all there on the surface. I didn't probe deeper. But I trusted you before that. Otherwise I'd never have asked you to become a member." And to cut her eyes out, but she wisely refrained from reminding him.

"I remember. You trusted me to join the Invisible Sword, but I also distinctly remember you saying you wouldn't risk your heart. Not until I proved myself to you. You know how I feel about you. Why didn't you say something? Why didn't you..."

Jump into his arms? Like she'd promised. Pain had replaced the anger in his voice, making it worse. "I..."

"You don't share the same feelings," he said. "That's why you've been keeping your distance. Why you didn't respond to that idiot in the common room."

"No. That's not... What about at the monastery?"

"What about it?"

"We..."

"Shared a sleeping cushion. To sleep."

He made it sound so...ordinary. "Yes, but I..." The right words remained elusive. She struggled to extract them from deep within her. Why was this so hard?

"You...what? You're embarrassed? Is that why you only showed me you care when the Invisible Swords couldn't see us? Or is it that you don't want my history to tarnish your leadership?"

"No! I..."

"That's what I thought. Excuse me, I need to get my team ready for our mission." Rendor strode from the room.

Shyla's mouth hung open, but a tight knot in her throat blocked all sounds and made breathing difficult. Pressure and pain filled her chest like a velbloud's air bladder. Still nothing escaped. Not even a squeak. She should run after him, grab his arm and tell him...what? That she believed if the others knew her feelings for him, they wouldn't trust him? Was that the real reason? Or was she worried they wouldn't trust her? No. They had faith in her. Then what?

Sitting on the mat, she cradled her head, trying to relax enough to draw in a deep breath. Was she having a panic attack? No. Perhaps she should have never made that damn speech. She recalled the words. Something in there niggled at her. A part of her must believe that the Invisible Swords would never accept Rendor. Then what would she do?

It struck her like an arrow to her heart. She didn't have to do *anything*. Rendor would never betray their trust. And he certainly wouldn't care what the others thought of him. So why should she?

She needed to find Rendor and explain. But was she ready to jump into his arms? What exactly did she feel for him? They'd flirted and she was physically attracted to him. Should she even be in a relationship? Her priorities had shifted from herself to all of Zirdai. Plus now she was responsible for the lives of twenty-nine Invisible Swords. Would being with Rendor be too much of a distraction? Or be too selfish?

This would be easier if she could peer into a mirror and read her own soul. But it hadn't worked. Yes, she'd tried. She sagged back on her mat. Pain pulsed in her temples. Despite her promise to take it slow, she'd overextended her magic. And here she was angsting over Rendor when she should be resting.

She pulled her sun cloak up over her shoulders. Closing her eyes, she decided to nap for a few angles and then talk to Rendor before he left for his mission. The right words were sure to come at that time.

* * *

By the time she woke, Rendor and the others had gone. She stood on the surface at angle one-seventy. No sign of their tracks marked the sand. Ximen had done a good job erasing ten sets of boot prints. The sun hung low in the pink sky. Shyla chewed on her lower lip. Worry and fear took equal turns squeezing her heart.

Jayden joined her.

"Why didn't anyone wake me before they left?" she asked him.

"No need. You put Rendor in charge. Unless you wanted to give him a kiss goodbye." Jayden studied her.

If he was hoping for a reaction, he was going to be disappointed. However, she suspected she'd have to endure similar comments in the future if she didn't put a stop to it right now.

"My *private* relationship is none of your business," she said.

He crossed his arms. "Oh, I think it is."

"Why is that?"

He held up his index finger. "First, you chose the worst person. No, falling in love with the Water Prince would have been worse." Another finger shot up. "Second, we really can't trust your judgment even if you say you read his soul. How do we know you didn't just see what you wanted to see?"

She mimicked him. "First, who is this *we*? Are you sure it isn't just you? You've been fighting me about everything. Is it because you're jealous of Rendor?"

He scoffed. "Hardly."

It wasn't because Jayden cared for her. He had made his opinion of her pretty clear, especially when he had called her a selfish sun-kissed. "Second, if you don't trust my judgment, you're welcome to leave and to take the others who are also concerned about my personal life with you." When he didn't reply, she continued, "I'll say it again, my personal life is none of the Invisible Sword's business."

"Then why did you assign Rendor to get us water when I repeatedly offered to take care of it?"

Son of a sand demon, he was jealous. "He had a better idea and he's a natural leader. I'm taking advantage of his skills, just like I do with Mojag or Ximen. And with you."

"Me?"

"Yes. I need to learn everything I can about my magic."

"Is that all you need me for?"

"Oh, for sand's sake, Jayden. No. You're vital to this organization for your connections with the vagrants, your knowledge of the hidden areas of Zirdai, your magical powers. Do I need to continue?"

"Well…"

She huffed. "I'm not stroking your ego anymore. Let's stop wasting time arguing and get to work. All right?"

"A truce?"

"I'd like nothing better."

"All right." He shook her hand.

She practiced working with the sand. Lots and lots of practice before full darkness. After third meal, she returned to her room. Soon after, Jayden brought her a bucket of sand.

"This is for—"

"Practice," she finished.

He grinned evilly. "Yup." At least Jayden had given her a distraction. She doubted she'd get much sleep.

And she was right. Shyla used up her energy to work with the sand. After that, she tried to rest. But despite the fatigue flowing through her body, every time she closed her eyes, Rendor's angry image rose. The pain in his voice echoed.

She glanced at the sand clock. Again. Angle three-twenty. Again, she swore the grains flowed up instead of down. Staring at the curved glass of the clock, Shyla pushed her will at it.

Stop.

The grains paused. Ha! She'd stopped time. Now the clock matched her mood. Too bad no one was there for her to tell. A pang of loneliness bounced in her chest. Her thoughts immediately went to Rendor. Argh. She couldn't wait any longer. Grabbing her sun cloak, she strode from her room and headed down to the dorms on level ten. Only a few had been cleared and Jayden shared one of them with Ximen, Mojag, and two others. Druk lanterns hung in the hallway, casting enough light into the rooms.

Not wishing to wake the others, she crept into the small space and whispered his name. Jayden woke with a jerk. He sat up and brandished a knife.

Whoa. Shyla held her hands up, leaning back.

He relaxed. "Don't do that."

"Wake you up?"

A grunt. "Is something wrong?"

"No."

"Then why—"

"I want to practice hiding in the sand."

"Now?" Incredulity laced his voice. "It's still dark and cold."

"I want to hide near the city's entrances. Is there a way to see through the sand? That would be a great way to spy on who's coming out without having to influence everyone."

"You're worried about Rendor's team."

At least he didn't just say Rendor. Progress. "Yes, but...I thought it might be a good idea to see if anyone follows them from the city."

Jayden considered. His blanket had slipped down to his waist, revealing his bare chest and defined abdominal muscles. Rendor also slept without a shirt despite it being ten degrees. She shivered. What was wrong with these guys? Did they enjoy showing off their muscles to sleep deprived and lonely sun-kisseds?

"All right," he said. "Give me an angle to get dressed."

She retreated to the common room. A few people sat at the tables, talking in low voices. Others hauled buckets up to the surface. While it was too cold to stay out there for long without being bundled up, short excursions were fine. Especially since lugging heavy sand was hot sweaty work.

Rae and Lian sat in the corner. The ex-acolytes waved her over. When she joined them, Rae said, "Worried about the team?"

"A little," she admitted.

"We're insulted he didn't ask us," Lian said. "We helped you get through all those guards and down to level seventy-three. That should count for something."

"It does. You have my eternal gratitude for helping rescue Banqui." Shyla wouldn't have gotten far without them, Jaft, and Elek. And that reminded her of another worry—where was Banqui? Was he safe?

"You know what I mean," Lian said.

"I do. And don't feel left out. Rendor did you a favor. Unless you wanted to climb ninety-nine levels carrying about twenty kilograms of water?"

Rae crinkled her small nose. Everything about the girl—yes, she was about the same age as Shyla, but she looked so young—was petite. Except her ability to fight. Nothing tiny about that.

Jayden arrived. "Ready?"

Shyla put on her sun cloak. The garment also provided warmth.

"Where are you going?" Lian asked.

"To do a little reconnaissance," Shyla said.

"Need backup?" she asked with a hopeful tone. Lian's pretty heart-shaped face held a wistful expression.

"I know everyone's sick of shoveling sand, but it's a necessary evil. And all too soon you'll be going on dangerous missions." Frankly, anytime any of them entered the city was dangerous.

"Promise?" Rae asked. Mischief sparked in her golden eyes.

"Yes."

"Goody."

Shyla and Jayden climbed from the temple and paused, allowing their vision to adjust to the darkness.

They weren't taking a druk. The lantern shone with a white light when it was on the surface. That shine would give them away.

The long fabric of her cloak flapped in the cold breeze. Above her head, the black sky glittered with millions of stars. A cluster of five large stars known as the brothers shone bright enough to illuminate their surroundings. Without the sun blazing overhead, the desert held no color. It rippled with various shades of gray.

Jayden erased their prints as they headed to the city. The sand crunched with a crispness underneath their boots. A quiet emptiness hovered over the landscape unlike during the sun's reign where the heat took up too much space, pushing and shoving at everything like a bully.

They passed a velbloud flock. The animals huddled together in one large mound. The warm air in their bladders kept them comfortable along with their white hair, which had the unique property of providing warmth during darkness and cooling the creatures during the killing heat. The people of Koraha revered the velbloud. When one died from sickness or old age, every part of it was used for the people's survival.

When they reached the city's outer limits, they circled the one-story structures, searching for the perfect vantage point. They chose a tall dune on the northeast edge. From that height, they would have a nice view of many of the entrances.

Jayden helped her float a Shyla-sized amount of sand. She lay on her stomach in the indentation. Holding out the hood of her cloak, she commanded the grains to settle. At first, it seemed like nothing happened, but then a weight pressed on her shoulders, back, legs and head. The starlight disappeared.

"How do I look?" she asked.

"A little too lumpy." Jayden's voice was slightly muffled. "Let me…" Sand shushed as it moved over her. "Okay, now lift your hood a bit and clear out two holes so you can see."

When she lifted the material, sand flowed toward her face.

"Not that much," Jayden said. "Push it away."

She cleared it and then created two small openings.

"Looks good. How do you feel?"

"Like a sand devil ready to pounce."

"Good. My turn."

Beside her the rustling sounds of moving sand didn't last long. Show-off.

As she waited for the sun to arrive, Shyla made a few discoveries. One, that the sand acted like a blanket, keeping her warm. Two, that remaining still for a few angles was harder than she thought. And the more she thought about it, the greater her desire to move, to stretch, to sneeze, to scratch since it seemed like every centimeter of her skin itched. Three, that breathing caused problems. Worried about taking too deep a breath and having someone notice the sand expanding and contracting, she tried to limit how much air she took in. But then that caused her to pant, which made her afraid she was running out of air despite Jayden's assurances and the fact there were two holes right in front of her.

"Breathe normally," Jayden said.

Surprised, she asked, "How did you know?"

"I can hear you."

Oh. Drawing in even breaths, she calmed.

The dark gray desert lightened in tiny increments. At first a blush of pink spread through the sands. It darkened, painting the surface with strokes of ruby, crimson, and orange until the desert was stained with color. When the sunlight struck the surface, it flashed with brilliance and snapped into the familiar reddish-orange hue.

Soon the cleaning crew appeared at the city's entrances, sweeping and shoveling the sand that had collected during the darkness. The constant wind only stilled during the killing heat.

Then the Heliacal Priestess arrived on the surface with a dozen deacons and four Arch Deacons in her wake. The priestess's green silk robe flowed behind her. The golden orbs embroidered on the fabric shone as she moved. Shyla squinted and spotted the platinum torque at the woman's neck. Sunlight glinted off the metal and the light silver color contrasted with her ebony skin. Bald and beautiful, the priestess walked with a confident grace, leaving behind slender footprints in the sand. The priestess worshipped the Sun Goddess every sun jump, performing a ritual and praying to the deity for…Shyla had no idea. Probably bountiful crops and help in gaining more power.

Shyla watched the priestess until she disappeared from sight. Then she scanned each deacon as they passed. The Arch Deacons were next. They wore green tunics and pants along with turbans and veils to hide everything but their eyes. Their torques glinted through the thin material of their veils.

Protected from her magic, there was no way she could sneak up on the Arch Deacons. Even though that wasn't what she intended to do on this sun jump, Shyla considered the problem. Perhaps if the Invisible Sword members arrived at the priestess's worship site before the sun and hid in the sand, they could ambush the Arch Deacons and take their torques.

However, that scenario didn't sit right. Interrupting a religious ceremony seemed dishonorable. Shyla hadn't believed in the existence of the Sun Goddess, but then she had been trapped on the surface and almost died of heat exposure. During that time, she had a conversation with the Sun Goddess who had asked her to save the people of Zirdai. Even though the encounter was probably a delusion, Shyla had been more open-minded about the Sun Goddess ever since.

The last of the Arch Deacons crossed her sight line. This one carried a sack over their shoulder—probably incense for the ritual. Shyla's focus returned to the entrances, seeking Invisible Swords. She spotted Elek's broad shoulders as he and Jaft strode from the north exit. They wore sun cloaks and carried shovels, not water.

She dug her fingers deep into the sand as her mind whirled with the implications. Was the mission unsuccessful? Needles of fear for Rendor and the others shot through her, leaving behind a painful pulse. At least no one followed them.

Then, despite the layer of sand, the high-pitched wail of a baby in distress reached her. The sound sliced right into her heart.

Son of a sand demon, that Arch Deacon hadn't been carrying incense but a baby. No doubt a sun-kissed to be abandoned on the surface to die.

In this case, she'd be more than happy to ruin the Heliacal Priestess's plans.

CHAPTER

7

Even though they were both hidden under the sand, Jayden managed to grab her arm. "Stay put." His voice was muffled but the order was clear.

"No." There was no way she'd let the Heliacal Priestess and her deacons abandon a baby. Another wail tore into her guts.

"We can't do anything until they're gone. We're outnumbered. Besides, we can't just appear from the sands. There's still too many people leaving the city."

She *hated* that he was right. Hated it with all her heart and soul. "As soon as—"

"Yes, *we* will."

How could he be so calm? A third and weaker cry skewered her. A physical need to move, to run, to swoop in and scoop up the baby hummed in her blood and drummed on her muscles.

"Look," Jayden said. "There's Nard and Lamar."

Shyla spotted the two men. No one paid them any attention as they strode away from the city in a different direction than Elek and Jaft. They too carried shovels. Except Nard's sun cloak appeared...odd. There was a... hump on his back. Not big as if— Idiot! They carried the air bladders full of water on their backs under their sun cloaks. Rendor was a genius!

A bit of pride pushed her other emotions to the side for an angle. He wasn't the second worst choice. In fact, she would no longer tolerate those comments. And it was time to stop trying to please everyone.

After a few more angles, Balin and Daksh slipped from a little used exit and soon disappeared from sight. Shyla and Jayden continued to wait, but none of the other Invisible Swords left the city. Soon, the flow of people stopped and the sweepers retreated underground. Had the rest of the team been caught? Or were they still collecting water? Instead of jumping to horrible conclusions, she'd ask Elek when she returned to the temple. But first the baby.

Jayden squeezed her arm. "Not yet."

She suppressed a growl. What were they delaying for? The baby shouldn't be out—

The Heliacal Priestess and her posse strode into sight. Oh, right. So anxious to rescue the infant, she'd forgotten about the seventeen people. Except only thirteen returned from the place of worship. The four Arch Deacons were noticeably absent. Seven hells. They'd remained behind to ensure the baby wasn't rescued. And with the torques protecting them from Shyla and Jayden's magic, they'd be hard to beat. Not impossible, but not a guarantee either.

Once the deacons and the priestess disappeared underground, Jayden said, "I'm not sure where the Arch Deacons are, so move the sand to the side instead of up into the air." He released his grip. "Try not to draw attention."

Shyla concentrated and envisioned the grains being swept aside as if she was slowly opening a set of curtains. The weight lifted from her back as the sunlight brightened. Interesting how the sand had also insulated her from the heat. The sand devils dug into the dunes to escape the killing heat, but they also had tough hides and special respiratory systems to aid in their survival.

Her stiff muscles protested when she pushed to her feet. Jayden stood next to her, brushing sand from his cloak.

Scanning the desert, she found the deacons' tracks. However, the baby hadn't made any more noise. Had the infant died already?

"We need a plan," Jayden said. "We can't just rush in there. Let's take a look first." He shrugged off his cloak.

Like Shyla, he wore the red tunic and pants that the monks donned when they were on the surface. Hanif had given them a number of used and worn sets. She copied Jayden. They folded the sun cloaks and then buried them under the sand. Without the protective material, the heat grew uncomfortable despite the early angle. Sweat collected along her brow.

Instead of following the tracks, Jayden led them to the southeast, looping around so they would approach the worship site from another direction. When they neared it, they crouched low, keeping a larger dune between them and the Arch Deacons.

Shyla spotted two monks lying in the sand nearby. And they no doubt noticed her as well. The monks or acolytes—hard to tell since their clothing, veils, and turbans blended in with the colors of the desert—appeared to be within direct sight of the worship site and probably the Arch Deacons. Either the Arch Deacons had chosen to ignore them or they hadn't seen them.

She tugged on Jayden's arm and pointed the monks out to him.

"Why are they here?" he asked, whispering in her ear.

Good question. Normally the parents of sun-kissed babies abandoned them in the desert well away from the public paths. In rare cases, some were given to the deacons to leave on the surface. "I think they're waiting for the Arch Deacons to return to the city so they can rescue the baby."

Jayden huffed. "So it's a waiting game? See who'll stay out here the longest without getting cooked?"

If the baby was unprotected from the sun, it would die well before the killing heat. "The monks are technically not allowed to interfere."

"So it's up to us?"

"Yes."

"We need to take a peek," Jayden said.

"How?" She gestured to their surroundings. "They'll see us and we can't influence them." Shyla stared at the monks. An idea formed.

"I'll go through the dune," Jayden said. "I'll just push the sand this way so they don't notice."

That would take him a fair amount of energy and time. "No. I've another plan."

"And…?"

"If it doesn't work, we'll go with yours." She crept to the edge of the dune, closing the distance between her and the hidden monks. Waving her hands, she hoped to catch their full attention and not just a glance. Lowering her mental shield, she prepared to act. The monk closest to her shifted his gaze and she made eye contact. Perfect! She picked up on his emotions and thoughts.

What did Shyla and her companion think they were doing? If they tried to get the child, they'd have to fight four Arch Deacons without his and Lota's help. Hanif would kill them both if they were seen aiding an abandoned child. At least Hanif's information that a sun-kissed had been born recently proved accurate. Appalled and disgusted, he hoped the Arch Deacons would leave soon, but the scorching sand demons seemed determined to wait until the poor child died. He also worried they'd been warned about the monks attempting to rescue the sun-kissed since the four deacons faced four different directions. And they each kept a hand on the hilt of their swords as if expecting an attack.

A scary thought hit Shyla. What if the baby was bait? What if this was a hideous attempt to get the Invisible Swords to come out of hiding? She returned to Jayden and told him what she'd learned and her fears.

"How would they know you were watching on this particular sun jump?" Jayden asked, questioning her theory.

"I don't know. Maybe they thought we had spies in the city. Hanif had known this might happen and sent the monks. Unless..." No, that was too terrible.

"Unless what?"

"Unless they've been doing this every sun jump since we attacked them at the old headquarters."

Jayden's horror matched her own. "That was five sun jumps ago."

Her next thought was equally ghastly. Did they bring the child back to the city when their trap didn't work only to take the poor thing back out the next sun jump? This had to stop. Now.

"Even if they're expecting us, we can't walk away," she said.

"Agreed. But unless the monks fight—"

"They won't."

"Then it's two against four and they'll see us coming." Jayden rubbed his hands together. "I'm okay with that."

Was she? They couldn't influence or manipulate the Arch Deacons, but they could move the sand. Perhaps a cloud to hide them or— "What an idiot!"

"I hope you're not talking about me."

"No." She rushed to explain her plan. "Do you think it'll work?"

"If it doesn't we can always fall back on plan B."

"Fists and feet?"

"And knives." Jayden pulled his from his belt and brandished it. "Might as well put on a show."

Shyla added learn-how-to-fight-with-a-knife to her list of things to do. Going up against two Arch Deacons without a weapon was a daunting prospect. She hoped her crazy scheme worked.

As she and Jayden crested the dune, Shyla didn't need to read the hidden monks' thoughts. No doubt they were questioning her intelligence.

The Arch Deacons spotted them immediately. The four formed a line between them and the baby on the sand. They drew their weapons—short swords, sharp and slightly curved. Jayden's knife looked like a child's toy in comparison.

"Ah, the Blessed One was correct that you wouldn't be able to resist," said an Arch Deacon. He stood on the far left and had to be the leader. "Come with us, Sun-kissed, and your companion can take the baby and go."

"That's a decent offer. What do you think?" Jayden asked her.

"I think the Arch Deacon is a son of a sand demon and should be left on the surface to die." She stared at the man but concentrated on his feet.

"Ouch." Jayden pressed his free hand to his chest. He turned to the Arch Deacon. "The truth hurts, doesn't it?"

"Enough of this," the man said, then to his companions, "Don't kill the sun-kissed."

The Arch Deacons stepped forward. Or, rather, they tried. The sand underneath them no longer supported their weight. Shyla increased her will, creating a deeper hole under the leader. Jayden focused on the other three.

Amid cries of disbelief and fear, the quartet sank up to their chests—a comical sight. Their arms remained on the surface and they struggled to break free. Jayden used the sand to yank the swords from their hands. The weapons disappeared into a dune. Then the grains trapped the men's arms.

Not wasting time, Shyla crouched in front of the leader. She yanked the torque from his throat, then met his terrified gaze.

"You should be scared," she said. Not bothering to question him, she probed the depths of his mind.

As she'd feared, they'd been setting this trap for the last couple sun jumps. They thought they'd be safe from her magic with the torques.

Shyla gave him a cold smile. "You're never safe from me. And inform the Heliacal Priestess that if she tries to abandon another baby, everyone will be dragged deep under the sand and left there to die."

Jayden removed the torques from the other three. Then they put the four Arch Deacons to sleep. Shyla scooped up the baby. Sweat glistened on its dark skin and the poor thing was overheated. Dehydrated, too—no tears leaked from its eyes and its wails were weak gasps. The blanket was twisted around the baby's body. Shyla pulled it off and paused. The boy wasn't sun-kissed. Outrage and horror filled her. The Heliacal Priestess had taken someone's baby to trap Shyla.

The monks approached but then stopped as if afraid to come any closer.

"Are they dead?" Lota asked, nodding at the half-buried forms.

"No, sleeping. Before we leave, we'll loosen the sand and wake them up so they can get inside before the danger zone."

"We can take the baby to the monastery," Lota said.

"He's not sun-kissed."

The monks glanced at each other.

Jayden peered over her shoulder. "Do you think they kidnapped the baby?"

"Knowing the Heliacal Priestess, she probably browbeat his parents to offer him to the Sun Goddess," Shyla said in disgust.

"We can't take him back to Zirdai until we find his family and determine what happened," Jayden said.

"Agreed. Can you take him for now?" Shyla asked the monks. "Tell Hanif we are searching for his family."

"All right." Lota took the baby and covered him in the blanket.

The other monk opened his water skin and dribbled a white liquid into the baby's mouth.

Surprised, Shyla asked, "Milk?"

"Yes. Unfortunately, we have experience with saving babies. Fortunately, it happens infrequently," he said.

The monks headed back to the monastery while Shyla and Jayden worked on releasing the Arch Deacons.

"They deserve to be cooked," Jayden said.

"That's a horrible way to die," she said. "Besides, we don't kill. And I'm sure they'll be punished by the priestess for failing to capture me."

He grunted, then focused on the dune behind her. She turned in time to watch the four short swords emerge from the sand. Jayden picked them up. "These'll come in handy." He inclined his head to the Arch Deacons. "They'll be awake soon. Let's go, I'm beat."

No need to tell her twice. Shyla hurried to catch up with Jayden as they retrieved their sun cloaks. She erased their tracks as Jayden's energy was clearly lagging.

"I must admit," he said, "that trick of trapping the Arch Deacons was a great idea. I've always viewed that skill as a way to hide and travel unseen." He remained quiet for a while. "Granted, we don't have many skirmishes on the surface."

"And now the Heliacal Priestess knows what we can do. Let's hope that prevents her from trying that again."

As Jayden's steps slowed, she glanced at him. "I wish I could have helped you more."

"You will. You're a fast learner, and, once you have enough practice, you'll be able to sink a dozen deacons."

Not sure she had the power for that many, she kept quiet. When they arrived at headquarters, there was a celebratory buzz in the air. In the common room, the six men from the mission stood amid a group of people all with smiles on their faces. Six previously empty water jugs were now full. Jaft spun around, showing off the air bladder that had been fashioned into a backpack.

Shyla gestured Elek over to update her and Jayden. "Where are the others? Did something happen?"

"No, the mission went off without a hitch. Rendor thought having all of us leave at the same time would be too suspicious. So six left this sun jump and the other four will go during the next."

"Any problems?" Jayden asked.

"None. We avoided all the patrols. Well, getting the water from the pipe was a bit tricky. The valve had rusted shut and was a devil to get open." He flexed his biceps. "But it was no match for me."

She raised an eyebrow. "For you?"

"Well, Rendor may have helped a little."

"Uh-huh. Where are the others staying while they wait?"

He shrugged. "Don't know. But I'm sure it's safe. Rendor knows all the places the guards check."

While she wished they'd all returned, overall it was good news. And she hoped that the other members would start to look at Rendor in a new light.

"Thanks," she said.

He nodded and joined the others. Shyla then relaxed—a mistake. Her adventures caught up to her and fatigue threatened to topple her. Before going to rest, she filled her water skin. Jayden did the same. He set the swords down.

"Do we have people who can fight with those?" she asked.

"Yes, most of the Invisible Swords can handle one. We prefer knives as they're easier to conceal and to fight with in a confined space."

Good to know. "Give me the rest of the torques. I'll take them to the monastery later. Plus I can check on the baby."

Jayden pulled them from his pack. "At least we reclaimed four more." Jayden inspected one in the druk light. The Invisible Sword symbol was etched into the metal along with other glyphs and symbols. Jayden turned it over. He ran a fingernail along the back, then squinted closer. A strangled sound escaped his lips.

"What's wrong?" she asked.

"This…" He held up the torque. "Is new!"

Not sure she understood, she said, "New as in—"

"As in somehow the Heliacal Priestess is making more. As in, she might have hundreds instead of the dozen original ones." Jayden slumped against the wall.

Seven hells. That was bad.

"Let's not panic." She guided him over to a table. "Sit." After fetching a couple rolls of jerky, she handed him one. "Eat."

As he chewed on his, she dug into her pack and removed the torque she'd taken from the Arch Deacon. She laid the four of them on the table. "Obviously the Arch Deacon I interrogated back at the old headquarters didn't know about these new torques or they didn't have them at that time." She considered. "Platinum is rare and expensive. If a large quantity was recently purchased, one of your contacts in Zirdai will know how much. Right?"

"Yes. It's hard to keep things like that quiet."

"Good. Once we know how much the priestess purchased, we can estimate the number of new torques she has." She gestured to the ones in front of them. "Are all these new?"

Jayden examined each one, turning them over. "Two are, the others are not."

"All right. Come with me to the monastery later to check the others. Once Mojag is back, you both can go into the city and ask about the platinum and see if anyone knows about a missing baby."

He rubbed a hand over his face. "Okay."

"First, get some rest."

"You, too."

* * *

After she woke, she collected Jayden and they headed to the monastery. This time she didn't waste energy trying to sneak up on the monks. The news of their approach reached the monastery well before they did. When they arrived, Hanif waited for them in the surface building.

"How's the baby doing?" Shyla asked.

"Not well. My healers are not sure what's wrong with him so I've sent for Zhek." He studied them. "Any news on the babe's parents?"

"Not yet. We need to take a look at those torques. Can you retrieve them for us?" she asked.

Now she received a shrewd appraisal. "I'm just about to assess three acolytes. If you're willing to help me out, I can spare some time to fetch them for you."

A niggling sensation warned her that this wasn't going to be that straightforward. "All right. What do you need?"

Seeming way too happy about her acceptance, Hanif led her down to the training room on level seven. "These three acolytes are almost ready to take the oath. They all arrived at the monastery over a short period of time four circuits ago. All on different sun jumps, but it's a bit odd for us to get that many so close together."

Ah, she sensed where this was going. "And you suspect they might be spies."

"Yes. We've had them in the past. Over the last twenty circuits, the people in power have sent a dozen or so of their loyal supporters to infiltrate us, hoping they'd become monks and steal all our secrets."

"The vagrants have the same problem. How do you catch them?" Jayden asked.

"We keep a close eye on the acolytes. They tend to reveal themselves by being just a bit more curious than their fellows, a bit more observant, a bit more...standoffish as if they're better than the rest of us. They also tend to be found in places that are off-limits to acolytes. These three, though, have not shown any of those signs, but the timing of their arrival also coincides with when the current Water Prince came into power."

"You want me to read them," Shyla said.

"Yes."

An uncomfortable twinge gripped her stomach. On the one hand, she wanted to help Hanif and keep the Water Prince from learning about the monks and, by association, her, but on the other hand, what if they were innocent? She'd hate to invade their privacy.

"Do they know she has woken The Eyes?" Jayden asked.

"Unfortunately, everyone in the monastery knows." Hanif shrugged. "Something that momentous can't be kept a secret for long."

"Then as soon as they see her, they'll know you don't trust them. You might lose three good people. But if they're working for the Water Prince, they might try to kill her."

Oh, she hadn't thought of that. And she needed to make eye contact to read a soul. Perhaps she could wear a turban and veil to hide her identity.

"She could assess their fighting abilities. The acolytes have a final match with a veiled monk before taking the oath." Hanif seemed to follow her train of thought.

Except she hadn't been practicing the Ways of the Yarin lately. "I don't know if I'll be a worthy opponent."

"It doesn't matter. I *know* they're good fighters, but I don't *know* if they're trustworthy."

In that case… "All right. But this is worth more than you getting the torques for me. You owe me another favor." A pause. "How about admittance into the Third Room of Knowledge?"

Hanif laughed. "Nice try. I agree to another favor, but not that. Pick something else."

"How about when the time comes, you allow Kaveri to help us with starting our own garden?"

He shot her a probing look, but she kept her expression neutral. Did Hanif really believe she hadn't figured out Kaveri was her mother?

"Okay, but that doesn't include providing plants," he said. "For that I'd need you to do another task."

Still a victory. She'd expected to have to do more for the plants. "Do you have a task in mind?"

"No, but I'm sure something will come up."

Jayden just shook his head over their negotiations. "Can you get the torques before the fights?"

While Hanif fetched the necklaces, Shyla changed into a monk's uniform. The stiff tan fabric was more tailored than what the acolytes wore—the tunic was shorter and it had a matching fabric belt that she tied around her waist. Shyla studied her reflection in the mirror.

She'd spent her entire childhood insisting she'd never become a monk. Not that she was one, but wearing the uniform and being a part of an assessment came close. At least the idea of being a monk no longer caused her to panic. She'd learned being a part of an organization was really just being part of a family.

She wound the turban around her short hair, keeping it small and tucked in close. Then she secured the veil so the material would not come loose while she fought.

Jayden waited for her in the training room. He met her gaze when she entered—the only part of her exposed. "I'm still having trouble getting used to your new eye color. Do any of the monks have blue eyes?"

"A couple." It was a good thing that blue eyes weren't that uncommon among the people in Zirdai.

Hanif returned with the torques. He gave them to Jayden and then shooed him from the room. "Only monks are allowed." After Jayden left, Hanif turned to

Shyla. "You're going to need to be on the offensive. Can you do that?"

Before her adventures with the Invisible Sword, she'd had a hard time being an aggressor since the Ways of the Yarin focused on defense—block and then punch versus punch and then block. However, she'd learned how to attack first and ask questions later. "Yes."

"Good." He left but soon came back with an acolyte and two other monks.

The two monks sat on stools along the far wall. The acolyte faced her. Shyla didn't recognize the monks, but she knew the acolyte—her name was Durva. It made sense once she thought about it. Durva and the other acolytes would have come to the monastery when Shyla was still living here.

Hanif served as the referee. "To me."

They bowed to him.

"To each other."

They bowed, but not as deeply. Shyla kept her gaze on Durva, making eye contact while removing her mental shield. The woman was nervous and excited and confident. Durva was five centimeters taller than Shyla, with longer limbs that she planned to use to her benefit.

Hanif held his hand between them and they shifted into fighting stances.

"Go!" Hanif jerked his arm up and backed away.

Shyla executed a front shuffle kick followed by a roundhouse kick. Durva sidestepped and snapped a side kick at Shyla's leg—the one that held all her weight. A good strategy for any other opponent, except Shyla hopped out of the way before Durva's foot touched her. Shyla attacked with two quick punches to Durva's ribs. Durva blocked both with her forearms and stepped close to launch an upper cut to Shyla's jaw. Shyla leaned back just in time for Durva's fist to sail pass. They disengaged and the two women circled each other.

Durva was quick and skilled. Shyla was out of practice and still fatigued from using her magic. However, being able to read Durva's intentions gave Shyla a big advantage. It was fun and Shyla almost forgot why they were sparring. With a renewed effort, she concentrated on Durva's deeper thoughts—ones not connected to the fight. That wasn't fun. Shyla's unease grew as she learned things about Durva that she was sure the woman would never have shared. Was she crossing a line? Abusing her power just so Hanif could uncover a spy?

Shyla won the match three points to two. They bowed again and Durva left. Hanif brought in the next acolyte—an over-muscled bruiser named Tobbar. He didn't waste energy blocking. Instead he absorbed the hits without slowing down. Tobbar only let her attack once, and then he went on the offensive for the rest of the match, winning it three points to two.

Chago was the third and last acolyte. He was a lanky young man who was freakishly fast even with his thoughts. Shyla just managed to stay ahead of him. And she had to sacrifice a couple points to probe his mind. By the end of the match, her energy lagged and Chago won four points to one. At least she'd held him off longer than he'd expected when he'd sized her up in the beginning.

Hanif consulted with the two other monks before they left. She ripped off the veil as soon as they were out of sight. The material had clung to her damp face while she fought. Then she pulled off the sweat-soaked turban. Ugh. She reeked.

"You need practice," Hanif said.

"Tell me something I don't know."

"You did better than I thought you would."

"Gee, thanks."

"Did you...?" He tapped his forehead.

"Is that code for 'read their souls'?"

"Shyla."

She enjoyed annoying Hanif much more now that she was an adult. "Yes. Durva and Tobbar are legit. Chago isn't. He's the Water Prince's cousin."

"Seven hells."

"He's very good. And you're going to have to decide what to do with him."

Hanif's gaze sharpened. "What do you mean?"

"If you kick him out, then he's going to suspect I was somehow involved. Which will no doubt bring Captain Yates back."

Another string of curses burst from Hanif.

"How long can you delay them from taking the oath?" she asked.

"Not long—five or six sun jumps. They've met all the requirements."

Too soon. "How about allowing him to become a monk and just keeping him from sensitive information?"

"That would be difficult."

"If you prevent him from passing along information, I can erase his memories later."

Hanif considered her offer. "How much later?"

"When we unseat the Water Prince."

"That's not what I asked."

Figured he wouldn't accept a vague answer. "I don't know. We're still rebuilding. We have limited resources and people. It might be impossible." She plopped onto a stool and rested her head in her hands. That was the first time she'd admitted out loud that the task of overthrowing the Water Prince and Heliacal Priestess may very well be unattainable for her and the Invisible Swords.

A warm hand rested on her shoulder. "You have a history of doing the impossible."

She lifted her head. "I do?"

"Yes. You survived on the surface during the killing heat. You woke The Eyes of Tamburah. You convinced Captain Rendor to turn his life around. You rescued Banqui. All things I would have sworn no one could possibly do."

"But this is different."

He raised an eyebrow—a familiar and exasperating gesture. "Is it?"

Yes. It was. Maybe. Scorching hells, at this point she'd no idea. And Banqui was missing. Again. She sighed.

He patted her shoulder. "You'll figure it out."

Easy for him to say.

"And I'll deal with Chago," he said. "Perhaps I'll feed him some misinformation for fun." An evil little grin spread across his face.

Shyla almost felt sorry for Chago. Almost.

* * *

After she cleaned up, she joined Jayden in Hanif's office. He'd spread the nine torques out on the desk. "Only the two are new, the rest are old."

Which didn't tell them much.

"I'd like to take these back to our headquarters. Maybe we can learn how they work and figure out a way to bypass it," Jayden said.

"What if we're raided?" She'd hate for the torques to be used against them.

"I can hide them in the sand. So can you."

True.

"And when I'm done I'll melt them down."

"Too bad we can't sell the platinum." Then she wouldn't have to worry about getting coins.

155

"It would be nice, but the priestess would just buy it and make more." Jayden gathered the torques and tucked them into his pack. "When the priestess is no longer in power, we'll sell it for a bundle of osees."

Shyla paused. This was the first time Jayden sounded confident that they would overthrow the priestess. She wondered what changed.

Unaware of her regard, Jayden said, "If we hurry we can get back before darkness."

They left the monastery at angle one-seventy. The sun squatted on the horizon. It had swelled into a giant red sphere that warped the pink sky into bands of purple, orange, and yellow. As they walked through the cooling sand, Shyla mulled over what had happened at the monastery.

She'd never considered that the Water Prince and the Heliacal Priestess would send people to infiltrate the monks. Growing up with the acolytes, she hadn't noticed anyone being too curious or too observant, which was more of an indication of her observational skills than theirs. The most alarming realization was that of the fifteen acolytes that had volunteered to be Invisible Swords, one or more of them could be spies.

After she'd woken The Eyes, they had rushed to rescue Jayden, then they'd hurried to move into the temple and had been scrambling to secure basic needs since. She'd never formally accepted them, nor had she asked them to pledge an oath—not that swearing to be loyal meant they would be. If Hanif allowed Chago to become a monk, the man would lie.

Shyla hadn't wanted to scare or upset anyone by abusing her power. But now that she thought about it, she needed to formalize the membership. At least for the acolytes since they weren't Invisible Swords before.

"Jayden, did the Invisible Sword require all members to pledge their loyalty to the organization? Does everyone have the mark on their shoulder?" It was an invisible mark that only other members could see.

"I was thinking the same thing. Yes, everyone who helped us pledged their loyalty. Only those in the upper levels bear the mark."

"We need to do that for the new recruits."

"I agree. Are you going to read their souls, too?" he asked casually.

"If I do, then I should do it for all the Invisible Swords as well. It's only fair."

He stopped. "No it isn't. They all swore their loyalty. If you do that, they'll be insulted."

Just like Jayden was at the very idea. Except they'd made their vow before Shyla woke The Eyes. "Yet someone betrayed us."

He rounded on her. "Not someone. *Banqui.* You just refuse to see it. Which is why no one believes you about Rendor."

This was an old argument, but she couldn't help saying, "There's no evidence Banqui did it. And why *would* he? He has no reason." Plus he'd promised her he'd say goodbye. And perhaps she was being naive, but she trusted Banqui to keep his promises.

"Coins are enough of a reason."

Tired of arguing, she headed toward the temple. No matter what Jayden thought, she was going to figure out a way to test all the Invisible Swords.

Before they reached the common room, Shyla said to him, "I want to hide in the sand again."

"You think the priestess will try to abandon another baby?"

"No, but I'd like to ensure no one is following our people."

"All right. I'll meet you here at angle three-fifty."

* * *

Shyla squirmed into a comfortable position before commanding the sand to cover her.

"Better," Jayden said of her efforts as he settled next to her.

It didn't take long before Shyla spotted Gurice and Mojag. The siblings slipped from the south exit. The tight pressure around her chest eased a fraction.

"There's Ximen," Jayden whispered a few angles later.

While happy that he was free of the city and that no one had followed any of the Invisible Swords, Shyla worried about Rendor. Why hadn't he left with Ximen?

They remained in place for another ten angles. Still no Rendor. The sweepers returned inside. Still no Rendor. The priestess finished her service. Still no Rendor.

When the area was completely deserted, Jayden said, "We better go back."

"You can go," she said.

"Shyla, he's not coming out. Not if he doesn't want to draw unwanted attention. I'm sure Ximen knows where he is and why he stayed behind."

He was right. Yet Shyla was almost afraid to find out why. The citizens of Zirdai hated him, the Water Prince had ordered his guards to kill him on sight—if they could—and the deacons would happily end his life for no reason at all.

Shyla and Jayden returned to headquarters. Gurice, Mojag, and Ximen were regaling the others in the common room with stories of how they spent the sun jump hiding from the various factions.

Unable to wait another moment, Shyla sent Ximen a silent command.

Come here!

He turned to her in surprise, but once he saw her expression, he hurried over to her and Jayden.

"What happened?" she demanded.

"The mission was a complete success. And, as long as we're careful, we can tap into that water source whenever we need it."

"A complete success?" she asked doubtfully. "Then *where's* Rendor?"

Ximen glanced at Jayden then away. "He…" Ximen fidgeted with the sleeves of his tunic.

She wanted to strangle him. "Spit it out, Ximen."

Ximen drew in a breath, then released it slowly. "He decided to remain behind. He said he's not welcome in the Invisible Sword and it would be better for everyone if he just disappeared." Ximen touched her arm. "Rendor did the right thing. It's best for all of us."

CHAPTER

8

It's best for all of us. Had Ximen just said that to *her*? She stared at him in shock.

Rendor had decided not to become a member of the Invisible Sword.

Rendor had decided not to come back to *her*.

His angry words—which she'd been avoiding thinking about—replayed in her mind. *You're embarrassed? Is that why you only showed me you care when the Invisible Swords couldn't see us? Or is it that you don't want my history to tarnish your leadership?*

Scorching hells, why did she have such a good memory? Each word stabbed into her heart. Why hadn't she chased after him right away? Why had she waited? Stupid, selfish sun-idiot. And now he was gone.

"Did you erase his memory of us?" Jayden asked.

The thought of Rendor not remembering her tore through her with sharp teeth. She glared at Jayden. He wore a pleased smile that Shyla wanted to slap right off his face.

"No," Ximen said. "He's been exiled. If the guards see him, they have orders to kill him. Besides, he doesn't have anyone to tell."

"What about his parents and older brother?" Jayden asked.

Stunned, she almost rocked back on her heels. Rendor had a brother? Why didn't *she* know? What else didn't she know about him?

Ximen shrugged. "They disowned him when he signed up to be a guard."

"How do you know this?" she asked.

"Rendor's been causing the vagrants and the Invisible Sword trouble since he joined the guards," Jayden said. "We were hoping to find some leverage to keep him from being such a heartless killer. When we threatened to harm his brother, Hastin, he laughed and told us to go ahead, and, while we were at it, to take out his parents as well and save him the trouble."

"Where do they live?" Shyla demanded.

Ximen glanced at Jayden as if seeking his permission.

"*I* asked the question, Ximen," she snapped.

"This really is for the best," Ximen said. "Think about it, even Rendor's parents didn't want him and they raised him."

"That's not what I asked." She stared at him. If she had to get the information by using The Eyes and taking another step down the path to Tamburah's madness, she would.

Ximen dropped his gaze. "They live on level eighty-four."

Only the very wealthy could afford to live below level eighty. She'd no idea. A self-absorbed *and* selfish sun-idiot. "What do they do?"

"They own a number of businesses. Hastin travels to other cities to purchase and trade goods. He's supposed to be some kind of prodigy." Ximen shrugged. "All we know is that soon after Hastin became an active part of their business, they were able to move down from level sixty-seven."

And Rendor's skills with a sword were not beneficial to his family. He'd told her his family thought he was worthless, but she'd never asked him…anything. Too concerned with the Invisible Sword. No wonder he didn't want to come back. Too bad. She'd find him and drag him back if she had to.

"Shyla, it's not worth the risk," Jayden said.

Was she that easy to read?

"You're vital to this organization. Without you, we can't free Zirdai," Ximen said.

Jayden touched her arm. "You can't be selfish."

Oh yes she *could*. And she *would*. It took every gram of willpower not to punch him in his you-can't-be-selfish guts. Instead, she turned from them both and hurried to her room before tears spilled. Once in the privacy of her room, though, her sadness turned to anger. She paced the tiny area.

At the first sign of trouble between them, Rendor bolted. He had known the Invisible Sword wouldn't welcome him right away, that he'd have to fight for it. So what changed?

You don't share the same feelings, he'd said.

How could he believe that when everyone else apparently thought she was in love with him? Had something happened on the mission? She needed to talk to Gurice. Of all the people in the Invisible Sword, she'd already accepted Rendor. Or so it seemed.

Shyla found Gurice dumping buckets of sand on the surface.

"You just came back from a mission. You don't have to work," she said to Gurice. "Aren't you tired?"

"Nah. We slept while we waited."

"Tell me how the mission went."

Gurice swiped a stray lock of brown hair from her light green eyes. "Ximen reported it all to Jayden."

Who was the last person Shyla wished to speak to. "Humor me."

She shrugged. "We entered the city the same as we left it, in pairs. Mojag and I were first in and we got to the black market before it closed for darkness. I bought the air bladders and then we met up with the others on level thirty-two. Then Rendor led us down to this creepy tunnel that had big pipes crossing through it. The noise of the water rushing inside them was deafening and we had to use hand gestures to communicate. We found a rusted valve and Rendor, Elek, and Ximen had to all grab it." Gurice grinned. "Lots of bulging muscles on display." She fanned herself with a hand.

"Focus."

Gurice laughed. "That valve opened with such a screech I thought it would bring every guard down on us. But nothing happened. We filled the bladders without a hitch and climbed back to the surface. That was the hardest part. Water is heavy!" She shook the empty bucket. "Not as heavy as sand, but I don't have to lug sand up ninety-nine levels."

"Did you see the prince's…special cells?" Shyla swallowed the bile that immediately rose when she thought of those rooms. The image of the naked dead woman hanging upside down had been seared into her mind.

"No. And we didn't see any guards. Rendor seemed to know exactly where they'd be. Even during the sun jump we had to wait before leaving, we encountered no one as we stayed in various forgotten spots and took turns sleeping."

Good news and another reason they needed Rendor. See, she wasn't being selfish. "Did one of the guys say anything…nasty to Rendor?"

Gurice's expression softened. "Before the mission there was lots of unkind and spiteful grumbling, but no one said anything to *him*—nobody's *that* stupid. And during the mission, everyone was quite impressed. I'm sorry, Shyla. I know you two were…"

Were. As in the past. "Did he say anything about… that?"

"Just what he told Ximen. He seemed pretty grim at the time, but he's not exactly the happiest person."

True. But she treasured those moments she'd made him laugh. "Do you know how to find those pipes again?"

"Both Ximen and Elek know how to get back to the pipes, but truthfully, I'd feel better if Rendor was with us."

"Did he mention what he was going to do? Where he might go?" Shyla remembered he'd planned to become a monk before she invited him to join the Invisible Sword. If she couldn't find him in the city, she'd check with Hanif.

"No. He said he'd keep out of our way and not to worry about him."

That wasn't going to happen. "Thanks, Gurice."

* * *

At the end of the sun jump, Jayden and Mojag headed to the city. Shyla joined them, ignoring Jayden's protests, which turned him sullen. He refused to discuss the mission with her.

Instead, she filled Mojag in on the new mission. "I need you to find out how much platinum has been sold recently, and if the deacons bullied a family to give up their baby."

"What are you going to do?" Mojag asked.

"I'm going to see if the vagrant network knows where Aphra or Banqui are." And Rendor.

Glancing at Jayden, Mojag said, "We could do that for you."

"I know, but if they know where they are, then I need to talk to them both." And talk to *him*...well, after she slugged the big brute.

The rest of the trip was quiet—unusual for Mojag, but the boy must have sensed Jayden's foul mood and had enough self-preservation instincts to tone down his normally chatty personality. They joined the flow of people heading back into the city after tending to the velbloud flocks and gamelu herds.

Jayden led them to Orla's commune on level thirty-nine. She had planned to scan all the people they passed, searching for Rendor, but, due to Jayden's knowledge of the city's twists and turns, they only encountered a few citizens. Frustrating and impressive. It was obvious the Invisible Sword needed Jayden. Was she risking alienating him by chasing after Rendor? No. She needed them both.

Orla welcomed them. The older woman fussed over Mojag, sending him to get something decent to eat—a kind and cutting gesture at the same time. Though maybe Shyla was just feeling guilty for not providing fresh food for her members.

"Oh my goodness, no," Orla said when they asked her about a missing baby. "I haven't heard anything about that. The deacons have done some questionable and downright horrific things over the circuits, but that's a new low." She paused. "I'd hate to think this of my fellow Zirdains, but there is a possibility that the babe was…donated by either a devout mother or a desperate one. We get many young mothers here who can no longer afford to pay taxes and tithes for two."

In that case, the mother would be harder to find and probably wouldn't want the baby returned to her. And that was another sad state of affairs that needed to be rectified. Children under the age of two circuits should be exempt from paying taxes and tithes. More guilt pressed on her shoulders as she wondered whether she was wasting time chasing after Rendor.

"Have you heard anything about large shipments of platinum?" Jayden asked.

Orla's gray eyes gleamed. "We've heard rumors from Petula. She said a single platinum ring sold for fifteen osees."

"Petula lives in my commune," Jayden said. "I'll go talk to her."

Shyla noted that he still considered the commune on level sixty-two as his. Was that due to a lack of community within the Invisible Sword?

"What about Aphra or Banqui? Any word?" she asked Orla.

"Talk to Adair, he thought he spotted the woman."

Ugh. Shyla would rather not. Adair had pushed her into an air shaft without warning her that there was a net twelve levels below to catch her. She glanced at Jayden. Did he remember helping to extract her from that net?

"We caught you fair and square." He grinned. "You protested that you weren't ours, and look what happened. You're ours now."

His statement caused a strange combination of emotions to tumble inside her. The Invisible Sword had become her family, yet she hadn't gotten that reciprocal sense from them…well, not all of them. Perhaps if she'd put in more effort.

Shyla returned his smile. "Surprised?"

He laughed. "Aren't you?"

"Very much."

* * *

Before Jayden left to visit the commune on level sixty-two, Shyla gave him a handful of osees. "Please purchase some fresh food for the group."

"You sure? Jerky is cheaper."

"I'm sure."

He hesitated but then nodded and called to Mojag, who was wrestling on the ground with a pack of small squealing children. The kids complained with one disappointed *awww* when Mojag trotted over to join Jayden.

Shyla searched the commune for Adair. As she walked through the various common areas and gathering places, she grappled with her emotions. Adair hadn't tried to kill her, he'd just been spiteful. Too bad that logic failed to change her opinion of the man. She spotted him talking with a group of young men. He still had his short black beard that matched the color of his tight curly hair. Thick eyebrows arched over dark brown eyes.

He scowled when she approached but excused himself from the conversation.

"What do *you* want?" he asked.

To remind you we are on the same side, but she clamped down on that comment. Instead, she asked about Aphra. "Have you seen her?"

"Yeah."

"And?"

He stared at her as if waiting. It took her a moment to understand. She dug into her pack and handed him a coin.

"The treasure hunter is now shoveling sand for Rohana, the Water Prince's new archeologist."

That was unexpected. Shyla had thought Aphra would avoid Rohana. Also why hadn't Fadey known that? He was Rohana's assistant. Unless Aphra was wearing a disguise and avoiding him… Considering the treasure hunters knew he sold them out, it would make sense.

"Do you know if they're out on a dig?" she asked Adair.

"Do I look like I care?"

Oh no, he wasn't getting away with that. She stepped closer, capturing his full attention. Pushing her power through her gaze, she said, "Let me remind you *who* you're dealing with."

Sweat.

His derision turned to fear as heat swept through him. Moisture collected along his hairline and inched down his back.

"A simple no would have sufficed." She turned and strode away. Only when she was well across the room did she glance over her shoulder and stop the command.

It was petty, but oh so satisfying. She should do it more often. In fact, it was time for her to be more… pushy? A leader? Confident? All of them? However, she needed to find the right balance between asserting herself without abusing her power.

It was angle one-ninety. If the diggers had returned from a site, they'd be in the dining cavern on level nineteen. Shyla covered her hair with her wrap, pulling the material low to keep her face in shadow. There were enough people around that she could blend in as she ascended the nineteen levels.

171

Keeping an eye out for Rendor, she scanned everyone she passed. They didn't so much as glance in her direction. At least the big man would stand out. Or would he? He'd managed to get around just fine the few times he'd been in the city since becoming a wanted man. How would she— She almost groaned aloud. And to think she had just decided to use her powers more.

Shyla lowered her mental shield. Her prior connection to Rendor may come in handy as his soul would be the only one she could read in the city. Now she avoided eye contact so she could concentrate on finding Rendor's soul.

Once she neared the dining cavern, she slowed. In order to see inside, she'd have to bypass the two deacons guarding the entrance. She gathered her will and directed it at them.

Look away.

They both peered to the left as if fascinated with the very air. Moving to the right, she entered the cavern. By this time, many of the tables were empty. However, a rancorous group occupied the back corner. Their rumpled, dusty, and ripped clothing gave them away— diggers. Before anyone could wonder why she was there, she strode over to a water jug, filled her water skin, and left.

Once out of sight, she considered the tunnels leading away from the cavern. If the diggers headed straight back to their quarters on level thirteen, they would most likely take a direct route. Shyla found an ideal intersection and waited. There were plenty of druks hanging on the walls, giving off enough light. When footsteps sounded close, she'd project the *look away* command.

After various random people used the tunnel, the diggers arrived. The noise of their arrival was unmistakable. When they reached her, Shyla pushed another command at them without stopping.

Not here.

Not here.

Not here.

She scanned each face as they crossed the intersection. Aphra almost slipped by her. The woman had cut her long brown hair short and walked slightly hunched over. Not like the confident and cocky treasure hunter that Shyla remembered.

Once Aphra neared, Shyla needed her—and only her—to break off from the group. It would be tricky. Projecting the image of a water skin, Shyla aimed her power.

Forgot.

Aphra straightened and stopped.

"What's wrong?" asked the digger next to her.

"I forgot my water skin. Go on ahead, I'll catch up." Aphra waved her companions on and turned around.

They countered with good-natured insults. When they were out of sight, Shyla dropped the *not here* command and called to Aphra.

Aphra whipped around so fast her hair flew up. "Scorching hells, where did you come from?" Then a beat later, "You shouldn't be here, you're wanted—"

"By everyone. I know."

She cocked a hip and squinted at Shyla. "Do you have a death wish?"

"No. Do you? You're working for the Water Prince's archeologist."

Aphra grimaced. "It's called hiding in plain sight and it's my only option other than being arrested and tortured. I don't have enough coin to leave. Besides, who'd think to look for me there?" Her forehead creased with apprehension. "How did you find me? Did that son of a sand demon, Fadey—"

"No. He didn't tell me. And I doubt he noticed you. He seemed pretty wrapped up in his own misery."

"Good. You didn't answer my question."

Shyla considered, then decided to go with the truth. "I asked the vagrants to be on the lookout for you."

"Why?"

"Because of your connections. I've some sweets to sell."

"Ah." Then she shook her head. "Can't help you. I'd be caught for sure. I'm barely surviving as it is and risk being exposed every sun jump. Once I've saved enough osees, I'm outta here."

Not what Shyla wanted to hear. Without coin, the Invisible Sword couldn't afford to feed themselves let alone help others in need. "Is there anyone still selling treasures on the black market?"

Aphra gave her a sly smile. "I may have a contact you can sell to directly, but I'm having trouble remembering the name." She scratched her head.

Cute. Shyla handed her an osee. "Maybe this will jog your memory."

Aphra scrunched up her pudgy nose. "Sorry, still not able to recall it."

Shyla briefly considered just taking the information from the hunter, but the woman was just trying to survive. However, she would ensure Aphra didn't lie to her by reading the woman's surface thoughts and emotions.

Handing her two more osees, she met Aphra's gaze and said, "I'm sure this will do the trick."

"Ah, yes. It's Professor Emeline from Catronia University."

"She's still here?" It seemed like it was over a circuit ago that the Water Prince mentioned meeting with the visiting professor. But it was only fifty, maybe sixty, sun jumps ago.

"She's a guest lecturer at the university, but I think she's due to leave soon."

Aphra was telling the truth, giving Shyla some hope. "Where is she staying?"

"In the visiting professor quarters on level forty-two. Right next to the entrance to the library. Do you know where it is?"

"Yes. What does the woman look like?"

"She's about five centimeters taller than you and thin—skeletal thin. And she has a long narrow nose. You can't miss that nose."

"Great. Thank you."

"Good luck."

"You, too." Hopefully everything would go well for the ex-treasure hunter. Then it hit her—perhaps Aphra would want to join them. She'd be a valuable asset for the organization. The woman had always treated Shyla like an equal and not some pariah. Plus Aphra wouldn't have to worry about surviving on her own. "Wait. Do you want to join us?"

"The vagrants? No, thank you."

"No, we're not…" How to explain? And could Shyla trust her? She kept a light touch on Aphra's emotions. If she spooked and planned to betray them, Shyla could erase Aphra's memories of their encounter. "We're the Invisible Sword." Shyla braced for laughter.

But Aphra peered at her. "Like in Tamburah's time?"

One of the benefits of being a successful treasure hunter was that you became an expert in history.

"Yes."

"You found The Eyes."

Aphra had been one of the few people who'd actually paid attention to a sun-kissed. Shyla stepped close to a druk, testing the woman's observational skills. "I did."

She studied Shyla. "You have pretty blue eyes. What would I have to do as a member?"

As briefly as possible, Shyla explained what they hoped to do.

Now the woman laughed. "Is that all?"

"It's going to take some time."

"You ain't kidding. Do your members get paid?"

"No. You get shelter, food, water, and a good feeling by helping others. And if we overthrow the Water Prince, the new leader will be in need of an experienced and trustworthy archeologist."

"If." She huffed. "And the risks?"

"Besides the obvious ones?"

"Yeah, sorry. Let me think about it."

Shyla didn't sense any duplicitous emotions. "All right. If you decide to join us, we'll be leaving Zirdai at angle zero, but not this upcoming one, the next one. Meet us near the north exit."

"Okay." Aphra hurried to catch up with the other diggers.

Shyla wondered if she'd just made a huge mistake. Would Aphra sell her out? The woman could earn enough coins to not only travel but live in luxury in her new city by telling either the prince or priestess where to find the sun-kissed. Aphra was telling the truth about the professor, and she seemed genuine in considering Shyla's invitation, but Shyla hadn't delved any deeper into the woman's secrets. Why not? Because she was too nice. She didn't want to invade anyone's privacy. Shyla needed to start being more...ruthless. Lives were at stake!

Shyla raced down to level forty-two, hoping to get to Zirdai's only university before the students and faculty retreated to their rooms for the rest of the darkness. She located the guest quarters then found a dark shadow where she could wait and watch. The majority of people who walked by were either deep in conversation or intent on a scroll in their hands. And the few who were more observant suddenly had the desire to look elsewhere when they passed.

She tried not to think about Rendor. Of course his image immediately pervaded her mind. His harsh words sounded in her ear. Pain and loss filled the vast empty space inside her. Shyla clamped down on those emotions. She'd find him and somehow convince him to return. The right words would come to her by then.

Professor Emeline entered her room at angle two-forty. Aphra had been right, the skinny woman was easy to recognize. It appeared as if someone had grabbed the tip of her nose and yanked it straight down.

Once the woman closed the door, Shyla debated her next move. She did have something to offer the professor, but should she? Aphra had said her contact's employer studied the artifacts to learn about their history, which was better than the Water Prince who kept everything in his private collection. However, the Invisible Swords needed coins and, if they overthrew the prince, all those treasures would be put on display and made available to the historians. Shyla would make sure of it.

When the corridor was empty, Shyla emerged from her shadow and knocked on the stained glass.

Professor Emeline slid the door open a crack. One eye regarded her. "Yes?"

"I've something that you might be interested in."

The eye narrowed. "Like what?"

"An artifact of great historical significance."

"Why come to me?"

"Aphra sent me."

The door slid wider. "Come in."

After Shyla entered, the professor glanced down the tunnel both ways before closing the door. Trol lanterns lit the room. Their bright yellow light illuminated a decent-sized living area with a desk and work table. She guessed the open archway beyond led to her sleeping quarters.

Emeline studied Shyla, her gaze sweeping her from head to toe. And by the slight sneer, Shyla guessed she was found lacking in some regard.

"What do you have?" the professor asked.

"I've a map of Gorgain's temple." The scroll had been in her pack since her original client accused Shyla of murder and theft. Although a little wrinkled, it was still legible.

"So?" She feigned a yawn.

"*So*, the location of his crypt is clearly marked."

This caused a sharpening of the woman's interest. "And his diamond and gold crown and ruby torque?"

"Still buried with him. You need only to dig it out."

"Then your map is worthless."

"Excuse me?"

"Your Water Prince has made it impossible for anyone to work a dig site within thirty kilometers of Zirdai except for his archeologist."

Seven hells.

"But if you bring me that crown and torque, and it's authentic, I'd be happy to pay you more coins than you've seen in your lifetime."

Perfect, except Shyla didn't have a crew to dig. Actually, she did, but they had so much to do already. And they hadn't *helped* anyone yet. Every sun jump people were being tortured, they were dying, and the Invisible Swords were shoveling sand.

"I'll see what I can do," Shyla said.

"Don't wait too long. I'm leaving for home in twenty sun jumps." Emeline hustled Shyla out the door.

The visit hadn't gone as she'd expected. Shyla spent most of the trip back to Orla's commune trying to figure out a fast way to reach Gorgain's treasures. Before she ducked down the tunnel that would lead her to the back entrance, Shyla paused and checked that no one had followed her or was watching the tunnel.

She reached with her magic and sensed—Rendor! Spinning around, she peered into every shadow, trying to determine his location. A brief moment of alarm flared from him before he moved away, increasing the distance between them until she could no longer sense him.

Son of a sand demon. Shyla wanted to call after him, but the hard stone walls would echo and amplify the sound. People would come to investigate. Plus the heartbreaking fact that he'd seen her and run away… that said a lot.

Disheartened, she returned to Orla's. The commune was quiet as most of the children were asleep. Mojag and Jayden hadn't come back yet. Not hungry, but realizing it'd been a while since she'd eaten, Shyla nibbled on a roll of gamelu jerky as she spread the map of Gorgain's temple on a table. Better to work than to replay Rendor's rejection.

She used four druks to hold the edges down. The extra light also helped to illuminate the faded ink. Tracing the tunnel the grave diggers used to escape the crypt, she found an entry point into the temple then calculated just how much sand would have built up over thousands of circuits—approximately six or seven meters. The air would be stale, perhaps even toxic or explosive or both. And there was always the danger of a cave-in. And booby traps.

Groaning, she rubbed her face. This was not her area of expertise. She needed Banqui. Not knowing where he was or if he even was alive dragged on her. He could be confined in one of the priestess's chapels or in one of the prince's black cells on level ninety-eight, waiting for her to rescue him again. Or he could be hanging upside down in one of the prince's special rooms that were on the same level as the cells. That possibility gave her nightmares.

Too tired to think anymore, Shyla rolled up the map and crawled under a fur in what she was beginning to consider her room.

* * *

She woke before angle zero determined to find Rendor. They would have another conversation. Although she knew he wouldn't be at his parents', her curiosity wouldn't let her not check out where they lived. Using the power of The Eyes, she tricked a guard into pointing out their suite of rooms on level eighty-four.

Once again she waited in a shadow like a creepy stalker. The double-wide stained-glass doors showed an idyllic and ancient scene of water flowing through a garden. Trol lanterns hung to each side. An expensive hand-woven rug beckoned visitors.

At around angle ten, a man exited the suite. Shyla had to clamp her hand over her mouth—his resemblance to Rendor was uncanny. A few centimeters shorter than Rendor, Hastin had equally broad shoulders, but he wasn't as muscular. Not as dark-skinned either, but with the same color hair and eyes. Hastin's powerful and confident stride carried him right past her hiding spot. He didn't pause or acknowledge her. Obviously she was far beneath his notice.

Shyla waited some more, but Rendor's parents remained inside. When she left the area, she sensed Rendor but was unable to locate him. Again. Then she spent the rest of the sun jump searching for him. Hanif hadn't called her stubborn for no reason.

But she couldn't find him. Admitting defeat hurt deep inside her. She returned to the commune near angle one-eighty. Jayden and Mojag had also come back. They exchanged information.

"The Heliacal Priestess is buying every bit of platinum she can," Jayden said. "We've estimated that she bought enough for another twenty torques, which means she has about two dozen."

"Not good," she said.

"It gets worse," Mojag said. "There's a rumor that she sent a couple of her Arch Deacons to Catronia to purchase more."

Catronia was ten sun jumps away. "Do you know how long ago?"

Mojag shrugged. "The gossip is still warm."

Warm? She glanced at Jayden.

"Two maybe three sun jumps at most," Jayden translated. "We have some time to experiment with the ones we have and hopefully figure out a counter strategy before the priestess makes more."

"All right, we'll leave at angle zero. What about the baby's mother? Any news?"

"Not a squeak," Mojag said. "We've the network on the lookout."

The vagrant network had come in handy a number of times and had found Aphra. "Can you ask the network to keep an eye out for Rendor?"

Mojag shot Jayden a look but then ducked his head. "Sure thing."

Mojag was a lousy liar. Did he not remember she could read his emotions? What had Jayden told him about Rendor? Sick to her stomach, she left them and found Orla sitting in her favorite nook. Shyla joined her and asked the woman to have her people look for Rendor.

"Do we have to worry about him giving us trouble?" Orla asked.

"No. But I don't know how he's going to find food, or what he plans to do. If you see him or find out where he's living, can you please let me know."

"All right." Orla paused. "Can I let you know when I see *other* things?"

Not sure where Orla was going with this, she said, "Of course. Do you have some information for me?"

"The deacons who are stationed at the chapel on level fifty-one are especially cruel. They recently rounded up a number of people for 'lack of proper devotion' and are rehabilitating them. I'm afraid some of the younger ones aren't going to survive."

Shyla shot to her feet. "Why didn't you say something sooner?"

"I've been debating whether the backlash is worth it," Orla said calmly.

"The backlash?"

"Yes. If you go in there and rescue those people, the deacons will retaliate. And I can guarantee you it will be worse."

"Oh no, I'll ensure there's no backlash," Shyla said.

"You can do that?"

Shyla had no idea. "I'm going to try."

CHAPTER

9

"Tell me again what we're doing here?" Jayden asked for the fourth time.

"We're going to rescue the people being tortured inside that chapel," she whispered with annoyance. Granted, she'd woken him up and yanked him from his cushion, but still...

They crouched in a shadow on level fifty-one, watching the chapel. It was angle three hundred. Two deacons stood guard outside. Since no one dared to attack a chapel, they were more for show. However, the deacons were quite capable of defending themselves. Plus they all carried knives.

The rest of her team waited in a nearby tunnel. Orla had recruited a number of vagrants to aid Shyla. They all could fight, but their main job was to free the victims and take them to the commune for medical care. Shyla and Jayden would tackle the deacons.

"What about Arch Deacons?" Jayden asked. "Any inside?"

"I've no idea."

"What about torques? Do they have any?"

"Don't know."

Jayden closed his eyes a moment. "Your plan…"

"Sucks, I know."

"Then why are we here?"

"We're *helping* for a change. If you want to sit this one out, go—"

"I'm not going anywhere," he snapped. "Let's just get this over with."

"All right." Shyla straightened, took off her wrap, and strode toward the chapel. It didn't take long for the two deacons to notice her, and less for them to spot her short blond hair.

"The sun-kissed!" the one on the left yelled, pointing.

"Give the man a prize," she said. "Gather your people. I'm going to make a confession." Shyla entered the chapel, crossed the nave, and entered the back hallway that led to the confessionals.

The deacons trotted at her heels, calling to the others. She kept a brisk pace despite wanting to stop and help those suffering inside the rooms. More and more deacons joined them and soon Shyla had quite the parade.

When she reached the end of the corridor, she spun around, holding out her open hands to show she was unarmed. The deacons all stopped as well. Six of them stared at her. Behind them, the vagrants and Mojag rushed into the rooms to free the occupants. Jayden waited with his knife drawn in case she needed him.

Gathering her power, she made eye contact with each one. None wore torques. Although, after this, she doubted the priestess would make that mistake again. And none were Iskemu, the deacon who'd backhanded her and cut off her hair. She made a silent promise to get him next time. Then she pushed her magic toward all of them.

"The Sun Goddess has sent me here to commend you on your efforts," she said.

The deacons preened.

"She applauds your ability to rehabilitate so many lost souls. You've done such a good job there are no more souls that need your dispensations and you've released them all." Shyla mustered her strength and targeted each deacon. She caught a glimpse of Mojag carrying a bloody child from one of the confessionals. Heat built inside her as her fury grew. She channeled it toward the deacons. "In fact, if you harm another person in the Sun Goddess's name, you will suffer as well. You will feel unspeakable pain as if your soul is on fire." The words seared the air and her throat burned.

Jayden glanced at her in surprise. She'd no idea where that came from or if it would work, but she was too angry to think clearly. The desire to stop their hearts pulsed within her. But she remembered her orders not to kill another unless it was in self-defense.

Instead, she dragged up the last of her energy and commanded them.

Sleep.

They dropped like a ceiling during a cave-in. Unfortunately, so did she. Jayden hurried over and helped her stand.

"What did I tell you about using all your energy?" he asked, wrapping her arm around his shoulders.

"Not to do it." The chapel spun around her.

"It was a rhetorical question. Come on."

"But...the people..."

"Are being helped by the others. We need to get out of the city before the next shift of deacons shows up."

They climbed to the commune on level thirty-nine and rested. She gulped a glass of yellow-colored water that Zhek handed to her before rushing to tend to the others. He'd mixed a restorative in the liquid. At least she hoped that was what tinted it yellow and not his sleeping drug. Good thing Zhek had returned from the monastery in time.

While she caught her breath, Jayden and Mojag gathered the supplies they'd purchased. They said goodbye to Orla, who thanked them.

"Feel free to spread the rumor that it was the Invisible Sword and not you," Shyla said. "I don't want you to experience any backlash."

"Don't worry about us, dear. We've handled worse." Orla shooed them out. "Better hurry."

They only had twenty angles to ascend thirty-nine levels. It was doable in most circumstances, but this wasn't one of them. Shyla soon lagged behind. Jayden tried to help her, but her legs wouldn't last long. If he had to carry her out, they'd draw too much attention.

"Go," she said when they reached level twenty-three. "Take Mojag and get to headquarters."

"No."

"It's not a request. And look for Aphra, she might be waiting near the north exit." Shyla described the woman.

"Why would she—"

"I'll explain later."

"I'm not leaving you." Jayden crossed his arms—the universal sign of male stubbornness.

"I'll find a place to rest. Don't worry."

"You can't protect yourself if you're passed out."

"I'm going to collapse right here if you don't stop wasting time. It's an order. Take Mojag and go."

"You're not in your right mind. I'm not—ah hells." Jayden looked over her shoulder. "What are *you* doing here?"

Huh? Now who wasn't in his right mind?

"I've got her. You go," Rendor said from behind her.

She spun so fast she ended up on the ground. Peering up and up, she met Rendor's gaze. She was so happy to see him that she didn't mind the pain in her hip from the fall.

Jayden cursed. "I thought that was you tracking us."

Rendor had been following them? She must have really depleted her magical energy.

Jayden sighed, then said, "Stay out of sight. There's going to be deacons searching the city for her and stationed at all the exits."

"She'll be safe," Rendor said.

"Make sure she's back at headquarters by the next sun jump."

"Only if she's recovered and it's safe."

Jayden grunted. "Come on, Mojag, we need to hurry."

The boy gave her a wide-eyed look before following Jayden.

Rendor crouched down next to her. "We have to stop meeting like this."

Oh no, he didn't get to tease her. Not after leaving her like that and not letting her explain. Despite being glad to see him, Shyla punched him on the arm, but the blow was weak. She opened her mouth to demand he explain why he'd left.

"Not here." Rendor pulled her to her feet. "Can you walk?"

"It depends."

"That's not an answer."

"Yes, it is. Are we going up, down, or lateral?"

"I can carry you."

She crossed her arms.

"Fine. It's two levels down and half a klick south."

"Then, yes, I can." She gestured for him to lead the way.

They walked in silence. Rendor adjusted to her pace as it changed from slow to lumbering to a painful trudge. The tunnel's walls and floor softened around her. When had her legs become so heavy? Perhaps she'd been overly confident about her energy level.

"We need to keep moving," Rendor said.

Huh? She had stumbled to a stop.

"This isn't the best spot—"

"Then go. I didn't ask for help." She didn't have the strength to glare at him even though a part of her acknowledged she was the one behaving badly.

He growled, then dipped down, swept her off her feet, and threw her over his shoulder. "We don't have time for this, either."

She squawked in protest, but he ignored her. Soon his smooth and silent ground-eating strides lulled her to sleep. A change in movement roused her enough to note she no longer hung off his shoulder. Instead a softness cushioned her prone body. A fur being pulled up to her chin was the last thing she remembered.

* * *

When she woke, she was comfortable, warm, and alone. Disappointment seared through her over that last one.

A druk glowed with a reddish light, illuminating the small room that barely contained the sleeping cushion. Her pack rested on the floor next to her. Sitting up, she dug for her water skin. Her sore muscles complained, but the bone-deep fatigue was gone. After gulping enough water to un-shrivel her tongue, she found a roll of jerky and ate it without really tasting it—a good thing.

Her thoughts swirled. What was she going to say to Rendor? During all those angles searching for him, she'd been too focused on the hunt when she should have been composing an…apology? Yes. An apology.

The food and water revived her further. She clambered from the cushion—an uncoordinated and graceless endeavor. A newborn gamelu gained its feet with more aplomb. Granted, she was unused to the cushion's extra thickness. She paused. Her thin sleeping mat at the temple was pathetic in comparison. Not much of an enticement for Rendor to return. And why the sudden focus on a cushion? Because it was easier than facing Rendor.

A narrow opening connected this room to another. She crossed through it. This one contained a couple cushions to sit on, a low table, and a trunk with a sand clock sitting on top. It was angle one-eighty—she'd slept the entire sun jump. Two druks hung on the wall. A rough stained-glass door meant there were no more living spaces. Nowhere else that Rendor could be. She peeked out the door just in case he was standing guard.

The tunnel was dimly lit and two distant figures headed toward her. Their voices echoed. She ducked back inside before they spotted her.

She wondered if this was his place or if he was squatting here. It was bigger than her tiny single room on level three when she'd been a legal citizen.

With nothing to do but wait, Shyla considered her apology. But soon her thoughts turned dark. What if Rendor didn't return? Now she fretted. What if he was injured? Or he was caught? She couldn't do anything to help him. Not yet. And she needed to leave at angle zero; staying in Zirdai any longer would be too dangerous. A million horrible scenarios played out in her mind.

To keep from obsessing over Rendor, she considered what had happened in the chapel. She hadn't planned on commanding the deacons to experience pain if they hurt another person, but the sight of that child had triggered such fury that she considered ending all their lives. Wished it. Would the temptation to force others to do her bidding grow until she no longer thought it was wrong? Was that what had happened to Tamburah? He hadn't started out as a despot. Had the power of The Eyes corrupted him? Or had they given him the power to do what he longed to do all along?

She sighed. Why couldn't anything be simple? Was it too much to wish The Eyes came with instructions that made sense? Right now, she felt as if she were stumbling around in the dark, hoping not to slam into a wall. Same with Rendor. What was she supposed to do in this situation? She'd never cared for anyone like this and it appeared she'd already ruined it.

What if he didn't want to talk to her? He had to know she'd try to convince him to return to the Invisible Sword. Or what if he thought she wouldn't, and he was saving himself the pain of another rejection? Or he was truly done with her? She hadn't even thanked him for helping her!

Seven hells. She'd rather be fighting an Arch Deacon than twisting herself into a giant knot of what-ifs. Eventually she burned through her energy. Putting the sand clock next to the sleeping cushion, she lay down. The blasted thing was so damn comfortable. Would Rendor choose a cushion over her?

A light knocking woke her at angle three-forty. She was halfway to the door before she realized Rendor wouldn't knock. Her next thought—deacons!—was also dismissed. They'd pound on it or break the door down. Same with the guards. Cautiously, she cracked it open.

A young boy around twelve circuits old stood there. He was a bit grubby but not a vagrant.

"Can I help you?" she asked.

"I've a message for you."

Oh no. Her heart shriveled. "Wait, please." She grabbed her wrap and covered her hair before letting the boy inside.

He gazed at her. If he noticed her blond eyelashes and eyebrows, he didn't react. "I've been paid to guide you to the surface," he said. "We should leave now in order to get there by angle zero."

"Who paid you?" Shyla lowered her shield to read his thoughts. This could be a trap.

"Some big guy. He said to tell you that this is for the best. And for you to stop looking for him."

The boy told the truth. The desiccated thing in her chest crumbled, leaving behind a huge emptiness.

* * *

Shyla had only a vague memory of the trip to the surface. The boy was good at avoiding other people and he didn't say a word the entire trip. He pointed down a tunnel, said it would lead to an exit, and disappeared.

When she exited the tunnel, she encountered a few others heading toward the surface. She joined them, tagging along near the back. No one gave her a second glance…or even a first glance. But the two deacons standing next to the exit studied each person intently as they passed.

Slowing down, Shyla craned her neck to get a better look at their throats. Scorching hells. One wore a torque. Just her luck. She couldn't use her magic to slip by them unnoticed. Well…she could for one of them if she had enough energy. A quick plan took shape and she targeted the unprotected deacon, sending an image.

The sun-kissed.
The sun-kissed.

The deacon on the left cried out. "It's her!" He lunged forward, grabbing a man who was a few paces in front of her. "I've got the sun-kissed!" Yanking the poor man's hood down, the deacon tightened his grip on the guy's shoulders.

"Are you blind? That's not the sun-kissed," his partner said.

"Yes, it is."

"No—"

The sun-kissed.

"Watch out. She has a knife!" He pulled his dagger.

"No. Stop, you idiot."

Shyla skirted the two grappling deacons and sent a silent apology to the man she'd used. Striding along one of the well-used paths to avoid leaving footprints, she stopped the image when she was a safe distance away. Then she ducked behind a dune to catch her breath. That little deception cost her. And she doubted it would work a second time. Once the two deacons figured out what had happened and reported it, the priestess would change tactics.

Even though she was tempted to head straight to the temple, Shyla took a more circuitous route. The effort to smooth out her tracks became a test of her will. The sand grains resisted and moved with a heavy reluctance each time she stopped.

Her tunic was soaked with sweat when she arrived at the temple. The early angle crew were clearing sand. Gurice dumped her bucket and intercepted Shyla before she reached the entrance.

"Where's Rendor?" Gurice asked.

A sharp pain ringed the empty spot where her heart had been. "He's not coming back."

Gurice was smart enough to avoid asking why. Instead, she squeezed Shyla's arm in support. "His loss." She returned to work.

When Shyla entered the common room on level eight, Jayden was at a table with Aphra. She considered it a win that the treasure hunter had decided to join them. As she approached, Jayden glanced behind her as though expecting Rendor to be there. His gaze returned to her and he studied her expression. He too was smart and didn't question Rendor's absence or celebrate it.

"I was explaining the rules to Aphra," Jayden said. "Which shift do you want her on?"

"None of them." Shyla plopped onto a cushion opposite the woman. She made eye contact, gazing into her golden-brown eyes. "Are you committed to helping us?"

"Yes," Aphra said.

The truth. "Good. I've a job for you." Shyla dug into her pack and removed the map to Gorgain's crypt. Smoothing it out on the table, she pointed to the grave diggers' tunnel. "This will lead you right to the crypt. I need you to recover his crown and ruby torque. Can you do it?"

Aphra studied the scroll. "With the right equipment."

"We have people, shovels, buckets, and pulleys."

"How many people?"

"Twenty."

"We can't spare anyone," Jayden said. "We—"

Shyla shot him a quelling glare. "This is a priority. We're running out of osees."

"What about the Water Prince's decree that no one can dig within thirty klicks of Zirdai?" Aphra asked Shyla.

"One or two of those twenty people will be able to hide your activities from any nosy neighbors."

She crossed her arms. "Yeah? How?"

Too tired to demonstrate, she cocked her head at Jayden.

"We'll make you invisible," he said and then disappeared.

Aphra jumped and gave Shyla a wild-eyed stare. "Where did he go?"

"He's still sitting there."

Jayden reappeared. "You're no fun."

"That's one of the reasons we're called the *Invisible Sword*," she said to Aphra, ignoring him.

"Can I do that?"

"No," Jayden said.

"Why not?"

Good question. Shyla waited.

"You don't have the potential." Jayden explained how magic worked.

Aphra studied him. "I'm confident, intelligent, and resourceful. And I've been in plenty of terrifying circumstances."

"You forgot modest," Jayden quipped. Then he sobered. "I just don't…feel the potential within you. It's hard to describe."

Curious, Shyla pushed him to put the feeling into words.

He shot her a sour look. "It's a gut instinct."

She recalled that not everyone who had been tested taps into the power. And Jayden had dismissed the possibility of Mojag having magic rather quickly. Perhaps his gut instinct wasn't that accurate. "What do you feel when you encounter another Invisible Sword who can wield magic?"

"Probably the same as you," he hedged.

"Humor me."

"There's an instant connection. Like we're family. But you have to remember, I know everyone who can wield magic." He paused and glanced at Aphra. "She doesn't have that essence that makes me think she could be family. That's what I mean by gut feeling."

Shyla had experienced a similar bond with the other wielders. But she never picked up on an essence of potential. Then again, she was new to magic. Perhaps she needed to experiment. She scrutinized Aphra. Did she have potential? Was her magic like a locked door inside her, just waiting for a traumatic event to crack it open?

"Are you doing that soul reading thing?" Aphra asked in alarm. "I like you, but I don't want you to read my innermost thoughts and feelings."

"No, I'm not. Sorry, just trying to pick up on Jayden's gut instinct."

"You know that sounds weird, right?"

"I do. Okay, back to Gorgain. Do you think you can get his treasures?"

"Shouldn't be a problem," Aphra said.

"Can you do it in eighteen sun jumps?"

"Now we have a problem."

Shyla tapped the map. "What do you need to get it done in time?"

"More people."

"There's thirty—no, twenty-nine of us. Will that be enough?"

"It'll depend on the condition of the site. Will your people follow my orders?"

"Regarding the dig, yes. If we need to hide from any patrols, then we're in charge."

"Fair enough." Aphra examined the edges of the scroll where a series of ancient symbols marked the geospatial location of the temple on Koraha.

"Do you need me to translate those grid lines for you?" Shyla asked.

"I wouldn't have been a very good treasure hunter if I couldn't do it myself." She winked then glanced at the sand clock. "There should be enough time for me to scout out the temple and mark the entrance to the grave diggers' escape route."

"Good. Jayden, go with her."

"Now?" he asked.

Aphra rolled up the scroll and stood. "Yes, now."

He wasn't happy, but he went to retrieve his sun cloak.

Aphra gestured to the table. "They saved some fresh fruit for you."

That was kind. Too bad she didn't have an appetite.

"I take it things like fresh food are rare here?" Aphra asked.

"For now. I've plans once we earn more coins." She waited for the familiar frustration to well up inside her, but, with their recent success in freeing those people from the confession rooms, it didn't push quite as hard. And perhaps doing small rescues or acts of kindness would balance the more mundane tasks like shoveling sand for the rest of the Invisible Swords.

After grabbing a few slices of melon, Shyla headed to her room, needing more time to recover her strength. She lay on her thin mat, intending to sleep, but thoughts of Rendor invaded.

He'd been willing to prove himself to the Invisible Swords before she'd made that stupid speech. She should have kept her mouth shut and let him figure out how to get people for his team. Still, she expected he wouldn't give up on proving himself so easily. Did he want her to chase after him? Had she given up too soon? Time was a luxury she didn't have and her first priority should be helping the people in Zirdai—not her love life or the lack of one. So she allowed the hurt and pain and unanswerable questions to fill her until she could no longer hold it in. Sobbing, she curled into a ball, purging all her emotions until nothing was left but grim determination. She'd focus on work and stop wasting time and energy on Rendor.

* * *

She woke at angle one-seventy and found Jayden in the common room. "Did Aphra locate the temple?"

"Yes. She already took a crew out to uncover the entrance to the grave diggers' tunnel. Ximen is with them."

"Good."

Jayden scrubbed a hand over his face. "We can't give her all our people, Shyla. We need to dig a tunnel to Zirdai. Going in and out through the surface buildings is becoming too dangerous."

"I know. We need to recruit more members."

"And how are we going to do that?"

"I've a few ideas, but let's wait until Ximen returns. They shouldn't be too much longer."

Jayden grunted. "I wouldn't be surprised if they worked well into the darkness." Then he leaned back.

"If we do get more members, where will we house them? We don't even have enough room for us."

A good point. She considered the problem. "Are there any abandoned vagrant communes?" she asked.

"Yeah, but there's a reason no one lives there—the guards know where they are."

"Perhaps Orla will rent us some space in her commune. Or she might know a good spot. It'll only be for a short time." She ignored his lack of enthusiasm. Instead, she searched for Gurice.

She found her playing a game of dice with Mojag in the room he shared with Jayden and Ximen on level ten.

"That's two peepers in a row. You're cheating," Mojag accused his sister.

"Hardly. It's all in the wrist." She demonstrated by rolling another set of peepers. "See?"

He crossed his arms and glared at her. "How do I know you're not using magic?"

"She isn't," Shyla said, coming into the small room.

"Says another magic wielder."

Gurice threw her hands up in the air. "See? This is why I didn't tell you about magic. I knew you'd accuse me of using it to influence you. And, as much as I was tempted, and believe me, I was *very* tempted a number of times, I never used it on you."

Mojag failed to appear mollified.

Gurice shook her head, then turned to Shyla. "Did you need something?"

"Yes, I was hoping for your help."

The woman sprang to her feet. "What do you need?"

"You and Mojag."

They waited for her to continue.

"You can say no. There won't be any hard feelings or a change in our…friendship."

"Just spit it out," Gurice said.

"I want to read your souls and see if I can find out why you have magic and if Mojag has the potential."

"I thought you already read mine," Mojag said.

"I only picked up on your surface emotions and thoughts. Nothing deeper."

Gurice laughed. "That's about right, there's *nothing* deeper."

"Hey!" Mojag protested. "Is this important?" he asked Shyla. "Will it help us?"

"Yes to both."

"All right."

She looked at Gurice who spread her arms wide and said, "I'm all yours. Just don't blame me if you start having bad dreams."

In order to have some privacy, they went up to Shyla's room on level nine.

"Gurice, you're first," Shyla said, sitting on a threadbare cushion.

Mojag leaned his shoulder against the wall, watching them.

"Lucky me." Gurice crossed her legs as she settled on another poor excuse for a cushion, facing Shyla. "What do I have to do?"

Shyla lowered her shield and stared into Gurice's light green eyes. Or, rather, she tried. "Relax. This won't hurt."

"I've heard that before," Gurice muttered, but she released a long breath and met Shyla's gaze.

Despite Gurice's bravado and dry humor, the woman was apprehensive about having Shyla read her soul. She liked the sun-kissed, even considered her a good friend, but what if her secrets scared her off?

"I'm not going to uncover all your secrets," Shyla said, trying to reassure her.

What about her fears about the viability of the Invisible Sword? Gurice worried they'd never return to full strength. Never achieve any of their goals.

"Stop fretting." All of Gurice's chatter was blocking her.

"Then stop reminding me that you're reading my thoughts," Gurice shot back.

Shyla paused. Was it nerves or Gurice's magic that prevented her from delving deeper? Perhaps she needed to change tactics. "Imagine you're standing in the desert, preparing to erase your tracks with magic. You can close your eyes if you need. I've already established a connection."

"Does that mean we'll be connected all the time?"

"No. After this, I'll break our link and I won't invade your privacy without permission."

Gurice bit her lower lip then touched Shyla's arm. "If something bad happens like we're being attacked and you need to…read me, you have my permission. I trust you."

And with that, Gurice finally relaxed. Shyla briefly covered Gurice's hand with her own. "Thank you. Now imagine—"

"Yeah, yeah." She closed her eyes and soon her thoughts filled with rolling dunes. "Got it."

Shyla let the scene encompass her as well. She stood next to Gurice. One set of footprints marked the otherwise smooth sand. Gurice held a hand out with her palm down.

"Now erase the tracks," she ordered.

They disappeared, but there wasn't a change within Gurice.

"Did you wield magic?" she asked.

"I pretended to. I can't use *real* magic on an *imaginary* desert."

Of course! Shyla bit down on a groan. "Mojag, can you bring that bucket of sand over here?"

He lugged the container and set it between the two women.

Gurice scrunched up her nose. "Uh, that's not exactly my forte."

"Doesn't matter as long as you use your magic on the sand."

"All right, but you've been warned and if sand gets all over your room, I'm not cleaning it up."

"Noted."

Gurice reached out so her hand hovered over the bucket.

"Why do you do that?" Shyla asked.

"It helps me focus and aim. Otherwise, I'll spray sand in your face." She gave her a pointed look.

"Okay, I'll be quiet."

After a few moments, a bright yellow glow filled Gurice as if someone had uncovered a druk lantern deep inside her. The light intensified and filled her, but Shyla only saw it through their link and not with her own eyes. An odd disconnection.

Soon, the sand grains lifted into the air and shifted, forming a...lumpy sleeping cushion...no...a...sand snake that had just eaten a rat? The glow disappeared and the sand sculpture thudded back into the bucket.

Mojag peered at his sister as if seeing her for the first time. "That was cool. But why did you make a dead rat with a really long tail?"

"It was a velbloud with a tether," Gurice said, sounding offended.

"Clearly." But Shyla couldn't suppress a grin.

"Everyone's a critic." Gurice crossed her arms. "Was there a point to this exercise?"

"Yes. Did you see a…anything unusual when you used your magic?"

"Other than the sand blob," Mojag added unhelpfully.

After shooting the boy a glare, she said, "No. Nothing different. Why?"

"Mojag, did you see anything?"

"Just the floating sand."

"Can you do it again?" Shyla asked. This time she put her shield back in place, blocking both the siblings' thoughts.

"All right." Gurice concentrated.

This time a…scroll formed above the bucket. No light emanated inside the woman.

"Jerky?" Mojag asked.

A sigh. "No. It was a shovel." She released it. "And, before you ask, no I didn't see anything unusual. Did this help you?"

"I think it did. Now, I just need to test my theory. Mojag?"

"Yes?" His voice squeaked.

"Your turn." She removed the shield.

He hesitated but then exchanged places with Gurice. Meeting Shyla's gaze with an almost bold defiance, he braced as if awaiting a blow. This magic thing was still new to him even though he had known Jayden and his sister were hiding things from him. Hurt feelings over not being confided in mixed with jealousy. Figured she'd be able to do magic. Things always seemed to work out for his sister. He knew he shouldn't be like that—she raised him after their parents were murdered—he was grateful and—

"Mojag, focus on…" Shyla considered. He couldn't manipulate the sand or influence anyone. But he had other…talents. "Can you slip out of the temple without anyone seeing you?"

He shrugged. "Maybe. It depends."

"How about you try?"

"Now?"

"Yes."

"What about you?"

"I'll follow at a discreet distance."

"And when I get out?"

Interesting that he used *when* and not *if*. "Just come back here."

"All right." Mojag scrambled off the cushion and paused by her door.

A faint yellow light shone from him right before he peeked through the curtain. It wasn't nearly as bright as Gurice's. Almost as if the druk inside him was only cracked open a hair. Shyla trailed him. Whenever he was in danger of being seen, that thin ribbon of light flared. Completely unaware he was using magic, Mojag left the temple without anyone the wiser.

He returned with a cocky smirk on his face. "That was too easy. Next time give me a real challenge."

"Are you going to explain what you're doing now?" Gurice asked.

"Not yet." She worked with them both until she was able to identify their inner...druk...without having to witness them using magic. Its heavy presence really reminded her of the lantern—it seemed a vital and solid part of them. And then she had to decide what to tell Mojag. Could she open that druk all the way? Shyla wondered what had happened to him to crack it. Perhaps it was the death of his parents.

When Mojag yawned for the third time, Shyla ordered him to bed. Gurice moved to follow, but she asked her friend to remain. She explained what she'd been doing.

"If it's foolproof, we just added another weapon to our arsenal." Gurice grinned. "That was worth making a million sand blobs." Then her smile faded. "Does that mean Mojag doesn't have the potential?"

"Actually..." Shyla told her about the crack.

"He'll be thrilled." Gurice cocked her head. "Though I'm not sure how I feel about it. I'm happy for him but also sad because it's a burden as well as a gift."

"And we need to decide what to do about it, and if I should try to open the rest of his magic so he can wield it with intent versus tapping into it unconsciously. I've no idea if it will work or what would happen."

"We should discuss this with Jayden and Ximen," Gurice said. "I don't want to hurt my brother, but I don't want to hold him back either."

When they arrived in the common room, Aphra and Ximen had already returned from the dig. They sat around a table, talking intently with Jayden. Shyla and Gurice joined them.

"What's the bad news?" Shyla asked.

"How did you know the news is bad?" Aphra asked. "Magic?"

"No, your body language."

"Oh. Well, we uncovered the entrance to the grave diggers' tunnel. About three meters in we hit a wall."

"A real wall or something not marked on the map?"

"The tunnel collapsed," Ximen said.

"Can you open it up?" Shyla asked Aphra.

"It's soft so we can clear it. But, because it's soft, we need to install extra supports as we go deeper or risk being buried alive. But there's no way we can reach the crypt in eighteen sun jumps."

10

Just when Shyla thought something was finally going their way, they hit a wall. Literally.

"How about if we remove the sand with magic?" Gurice asked Aphra. "Would that make it go faster?"

"It's not the sand that's the problem, it's the time needed to ensure our safety," Aphra said.

Which was important. Shyla slumped over the table and rested her head in her hands.

"What do you want me to do?" Aphra asked.

There really was only one option left and Shyla hated to do it. "We can sell the map to the Water Prince's new archeologist."

"You want to sell the map to Rohana?" Aphra whistled. "Bold."

"Too dangerous," Jayden said. "She'll alert the guards."

"She won't," Shyla said. "The archeologist is under a great deal of pressure to procure artifacts for the prince." And the thought of the prince owning more of Koraha's priceless treasures made her sick to her stomach. But she had to feed her people.

"Still too risky," Jayden said. "Is there anyone else we can sell the map to?"

"Not in Zirdai," Aphra said. "Since we can't get to the treasures before Professor Emeline leaves, perhaps we could take them to Catronia."

Not a bad idea. "How long before you reach the crypt?" Shyla asked.

Aphra drummed her fingers on her thigh. "Twenty-five…maybe twenty-eight sun jumps. It'll depend on how many booby traps we'll need to disable."

If she added in twenty sun jumps of travel round trip and a couple more to find the professor and negotiate a price, it meant a total of fifty sun jumps. After they paid the travel fees, could they last on the coins they had until then? No.

"Any other ideas on how to earn coins while we wait to sell Gorgain's crown and torque?" Shyla asked the group.

"What about selling water to Orla's commune?" Gurice asked.

"That pipe is in a remote location," Ximen said. "Rendor warned us not to make too many trips down there or we'd eventually be noticed by the guards." He rubbed his hand on the stubble on his chin. "We could divert a few bladders to Orla, but that's not going to bring in enough coins."

"Is there another temple or site that has treasures that are easier to get to?" Jayden asked.

"Wouldn't you know?" Shyla asked. "You said the Invisible Sword members also worked as treasure hunters. Where did they get their information?"

"I don't know. Kantu, one of our commanders, used to handle that. Did you ever work with him?" Jayden asked Aphra.

"No, I didn't work with him. I didn't know Kantu was an Invisible Sword. There were two…factions selling and procuring artifacts. Fadey's and Kantu's. I heard he disappeared soon after the Water Prince cracked down on the illegal treasure hunting."

Another dead end. Shyla gripped the edge of the table as a wave of fatigue hit her. Experimenting with Gurice and Mojag must have sapped more of her strength than she'd thought. Jayden glanced at her in concern.

"Did Kantu have a storeroom or a place to hold the artifacts until he sold them?" Aphra asked.

"We had a bunch of places to store things in our old headquarters." Ximen looked at Jayden. "Do you think one of them could have something valuable?"

"No. They were for food, water, and supplies. Kantu was very careful. All of the commanders were."

Which was why they could hide in the forgotten deep levels of Tamburah's temple for so long without being discovered. That thought triggered another. When Banqui uncovered the building, only The Eyes remained. But they'd been fakes. What happened to Tamburah's legendary riches? Had the Invisible Swords sold them all? She asked Ximen.

"Yes, our predecessors confiscated all his wealth when they usurped him and spent it on helping the people recover," he said. "The only thing they couldn't locate was his vault."

That didn't make sense. "But you found it. It's where you put the fake Eyes for Banqui to find." According to Banqui there'd been nothing else but a skeleton inside when he'd first opened it.

"That was his personal vault. He supposedly had another one that wasn't marked on a map."

Supposedly. One of the words Shyla hated most as a researcher. "Is its existence written on a scroll or tablet or is it one of those legends?"

"It's from our oral history," Ximen said with an edge to his voice.

Which tended to be exaggerated and embellished during each generation. Since the Invisible Sword was about five hundred thousand sun jumps old, that was a great deal of time for their history to change.

"Don't forget, Shyla," Jayden said. "The Eyes are part of that history and they ended up being exactly what our history claimed."

True, but information about them was also written down. However, she didn't remind him. Instead, she asked, "Did you explore all of Tamburah's temple?"

"Of course. The vault's not there. Tamburah had a number of residences while he ruled. He was the king after all."

Yet, according to the records, he spent most of his time in his temple. He'd believed he was the Sun Goddess's son and therefore divine. Again, it wasn't worth arguing over.

"Back to my original question," Shyla said. "Any ideas on how to earn some coins now?"

Jayden hunched his shoulders. "I can work for the black-market dealers. I've done it before. They appreciate my abilities to get around Zirdai unseen. It won't bring in much, but enough to last until we uncover the crypt."

"Mojag can help you," Gurice said.

"The risk of getting caught by the guards or the deacons is high and I don't want him in danger."

She glanced at Shyla who shook her head slightly in a we-can-discuss-it-later manner.

Shyla said, "I can do some research and maybe find the location of the other vault. And while I'm at the monastery, I'll look for another site that may have a valuable artifact we can uncover faster."

"Do you want me to continue clearing the tunnel at Gorgain's?" Aphra asked her.

"Might as well until we have another possible dig site. But you're not going to have the full complement of Invisible Swords."

"I figured. Better some than none." Aphra stood and stretched. "I'd better get some sleep."

It sounded like an excellent idea.

"What was that look for?" Jayden asked Gurice once Aphra had left. "Do you really want to endanger your brother for a few extra coins?"

"Mojag might be better at avoiding the guards and deacons than you think," Shyla said. She explained about her experiments.

Instead of being happy, Jayden growled at Gurice. "And you let her do that to him? He's just a boy."

"He's old enough to make his own decisions," Gurice shot back. "Besides, it's a good thing. We need more people who can wield magic."

"He's not mature enough. He's already cocky and takes unnecessary risks. If he learned how to wield magic..." Jayden sighed.

"What's really bothering you, Jay?" Gurice asked in a soft voice.

"When I was the priestess's...prisoner...one of the things that got me through their...questioning..." He swallowed.

Ximen put a hand on Jayden's shoulder, squeezing it in support.

Jayden gave him a wan half smile that quickly faded. "I endured because I knew Mojag escaped. I thought the Invisible Sword was gone and that he would be able to return to the commune and not be recruited. He'd have…well, not a normal life, but a safer one." He swept an arm out. "And here he is. Still in danger."

It was obvious that Jayden and Mojag were more than friends, more than mentor and student—they were brothers of the heart.

"I'm glad you're worried about him, but that's not for you to decide," Gurice said. "It's his choice. He knew he could have returned to the commune back when we were hiding at the monastery. At any time, really. Unlike us, no one knows he's involved with the Invisible Sword. He's chosen to stay with us despite the danger. If Shyla can unlock all his magic, that will make him safer."

Jayden's shoulders sagged. "You're right." He focused on Shyla. "You said you could see a glowing ribbon of magic inside him when he tried to wield magic. Did you see it with The Eyes?"

"Yes. I had to lower my shield." She described what she had done in more detail.

"And you think you can unlock the rest of his magic?" he asked Shyla.

"As I see it, it's more like…opening it up to its full potential. Like widening that crack. I've no idea if it'll work, but I think it's worth the effort if Mojag agrees."

"When are you going to…you know…try?"

"Not for a couple sun jumps," Shyla said. "I need to recover."

"All right. I'll take him with me to the black-market dealers while you rest." Jayden glanced at her. "What about your ideas to recruit more people?"

Ximen straightened. "You have ideas?"

"A few. One of the reasons I experimented with Gurice and Mojag was to see if The Eyes could recognize a person's magic. Since they can, I thought I'd start with the deacons who've been tortured. Perhaps some cracked while being rehabilitated, and they might be interested in joining us."

"And if they're not, they'll alert all their deacon friends," Gurice said.

"Of course there's a risk," Shyla said. "I'm hoping once I read their souls, I'll know the likelihood of them joining. And if they're truly devoted to the Heliacal Priestess, then I'll erase their memories before they yell for help."

"How are you going to find them?" Ximen asked. "It's not like they have 'I've been beaten into submission' written on their robes."

"I know they're not the ones guarding the chapels or the dining cavern or working in the confession rooms. They tend to hold the lowly jobs. They're the gardeners, the cleaners, and the kitchen workers."

"What about the people you freed from the confession rooms?" Gurice asked her. "They're probably grateful."

"That's a possibility."

"We could free more," Ximen said.

She'd like to rescue them all. "Not for a while. The deacons will be on guard for another ambush."

"What are your other ideas?" Jayden asked.

"The vagrants. We could recruit from the communes."

"You mean *I* could," Jayden said. "They won't trust an outsider. Well, most won't. Orla's know what's going on with the Invisible Sword. They're already helping us, but I guess it won't hurt to ask if anyone wants to join. With Orla's permission, of course."

"Of course. Did the Invisible Sword ever recruit from the communes?" Shyla asked.

"Only a select few who could be trusted. And those who had the potential for magic were kidnapped and put through the test."

Which, if she learned how to unlock a person's power, wouldn't be necessary.

"I'll make some inquiries while I'm working for the black-market dealers," Jayden said.

"Thanks. And I also thought about recruiting from the guards."

The response was instant and unanimous—it was a terrible idea.

"I'm sure there are many guards who are unhappy with the state of affairs," she tried.

"There may be, but they won't let you get near them to ask," Jayden said.

Still worth the effort. But Shyla realized they'd never agree, so she moved on. "What about the citizens? Will some of them be willing to join?"

"No," Gurice said. "Those that are disgruntled enough to do something usually become vagrants, refusing to pay taxes and the tithe. The others are either content, complicit, or not miserable enough to make the effort. All useless."

"Let's start with the vagrants and see how many are willing to join us," Shyla said. "Ximen, you keep work-ing with Aphra to ensure the dig stays hidden. Take half of our members. Gurice, I need you to organize the other half and start excavating a tunnel to Zirdai."

"What are you going to do?" Jayden asked.

"I'm going to do what I do best. Research. I'll search for information on Tamburah's other vault and look for another dig site that might be easier to access."

* * *

Shyla started with the First Room of Knowledge. After collecting all the tablets and scrolls with any reference to King Tamburah, she piled them on a low table in the reading area along with four druks. She squirmed into a comfortable position on the cushion and set to work.

After the meeting with her...lieutenants, Shyla had returned to her room. She'd slept until angle zero then packed enough supplies to last her a couple sun jumps. Stopping to say hello to Hanif, she'd informed him that she planned to spend a significant time in the two Rooms of Knowledge. He'd already known that she'd arrived. The monks on guard had beaten her to his office.

When she had researched Tamburah for Banqui's mission to uncover The Eyes over a circuit ago, she had gone to the University of Zirdai's library. The resources there hadn't mentioned or implied there was another vault.

And, as she slowly lost feeling in her backside during the dozens of angles she spent reading, she failed to find any reference in the monks' collection to a second vault or to another building that Tamburah might have lived in or frequented.

Shyla stood and stretched, rubbing her stiff muscles. Time to explore the map room. Taking a druk, she found the hidden opening and wriggled on her stomach through the small half-moon gap. She'd recently rediscovered it. A sharp pang of loneliness gripped her. Rendor had been with her. He'd stuck his head into the gap, all that he could fit. She wished she could go back to that moment and start over with him.

Focusing on the task at hand, Shyla brushed dirt and sand from her clothes and straightened. None of the monks, including Hanif, knew about this shortcut and she hoped they never did. Otherwise, they'd seal it up and Shyla would be out of luck. No doubt getting permission to enter the map room would be difficult.

A large domed ceiling arched over the octagonal room. Shelves filled with maps lined seven of the eight walls. Beautiful stained-glass doors comprised the final side. Standing in the middle, she held up the druk, illuminating the stacks of scrolls.

The good news—one or more of them was bound to be a map of an ancient site filled with treasure.

The bad news—she didn't know which ones.

And she wasn't going to find one just by standing there. She strode to the closest shelf, grabbed the first scroll and examined it. One down, a couple thousand more to go.

She lost track of time as she studied map after map. None of them met her criteria: close to their headquarters, shallow enough to be accessed in a reasonable amount of time, and *allegedly* filled with treasure. If she found a structure that met the first two, then she would investigate its history to determine the possibility of the third.

When her vision blurred with fatigue, she returned to the First Room of Knowledge for a break. Research was not for the impatient. She returned the materials she'd collected on Tamburah and decided on a change of scenery…well not quite as the layout of the Second Room of Knowledge mimicked the First. Only the information held inside was different.

As she crossed to the northwest corner of the monastery and descended two levels, she recalled that Banqui had only been focused on Tamburah's temple when he had worked to uncover The Eyes. And not for the first time, she wished she could talk to the archeologist. Shyla would bet he'd know the location of a few nearby treasures. She hoped he was well and not imprisoned in a black cell.

All this hoping and wishing and yearning for both Rendor and Banqui drained her energy. She had people depending on her. As much as it tempted her, she could *not* wallow in self-pity. Instead, she pushed those complicated emotions deep within her. She would deal with them later. Much later.

She entered the Second Room of Knowledge and collected all the tablets and scrolls that might contain a reference to Tamburah's vaults. It was quite a large pile and bigger than the one in the First Room. Sighing, she settled in and read.

It was well into the darkness when Shyla, half asleep and bleary eyed, found a comment that might have been an allusion to other vaults. Suddenly awake, she scanned the passage a couple times. It had been written by the official scribe, but for his own personal account. The scroll chronicled Tamburah's increasing paranoia. How he had doubled his guards, switched sleeping rooms, arrested his advisors and hired all new people, and became obsessed with his wealth. Tamburah had ordered his servants to move his valuables to different locations until he found one that he believed was secure, then he killed them all so only he knew where his treasures were. When one of his generals had expressed concern that the king wouldn't remember, Tamburah had pointed to his left temple and said, *It's all right here.* Then he had the man put to death for his impertinence.

At first, Shyla thought Tamburah referred to his memory. Then she suspected it might have to do with The Eyes. Either way it wasn't going to help her. She continued to read the scribe's journal. It detailed Tamburah's decline into madness, his increased blood lust and obsession with eyes. Nausea churned in her stomach as she learned that the king had delighted in personally gouging out the eyes of his enemies, which sounded like anyone who had dared to even look at him.

She hunched over and hugged her arms to her chest. Was that her fate? According to the written history, Tamburah had been about thirty-one circuits old when he'd assumed power and allegedly The Eyes. Signs of his unbalanced mental state had been mentioned approximately ten circuits later. He'd been assassinated nineteen and a half circuits after he'd been crowned. Did that mean she only had ten circuits of lucidity? And would Rendor keep his promise to remove The Eyes when— *if*—she turned into a tyrannical maniac like Tamburah? Probably not. Rendor no longer wished to be with her. She needed to ask another to ensure she didn't become a monster.

Resting her forehead on the edge of the cold stone table, Shyla endured a moment of overwhelming sadness despite her earlier resolve. Being the leader of the Invisible Sword hadn't pressed as hard on her shoulders when Rendor had been a member. At least Jayden would be more than happy to take The Eyes from her should she go rogue. In fact, he might be too willing. Perhaps Gurice or Ximen would be a better choice.

When she'd indulged in her self-pity long enough, Shyla returned to the scroll, skimming Tamburah's long list of horrors and increasingly erratic behavior. One comment snagged her attention. The scribe claimed Tamburah frequently stared at his sculpture—the oversized relief of Tamburah's face carved into one of the walls of his judgment room. The king had referred to his sand visage as his legacy many times. The scribe had assigned the behavior as another sign of the king's megalomania, but Shyla wondered if there was more to it.

A memory tugged. She'd studied the carving closely when she had waited for the Invisible Sword. Something about Tamburah's face…the configuration of the blue and purple sand had reminded her of a map. Excitement pumped through her. If she examined the pattern with her new sight, would it reveal more?

Of course no one would agree that it was worth the risk to go to Tamburah's judgment room to examine it. Both the Water Prince and Heliacal Priestess might be watching the temple. However, the Invisible Sword's old hideout was in the lower levels so the upper ones might be safer.

She sensed that pattern might be a key. To what, she'd no idea.

Good thing she didn't need anyone's permission.

* * *

Instead of dashing off to Tamburah's temple, Shyla remained in the Second Room of Knowledge until she read through all the scrolls and tablets she'd collected on Tamburah. It took the rest of the darkness to finish. Nothing else mentioned or even hinted at the existence of another vault or buildings. Because that would just be too easy. She returned the materials to their proper shelves.

Stiff, sore, exhausted, and with a headache that throbbed behind her eyes, Shyla staggered to her room in the empty wing of the monastery. Sinking into the soft sleeping cushion, she wondered if anyone would notice if she stole it. An image of her hunched over with the cushion on her back as she trudged through the desert made her giggle. Perhaps the monks on guard would think she was an oversized velbloud looking for its flock.

She dreamed she flew high above the sands, connected to the ground by a thin thread. Her pleasure over the view warred with her fear as the fibers in the thread slowly unraveled. She woke the instant the thread snapped. Or was it the sound of her door opening that had jolted her from sleep?

Either way, she was on her feet when Easan entered her room. He held a druk and the young monk's face was creased with worry.

"What's wrong?" she asked.

"Captain Yates is here with a platoon of guards. They've orders to search the monastery for you."

Son of a sand demon. Her memory wipe must have not lasted on that thick-headed man or else someone had tipped him off that she was here. She glanced at the sand clock—angle sixty-five and too close to the danger zone for her to leave the monastery through one of the escape tunnels. "I can hide in the First Room—"

"Yates has permission to search the Rooms of Knowledge." Easan's voice was strident with outrage. "*All* of them."

"The Water Prince doesn't have that kind of power."

"No he doesn't, but the King of Koraha does."

"The King gave the Water Prince permission?"

"Yes."

Shocked, she stared at her childhood friend. "Wait. How did the prince manage that? Qulsary is over seventy sun jumps away. Unless the King isn't in the capital?"

"He's there. The prince has a special dispensation from the King. It's to be used one time only for an emergency."

"I'm considered an emergency?" She didn't know whether to be flattered or terrified.

"Apparently. Aren't you special." He gave her a tight-lipped smile.

It was bad, but it still wasn't dire.

"Also the guards have formed into six eight-person units for the search."

Now it was dire.

CHAPTER

11

Seven hells. An eight-person unit was too many for Shyla to influence right now. If she'd had more sleep, then maybe. She still couldn't believe the King of Koraha had given the prince permission to enter all the Rooms of Knowledge. She wondered how close the prince and King were. He had to have impressed the King at some point to win that dispensation. Had the prince sent a message to the King about Shyla? Did she have to worry about his men coming to Zirdai? Perhaps she should concentrate on surviving the problem at hand.

"Is there any place to hide down past level twelve?" Having grown up in the monastery, she knew there weren't any hiding places in the upper levels. Not ones that Hanif or one of the other monks hadn't found her in pretty quick.

"No. There's nothing. Sorry," Easan said.

"Do you have any rooms with loose sand?"

"Not below level one. But if you need sand…" He pointed to the sand clock. "We've a bunch of those."

Not enough for her to hide under. Plus it would look suspicious—a mound of sand right in the middle of an otherwise clean room. She sorted through her childhood memories. Perhaps something would trigger a brilliant plan. No luck. "How long have they been here?"

"About five angles. They've already searched the top six levels. Good thing I checked your room first."

"Any gaps between units that I can slip through?"

"They're being rather thorough. What do you want to do?"

Only one thing to do. "I'll find a way to stay hidden until they leave."

"Where?"

"It's better you don't know." Shyla grabbed her pack and headed to the First Room of Knowledge. Hopefully being able to go between there and the map room would allow her to remain undetected. She had enough energy to hide the shortcut from one or even two, three if she was desperate. Although she doubted that many would find the hiding spot under the table. The maze of shelves and sudden dead ends should be confusing to the guards. Overall, not the best plan, but it was all she had.

At least she didn't have to guess when the unit entered. Their boisterous voices echoed off the stone walls and their irreverent and smug comments grated on her sensibilities. They didn't belong here and they knew it. Hanif must be beside himself over being forced to allow the guards into the Rooms of Knowledge.

Then a voice that sent a knife of fear straight to her heart said, "Fan out, and don't trust your eyes. Search with your hands. I'll wait here in case you flush the sun-kissed out."

She shouldn't have been surprised. Of course Yates would be with this unit. He wouldn't be able to resist going into a place that was normally off-limits to him. Not waiting any longer, she hurried to the map room. Once inside, Shyla crouched to the side of the opening and just out of sight. If she sensed anyone nearby, she'd project a solid wall.

As she waited, she counted her heartbeats, which seemed to echo loudly in the room. It didn't take long for the sounds of boots and voices to reach her. Two, maybe three guards approached the table.

A male voice said, "If I encounter one more spider web, I'm gonna charge the monks a cleaning fee."

"I don't know what all the fuss is about these rooms," said another man. "There's nothing here but a bunch of dusty old scrolls and tablets."

"What did you expect?" a woman asked.

"Golden chalices, bowls filled with precious gems, ancient artifacts."

"You certainly have quite the imagination," she said, and her tone implied it wasn't a compliment.

Weak druk light pierced the map room. Shyla gathered her magic as the light brightened.

"Ugh, there's a gap under the table. Check it out, Gafna," the first man ordered.

"Why me?"

"You're smaller than we are."

"And smarter, too," she said, but then she sighed. "You owe me."

A scrape of a boot was followed by a grunt. Shyla aimed her magic at the woman.

Wall.

But without making eye contact, Shyla had no way to know if her magic was working.

Wall.

"There's nothing here," the woman said.

Phew.

"Did you do a hand check?"

Oh no.

Another sigh. "You really want me to get bitten by a spider, don't you?"

"Better you than me."

Solid wall.

A hand poked through the shortcut. Shyla bit down on a curse.

"Huh? What the— Uri, get down here and bring that druk!"

"What did you find?" Uri asked.

Shyla sent her magic to the man as well.

Solid wall.

"I don't know, you big lug. Give me the light."

A druk was thrust into the map room. Shyla backed away from the shortcut.

Not here.

The female guard stuck her head in. "That was weird."

"What in seven hells, Gafna. Where's your head?"

"In some kind of room." She withdrew. "See for yourself."

"That's a solid wall."

"It looks like one, but it's not. Isn't this what Captain Yates said to be on the lookout for?"

This wasn't going to end well, but Shyla didn't know what else to do.

Not here.

A big hand with calluses appeared followed by a scowling guard's face. His surprise didn't last long. He retreated.

"Block that opening," he ordered Gafna. "I'm going to find out about that room."

Not here.

Gafna reappeared, but she stopped so half of her body remained in the First Room. She held her sword and scanned the octagonal space.

Sleep.

The woman blinked a few times and yawned, but she shook off the command. Shyla increased her will.

Sleep.

Gafna's head dropped. Not wasting time, Shyla raced over to the double stained-glass doors. They were locked. Scorching hells. After a moment of panic, she remembered that this room was guarded like all the others. Reaching out, she sensed the two monks on the other side.

Open doors.

Nothing.

Open doors.

"Hey, what are you doing?" a muffled voice on the other side said.

A key rasped in the keyhole. "Unlocking the door."

"Why?"

She didn't have time for this. Using more of her waning energy, she pushed it at the two monks.

Open doors.

A metallic snap broke the quiet. The doors slid apart. Both monks peeked inside.

Not here.

She darted into the hallway.

Lock doors.

They did as instructed. Shyla hurried away. She was on level nine. And probably so were the other units. If she only encountered a few guards she could slip by them and get higher. If not…she'd be caught. Best to think positive.

Voices alerted her before she turned the corner. She skidded to a stop and backtracked to the intersection she'd just passed. Ducking down the left tunnel, she pressed against the wall just as the group walked by. Hanif led Captain Yates and four guards. They were so focused on getting to the map room that none glanced her way. She remembered to breathe. After waiting for what seemed like a couple thousand angles, she ventured out and tried to find a route free of guards.

She managed to reach level seven, but Yates must have brought more than a platoon because there were plenty of guards stationed at the various ramps to the upper levels. Too many for her to handle. Besides, it was still too hot to be higher than level six. Shyla considered borrowing a robe and trying to sneak by them, but as she watched from a hidden spot, the guards yanked the hoods down on all the monks who had them up.

Her only option was to stay hidden until the surface cooled enough for her to use one of the escape tunnels. Except she soon learned that guards blocked those as well. She had to grudgingly admit Captain Yates wasn't an idiot. Panic churned and bubbled up her throat. She swallowed it down.

Hoping the guards had already searched level seven, Shyla sought a place to hide. The kitchen and dining area were nearby, but second meal would be in full swing. Perhaps if she found a robe, she could blend in with the monks there. Too bad there weren't robes just lying around.

She spent the next ten or twenty angles dodging guards. Each close encounter sapped her strength a little more. At this rate, they would find her curled up in a corner sound asleep.

At a loss for what to do, she kept moving until she realized groups of monks had joined in the search for her. They weren't obvious about it, but she sensed their intent to find her. Too tired to figure out why, and hoping it was for a good reason, she trailed one of them until she thought it was safe to reveal her presence.

The five of them quickly surrounded her—not to attack, but to hide her. Without a word, they headed to the kitchen where they left her. Huh? After glancing briefly in her direction, the staff returned to their duties. The savory scent of roast gamelu enticed her to the stew pot despite her unsettled stomach. She helped herself. Why not? This might be her last meal.

Soon a group of three monks entered the kitchen. This time, she recognized Kaveri.

"We don't have much time," Kaveri said.

An understatement. "What's going on?"

"We've a plan to help you." Kaveri took off her robe. Underneath she wore a plain tunic and pants much like the ones the citizens wore. Actually, very similar to what Shyla wore.

"Here." Kaveri handed her the robe. "Put that on."

"But—"

"Trust me."

And since the woman was her mother, Shyla did.

Kaveri handed a pair of scissors to another monk. "Be quick."

Shyla watched in fascinated horror as the monk cut Kaveri's hair short. Long strands of beautiful yellow hair floated to the floor. "You..."

"Don't worry, it'll grow back," Kaveri said, unconcerned. Unlike Shyla who had been upset when the deacon had chopped off her long locks. Soon Kaveri's hairstyle matched Shyla's. And a strange sensation swept through her as the resemblance between the two of them was undeniable. Shyla stared into her future.

"You..." Again words failed her as Shyla tried to speak.

"We'll talk about it later," Kaveri said, cupping Shyla's cheek for a moment. "Now, let me tell you the plan."

As far as plans went, this one was rather simple. But it put Kaveri at considerable risk. Shyla argued that Captain Yates might arrest the woman out of spite.

"He can try, but he won't succeed. I am a monk." Kaveri's confidence was unshakable.

Shyla wondered if she'd ever be that...comfortable with her role in their world. At least, if she survived, Shyla might learn more about the woman who gave birth to her. The two of them crept back up to level seven. By now, enough time had passed and the surface would be safe...sort of. It wouldn't be comfortable, but it wouldn't kill her either.

They stopped at a collection station before splitting up to implement Kaveri's scheme at one of the ramps to level six. From a hidden vantage point, Shyla held her breath and watched as her mother rounded a corner as if being pursued. Kaveri halted when she spotted the six guards. They stared at each other for a few stunned heart-beats. Then Kaveri spun on her heel and dashed away.

"It's the sun-kissed," one guard cried. "Baru and Lute, stay here. The rest with me."

Four guards raced after Kaveri, leaving two behind.

If all went according to plan, Kaveri would lead them deep into the monastery before allowing them to catch her.

The guards that remained at the ramp buzzed with a new sense of purpose. Shyla waited about three angles. Covering her hair with the robe's hood, she hefted the heavy bucket and strolled toward the two guards.

They wrinkled their noses at the foul odor and parted, allowing Shyla to pass without questioning her or even looking closely at her. She didn't even need to use her magic. In fact, everyone gave her a wide berth as she carried that noxious bucket up to the growing cavern on level six. Wow. Who knew the power of poop?

She set the container in the back room for Kaveri to turn the contents into fertilizer. On the way out, she stopped and bent close to one of the plants, breathing in its fresh scent to purge the stink of excrement from her nose and lungs. Then she hurried to the surface. The temperature increased with each level, until she pushed through the hot thickness.

When she reached the surface building, the sunlight blinded her. And the heat immediately closed in, baking the sweat from her skin. Invisible fire burned with each inhalation. Soon her eyes adjusted to the brilliance and she changed into her sun cloak, leaving Kaveri's robe on the bench. The monks who guarded the entrance hadn't returned yet.

Out in the full sunshine, the velbloud fibers of her cloak helped lessen the intensity of the sun, but the desert's bright colors hurt. Which didn't make sense. Colors shouldn't be painful.

Yet, as she sloughed through the blistering sand, various aches woke. The fiery press of heat on her head and shoulders increased her fatigue. And the effort to erase her footprints caused her muscles to tremble so much she had to quit hiding them once she was half a kilometer away. The distance to the Invisible Sword's headquarters stretched toward impossible. She'd almost halted in defeat. But, in order to keep moving, Shyla set small goals.

Just get to the top of this dune.
Ten steps.
Twelve more steps.
Just reach that patch of shade.

The heat had thinned slightly by the time she arrived at the entrance. She staggered to a stop, gathering the last dregs of her energy to mount the ladder. The lookout climbed from the temple. He jerked in surprise when he noticed her standing there.

"Are you all right?" Balin asked.

"I'm fine," she croaked.

Dubious, he raised his thick black eyebrows at her. "What are you doing out here?"

She considered a sarcastic reply, but it was a legitimate question. "I just came from the monastery." Overlooking how his eyebrows lifted even higher—a rather amazing feat—she gestured to her tracks and explained about the guards. "Keep an eye in this direction in case they find them and follow me. I'll send someone to erase them."

"All right."

If the guards appeared in the distance, Balin would sound the alarm, and those who had magic would cover the entrance, the ventilation shafts, and any tracks with sand. That was, if any of them were here. Between the city and the dig site, there weren't many around. More reason to increase their numbers.

After the ridiculously complex task of descending the ladder, Shyla found Gurice, ignored her questions, and sent her to the surface. Then she gulped half of the water in her water skin and collapsed onto her mat with a groan.

Despite her near miss with the guards and the exhaustion that had sunk deep into her bones, she still wished she'd stolen a sleeping cushion from the monks.

* * *

"You do understand that you're not only endangering yourself but the rest of us as well?" Gurice asked.

"I'm aware of the risks," Shyla said, swallowing down a sigh. No surprise that she'd encountered resistance to her plan to visit Tamburah's judgment chamber.

They sat at a table in the common room. Shyla had slept for a long time, scaring everyone. Gurice had been about to send for Zhek when she woke. Even now, after another full sun jump of rest, fatigue still tugged on her muscles.

"Let me come with you, then," Gurice said. "Or take Titus. He has magic."

"No, you're both needed here in case our hideout is discovered."

"At least take a couple of the acolytes with you. Jayden will kill me if he finds out you went alone."

Shyla considered. "All right."

Gurice pressed a hand to her chest. "You *can* be reasonable. Praise the goddess."

"Cute."

* * *

"Finally, a challenge," Lian said. "I'm sick of shoveling sand."

"My blisters have blisters," Jaft quipped.

"All part of being a member of a not-so-secret organization," Elek said.

"Are you done complaining?" Rae asked her friends. "Shyla hasn't finished explaining the mission."

Shyla didn't mind their banter, although she'd never tell them that or they wouldn't shut up. Their easy friendship and loyalty was what she hoped all the members of the Invisible Sword would eventually feel toward each other. A big family, working together, fighting together, helping others.

They had agreed to accompany her to Tamburah's temple without knowing all the details. Dressed and ready to go, they had met her in the common room at angle three-fifty-five for a quick briefing.

"This shouldn't take long," Shyla said. "The hardest part will probably be finding the escape tunnel."

"Are you expecting trouble?" Elek asked.

"I'm always expecting trouble. However, I'm hoping that we'll be disappointed."

They left at angle zero. Shyla erased their tracks. The action reminded her of her escape from the monastery. It was too dangerous to send a runner to check on what happened there after she'd left three sun jumps ago. Worry for her parents and the monks pulsed in her chest. If the Water Prince contacted the King about her, it could mean trouble for the monastery. Would he send his elite soldiers to investigate the dangerous sun-kissed? What if the King ordered the monks to turn Shyla over to the Water Prince if she ever returned? Best to stay away for a while. She'd wait until Jayden and Mojag returned from Zirdai and ask if they'd heard any rumors.

Despite their earlier chatter, the four ex-acolytes settled into a quiet, highly focused team, scanning the desert for potential problems. Jaft and Elek carried shovels. A sense of readiness and competence oozed from all of them, their smooth gaits and graceful movements reminding Shyla of predators.

As predicted, the hatch covering the safety tunnel was difficult to locate. It'd been thirty-nine sun jumps since it was last used and the constant blowing sand had reburied it. They used the handles of the shovels to puncture the loose sand, listening for a hollow *thunk* that would mean they'd hit the hatch.

"Found it," Jaft shouted.

They removed the sand and opened the hatch. Stale air rushed out. Shyla dropped into the hole first, ensuring the tunnel hadn't collapsed since it wasn't part of the temple. Strong emotions welled as she shone the druk on the sand walls. The last time she was here, she'd run from the deacons and embraced the sun, knowing full well the heat would kill her.

"It's clear," she called.

Soon the others followed her deeper into the temple. They reached the faces of the dead. Carved into the sandstone were the eyeless visages of Tamburah's victims. Their mouths were open in silent wails of anguish, desperation, and fear. The carvings covered the walls from floor to ceiling.

"Is anyone else creeped out by all these people?" Jaft asked.

"Even though they don't have eyes, it seems like they're staring at you," Rae said with a shudder. "Are they just decoration?"

"No," Shyla said. "They were real people who King Tamburah judged as not trustworthy. He removed their eyes as punishment. Proud of his handiwork, he had an artist carve their faces into the walls so he could admire them. Banqui called this one of the hallways of the dead."

"You mean there are more?" Jaft asked.

"Lots more. The temple is filled with them."

"He makes the Water Prince seem like...well, a prince," Lian said.

"The Water Prince tortures people by hanging them upside down and cutting into their flesh, including eyeballs, and male genitalia." Revulsion coated her mouth with bile as the vivid memory of the naked vagrant flashed.

"If given the choice, I'd choose my eyes over my—"

"That's enough," Elek said, interrupting Jaft. "I just ate."

Tamburah's judgment chamber was located on level five. They covered the druks and slowed as they neared the entrance, their footsteps almost silent. Shyla stretched out her senses, seeking that bump of others. Was an ambush waiting for them? Not one comprised of guards. Deacons were another matter. If they wore torques, Shyla and her friends would have to fight their way free.

Taking a chance, she said, "Uncover the druks."

Light illuminated the threshold and, beyond that, the chamber. No sound pierced the quiet. No deacons attacked from the shadows. Not yet. She'd been surprised twice before in this very location and didn't wish to add a third. The five of them entered and spread out. Stone benches and a large stone altar decorated the hexagonal room. Behind the altar, King Tamburah's smug face filled the wall. Blue and purple sand lined his skin, and red grains of crystal filled his empty eye sockets and dripped down his cheek, indicating blood—it was all very dramatic.

"Let's check the other hallways of the dead," Shyla said. Six doorways led to other areas of the temple, but she wanted to ensure they were empty of attackers. Satisfied they were alone, for now, she took a druk and examined Tamburah's giant face while the others guarded her back.

Like she'd suspected, the lines formed a pattern that resembled a...maze...or it could be a complex map. Either way there wasn't a big X marking the location of another vault or anything else. Studying it with the power of The Eyes also failed to reveal any secrets—because that would have just been too easy. Still…the design seemed clearer than before.

Shyla dug into her pack and removed a blank scroll, a stylus, and a vial of ink. She copied the pattern. As the lines filled the velbloud skin, a nagging sense that she'd seen this before grew. It was a map to a maze, and at the center of the maze should be the prize, whatever that was. Yet the problem still remained of where in Zirdai or the surrounding desert the map detailed. It could be anywhere. Also there wasn't a key or a compass rose. The area might be kilometers wide, or all contained within a single level. Except…

Tamburah considered the temple his seat of power. Following the logic that he wouldn't want anything important to be too far away from him, the map would start in the temple. But where?

When she finished the copy, she let the ink dry. She stepped back from the carving. Once again she studied the pattern. Tamburah's obsession with eyes meant they would be a focus point—an important part of the map. Perhaps the location of the maze. So where was the starting point? The judgment room! She glanced around. Six possible directions. She would have to explore each one, following the map. Too bad she no longer had the map to Tamburah's temple. The last time she examined it the map had been in Banqui's work rooms on level thirteen. No doubt Rohana and her diggers now occupied the three large caverns.

"Are you done?" Lian asked. "It's getting late."

Shyla debated. They could retreat deeper in the temple and Shyla could explore. Or she could return at another time with Jayden. He had to be well acquainted with the temple's layout. Plus Banqui had disabled a few booby traps. Perhaps the Invisible Sword had kept some traps active to keep the curious or the treasure hunters away. The smart thing would be to come back with Jayden, even though it would probably start a fight between them.

"All right. Let's go," Shyla said.

They returned to headquarters well before the danger zone. And, as if he'd read her mind, Jayden waited for her in the common room. He and Mojag had earned a small pile of coins, but that wasn't why they'd returned.

"I've news," Jayden said.

And by the wary way he gazed at her, Shyla knew it wasn't good. "Just tell me."

"Captain Yates arrested Hanif and another monk. They're in the black cells."

CHAPTER

12

Shyla stared at Jayden in stunned silence. Hanif arrested? Locked in the black cells? Grief cracked through the surprise and the full implications of his news hit her. She rocked back on her heels. "Another monk? Do you know who?"

"The rumors said she's a sun-kissed. I thought it was you. That's why I came back here as soon as I could." He shot her an annoyed glare. "To find you missing."

She ignored him. The other monk had to be Kaveri. All of her energy drained and she sank onto a cushion. It was her fault they'd been arrested. Memories from when she'd visited Banqui rose—the foul odor of excrement and piss, the cold dampness, the wails of the other prisoners, and not a single beam of light.

"We have to rescue them," she said.

"We don't have the resources," Jayden said. "Besides, they're under the protection of the King. They won't be there long."

She jumped to her feet. "Being in there one single angle is too long! And the King gave the Water Prince *permission* to search the monastery, including the Rooms of Knowledge. That must mean they've a good relationship. The monks have helped us so much. We have to *do* something."

Jayden held out his hands. "Calm down. We'll find out why they were arrested and see what we can do."

Not good enough. They needed to act now. "We can get into one of the prince's empty special rooms and find a way into the black cells from there."

"It's not that simple, otherwise we'd have done it before."

At that moment, she hated Jayden. Easy for him to be logical and calm, it wasn't his parents who were in trouble. Except, no one besides Rendor knew they were her parents. Everyone still believed she'd been abandoned in the desert as a baby. Hanif had asked her to keep it a secret.

"I'll send Mojag and Gurice to the monastery as soon as it's cool enough," Jayden said. "We can discuss options once we learn more. In the meantime, you can explain to me why you thought going to Tamburah's temple was a good idea."

A childish retort—*I don't have to explain myself to you*—pushed up her throat. Instead, she detailed her reasons and showed him the map. "I think it might lead to a maze of hidden tunnels and rooms. Do you recognize anything?"

He studied the scroll with his forehead furrowed. A pang gripped her. Underneath his eyes were dark smudges like faded bruises. He hadn't been getting enough sleep.

Finally, he met her gaze. "We've had our headquarters in the temple for hundreds of thousands of sun jumps. If there was something like this in there, the Invisible Sword would have found it by now."

"It has to be well concealed. And perhaps only I'll be able to see it."

"Still dangerous just for a perhaps."

"We'll go along as backup," Elek said, gesturing to the other three who nodded in agreement.

His comment eased some of the pain in her chest. "And I'll need you, too, Jayden. I think it's worth the danger." However, if he didn't agree to accompany her, it would be too hazardous to go.

"I'll think about it. For now, let's deal with the problem at hand."

"Which one?" she asked.

Jayden ignored her sarcasm. "The one associated with the other bit of news I picked up while working for the black-market dealers."

She settled back on the cushion. "How bad is it?"

"There's a trading caravan coming in from Tarim in a few sun jumps. The dealers say the leader of this cavalcade, Zimraan, is fond of precious metals and is well known to have ingots of platinum for sale."

"How well known?"

"The Heliacal Priestess is probably already planning on sending a couple of Arch Deacons to the man's market stand."

Scorching sand demons. "We need to stop that sale."

"Exactly."

Shyla mulled it over. "When are they due to arrive?"

"In the next four to six sun jumps, but it could be longer."

"At least we have some time to plan. But that will take away from all the other things we need to do!"

"You can't save the city in a couple sun jumps, Shyla," Jayden said before leaving to find Mojag and Gurice.

But it'd been more than a couple. An eternity of them weighed on her shoulders. To be fair, it was only twenty-six sun jumps since she'd sacrificed her eyes, but she'd expected to have accomplished more. Jayden was right. They lacked resources. They needed to strengthen their numbers. Especially if they were going to rescue Hanif and Kaveri, find the hidden maze, and stop a merchant from selling his valuable goods. She studied the four ex-acolytes.

"Oh no, do you see that look on Shyla's face?" Lian asked her friends. "She's up to something. Well, it's been nice, but I've sand to shovel." She gave a jaunty wave.

"Nice try," Shyla said, tugging Lian back. "Sit down." She explained her experiments with Mojag and Gurice to them. "I'd like to see if you have the potential to wield magic."

"Does that mean you'll read our souls?" Rae asked. She pulled her knees up to her chest and hugged them.

"No. Yes. Not exactly."

"That was clearly confusing," Jaft said.

"I won't dig for your innermost desires and secrets. I'm searching for your potential. I might learn something about you, but it's usually just surface thoughts and emotions. It's up to you."

"I think knowing I have potential to wield magic is worth Shyla knowing I hate my father," Lian said.

"We *all* know you hate him," Elek said. "If I ever meet him…" He punched a fist into his hand. "I'm going to pummel him."

"*After* I'm done with him," Lian said.

"What if we're cracked? Then what?" Rae asked.

"I'll try to open it. Expand it." Shyla mimed pulling apart a druk.

"Try to? That doesn't sound very reassuring," Jaft said.

"I'm still working on that part. Once I figure it out, then I'll open everyone with potential."

"I'm feeling better already."

"Ignore him, we always do," Lian said. "I'm in."

The other three also agreed.

"What do we need to do?" Rae asked.

"Relax." Shyla grabbed a handful of sand and poured it on the table. "I want you to gather your energy and try to move the sand." She explained the process of using magic as best she could.

Lian went first, then Jaft, Elek, and finally Rae. Nothing she encountered while searching for that inner light surprised her, except for Rae.

The petite woman was a sun-kissed. Burn scars marked her skin from when she'd been abandoned in the desert. Rae dyed her hair, eyebrows, and eyelashes in order to blend in. Only the monks knew what she was and she wanted to keep it that way. And, of the four, Rae was the only one with potential. As Rae focused on the sand, a sliver of light glowed inside her.

"Figures," Lian said when Shyla told them.

"At least I'm still young and handsome," Jaft said, eliciting groans all around.

Unconcerned, Elek shrugged his big shoulders.

Rae, though, curled tighter. "Are you sure? The sand didn't move when I stared at it."

Sensing Rae's distress, Shyla put her arm around the young woman's shoulders. "Yes, I'm sure. And you don't have to do anything you don't want to."

"I'm okay. Just getting used to the idea. Besides, nothing bad ever happened to…crack me."

Perhaps the trauma of almost dying as a baby had unlocked Rae's magic, or maybe being sun-kissed was a factor. Shyla wondered if her mother might have the potential. Claws of fear sank into her stomach. What if something terrible happened in the black cells that unlocked Kaveri's magic?

To keep from useless worrying, Shyla scanned the common room. Many people had congregated there for second meal. She asked Elek to gather the rest of the ex-acolytes so she could test them. He went over to a table of them. She was struck by how the members had sorted themselves into groups of ex-acolytes and original Invisible Swords. Even she thought of them that way. That wasn't good. She needed to fix it. Yet another problem to add to her ever-growing list. At least they had a steady supply of clean water thanks to Rendor. Thinking of him sent a bolt of pain right through her. She quickly refocused on the Invisible Swords.

Elek sent Balin, Nard, and Daksh over and then went in search of the others. Shyla explained to the three men what she was doing and why. They'd all seen magic in use and all were willing to allow her to access their souls. Too bad none of them had potential.

Of the remaining ex-acolytes, only Yoria had potential. The woman was thirty-eight circuits old and she wasn't surprised to be...cracked. Shyla needed to come up with a better word.

"My tyrant of a husband drove me to leave Zirdai and join the monks," Yoria said. "I should have done it sooner, which is why I'm helping others as an Invisible Sword. The citizens of Zirdai need to realize they've waited too long. It's time to change the status quo. I consider my experiences a mixed blessing from the Sun Goddess."

"She tends to do that," Shyla said, remembering her own "conversation" with the goddess.

Being sun-kissed is a gift, the goddess had said. *I do not enjoy seeing my people suffer. Make it stop.*

The Sun Goddess must be very disappointed in Shyla.

* * *

After the danger zone had passed, Mojag and Gurice left for the monastery and Shyla pulled Jayden aside.

"Besides Mojag, two of our members have the potential," she said to him. "I want to examine the original Invisible Swords."

"Waste of time and energy," he said. "They've all been through our assessment and failed."

"But you might have cracked them." Again, she needed a kinder descriptor.

He opened his mouth but then paused. "Good point."

Progress! "I'm also thinking we need…something to bring everyone together."

"Something?"

They'd discussed this before and Jayden had gotten angry, but she was tired of worrying about Jayden's moods. "Yes, a new oath for a new archive of the Invisible Sword."

"A new archive?"

"Yes, since the organization has gone through a major change, it's a new era."

"I like that."

She put her hand to the wall as if to keep from falling over. "Whoa. Next time warn me before you agree with me."

He flashed her a smile, and damn, the frustrating man was handsome. "Don't get used to it."

"Wouldn't dream of it."

Jayden huffed in amusement. "Are you going to gather everyone or do it individually?"

"I think everyone should be together. But I'm still working out the details. For now, I'm going to concentrate on testing everyone."

Over the rest of the sun jump, Shyla examined the remaining members. Or she tried. A few kept dodging her, and she assumed they didn't wish for her to test them but were too polite or too scared of her to say no. At least she found one more person with potential. Lamar, a quiet young man, told her the trauma of the priestess's ambush and seeing his friends in the Invisible Sword killed by the deacons must have caused him to crack.

"Up until then, I was lucky and didn't think anything would harm us." He hunched his thin shoulders.

"You were lucky to escape," she said.

"I guess."

One thing she'd learned was that magic came with a cost. She wondered why the other survivors of the massacre hadn't also tapped into their power. They had to have been traumatized as well. Did that mean they didn't have the potential? Or were they stronger and hadn't needed to tap into their inner reserves? She wished there was a way she could connect to that closed lantern that was supposed to be inside those people born with magical potential, but, so far, only the ones that had been cracked open were visible. At least Jayden had been right about Aphra, though. She didn't pass, and she wasn't happy about it either.

Overall, Shyla was pleased with finding three more. Including Mojag, that would bring the total number of wielders to nine if the new ones could access their full power. Perhaps a few lessons would do the trick. Or would she need to fully engage their magic? Once Mojag and Gurice returned, she'd talk to all four and discuss options.

Exhausted, she went to her room to lie down. She'd told Jayden to wake her as soon as they came back. But when she closed her eyes, the cries of the prisoners in the black cells filled her head. How could a memory be so loud? And what if the Water Prince had Hanif and Kaveri in one of his special rooms? Worry and fear pumped through her. In an attempt to distract her thoughts from conjuring up more horrible scenarios about her parents, she focused on other problems, which led to making a mental list of everything she needed to accomplish. It was overwhelming. So why was she wasting time trying to sleep?

Giving up, she took the map from her pack and examined it. That nagging feeling once again poked her like an annoying younger sibling.

Poke—*remember this?*

Poke—*come on, you know it.*

Poke—*how stupid can you be?*

Poke—*no wonder Mom loves me best.*

The desire to crumple the skin into a tight little wad twitched along her fingers. Instead she stared at it, imagining her eyes had turned to lava stones and could set the damn thing on fire. Too bad she couldn't read the map like a person's soul. What would happen if she pushed with the magic of The Eyes while looking at an inanimate object? Probably nothing. At least she wouldn't be disappointed as that was all she'd managed to get from it so far.

Feeling a bit silly, she gazed at the map using her magic. As expected, nothing happened. Then she blinked. The lines shifted. Suddenly another map rose. A three-dimensional shape of a maze with twists and turns and dead ends. And in the center, the prize. Was that what Tamburah meant when he pointed to his temple and said, *It's all right here?* Perhaps he was really pointing to his eyes, indicating that his power would show him the right way. Excitement replaced her frustration. Now she just needed to find the entrance into the maze.

When her eyes crossed with fatigue, she returned to her sleeping mat. Jayden woke her a few angles later. Mojag and Gurice were back.

They'd arrived just before darkness along with the crew from the dig site. The diggers hadn't reached deep enough to safely remain on site. Gurice went to check on her team working on the tunnel to Zirdai, leaving Mojag to report the news.

Ximen joined the three of them in a corner of the common room. Not for the first time, or the last, she was sure, Shyla wished for a cup of hot tea.

"The monks are in a tizzy," Mojag said. "Seems the big arrest is unpress…unprez…er…never happened before."

"What was the reason for the arrest?" Shyla asked.

"Hiding a known criminal, and collusion, whatever that means. Yates said if the monks told him where the sun-kissed is hiding, he'd let Hanif go. The other monk was arrested for obstruction." Mojag perked up a bit. "Good call on not telling them where we are."

"What about the King? Has he been informed?" Jayden asked.

"They sent a messenger. And the monks said they argued with Yates that he didn't have the power to arrest them, that he used up his one exemption. But he said that it was used to search for the sun-kissed, which also meant the monks had to cooperate and, when they didn't, he was within his rights to arrest them."

"I'm surprised the monks allowed the guards to leave," Ximen said. "From what I've seen, they're more than capable of handling them."

"Hanif told them not to fight. He said to contact the King." Mojag rubbed his arms with short agitated strokes. "Do you think the King will send his army? What if they side with the Water Prince?"

"It will take at least seventy sun jumps for a message to reach the King," Shyla said. "I doubt he'd do more than send a message back ordering Hanif and Kaveri's release, which will take another seventy sun jumps if the King responds right away, otherwise it could be even more." Any amount of time was unacceptable to her.

"Do you think the monks would be willing to help us?" Jayden asked her.

"Help us how?"

"We need more people. The monks are well trained. We could join forces and attack the Water Prince."

That would be wonderful. "They might want to, but they're not permitted to interfere."

Jayden pounded his fist on the table. "That's just an excuse."

"They work for the King."

He was not appeased. "Then we can't help Hanif. Not yet."

Shyla wasn't going to give up. "We managed to get to the prince before. We can do it again."

"The only reason that worked was because the Water Prince thought you had The Eyes. This time, he'd just overwhelm us with sheer numbers. And that is if we even get down there. If the priestess hears we're on the warpath, she'll send Arch Deacons after us."

"We can wield magic and remain hidden."

Jayden leaned forward. "It's too exhausting. The Invisible Sword's leaders brainstormed various strategies to overthrow the prince. The best they came up with is tricking him with The Eyes." The unspoken *and you ruined it* flared in his pointed gaze.

"He's right," Ximen said.

"But you didn't have a leader who woke The Eyes. I'm—"

"Still learning how to use your magic," Jayden said.

She wilted. True.

Mojag yawned and left to get some rest. Shyla watched him go. "You might have more students to teach." She filled them in on the results of her test.

"Lamar? Wow, I never would have guessed," Ximen said. "And Mojag's going to be...obnoxious."

"Except they still need to be opened. I was thinking if they learn how to focus their magic, that might work to expand their abilities."

"And if it doesn't?" Ximen asked.

"Then I'll ask for a volunteer and use The Eyes."

"You have to be careful, Shyla," Jayden said. "Remember when you took the oath and the magic slammed us all into the walls? There are other consequences to using magic aside from exhausting yourself. Some people's minds are fragile."

"Then I'll be cautious. It's just too important not to try."

"What about that caravan?" Ximen asked. "How are we going to get that platinum when we don't have enough coins to buy it and we won't steal?"

Shyla met Jayden's gaze. "Come with me to Tamburah's temple. Give me one chance to find that maze."

"You know you can order me to go with you," Jayden said.

"Do you want me to? Will that help?"

"No to both. All right, I'm in. When do you want to go?"

"Angle three-forty-five. Ximen, I want you to work with the potentials, see if any of them can wield magic."

"Does this mean I'm the one who gets to tell Mojag about his magic?" Ximen asked.

"No." Jayden stood up. "I'll do it." He left.

"What about the dig site?" Ximen asked.

"Gurice can take your place for a sun jump."

"She's not that good with moving sand."

"What about Titus?"

"He's better. Can you send them both?"

"Yes, let them know, and I'll round up my backup. Rae isn't going to be happy about staying behind," Shyla said.

"Tell her that we'll start at angle zero. I'm beat."

"Get some rest, Ximen."

He gave her a two-fingered salute. Shyla found Rae in the small room she shared with Lian and two other women who were also ex-acolytes.

As expected, Rae protested. "Who are you going to take instead?"

"I'll take Vashi. I hear she's a pretty good fighter."

Lian snorted. "Those Invisible Swords all think they're good, but compared to our training..." She spread her hands and turned her palms up—unimpressed.

"You're Invisible Swords now," Shyla reminded her. "And we need to all work together."

"That's the thing," Lian said. "We don't feel like one of them."

"I know. I'm working to rectify that." Shyla paused. "When I have time."

Shyla made one more stop.

"A hidden maze with booby traps? Count me in," Aphra said.

"*If* we find it. And just being in the temple will be dangerous," Shyla said.

Aphra arched an eyebrow. "And how is that different from my life as a treasure hunter?"

"Fair point. But do you even know how to fight with that knife you carry?"

"You want to try taking it from me?" Aphra shifted her weight to the balls of her feet.

"A simple yes would have sufficed."

"But it's not as fun."

Shyla grinned. "Another time then."

"No magic. That's cheating."

She agreed. "No magic."

While walking back to her room, Shyla considered her brief conversations with Rae and Lian and Aphra. Perhaps they should all train and spar together. They could spare fifteen angles a sun jump. Not only would it keep their skills sharp, but it would create a sense of kinship. Like all good ideas, she wished she'd thought of it sooner. Maybe then Rendor wouldn't have left.

She pulled her thoughts from that direction. Those "should haves" and "could haves" would only drag her into despair. Instead, she focused on the mission, and was surprised to find Mojag waiting for her in her room.

He played with the sand in her practice bucket, molding shapes with his hands only to squash them and create something else.

"Is it true?" he asked without looking up.

No need to ask what he referred to. "Yes."

"What if I lose my abilities to…sniff out people by opening up my magic?"

"I think it would enhance those abilities."

"What if it changes me?"

"You don't have to do anything. If you're happy to remain this way, I won't force you. No one will."

Now he looked at her. "I can't do that. It might help us."

"Might is the key word, Mojag. No guarantee."

He jumped to his feet. "You sacrificed your eyes for us. Your eyes! No guarantee then either! It's the least I can do."

A very mature reaction. She wondered what Jayden had said to him. "Why are you afraid of changing?"

"You and Jayden and the others are so…serious and worried all the time. You have so much…responsibility. No one is happy."

She'd been ready to explain until he reached the last point. Thinking quickly, she said, "We're unhappy with the situation, which is why we're working so hard to change things."

"Nah, that's not it. You haven't been happy since Rendor left."

"That has nothing to do with magic, Mojag. And you already have serious responsibilities which you are handling so well. When I was your age, my biggest worry was handing in my assignments on time."

"Sounds boring."

"It was."

"Okay, I'll do it. And if the magic lessons don't work, I wanna be first."

"First what?"

He tapped a finger on his chest. "The first person you open."

Mojag left before she could respond, which was a good thing as she didn't want to upset him by refusing.

* * *

Jayden didn't comment when Aphra joined their group at angle three-forty-five. Elek and Jaft scowled at Vashi, who ignored them both. The tall woman's long brown hair had been braided and twisted into a knot at the nape of her neck. Her tawny-colored eyes sparked with disdain as she scanned the others. Except for Jayden. A softness eased the strong lines of her face when she gazed at him.

They climbed to the surface. The sharp cold of the air chased away the last tendrils of sleep, and Shyla drew in a deep cleansing breath. It energized her. But she knew the bite in the air would eventually cause shivers and numb fingers.

When her eyes adjusted to the starlight, Shyla turned to the group. Mojag was right, everyone was so serious all the time. They had good reasons, but if there was too much pressure they'd all break. They needed to warm up. Might as well make it fun.

She pulled in a deep breath and said, "Last one there is a rotten velbloud egg!" She took off running. Suddenly feeling six circuits old, she laughed. The sound was carried by the wind.

For a few meters she worried that no one had followed her. That they all stood there staring after her as if she'd gone insane. Then a whoop sounded behind her along with the crunch and thrum of boots on the sand.

Jaft soon caught up to her. He flashed her a big grin. "You run like a gamelu with a sore hoof."

"Better than smelling like one," she countered.

"Yeah, well, enjoy the aroma, because you'll be downwind of me from now on." With a burst of speed, he pulled ahead.

Lian came up beside her and slowed to Shyla's pace. "We'll let that idiot burn up all his energy and then we'll pass him while he's bent over sucking in air."

"Sounds like this isn't the first time you've raced him," Shyla said.

"Let's just say he has issues with pacing himself."

"Oh?"

Lian winked at her.

"Oooh."

Vashi drew up on Shyla's right side. "This is fun. I really needed to stretch my legs."

"With those long legs, you have an unfair advantage," Lian mock groused.

"And they're handy in a fight."

"Modest, too. I'm beginning to hate her," Lian said, but without any malice.

Soon, they were too winded to talk. Shyla glanced behind her. Elek was a few meters back, while Aphra and Jayden jogged side by side. She wondered if they were biding their time. Or was Jayden keeping a slower pace for Aphra? The treasure hunter probably didn't have the training the rest of them did.

As predicted, they passed Jaft about a kilometer from Tamburah's temple. While far from bent over, he puffed and complained with each step. "Stupid...sand... sucks...all the...energy...from my...legs."

When the temple was within sight, Lian and Vashi increased their speed. Shyla kept her slower pace to avoid expending too much energy. Elek passed her a few meters from the escape hatch. Vashi reached it first, then Lian, Elek, Shyla, Jaft, and Aphra. Jayden was the rotten velbloud egg. They all collapsed in the sand. And even while huffing for breath, they were still able to give Jayden a hard time over being last.

"Someone had to erase our tracks while running at the same time," he said in his defense, but otherwise didn't seem to mind the good-natured ribbing.

It didn't take long for them to recover. After removing closed druks from their packs, they opened them and entered through the escape tunnel.

Aphra stopped to admire the faces. Exploring the carvings with her fingertips, she said, "These might be worth a few osees if you could remove them without damaging them."

"Really?" Jaft asked. "Who would buy them? They're hideous."

"You'd be surprised what people will buy if they think it's old and rare," Aphra said.

"There are thousands of them," he countered.

"Except the buyers don't know that, do they?" Aphra smirked.

"Ah, tricky."

They continued on to the judgment room. Shyla removed her copy of the map and spread it out on the altar. Jayden stood next to her.

She pointed to Tamburah's chin. "This is the starting point and I think that's here in his judgment room. His eyes are where the maze is located. We just need to figure out which of these hallways is this line that leads from the starting point. We could try all six, but that would take too long. Do you remember the layout beyond each one?"

Jayden picked up the map, holding it out in front of him. He glanced at each hallway, then back at the map.

Aphra moved closer to Tamburah's face. She poked the tip of her knife into one of the red tears on his cheek. "These are ruby chips. Also worth a couple osees."

"Can you sell them in Zirdai or would you need to go to Catriona?" Shyla asked.

Aphra considered. "The prince stopped all the hunters here, but he didn't arrest any of the buyers. I'm sure they'd be interested. As long as it's not something big or significant. Why?"

"Just in case we're desperate."

Jayden finished his assessment. "That hallway matches the best. I don't remember anything interesting beyond." He shrugged. "I guess it could be hidden."

"Elek and Lian stay here," Shyla said. "If anyone arrives, you can either fight or hide."

"Or come warn us," Jayden said.

"Use your judgment," Shyla said.

Aphra said, "Jayden and I will go first. There might be traps. Shyla, you read the map and tell me which way to go. Then the muscles can follow to watch our backs."

"Why am I with you?" Jayden asked. "Are you going to use me to trigger the booby traps?"

"Aren't you the one who knows this place the best?" She didn't wait for an answer. "You can point out anything that doesn't look right."

"Oh. Okay."

"*And* you can trigger the traps," she teased.

"Not funny."

Shyla directed the group through a number of hallways of the dead. Their boots scraped on the rough stone floor. The air smelled of dust and abandonment. And that was another potential hazard—bad air. Gases might have built up in various pockets.

Aphra held the druk out in front of her, shining the light on every crack in the floor and walls. She paused often, holding up her free hand, stopping them. Once she crouched down and tapped the hilt of her knife on the floor. When nothing happened she straightened and continued.

The slow pace and the knowledge that a trap could spring at any moment created a tension so thick it tasted bitter on Shyla's tongue. Only Jayden seemed unaffected, watching Aphra's cautious movements with an amused disdain.

That was until she cried out and tackled him, knocking him down right before a sword shot out from the wall he'd just been standing next to.

"Scorching sand demons," he said.

Aphra shushed him and they remained quiet. Shyla and the others stood frozen in place. Afraid to move, she noted Vashi had drawn her short sword.

"All clear," Aphra said, rolling off Jayden.

He regained his feet, brushing the sand off his pants. "That happened so fast. How did you know?"

"I heard a click. These traps are old and many times there's a delay. And sometimes they fail to trigger. Other times…"

"Other times?" Jayden helped Aphra to her feet.

"They skewer you without warning."

He shuddered and scanned the walls. "When the Invisible Sword had their headquarters below, we hardly came up here, but I was certain there weren't any traps left."

Aphra glanced at Shyla. "We must be getting close."

"A few more turns," she said.

"Stay behind me," Aphra ordered.

No one argued.

After a few angles and a half dozen more traps, which Aphra triggered so they weren't surprised on the way out, they reached an empty hexagonal room. About four meters wide, it was smaller than Tamburah's judgment chamber and a layer of loose sand covered the floor, but, instead of six doors, it had only one. The room was a dead end. Aphra checked it for traps as Shyla consulted the map, but it appeared they'd arrived at the area of Tamburah's left eye.

"Now what?" Aphra asked after she declared it safe.

Shyla examined the room. There were no symbols or markings on the walls or floor, no switches or even cracks. Everyone waited for her. But she saw nothing. After another frustrated angle, she remembered. Shyla needed to *see* with the power of The Eyes. Gathering her will, she added…heat…to her gaze and scanned the walls.

Yellow symbols glowed—one on each wall, five total.

"Do you see them?" she asked, digging into her pack for a piece of chalk.

"Them?" Jayden asked.

She swept a hand out. "The glyphs?"

"No."

The rest shook their heads.

"I do." The others watched her as she traced them with the chalk. When she finished all of them, she relaxed and the glow faded. The white chalk marks stood out clearly against the reddish-brown walls. The curved graphics tugged at her memories. She'd seen these before.

"That was…interesting," Aphra said. She moved closer to study one. "This is familiar."

Shyla joined her. "I thought so, too."

"These crossed and hooked lines remind me of Wequain's reign. It's part of his crest. He had everything branded with his crest."

"Even his family and servants," Shyla said, then tapped the middle of her forehead. "Right here."

"That's horrible." Jaft rubbed his arms.

"Hence the moniker, Wequain the Horrible." The king had done a few other notable things as well. "He also started using osmium as currency. And—" She stared at the symbol as its meaning clicked in her head.

"And?" Jaft prompted.

"And it's the number three!"

"Great. How does that help us?"

"Patience, Jaft." Shyla examined the others. "Here are numbers one, two, four, and five."

"It's a code. Get the right combination and…something happens," Aphra said.

"Something good or something bad?" Jayden asked, no doubt remembering his near miss with the blade.

"It's usually a surprise."

"Fun." Jaft's dry tone indicated he thought the opposite.

"There are one hundred and twenty combinations with five numbers if you don't repeat a number," Vashi said. "But if you do, then it's in the thousands. If the code is longer than five digits, then the possible combinations can be in the millions."

Shyla flipped between being impressed by Vashi's math skills and despairing over the sheer number of possibilities.

"Vashi was in charge of our treasury and ensuring we had enough supplies," Jayden said.

While interesting, it wasn't helping. Shyla concentrated on the glyphs. The numbers weren't in order on the walls either from left to right or right to left. Only Tamburah would be able to see them, so why not make it simple?

Since she needed magic to find them, Shyla guessed she needed to use her power to...what? Touch them? It'd be a start.

"I'm going to try pressing them from one to five in ascending order. You need to leave the room just in case there's a bad surprise," Shyla said.

They moved to the doorway but remained there.

Shyla went to number one and pulled her magic into her right hand. Taking a deep breath, she said, "Yell if you see or hear anything." She placed her palm against the symbol. The rough wall was cool to the touch. Moving onto two, she repeated the action. Then three, four, and five. She kept her weight balanced, ready to dive or dash.

Nothing happened.

All right, what else was simple? "Now descending order."

"Are you going to try all hundred and twenty combinations?" Jaft asked.

Was she? "Yes." She touched five, then four, three, two, and one.

A deep boom rattled the room. Then, starting in the middle of the floor, a line appeared in the sand and spiraled outward, growing larger with each rotation. It looked as if a giant invisible finger was drawing it.

She looked at the others. "Can you see—"

"The creepy death spiral? Yes," Jaft said.

Shyla joined her friends as it grew. With a thud, the middle of the room sank. Sand sizzled through the cracks in the floor as it continued to go down. The grating sound of stone scraping stone filled the air. The next spiral sank a moment later, then the next, and the next followed. Another boom vibrated through the soles of her boots. After a few heartbeats, the sand stopped. Silence descended.

Instead of a flat floor, before them was now a ramp that corkscrewed down into the blackness.

CHAPTER

13

The five of them stared into the darkness. For the floor to just drop away…that was impressive. She'd never witnessed anything like that before.

"Who wants to climb down into the seven caverns of hell first?" Jaft asked.

"Are you always this melodramatic?" Vashi asked him.

Shyla glanced at Aphra. "Do you think there will be booby traps?"

"It depends if Tamburah believed someone could get this far. Considering only he had been able to see the symbols, I doubt it. But I'm not relaxing my guard."

"Then you first."

"Thanks." Aphra approached the lip of the ramp as if a venomous snake was coiled inside. She held a druk in one hand and her knife in the other. Winding around the steps, she slowly disappeared.

The tension increased as Shyla waited. Perhaps she shouldn't have sent Aphra down there. What if only someone with the power of The Eyes—

"All clear," Aphra called.

Everyone let out a collective sigh of relief. With Shyla in the lead, they stepped down the series of ramps, each one smaller than the last, until they reached the end which rested on the floor a level below the hexagonal room.

Aphra waited for them. She jerked her thumb behind her. "The maze awaits."

"What happened to your arm?" Jayden asked.

Her sleeve was ripped and blood welled. "There are nasty traps in there."

"What a surprise," Jaft said dryly.

To Aphra's evident amusement, Jayden inspected the wound and declared it shallow. He removed a bandage from his pack and wrapped it around her bicep.

The action reminded Shyla of Rendor, who would have done the same thing if she'd gotten hurt. Or perhaps not. He might be glad not having to worry about her anymore. Silencing those depressing thoughts, Shyla strode over to the maze's entrance. "Bring that druk, Jaft."

He stopped right behind her. She took the lantern from him and held it up. The walls were identical to all the others in the temple. There were two ways to go, left or right.

"Don't go left," Aphra said.

Wondering if Tamburah had memorized the correct route or marked it as he had with the symbols, Shyla used her magic. Sure enough, an arrow pointed right. It seemed too easy.

"Would the correct path have booby traps?" she asked Aphra.

"No. Otherwise, Tamburah would have to disable them every time."

"He was paranoid about thieves finding his valuables," Shyla said.

"In that case, we should proceed with care."

"Wait," Jayden said. "Do we need to solve the maze? We don't have enough time to figure it out."

"No. Tamburah marked the route," she said.

"Right then?" Aphra asked.

"Yes."

Aphra once again took the lead. Shyla directed her and they moved slowly. When Aphra held up a hand, they halted. When the hunter crouched, Shyla spotted another symbol on the wall. And there were four more on the floor. It took her a few moments to decipher it.

"There's a safe path through the trap," Shyla said.

"How do you know?" Aphra asked.

"I can see it."

She moved aside. "You first."

"Are you sure?" Jayden asked.

"I'm pretty sure."

"Such confidence," Jaft muttered.

Shyla stepped on the first graphic on the floor. When nothing happened, she released her breath, bent down to trace her boot with the chalk, and moved to the subsequent one. After she finished, she spotted the next arrow.

"Follow my footprints *exactly*," she instructed.

Without hesitating, Aphra went, then Jayden and Vashi.

"And to think," Jaft said, stepping onto the first print. "My parents encouraged me to join the monastery because I had dangerous friends. If only they could see me now."

After Jaft joined them, Shyla led. With the booby traps marked, she was able to increase their pace. As she navigated the twists and turns, she wondered how Tamburah had been able to create symbols only the power of The Eyes could detect. Had he used a special ink or chalk? Whatever it was, it had lasted for over thirteen hundred circuits.

So intent on searching for more symbols, Shyla barreled into another hexagonal room without noticing the skeletons at first. They sat on the floor with their backs resting on the walls and their legs splayed out in front. There were ten of them.

"Friends of yours?" Jaft asked.

"Maybe it's a warning." Aphra knelt next to one.

"I think they were Tamburah's servants who helped hide his treasure." Shyla pointed to a rusted knife lodged between one of the skeleton's ribs.

"Speaking of treasure, where is it?" Jayden asked.

Increasing her magic, she scanned the walls. Nothing.

"Don't tell me someone already took it?" Aphra's voice held disappointment. She straightened. "Unfortunately, it happens more often than not."

No. Shyla refused to believe that they'd come all this way to find nothing. She paced around the room, almost tripping over the skeletons' feet. That gave her an idea. Sweeping the sand away from the center of the floor, Shyla revealed a symbol. This one was a simple swirl.

Shyla set her druk down, crouched and pressed both her palms to the swirl. She pushed with her magic and the ground collapsed underneath her.

With a cry, she tumbled forward. Jayden shouted her name as she fell into a hole that expanded into steps. Rolling down the hard stone staircase, she kept her chin tucked close to her chest so she wouldn't break her neck. She landed hard, sprawling at the bottom with a thump. Pain radiated up her back and ringed her ribs. Her lungs refused to work.

Jayden rushed down the steps then bent over her. "Are you all right?"

Unable to speak, she nodded. Aphra, Jaft and Vashi soon clustered around her in concern. The added light illuminated the room. Shyla caught a glimmer from the corner of her eye. She sucked in a breath and labored to sit up.

Jayden helped her. "What's wrong?"

Pointing over his shoulder, she gasped, "Tamburah."

Everyone spun to look. A life-sized, golden statue of Tamburah sparkled in the druk light. Behind him were shelves filled with treasure.

* * *

Whoops of joy echoed in the small room. Finally something that went right! Shyla was abandoned as everyone raced over to inspect the items on the shelves. Even though pain still pulsed, she struggled to her feet and joined the others. Everyone grinned and hugged as they celebrated. While thrilled they'd solved one of their biggest problems, there was a part of Shyla that longed to share the good news with Rendor.

Aphra donned a crown of gold, platinum, and silver all twisted together with emeralds decorating it. It was one of many crowns and scepters. Chalices, bowls, jewelry, hairpins, an army of smaller Tamburah statues—Shyla added narcissistic to his long list of faults—all sparkled in the yellow druk light. The collection filled five deep shelves. Too many items to count, but that didn't stop Jaft from trying.

Jayden shook his head in amazement. "I'd no idea this was here."

"I think that was the point," Jaft said. Then he hefted one of the Tamburah statues. It was a nude. "Nice of the king to exaggerate his…er…male attributes. Extra gold for us! We should melt this one down first because of the ewww factor."

His comment reminded everyone that finding the treasure was just the start. They filled their packs with a variety of items, leaving the bigger treasures for later. What they grabbed would feed them for circuits. Aphra offered to sell the ones that held less value to avoid drawing attention, and Shyla planned to visit Professor Emeline before the woman left Zirdai. The crown would be a perfect replacement for Gorgain's.

They climbed the steps to the skeleton room. Shyla puzzled over how to close the hole in the floor. She pressed a number of locations but nothing moved. The swirl was on the last step, so she touched it and then bolted up as the staircase retracted, making it to the top before it closed. At least the ramp outside the maze was easier. Shyla pressed the numbers in ascending order and the floor returned to its original position. She and Jayden used their magic to smooth the remaining sand, covering the pattern of thin swirling lines.

Before they reached Tamburah's judgment room, they slowed. Apprehension filled her. Since one thing had gone in their favor, she expected the next ten to be a disaster. Except Elek and Lian reported being "utterly bored" while the others were having a "grand adventure." They quickly forgot their petulance when shown a few of the treasures.

"Does that mean we don't have to clear that tunnel at the crypt anymore?" Elek asked.

"For now. I'd like to go back to it," Shyla said. "But it also means we'll have double shifts working on the tunnel to Zirdai."

Everyone groaned.

* * *

When they returned to headquarters, it was angle seventy—closer to the danger zone than they'd have liked. The good news about the find energized everyone, lifting the constant worry from all their shoulders. Happy sounds and laughter filled the common room. Smiles and slaps on backs echoed. And Shyla figured this would be a perfect time to have them all pledge an oath to the new Invisible Sword, but she needed to consult with Jayden and Ximen first.

The three of them went to Shyla's room. Except for a few items that Aphra planned to sell, Shyla had collected all the treasures and put them into the trunk in her room. It locked.

"We can't flood the market, and we need to be careful with our purchases as well," Jayden said. "We don't want to draw any attention by buying large quantities."

"All right. Would you like to oversee that, Jayden?"

If he was surprised, he didn't react. "Yes. What about the professor?"

"I'll work with her since she knows me, but you can handle the rest. However, that's not why I asked you to accompany me." She turned to Ximen. "How did the magic lessons go?"

He frowned. "Not well. If I didn't know any better, I'd say they showed an utter lack of magical ability."

"That bad? What about Mojag's sensing ability?" she asked.

"When he tried to use it, he couldn't sense anyone. It was only when he wasn't paying attention that it worked."

"Plan B?" Jayden asked.

"Yes, I'll ask for a volunteer."

"Not Mojag."

"Did you know he already volunteered?" she asked.

"Figures. You didn't take him up on it, right?"

"Of course not. Did you really think I would?"

"I think you would do what is needed for this organization to survive," Jayden said.

Interesting. "There's another matter. I want to have everyone take the oath at the sun's apex. The pledge will be almost identical to the one you used, and I plan to give everyone that symbol on their shoulders, but I'm going to alter it to reflect the new archive."

Jayden and Ximen exchanged a look. Finally Ximen said, "That symbol only works for those who have magic."

"They only need magic to see it. Right?"

"No. They need magic for it to heal so quickly and for the symbol to remain on the skin. When a wielder takes the oath, it creates a magical reaction." Ximen rubbed his shoulder. "We're really not sure how it works."

That was disappointing, but Shyla thought if she could figure out how Tamburah marked those walls, perhaps she could mark the members.

Ximen left to find her a volunteer for plan B.

Jayden remained behind. "You don't have to mark everyone. Swearing an oath is a powerful thing, and for most people it is enough."

She remembered Chago at the monastery, spying for the Water Prince. Perhaps he'd told Captain Yates about Shyla's visits and it had led to the search and her parents' arrest. "But not for everyone."

"You still think there's a traitor in our midst." His anger heated the air between them. "Why don't you just read everyone's souls and stop with all this taking-an-oath nonsense?"

"Do you want me to read your soul without your permission?"

"You know I don't."

"So that must mean you have something to hide?"

"It just means I value my privacy. I get it. Okay? But how is taking an oath going to reveal a potential spy?"

"As you said, taking an oath is a powerful thing, and, in that case, I don't need to read a person's soul to know if they're telling the truth. It'll all be right there on their surface thoughts. In their body language."

"And that's not reading a soul?" he asked.

"Yes. Reading a soul is going deep, learning secrets, learning the full measure of a person, what they've done, what they think and believe. Who they are."

"I still think you're walking a thin line."

"And I think it's something I need to do for this organization to survive." She used his words against him.

"Fair enough." He turned to leave.

"Jayden."

He paused on the threshold.

"I haven't read anyone's soul. Not to that depth. But I will if I have to. I'll cross that line and not apologize."

Jayden glanced over his shoulder and met her gaze. "Good to know." Then he left.

She plopped onto her sitting cushion. He had a point. It would be easier for her to read everyone and be done with it, but they'd never trust her again. And that reminded her too much of Tamburah. The last thing she ever wanted was to be like him.

While waiting for her volunteer, Shyla spent the time reading over the scroll of maddeningly vague instructions about using The Eyes. She'd learned she could push her power through her hands, but nothing in the text suggested that was possible. Unless the linking and creating a connection passage referred to that skill. What if she pushed her power while making a mark? It couldn't hurt to try.

Shyla retrieved her chalk from her pack. Feeling a little silly, she rubbed the chalk over the rough stone, writing her name on the wall of her room while adding magic through her fingertips.

"Are you afraid someone is going to take your room?" Gurice asked with amusement. She stood in the doorway with Mojag pressed against her.

The two of them together didn't bode well. "I'm experimenting." Shyla used a corner of her sleeve to erase the letters, but a faint dusting of white remained. Hating to use water but unable to think of something else, she picked up her water skin and washed off the rest of the marks. Now she'd have to wait until it dried.

"Okay," Gurice drawled as if humoring a crazy lady. "Does this have anything to do with opening a person's magic?"

Shyla muttered a curse. "No one volunteered?"

"I did!" Mojag said, affronted. "Don't know why you asked the others. Am I not good enough for you?"

Sigh. "Mojag, you're *too* good for me. I don't want to hurt you. You're *too* important."

"*Too* bad. I'm here." He grabbed a handful of sand from the bucket. "And I want to make this sand fly."

She met Gurice's gaze.

"Our family line has magic so he would have been tested in the chamber," Gurice said. "Some people change after being chained that long in the dark."

"All right." At least she could stop if he showed any signs of distress. "Sit down."

He settled next to the bucket.

"Should I go?" Gurice asked.

"No, stay." Shyla knelt on the other side of the bucket, facing Mojag. "Did Ximen teach you how to gather your will?"

"Yes, but it didn't work," Mojag said. "Or I didn't do it right. It's hard to gather something that's not… something."

Shyla lowered her shield. Despite Mojag's brave words, he was scared. Gurice, too, but she kept her posture relaxed so she wouldn't upset him. Despite their bickering, they loved each other deeply.

"How about pulling it? Can you pull it from inside…" She tapped her chest. "…and aim it at the sand in the bucket?"

"You mean to stare at it with intention?"

"That's one way to describe it."

"Okay." Mojag's eyebrows crashed together as he squinted at the sand.

The ribbon of magic glowed inside him. Once again it resembled a druk lantern only opened a crack. The edges around that gap were sharp and ragged. Shyla reached toward the glow as if seeking his thoughts. She grasped the ends of the lantern and pulled them apart.

Memories gushed from the opening as it widened. *A vagrant woman lies broken and mutilated, blood pooling under her body. Her head lolls to the side and she meets Mojag's gaze right before the light in her eyes dies.*

A man—no, a guard—straddles her, raising his knife for another unneeded strike. An anguished cry slices the air as another man tackles the guard to the ground. They fight until two more guards arrive and drag the man to his feet. Then they beat him to death right in front of his son who is hiding in a dark corner.

"Mom! Dad!" Mojag cried as the scene repeated. Pain and grief surged through his body, rubbing him raw.

"What's going on?" Gurice demanded. She grabbed her brother, hugging him close.

Shyla reversed her efforts, closing the lantern.

Mojag's hand shot out and clutched her wrist. "No. Don't. Keep going. Let it out. Let it *all* out."

She exchanged a look with Gurice, seeking his sister's permission.

"Please," Mojag said.

Gurice nodded and Shyla pulled the lantern wide open. Mojag jerked as more memories poured from the rift. Horrible images of all the terrible things he'd witnessed since his parents' murder. Then came the guilt over what he'd done in his short life, including when he sold Shyla to the deacons.

The poor boy thrashed and wailed and cried. Tears streamed down his face and he clamped onto his sister as if she alone could keep him from being washed away. Sobs racked his body. Then the images faded. The painful memories dulled to a throb. Mojag sucked in a deep breath, relaxed, and fell asleep.

Gurice held him tight. "Did it work?"

"I don't know." Shyla wished she could forget Mojag's terrible memories. She understood why he'd want to get rid of them. Despite the purge, they still remained with him. At least they weren't nearly as sharp. "We'll find out when he wakes up."

"Son of a sand demon, you did it, didn't you?" Jayden demanded from the doorway. "He's just a boy."

"No, he isn't," Shyla said. "He hasn't been since his parents died."

Jayden glared at her. Then he swooped in and picked Mojag up in his arms, cradling him to his chest. "If you harmed him, we're leaving." He turned his anger on Gurice. "And you're not invited."

14

Jayden carried Mojag from Shyla's room. Gurice stared at the doorway. "After our parents died in one of the Water Prince's raids, Jayden helped us so much. Mojag was unruly, sullen, prone to angry outbursts, and I didn't know what to do with him. Mojag considers Jayden his brother." She huffed. "A better sibling than me, that's for sure."

"No." Shyla put her hand on her shoulder. "You're doing a good job. He had a traumatic experience at such a young age. Witnessing your parents' murder is not something you recover from without some permanent scars."

"Wait." Gurice turned to her. "He saw them being killed?"

Oops. "You didn't know?"

She slumped. "We found him hiding in a trunk. I'd assumed our dad told him to stay there and not to come out no matter what. He wouldn't come out for a long time. And, when he did, he didn't talk for a circuit afterwards. I never asked if he saw anything."

"He's been holding that inside for a long time and needed to release it. You did a good thing, Gurice."

"I hope so." She tilted her head at the wall. "It's dry. Does that prove something?"

Shyla added heat to her gaze. Her name shone on the wall. "It does!" She grinned at her friend.

"Uh-oh. Why do I have a feeling I'm not going to like what's next?"

"How would you like to be the first person to take the oath for the new archive of the Invisible Sword?"

"Like a new beginning?"

"Yes. Exactly."

"Is it going to hurt?"

"I've no idea."

"Funny, but really…is it?"

Shyla laughed. "Roll up your sleeve."

Gurice grumbled but pulled the fabric of her tunic up over her shoulder. Her Invisible Sword symbol shone on her chestnut-colored skin. Only another sworn Invisible Sword member with magic could see it.

The mark wasn't that complex. There were two crossed swords. They overlapped about a quarter of the way down from the tips. A line curved through both hilts and flared out to the sides. It bowed away from the tips, while a second line arced in the opposite direction between the two blades. The two curved lines had an oval shape, and, from a distance, resembled an eye.

Shyla considered. If she drew a circle inside that oval to represent an iris, and then a solid circle for the pupil, then there'd be no doubt it was an eye. Fitting. Except adding those extra lines with chalk seemed silly. She needed something else that was thin that she could push her magic through. Her stylus!

Rummaging through her pack, she found the instrument. The metal tip should be small enough and the slightly flattened end wouldn't scratch skin.

"Are you going to write your name on me?" Gurice asked.

"No." She explained her plan. "What do you think?"

"I think you should draw it out and show everyone so they'll know what it looks like."

"Good idea. And I think you should take the oath along with everyone else. But, if you don't mind, I'd like to try to add the extra embellishments now, because if it doesn't work, I'll have to figure something else out."

"Does that mean I'll have to do it twice?"

"Yes."

"It's a good thing I like you. All right, what do I do?"

Shyla brought the tip close to Gurice's shoulder and pushed her magic into the stylus. "Repeat after me. As a member of the Invisible Sword, I swear that I will embrace the beliefs and tenets of the organization and fully support its efforts to help those in need."

As Gurice recited the words, Shyla traced the two sword blades on her shoulder.

"As a member of the Invisible Sword, I swear I will not betray the location of our headquarters or the identities of our members to our enemies and would give my life to keep its secrets."

"Our enemies? That's new. Before we didn't tell anyone outside the organization."

"It'll be hard to recruit people without telling them about it."

"Good point." She repeated the second phrase while Shyla traced the two curved lines of the symbol.

"As a member of the Invisible Sword, I swear not to harm or kill another unless it is absolutely necessary or in self-defense."

Gurice raised her eyebrows but echoed Shyla's words. Shyla drew a big circle in the oval shape.

"As a member of the Invisible Sword, I swear allegiance to my fellow Invisible Swords."

When Gurice recited that sentence, Shyla met her gaze and the truth of her oath blazed through Shyla. She channeled it into the stylus and colored in a smaller circle in the middle of the oval.

"Ow!" Gurice jerked away, covering her shoulder with a hand. "Did you just stab me?"

"No."

"What happened?"

"If you put your hand down, I'll tell you if it worked."
Although she was pretty confident the oath was genuine.

When Gurice uncovered the symbol, it now glowed
with Shyla's eye. "It worked. Congratulations, you're now
a member of the new archive of the Invisible Sword."

"Should we hug?"

"Do you need a hug?"

"Who doesn't?" But Gurice rolled her shoulders. "I
don't feel any different."

"Good. Then you can get back to work."

She huffed. "And after all I've done for you."

"You have my gratitude. And you've earned a gold
statue of Tamburah. We've lots."

"Ugh, I'll pass on the statue."

"He's not naked in all of them."

"Still no."

"Yeah, I don't think they're going to be popular."

* * *

Shyla wanted to get everyone sworn in right away, but
Mojag still slept and she didn't have the heart to wake
him. Plus, if she was being honest, the effort to open
Mojag's magic had used up quite a bit of her energy.
Instead, she decided to wait until after she returned
from the city. She planned to go into Zirdai at angle
one-eighty to sell one of Tamburah's crowns to the professor. It had been about nine sun jumps since their last

meeting and the woman could have decided to leave early. Also they needed the coins to buy the platinum from Zimraan. And, since she was being honest, she might catch a glimpse of Rendor. It was pathetic, but she missed him.

Ximen elected to accompany her when Jayden chose to remain at headquarters with Mojag. Elek and Jaft also tagged along. They were scheduled for a water run. In order to keep the jugs filled, teams of two had been making trips to the bowels of Zirdai with the velbloud bladders every five or six sun jumps.

Right after the group climbed to the surface, Jayden called up to Shyla. "Mojag's awake." His face creased as if he was in pain.

She waited.

"He moved the sand with magic."

Relief and joy swirled in her heart. She hoped Mojag recovered from the ordeal, but it seemed her plan to expand their number of wielders worked.

"You know he'll be impossible to live with now," Jayden said.

"And how is that different than before?"

Jayden just shook his head. Shyla joined the others. She walked beside Ximen, striding easily through the sand as if she were a velbloud ready to lift into the sky. Her thoughts focused on how to find others who had the potential to wield magic.

When they reached the city, Elek and Ximen headed for a different entrance than Shyla and Jaft. They planned to meet up once inside. There were a few deacons watching the people returning from the desert. Some of them wore protective torques.

Ximen created a small whirlwind of sand. It buzzed through the one-story buildings. Sand whirls were a common enough occurrence to not be viewed as suspicious, but interesting enough to provide a distraction for Shyla and Jaft to get inside.

"Handy," Jaft said once they were through. "Will Rae be able to do that?"

"Depends."

"Wow, that's vaguely specific."

"It's up to Rae if she wishes to access her magic and, if she does, it will depend on how strong she is and if she even has the ability to move sand."

"Oh."

Thankfully, Jaft didn't ask any more questions. They rendezvoused with Elek and Ximen. After agreeing to meet Elek and Jaft back at the same location on level ten at angle three-fifty-five, they split up. Ximen headed to the markets to determine the time—or as close to it as possible—that Zimraan's caravan was scheduled to arrive while Elek and Jaft took Rendor's route to his water source. Shyla kept to the edges of the city as she descended to Professor Emeline's quarters on level forty-two. When her and Ximen's tasks were finished, they would meet back at Orla's.

Shyla waited in the same dark nook for the professor to return from third meal. The temptation to seek Rendor with her magic pulsed in her veins. She had found if she kept busy, the memories of his kiss and the longing for his touch wouldn't ambush her as often. To keep from thinking about him, she focused on the people in the tunnels nearby. Students mostly, but a few professors and a couple of guards patrolled. Not the guards who had helped her when Utina had accused her of murdering Banqui and stealing The Eyes from him. She wondered if those two would be receptive to changing their allegiance. Probably not, but it wouldn't hurt to ask.

Emeline arrived at angle two-forty-five and Shyla stepped from the shadow.

The woman started but recovered with a nervous laugh. "You certainly like to make an entrance. Do you have something for me?"

"Yes."

"Come on in." Emeline unlocked the door and swept a bony arm out, indicating Shyla should precede her.

She entered the dark room and waited near the door while the professor uncovered the trol lanterns, then slid the glass panel closed.

"Did you recover Gorgain's crown and torque?" Emeline's eyes glowed almost as bright as the lanterns.

"No, but I found something better."

The woman deflated. "There's not much that's better."

"Oh, I think you won't be disappointed." Shyla removed one of Tamburah's crowns from her pack. This one resembled a ring of vines with berries interspersed throughout. The leaves and stems were made of gold, and rubies provided the vivid red color of the berries.

Emeline sucked in a breath. "Whose is that?"

"King Tamburah's."

"But his tomb and vault were looted thousands of circuits ago."

Shyla told her about Tamburah's increasing paranoia and the existence of a second vault.

"May I?" She held out her hand.

"Of course."

The professor brought it to her desk and examined it under the light. Then she put a glass monocle to her eye and peered at the rubies. Fascinated, Shyla watched as the woman brought out a set of delicate tools and tested the gold by trying to scrape off the color. Emeline performed a few more assessments before weighing the crown.

"It's certainly valuable. But I'm not convinced it was Tamburah's. Do you have proof?"

"Isn't there an analysis that can determine an artifact's age?"

"Yes, but it takes a long time and I don't have the equipment here."

"Why does it matter? The gold and rubies alone are worth plenty of coins."

"True, but if it really is a historical artifact that can be studied and displayed, then it's worth more."

"How much more?"

"Double."

Ah. Was it worth the risk? But, more importantly, did she want the crown to be disassembled and melted down? "I've a statue of Tamburah that was found along with the crown."

Emeline perked up. "That would be perfect! Do you wish to sell that one as well?"

"Do you have enough coins to pay for both?"

"Please don't insult me, girl."

Shyla waited.

The professor unlocked a small trunk and pulled a big pouch out. It jangled and clanged when she handled it. She untied it and then spilled dozens and dozens of osees onto the desk. "As you can see, I've plenty." Picking up the now empty pouch, she met Shyla's gaze. "How about I pay you now for the crown at the current black-market value and, when you return with the statue, I'll double that amount and we'll negotiate a price for the statue?"

It sounded reasonable. Aphra had warned her that she wouldn't get full market value because the sale wasn't legitimate. "What are you offering?"

"One hundred osees."

Aphra had also taught her to never take the first offer. It would be insultingly low and a test to see if Emeline could take advantage of Shyla.

"Seven hundred osees," she countered.

"Ha! That's robbery. Two hundred osees."

They went back and forth until they agreed on four hundred osees. Shyla kept her expression neutral, but inside she celebrated. That amount would go a long way and when she returned, she'd double it along with the value of the statue.

After Emeline paid her, Shyla headed to Orla's commune.

Ximen was already there, waiting for her. "The merchants expect Zimraan's caravan in five sun jumps."

"How do they know he's coming then?" she asked.

"Most big caravans send runners a few sun jumps ahead to inform the next city of their arrival, to hire muscle to carry their goods down to the market, and to arrange for someone to care for their gamelus while they're in the city." Ximen looked at her in amusement.

"What?"

"You know all this history and how to read ancient languages, but not the mundane workings of the city."

"That's what happens when you grow up in a monastery. What else do I need to know about these caravans?"

"They're guarded. And Zimraan won't want to upset the Heliacal Priestess by selling the platinum to us."

She jingled the osees in her pack. "I'm sure he'll get over it."

Ximen smiled. "I take it your visit went well."

Shyla handed him the pouch of coins minus a handful for her to spend. "Yes. I want you to take this back to headquarters and fetch one of the Tamburah statues." She explained about the deal. "You'll have an easier time leaving and returning. I can take care of some business while I wait."

"All right."

"And can you check on Mojag? Make sure he's still okay."

"Will do." Ximen left to meet up with Jaft and Elek.

Shyla searched for Orla. The woman was happy to see her and quickly filled her in on the news. The vagrants hadn't found the mother of the infant left in the sand and they didn't know where Rendor was staying. The city was buzzing with talk about the arrest of the monks, and the Heliacal Priestess's obsession with purchasing platinum was still an active source of gossip.

"We believe they're melting the platinum down in the chapel on level seventy-one. One of my people caught a whiff of molten metal. The priestess has also doubled the number of deacons guarding all the chapels," Orla said.

"That's not a surprise. Did you get any backlash from the rescue?" Shyla asked.

"No. In fact, the search for the members of the Invisible Sword has taken priority and both the guards and deacons have stopped harassing the vagrants for now."

At least Shyla was able to make a difference for the communes. *Baby steps* was what Ximen had said about learning magic, but it could be applied to their efforts to help others as well. Eventually, they'd be in a position to effect real change. That thought reminded her.

She asked about the people the deacons had tortured. "Are they fully recovered?" It'd been eight sun jumps since the rescue.

"Some are. A few need more time, but Zhek is satisfied with their progress."

"Once they're better what happens to them?"

"They are afraid to return to their lives, so they've asked to remain with us. As long as they contribute to the commune, they're welcome to stay."

"I'd like to talk to them," Shyla said.

"They're asleep right now, but I'm sure they'll be happy to see you when they wake. How long are you staying?"

"Just another sun jump." Sleeping sounded like a good idea, so she headed to her room. As she sank into the cushion, she wondered if she could justify using her newly acquired coins to buy a couple sleeping cushions. Would Zimraan have any to sell? And why was she obsessed with this? Perhaps thinking about obtaining a comfortable cushion kept her from contemplating the fact she had no one to share it with. No one had seen Rendor. Did that mean he'd left the city? And why did that notion hurt so much?

* * *

Orla was right. The group she'd helped rescue cheered when she entered their quarters around angle twenty. A dozen total—part of an extended family that had gotten on the priestess's bad side—they stayed in a large room that had sleeping cushions, furs, tables, and a sitting area. They also cared for the four that still required assistance.

After she explained about their potential to have magic because of the trauma they had experienced, they all immediately agreed to allow her to test them, even those four who couldn't stand.

Of the twelve, only two had been cracked, and one was younger than Mojag. Too young, but she was determined to be a part.

"When you're older," Shyla said to her. And she explained to Wazir, the other one, that he'd have to relive the horrors he had experienced in order for her to fully open his magic.

"You saved my son. I'll do whatever it takes to help you," Wazir said.

The mention of his son sent a jolt of alarm straight through her along with a sudden realization. The other Invisible Sword members didn't have children, which she was very glad about. And she didn't want Wazir's son to grow up without his father. Or for his wife to lose her husband.

"You can help by taking care of your son. I'll find another—"

"Do you think I want him to grow up in a world where your family can be arrested or grabbed by power hungry deacons for little to no reason? He will be safe here in the commune while I fight to make Zirdai a good place to raise a family."

"We will fight." Another man stood next to Wazir. "I might not have magic, but I have a strong back."

Two young women joined them.

"Us, too," one of them said. "If we want things to change, we have to stop waiting for someone else to change them."

Hard to argue with that. "Welcome to the Invisible Sword."

* * *

Shyla spent the rest of the sun jump stalking deacons. While she couldn't get near the ones in the chapels due to the deacons guarding them—at least one and sometimes two of the four wore a torque—she followed the deacons leaving. None showed any signs that they wielded magic. Most of the citizens parted or stepped out of their way, but that was probably due to fear.

Giving up on them, Shyla slipped inside the dining cavern on level twenty-nine during second meal and observed the kitchen staff. There she noted a few people with scars circling their wrists. Even though they were technically deacons, they wore light green tunics and pants instead of the robes. And most of them wore white aprons.

When one of the deacons who'd been outside guarding the dining cavern came into the kitchen, Shyla experienced a strong desire not to look in certain areas. Brushing the magic aside, she marked the two female workers who had frozen in place. Their fear was evident in their postures and darting glances. The women only relaxed once the deacon left the kitchen.

After the kitchen staff cleaned up, the workers returned to their dorms. They only had about thirty-five angles before they needed to return to set up for third meal. Shyla shadowed the two women. It wasn't long before they entered one of the rooms along with two others. Most of the priestess's deacons lived in dormitories near where they worked. The higher-ranking deacons stayed in apartments near the chapels.

When the tunnel emptied, Shyla strode to their room and knocked on the door. The sudden knowledge that the room was empty pressed on her along with the need to leave. Her stomach churned as she realized these women were still being abused. She blocked their magic and projected her own.

Friend.

The door slid open a crack. "I don't know you," the woman said so low it was almost a whisper.

"You don't, but you will. Can I come in?"

Friend.

A hesitation, but then she widened the gap and let Shyla into the small room. She remained by the now closed door as if she planned to dash out if Shyla tried anything untoward. The room contained two druks, four sleeping cushions, four trunks, and four scared women. The two on the right pushed, *go away, go away, go away.* Shyla deflected the magic as she met each of their gazes, taking their measure.

"What do you want?" the lady on the far left demanded. She had her hands on her cocked hip—the unofficial leader.

"To help."

A bitter laugh. "Go sign up at the chapel. The deacons are always looking for new recruits."

"Not that kind of help." Shyla pulled her wrap down, revealing her hair.

The four women stared at her as if she'd just uncovered the sun.

"You're…"

"You can't be here," the woman by the door said. "They'll kill you."

"And us," the leader added.

Go away.

Go away.

Go away.

Shyla turned to the two using magic. "I'm not going away. You can't make me, nor can you disappear. Do you want to know why?"

Stunned silence.

"Because I know what you two can do. You're using magic."

The women glanced at each other.

"Yes, that's what you've been doing. It's real. I'll demonstrate to make this go faster." Shyla gathered her will and aimed it at all four.

Gone.

Gasps and confused exchanges followed, confirming that they all witnessed her disappear. Shyla stepped to the back of the room and stopped the magical command.

"You have three choices," Shyla said.

They started and spun around to face her.

"We haven't had a choice since being *rehabilitated*," the leader said.

"Well now you do. The first one is that you can do nothing, keep working in the kitchen, keep cowering in your room. Or you can run to your boss and report that you've seen the evil sun-kissed. You might get a pat on the back, but when they can't find me, you'll probably be in trouble."

"No probably about it," muttered the leader.

"The third choice is to join me. You can help stop the deacons from *rehabilitating* more people. I'm gathering an army and we're going to change the leadership of Zirdai." Might as well be optimistic that she would soon have an army.

"Say we do join you. What would we do?" the leader asked.

"For now you would learn how to fight and shovel lots of sand, and for these two..." She pointed at the women on the right. "They would need to open the rest of their magic and learn how to use it." She explained what that would entail.

They both paled several shades.

"And the dangers?" the woman by the door asked.

"Deacons and guards. Everyone is after me and my people. If you're caught, you'll be tortured for information and killed." No sense dancing around the truth.

"We need to think about it," the leader said.

"Of course." Shyla told them where to meet. "Be there by angle three-fifty-five. If anyone else trustworthy wants to join, they're welcome. And I'll know if there's an ambush of deacons waiting for me." Although she doubted they would rat her out. "So be prepared for any backlash that will cause."

"From you?"

"No, from the deacons. I don't think they'll be pleased that your information was inaccurate. I won't cause you any more trouble. I suspect you've already had more than your share and that's what I'm trying to stop." Shyla left.

During third meal, Shyla observed the kitchen staff in the dining cavern on level thirty-nine. There she spotted a young man using magic. She trailed him to his room and repeated her recruitment spiel to him and his room-mates. Except this time one of the men contemplated how to report the sun-kissed to his superiors. So she erased his memories of her visit and sent him to sleep.

"He'll betray you if you tell him about me. Decide to come or stay, but don't reveal your plans to him."

"How do you know he planned to betray us?" one man asked.

"The same way I know you're thinking of finding your sister, Karrah, hoping to convince her to come with you."

He straightened in surprise. "Oh."

"And, by the way, she's welcome." Although where Shyla was going to fit all these people she had no idea.

She wished she could visit the other six dining caverns. Because once these people disappeared, she doubted she'd be able to get near the kitchen workers again.

* * *

Jayden arrived at Orla's commune after darkness.

Surprised, she asked, "Where's Ximen?"

"Good to see you, too," he snarked. Then he sobered. "Mojag is driving me crazy. The kid is inexhaustible and wants to learn everything about magic. Right away! For the first time in his short life, Mojag is focused and determined."

"That's wonderful news."

"For you," he mock-grumbled. "Not for me. I needed a break so I asked Ximen to take a turn with him."

"Good idea. Did you bring a statue?"

Jayden dug into his pack. "I thought this one makes him look the most kingly." He handed her a statue of Tamburah wearing a crown and elaborate royal garments.

It was about thirty centimeters high and weighed around two kilograms, which meant it was hollow. If it'd been solid gold, it would be much heavier.

She updated Jayden on the new members. "We'll take them with us when we leave at angle zero. In the meantime, I'm going to visit the professor." She grabbed a handful of coins and gave them to Jayden. "Here. We're going to have twelve more people to feed. Please buy some fresh food."

He stared at the coins in his palm. "Twelve?"

"So far. I've been recruiting and I plan to get a dozen more." She slapped him good-naturedly on the back before hurrying to level forty-two to finish her business with Emeline.

After dodging a couple guards, Shyla slowed. No sense running straight into the enemy. When she reached level forty-three, she paused as a familiar set of…bumps touched her. Pressing against the tunnel's wall, she peered around the corner. About three meters away were Nuru and Vallie—the two guards who helped her when Utina, the historian, demanded that she be arrested. They had seemed open-minded and intelligent when they escorted her to the library. Would they be open to the idea of joining the Invisible Sword?

Shyla drew in a breath. Only one way to find out. Gathering her courage, she rounded the corner and strode to the pair. It took them a few heartbeats to notice her, and then a couple more to recognize her.

"Hey!" Nuru shouted, pulling his sword. "You're under arrest."

She held her hands out to show them she was unarmed. "I'm not running away."

Vallie had also drawn her weapon. "Good, then we won't hurt you."

"I just want to talk to you," Shyla said.

"Fine. You can talk all you want on the way down to the Water Prince. Turn around and put your hands behind your back." Nuru gestured with the tip of his blade.

"No." She made eye contact with each of them. Both were confused by her behavior, but excited to have caught the sun-kissed. "You know the Water Prince will torture me and eventually kill me."

"He might spare you," Vallie said.

"You should have thought of that before you stole The Eyes from him," Nuru said.

"The Eyes were never his. But if he gets them, he will have a great deal of power. And what do you think he'll do with this power?"

"Not our concern," Nuru said. "Now move, or I'll—"

"When will it become your concern? When the prince targets your family? Your friends? Your partner? When your mother is hanging upside down being tortured because your thoughts were not what the prince wanted to hear?"

They both stared at her.

"Yes, The Eyes will give him the power to read your minds, your emotions, your souls. You won't be able to lie to him. Ever."

Vallie sheathed her sword and pulled out a pair of manacles. "Nice try, Sun-Kissed. But we don't scare easily."

"I'm telling the truth. And you can help me to overthrow the prince. I'm—"

"A delusional sun-kissed whose brains have been fried by the sun. No, thanks," Nuru said.

"You've no idea what you're talking about," Vallie said. "There's no reason for us to trust you."

Their emotions matched their words. The idea of working with a sun-kissed or anyone to overthrow the prince would be suicide. Too bad. Shyla summoned her will.

Stop.

They both froze. Vallie's arms were extended as she reached for Shyla. Pushing her arms down, Shyla

315

hooked the manacles back on the woman's belt. Then she took Nuru's sword and slid it back into its sheath. Shyla stepped behind them and erased their memories of the encounter with her. Only when she was out of sight did she release them.

She climbed to level forty-two. After ensuring there was nobody in the tunnels around the professor's room, Shyla knocked on the door.

Emeline invited her inside. "I didn't think you'd be back this quick."

"No sense waiting." Shyla pulled the statue from her pack.

"Oh my." She took the golden figure almost reverently. Holding it near a lantern, she examined it carefully, once again using her tools. "It's genuine." Emeline glanced up. "Well done. How many artifacts did you find in Tamburah's second vault?"

"I've a few more pieces," Shyla hedged. "Are you interested in buying them?"

"I doubt I have the coin for such historically valuable items. But the Water Prince is very curious where you found these. Guards!"

Shyla started as guards rushed from the professor's sleeping chamber. So focused on potential ambushers outside the room, she'd never considered seeking them inside. A deadly mistake.

15

Shyla recovered from her shock and held her hands up. Not to surrender, but to push her magic at the six guards.

Stop.

They halted.

The professor clutched the statue of Tamburah to her chest as she glanced at the guards. "What are you waiting for? Grab her!"

Sleep.

The four men and two women collapsed to the floor.

Emeline backed away from Shyla. "What did you do to them?"

Shyla stepped toward the deceitful woman. "You'll find out if you don't pay me what you owe for the crown."

"She's bluffing," a familiar and rather terrifying voice said. The Water Prince stepped from Emeline's sleeping chamber with Captain Yates right behind him. "Shyla won't hurt you." He met her gaze.

Big mistake as that allowed her to read his soul. The prince gaped in shock as he noticed her new eye color. His surprise transformed to fury in a heartbeat, but he recovered, burying his anger deep and resuming his neutral expression. He studied her as if appraising a gamelu herd. As much as she was tempted to go deeper into his thoughts and emotions, she kept her focus on his surface emotions only. For now.

"I wouldn't be so sure of that," Shyla said. Her voice remained calm despite the tight fear ringing her throat. Gauging how much strength she needed to knock both the prince and Yates unconscious, she collected her will. From past experiences, Yates would be hard to influence. Perhaps she should just bolt. But would she make it to the door before Yates caught her?

Still clutching the statue, Emeline pressed into a corner, staying out of the way. The prince and Yates kept their distance from her. The Water Prince wore an unremarkable tunic and pants that showed off his athletic build. At twenty-five circuits old, he was young for such a powerful position, but his ruthlessness had developed at an early age.

Holding his hands out to the sides, the prince said, "Relax. We're here to talk."

The truth. Yates' massive fists were pressed to his hips, but he hadn't drawn his sword. Or his knife. His fierce glower warned her that he could grab both at any time.

She gestured to the six guards on the floor and edged closer to the door. "Sure doesn't seem like it."

He gave them a disdainful look. "They're for my protection." Then he returned his full focus on her.

Even though she knew he was evil to his core, she was still struck by his handsome features, the deep emerald of his eyes flecked with silver, his black hair contrasting with his tan skin. Like many others who lived deep in the bowels of Zirdai, the prince spent little time in the sun, while Yates could almost be his shadow.

Subtly she shifted, increasing the distance between them. The door loomed behind her about two meters away. But then she sensed more guards on the other side. They filled the hallway in front of Emeline's quarters.

Scorching sand rats.

"What did you want to talk about?" she asked, delaying the inevitable. Her best chance would be to dive into the hallway, surprising those waiting, and hope to sprint away without having to send them all to sleep. She inched closer.

"About a possible exchange."

She froze.

He smiled, but the sharp lines of his face didn't soften. In fact, they appeared even more severe, and she wondered how she could have ever thought this man attractive.

"It's your turn," he said. Then after a moment, he continued. "No? All right then, I wish to discuss the fate of the two monks in my custody—your parents."

She kept her expression impassive despite her heart's frantic beats. "My parents abandoned me in the desert. You are mistaken."

"Oh, come on, Shyla. You'd have to be blind not to see the resemblance."

Considering she was raised in the monastery and spent eighteen circuits with Hanif, blind was an apt description. "What do you want?" Although she had a good guess.

"I want The Eyes of Tamburah." He swept a hand out, indicating the sleeping guards. "But you've already claimed them and somehow woke their power." His tone almost filled with awe until it sharpened. "You lied to me. You said The Eyes held no magical powers. That you didn't seek power. Yet, here you are."

"I didn't lie. At that time, I thought both statements were true. But now…"

"Now?"

"By assigning me the task to find The Eyes for you, you made me see the real city of Zirdai, and not the one I'd built in my childish fantasies. I saw the rot, the corruption, and the horrors of your rule. I saw a city suffering. And when I held the means to change it in my hands, I found the strength to claim it."

"Nice speech. You may have The Eyes, but you don't have much else. You may be able to put my guards to sleep, but I've an army of people. And if you could render them all unconscious, then we wouldn't have almost caught you at the monastery."

Shyla thought it best to remain silent. If he was hoping she'd reveal the limits of her power, he was going to be disappointed. She concentrated on the guards outside the door, counting them and devising an escape plan.

"What I want"—the prince stepped closer—"is for you to work for me. I want the Invisible Sword to disappear for good—never to be seen again. In exchange, I'll release the monks and anyone else you care about."

Not quite what she'd expected. At least cutting her eyes out wasn't part of the deal. Not yet anyway. Not until he learned how to claim the power for himself.

"Anyone? Including Banqui?" she tried.

The prince glanced at Yates in genuine surprise. The captain shook his head.

"Have you lost your friend again? That's rather irresponsible of you," the prince said.

At least Banqui wasn't locked in a black cell. Then where was he? Bringing her attention back to the prince, she asked, "What would I do if I worked for you?"

He tilted his head at the prone forms on the floor. "You'll be one of my protectors. You'll also be my advisor. You can tell if someone is lying, right?" He didn't wait for an answer. "You'll help me usurp the Heliacal Priestess. The city doesn't need two rulers. Everything will be better with just me in charge. And…" The prince moved closer and lowered his voice. "I'll stop torturing people for information."

That was too good to be true. There had to be some trick despite his honesty.

He leaned in. "Think about it. Why would I need to torture anyone when you can read their souls and learn all their secrets?"

Stopping the torture was her top priority. And working for the prince would solve a number of other issues and avoid a battle where there would be casualties. A cold pulse of shock slammed into her when she realized she was tempted. It allowed the rational part of her to override her emotional first reaction. What the prince proposed she'd do instead of hurting his prisoners was exactly what Tamburah had done. Besides, the prince had to release her parents eventually or risk upsetting the King.

Then it occurred to her that she could capture the prince right now. Except she doubted his guards outside would allow her to leave with her prisoner. Unless she knocked them out, which would take too much energy because Yates was thick-headed and would require most of her strength.

The prince watched her. "Do we have a deal?"

"I need to think about it."

"Then sit down and have a think." He gestured to a cushion. "Professor, do you have any refreshments for your guests?"

Emeline let out a squeak of surprise before dashing over to a water jug. Shyla didn't move. Obviously the prince wasn't going to let her leave without an answer. And she wasn't about to give him one. Both led to trouble.

As the prince made a show of settling in with a glass of water in hand, Shyla's thoughts raced. There were about eight guards in the hallway. Too many to put to sleep, but perhaps she could influence them.

She accepted a cup from Emeline but didn't sip the water. The professor might have served her holy water. Why not? She'd betrayed Shyla to the prince, she could be working for the priestess as well. And that thought gave her an idea. Gathering her power, she sent it to the five men and three women waiting outside.

Arch Deacons.

Shyla envisioned half a dozen well-armed Arch Deacons approaching the guards from both sides.

Arch Deacons.

Shouts pierced the tense silence. Then a rustling and the unmistakable ring of swords being drawn. The prince and Yates exchanged a concerned glance before the huge man strode to the door and slid it open with more force than needed. A crack zigzagged along the colored glass.

The guards had split into two groups of four. They stood back to back, facing the Arch Deacons.

"What's going on?" Yates demanded.

Arch Deacons.

Shyla pictured them advancing on the guards.

"Arch Deacons are attacking, sir!" one man said as he blocked an invisible weapon.

Taking advantage of the momentary confusion, Shyla used the *not here* command and took off down the tunnel. Only Yates spotted her. The captain cursed and the sound of his boots pounded after her. Once she was out of sight of the guards, she dropped her mental suggestions, then poured all her energy into staying ahead of Yates.

From the brief glances over her shoulder, Yates wasn't far behind. In fact, for a man his size, he was rather quick. There was nothing worse than being chased through an underground city. Eventually, they'd run into more guards or a group of deacons or a dead end, which was very likely as she wasn't familiar with this particular level.

The few people she passed just pressed against the walls, giving Yates room. They wouldn't dare try to stop him, but they wouldn't interfere with her either. Unless they decided helping the Water Prince's captain would benefit them. All she needed was a fraction of an angle to disappear from his sight so she could lose him before that happened.

Shyla aimed her magic back at Yates.

Gone.

Nothing. Not even a hitch in his stride. She added more force.

Gone.

And a bit more power.

Gone.

Her commands just bounced off his broad chest. Or so it seemed. And to add to the fun, another set of boots sounded behind Yates—probably the fastest of the guards rushing to catch up. She ceased her efforts to use her magic and concentrated on her direction. Aiming away from the populated areas, Shyla turned to dart down what she hoped—

Pain exploded in the back of her right thigh. She sprawled forward, skidding over the stone floor, scraping her palms and forearms raw. But that was minor compared to the agony that gripped her leg muscles. She looked back and wasn't sure what was scarier. The knife sticking out of her leg or Captain Yates standing next to her with the tip of his sword descending slowly toward her. Desperate, she sent all her magic at him.

Stop!

Nothing. She tried to scramble away from the weapon, but the fire in her leg prevented her. The sharp point of the sword touched her back. She froze—all pain forgotten as it pierced her tunic and skin.

"The prince doesn't care if you die," Yates said. "As long as I don't damage your eyeballs." He twisted the sword, creating a bigger gash.

Shyla bit down on a cry.

"Go ahead, Sun-Kissed. Stop me from killing you with your magic."

She'd like nothing better. But the beast seemed immune.

He knelt next to her and tugged down the collar of his uniform, exposing a platinum torque. "Took this from an Arch Deacon." He grinned.

Terror seized her lungs, forcing all the air from them. And while she couldn't read his soul, there was no doubt that he not only planned to kill her but would enjoy it.

"This is going to be our little secret, something you can share with the Sun Goddess when you see her. Because you can't stop me."

"But I can," Rendor said.

Yates straightened, yanking his knife from Shyla's leg. A hiss of pain escaped her lips. But when he pulled his sword free, she sucked in a deep breath. Without the blade in her leg, she was able to roll over and prop up on her elbows.

Rendor faced the captain. He too held a sword and a knife. His hard gaze promised no mercy. Her relief over his arrival was short-lived as worry for him dominated.

No way was Rendor fully healed from being skewered by two swords even though it had been over sixty sun jumps ago. Also, as the captain of the guard, Yates was the best swordsman in Zirdai.

She wanted to tell him to leave, to save himself, but his posture radiated stubborn determination, which meant she'd have more luck convincing a stone statue than Rendor.

The two men stood in the middle of an intersection. Shyla hadn't noticed before—probably due to running for her life—but it was one of the bigger ones with tunnels branching off in six different directions. Two druk lanterns illuminated the space and glinted off the blood pooling under her knee. She sat up and bent her injured leg. Lacing her fingers together, she pressed her hands to the wound to staunch the blood, pulling her thigh against her chest for added pressure.

"You've been replaced, Rendor. You're weak. A traitor," Yates said.

"And you're not the true captain of the guard, Yates. You were *appointed*." Rendor's derision was clear. "All the guards know you never fought for your position so you'll never be their captain. Not while I'm still alive."

"I can fix that right now." Yates lunged, stabbing his sword toward Rendor's heart.

Their blades crossed with a loud clang as Rendor blocked the thrust. Yates stepped in close and jabbed with his knife. Rendor pivoted his hips. Shyla's blood on the tip of Yates' weapon left a streak of red on Rendor's tunic. Then the fight began in earnest.

Both large and muscular, they were evenly matched and equally well trained. Yates was stronger, but Rendor was quicker. They fought with brutal, efficient strikes, not wasting energy, not even speaking. It was silent except for the ring of steel, the shuffle of boots, and the grunts of the men that echoed off the hard stone walls. No finesse touched their moves, just a mindless drive to get past the other's defense and kill him.

Shyla watched with fascinated horror. The air heated with their exertions. The musky odor of male sweat reached her as their tunics dampened and their faces shone. Their breaths rasped. As the fight extended, Rendor's injuries became apparent—a weakness in his left arm and a slight hitch in his right leg. Yates wasted no time in pressing his advantage. He knocked the sword from Rendor's hand. It landed on the opposite side of the intersection. In other words, as far from Shyla as possible.

Fearing for Rendor's life, she rummaged in her pack—not caring about her bloody hands—searching for a weapon or anything she could use to help him. There was nothing but her water skin and scarf. The water might make Yates slip, but it would also endanger Rendor. She wished she still had Tamburah's statue. It was heavy enough to knock Yates out. If she could stand, she could wrap her scarf around his neck—

She almost smacked herself. Why didn't she think of this before? She needed to get Rendor's attention but didn't want him to lose focus either—it could cost him his life. Using the wall to keep her balance, Shyla lurched to her feet. A hot poker of pain shot through her leg.

A loud clang sounded and Rendor's knife went flying. Rendor grabbed Yates' wrists and moved in close to him—too close for the captain to use his sword. Yates dropped the sword and broke Rendor's grip on his right wrist. Then both men struggled for control of the remaining knife. Rendor dug his fingers into Yates' forearm. Yates fought to break free, swinging Rendor around. They both hit the wall and the knife was knocked loose.

The fight turned into a wrestling match. But Yates was stronger and knew where Rendor's weak spots were. He slammed Rendor into the wall. Shyla winced in sympathy as Rendor's head bounced with a horrible thud. Dazed by the blow, Rendor lost his grip on Yates' wrists. The captain wrapped his hands around Rendor's neck and squeezed.

Rendor finally looked over Yates' shoulder and met her gaze. Regret filled his. She yanked at her collar. "Pull it off!" she yelled.

Rendor stopped trying to pry Yates' fingers from his throat—which he should have known not to do, but he did just suffer a blow to the head. Instead, he reached for Yates' throat and ripped off the torque.

Drawing all her strength, she thrust out both hands and pushed with all her might.

Sleep!

Yates toppled to the ground, pulling Rendor down with him. Shyla limped over to help. By the time she reached him, he'd already removed Yates' hands from his neck. He lay there panting.

"How long...will he...sleep," Rendor asked between gasps.

"Not long."

Rendor clambered to his feet, but he swayed as the color leaked from his face. She tried to steady him but with only one good leg she couldn't support his weight let alone her own. They both toppled to the ground. She landed on top of him and he grabbed her instinctively.

"Maybe you should catch your breath before trying to stand," Shyla said.

He grunted and closed his eyes.

"My weight on your chest is probably not helping."

Instead of releasing her, he held her tighter. His body heat warmed her and, surprisingly, she didn't mind the strong sweaty odor of Rendor—a mix of male musk with a hint of ginger. She breathed it in. It was a nice distraction from the throbbing in her leg. The hard vibrations from Rendor's heart eased after a few moments. He opened his eyes and relaxed his grip.

"Better?" she asked, sliding off him.

"Yes." He sat up and stood. This time he remained standing. "Can you walk?"

She held a hand out. Rendor grabbed it and pulled her, gently, to her feet. Putting weight on her bad leg caused considerable pain but it didn't collapse under her—a small victory. She tied her wrap around her leg to staunch the blood and tried a few steps on her own. "Yes, but not far."

The good news—Orla's commune was only three levels away. The bad news—they had to climb up.

Rendor supported her as she limped with slow agonizing steps. His desire to just carry her was obvious with every flex of his muscles. They finally reached the commune.

"Get Zhek," Rendor barked at the first person they encountered. He escorted her to one of Zhek's examination rooms and helped her onto the table. Once she was settled, he pulled away.

"Don't go," she said to him, grabbing his hand.

He hesitated. That hurt more than the knife wound. Yet, he had come to her rescue, almost losing his life in order to save hers.

"Guess I'll just have to get into trouble again," she said and released her grip. "Do you think Yates—"

"Don't joke about that." His harsh words rasped with fear and anger.

Exhaustion had caught up to her, making it difficult to block his emotions. "Then stay."

"I can't."

His conflict was clear, though it was mixed with another deeper longing and, underneath it all, passion, maybe love. It was too complex to sort out and she wouldn't intrude by probing his soul.

She met his gaze, remembering the argument they'd had—it seemed like circuits ago. She didn't have the words then, but she knew what to say now. "I'm sorry."

"For what?"

"For not responding to the idiot in the common room. For worrying about what the other Invisible Swords thought about us. For not jumping into your arms when I had the chance."

He stared at her for an eternity. "You—"

"Out of the way, you big brute," Zhek said, pushing past Rendor.

Orla followed the healer, crowding into the small room. Zhek grabbed Shyla's hands and tsked over her raw palms. But when he spotted the wound in her leg, he ordered everyone out. Rendor left with Orla, taking his unspoken words with him. She doubted he'd return. And while that knowledge ached deep inside her, it no longer cut as sharply into her heart. She'd said what she needed to say. Although she never thanked him for saving her life. Actually...she had when she saved *his* by sending Yates to sleep.

Zhek's administrations yanked her painfully into the present. He grumbled as he washed her wounds. When he examined the gash on the back of her leg, she about jumped off the table. He rubbed a numbing paste on it and she showed considerable restraint by not snapping at him for not doing that *first*.

"At least the blade went in and out clean," he said.

"Clean?"

"It wasn't twisted while inside you. That would have caused more damage and extended the time you needed to heal." He sighed loudly. "Not that you'll allow it to fully heal before injuring yourself again."

He made it sound as if she did it on purpose just to annoy him. She wisely remained quiet while he finished patching her up. He called for one of the vagrants to help her to her room. As the young man supported her through the common areas of the commune, she searched for Rendor. Shyla noted the time—angle two-ninety. But, as she had suspected, Rendor was gone. For once, it would have been nice to be wrong.

When they reached her room, she remembered her recruits and Jayden. "Do you know where Jayden is?" she asked the young man.

"I think he left to gather information."

"Can you tell him to come to my room when he gets back?"

"Sure." He helped her onto the cushion and left.

Shyla squirmed into a comfortable position. Pain bit into her each time she moved her leg. Soon after she settled, Zhek arrived with a cup of his special tea.

"I promise to drink this once Jayden returns," she said.

"That might not be for a while."

"Do you have something for the pain?"

He considered. "You promise to stay put while waiting?" He fluttered a hand toward the door. "And not go out visiting?"

"Yes."

Zhek grunted and left. When he didn't return, she eyed the tea. Her encounter with the guards and Yates had left her without any energy. Sleep would be best, but she needed to talk to Jayden. Before she could decide, Zhek returned with glass of red water.

"Red?" she asked when he handed it to her.

"For the pain."

"Thanks." She drank it.

He jabbed a finger at the cooling tea. "Remember your promise."

It didn't take long for the pain to lessen and disappear. No wonder Zhek worried she'd leave. But her exhaustion caught up to her and she dozed until Jayden woke her around angle three-forty.

"What happened? Zhek said you were stabbed. By who?"

"Long story. I'll tell you about it later. Right now I need you to meet with the recruits at angle three-fifty-five and escort them to our headquarters."

"All right, but I want a full report when I return."

She raised the cup of Zhek's now cold tea and saluted him.

"Cute." He left.

After downing the liquid, she set the cup on the floor and waited for the peace of oblivion to overtake her.

* * *

When she woke, Jayden was sitting by her door. He leaned against the wall and looked exhausted. "How do you feel?"

Shyla rolled over and groaned as all her injuries flared to life. Stiff and sore, she tried to sit up but then gave in, plopping back.

"That good?" Jayden stood. "Should I get Zhek?"

"No. I'm fine." To prove it she managed to sit up without wincing. "How long did I sleep?"

"An entire sun jump plus sixty angles."

Angle forty already? She'd slept through her chance to leave Zirdai at angle zero.

"Have you gotten any sleep?" she asked him.

"Some."

"The recruits?"

"All safely transferred to headquarters." He frowned. "You could have warned me there would be so many."

"Did all twelve show up?"

"There were sixteen."

"Sixteen? Does that include Wazir and his three family members?"

"No, they wanted to stay here a couple more sun jumps."

"Sixteen? Are you sure?"

He held up his hands and wiggled his fingers. "I count good."

"Sorry. It's just—"

"You weren't expecting so many?"

"An understatement."

"I doubt we'll get any more. The deacons are furiously searching for their missing members. You probably should stay here a few more sun jumps."

"There's too much to do."

"Like figuring out if Yates told the Water Prince about the torques?"

"How do you know Yates had a torque?"

Jayden reached into his bag. "Rendor told me when he gave me this." He pulled the broken platinum necklace from it.

"From what Yates said and the fact the prince wasn't wearing one, I don't believe he's shared his knowledge about the torques."

"Ah, the captain might not be as loyal as we thought." Jayden fiddled with the torque as his gaze grew distant. "Perhaps we could recruit him."

"We can't. Yates is very loyal…to Yates."

"That could still be beneficial. At a crucial moment, he might decide to save his own skin instead of the prince's."

"We can hope." They shared a grin.

"Tell me what led to you getting stabbed by Yates."

She filled him in on the professor's ambush and the prince's offer. "An exchange—me for Hanif and Kaveri."

"He's bluffing. He won't harm the monks," he said.

"Not yet. But I fear if he gets desperate he will." And she couldn't allow that to happen.

Jayden was quiet a moment. Then he said, "Since we're stuck here another sun jump, I'm going to visit my commune and get some sleep. You probably should rest as well or Zhek won't be happy." He headed for the door.

"When is Zhek ever happy?" she asked in frustration.

He paused and glanced back. "After a successful birth. He's all smiles."

It was hard to imagine. And she wasn't going to have a baby just to witness it. Anyway, it wasn't like she had to worry about that as Rendor...well, she'd no idea if she'd ever see him again, much less do...that. Besides, there was something that men did to prevent pregnancy. Would Rendor know? Argh, why was she thinking about this? About him? She needed to focus on the heaping mound of problems the Invisible Sword still needed to solve. And she wasn't going to solve them lying here all sun jump.

Moving was difficult, but she managed to get upright without falling over. Putting her weight on her injured leg ignited a fire behind her thigh. She ignored it and took a few lurching steps. Shyla worked the stiffness from her limbs but was unable to walk without a considerable limp. She needed—a cane!

She hobbled from her room and aimed for one of the tables in the large common room. Only a few people milled about. Most were either out or asleep. She spotted a familiar figure.

"Ilan," she called.

The boy skidded to a stop and came over. "Do you want to buy some rats?"

Did she? Their water supply was safe for now. "Not yet. But I need a cane. Do you know if there's one I can use?"

"Oh, yeah. I'll be right back." He dashed off.

While she waited, she spotted Zhek carrying a tray of food into her room. This was going to hurt more than the stab wound. Sure enough, Zhek stormed out. He glanced around, found her, and strode over. She braced for the lecture and wasn't disappointed. At least he brought the food with him. Except she remembered that he had no qualms about putting his sleeping medicine into a patient's food.

At the end of his tirade he said, "Well? What do you have to say?"

"Can you please give me more of that red water for the pain?"

Zhek sputtered. When Ilan arrived with a cane, it was too much for the healer. He pressed his lips together and left. Guess that was a no to the pain relief.

Ilan knew better than to ask about Zhek. Instead, he handed her the cane. Made of blue alabaster, a lightweight but strong stone, it hooked at the end to form a handle. There were small ridges on the underside that helped her get a better grip. A leather plug covered the bottom of the cane to reduce noise.

"Twist the handle and pull," Ilan said.

She did as instructed and revealed a surprise. A thin blade about thirty centimeters long slid out. "Oooh. I like this."

"Thought so." He beamed.

* * *

Slightly hunched over, Shyla walked with her cane. It took her a few angles to find a rhythm and she still wasn't smooth or very fast. But that didn't matter as her ungainly gait matched her disguise of an older woman. She'd covered her hair and half of her face with her wrap. The best part was that the cane kept most of her weight off her injured leg.

Ilan accompanied her, playing the role of a dutiful grandson. She'd argued with Orla that she was just going on a reconnaissance mission, but the woman had insisted that, with the deacons searching Zirdai, Shyla needed backup.

"But he's only ten circuits old," she'd said. "I don't want him to get caught or hurt." She'd feel awful if that happened. His rats would miss him.

"He's eleven and the boy's better equipped at avoiding a deacon than you are right now," Orla had said. "Take him or you can't go."

And here they were. Shyla found it interesting and a little sad that most people ignored her. Instead, they nodded to Ilan with approval. Not that she was complaining—going unnoticed was her goal. They descended to level seventy-one where blending in became harder to do. The quality of their clothing didn't match that of the people who lived in the seventies. Though not nearly as wealthy as those living below level eighty, they still had extra coin to purchase finer fabrics that were custom tailored.

Avoiding guards was also challenging as teams of them patrolled these tunnels and the presence of the costly trol lanterns hindered them. The bright light of the trols chased away the shadows. Shyla preferred the druks with their weak purple glow.

They took a circuitous route to the chapel, keeping a lookout for both guards and deacons. Not many people traveled in this part of the city. Shyla wondered if it was due to the chapel nearby—out of sight equaling out of mind—or if it was due to the warmer air and strange odor. It had a hot metallic tang and left a bad taste in her mouth. People living underground learned a long time ago that pockets of foul air or unusual hot or cold spots were signs of toxic gases. And if they had collected in one place, there was a good chance they might ignite in a powerful explosion. This scent, though, reminded her of the foundries in the upper levels.

Finding a location to watch the chapel without being seen was difficult. They ended up in a tight corner, but it had a clear view of the main entrance. Too bad it was guarded by six Arch Deacons. If that didn't tip her off that something big was going on inside the chapel, she needed to find a new profession.

As a mental exercise, she considered how she'd attack the chapel. The well-armed men wore torques, rendering her magic useless. The Invisible Swords could fight one-on-one and take their torques like Rendor had done to Yates, but she had no idea exactly how many deacons were inside. If this chapel had another entrance like the one on level fifty-two, she could send her people in that way to try for a surprise. Again, how many would she need? She wished for a way to neutralize the deacons without fighting. A vision of striking them on the head with a statue of Tamburah flashed. Not a terrible idea, except she'd have to get close.

Perhaps she could invite them for drinks and serve them some of Zhek's special tea. Imagining them toppling over, she swallowed a giggle. Ilan glanced at her in concern.

As they watched, a handful of people passed by at various times, a quartet of deacons arrived, and the Arch Deacon on the far right scratched his nose seventeen times.

"How long are we going to stay here?" Ilan whispered to her.

"Until I figure out what they're doing inside."

"They're melting platinum." He wrinkled his cute little nose. "Can't you smell it?"

"Yes, but I need more information." She sensed about a dozen inside, but, with all that platinum, there could be a dozen more deacons. And without a constant watch, she'd never learn what was really going on inside. She needed to hire a couple vagrants to collect the information.

"All right, let's go," she said. Her injured muscles had stiffened with the inactivity and her leg almost buckled underneath her when she moved.

Ilan grabbed her just as a group of six deacons left the chapel. He pulled her back into the shadow. She watched as the deacons sorted themselves. Two carried about ten platinum torques each and the other four formed a defensive circle around them.

But it seemed odd that they were worried about being attacked. Or were they just trying to hide the torques from view? Did the priestess suspect the Invisible Swords would be very interested in her operations here? It was almost as if they were putting on a show. Did the priestess want them to know they were making more torques?

Then the group disappeared. Not gone as in around the corner or down a tunnel.

No. They literally disappeared.

Ilan sucked in a breath. "They're gone."

Shyla recovered from her shock. She knew only one way to disappear from sight like that. Magic. Concentrating, she located the chanting rhythm of a magical command pressing on her. She shoved it aside. The group of deacons reappeared.

Scorching hells. The deacons had wielded magic. Somehow the Heliacal Priestess had figured it out. Somehow she'd recognized the magical potential in her conscripted deacons and had taught them how to direct it.

How in the seven hells did the priestess learn— Shyla almost groaned at the depth of her idiocy. Someone in the Invisible Sword had passed that information on to the priestess. She'd suspected a traitor all along. So why hadn't she done more to find the person? She hadn't wanted to upset Jayden. And look at what happened.

They were cooked.

* * *

"Can you explain your logic?" Jayden asked after she'd filled him in on all that she'd learned.

They were in her room at Orla's commune.

"I shouldn't have to, Jayden," Shyla said in annoyance. While the cane helped, her leg still throbbed.

"How do you know the traitor's one of us and not one of the vagrants or deacons? You've been telling everyone about us. Maybe you told one of them your theories about cracked deacons."

She clamped down on a nasty reply. Instead, she drew in a breath. "I only told trustworthy people, Jayden." She held up a hand. "Trustworthy, because I read enough of their souls to know their intentions."

He scrubbed a hand through his hair. "All right. Say you're right and the priestess found out about the potential magic wielders in their midst. Then why did the deacons wield magic at that moment? They could have just hidden the torques under their robes or in a basket. There was no need to use magic to hide from the prince's guards or any other watchers."

"It almost seemed rehearsed, as if they were performing for an audience. I think they knew we were watching."

"How? You were well hidden, right?"

She ignored the implication that she'd let them spot her. "You're thinking about it the wrong way. Now that the deacons can wield magic, it changes everything. They *sensed* us. It's an easy skill to learn even for the newest of beginners." She rubbed her temples. "They correctly guessed we were affiliated with the Invisible Sword. It's logical that we'd consider shutting down their torque-making operation. In fact, that's why I was there, to check it out and see if it was possible to stop them or to steal their platinum. When they sensed us nearby, they staged that little demonstration just for us."

"Why would they tip their hand? Surprising us with their own wielders would give the priestess a big advantage."

True. A sudden thought occurred to her. "We need to act quickly."

"What?"

"The priestess only has a few wielders. Otherwise she wouldn't have shown them to us."

"Wait. Where's this logic coming from? How do you know she only has a few wielders?"

"You asked why she showed us at all. There's only one reason to tip her hand. Because she wants to scare us off. Make us hesitate and wait so she can find and train more of her deacons. Which is why we need to act quickly."

"Doing what?" Jayden asked.

"Getting to those deacons before she does."

"Do you think you can after those sixteen people left?"

"It'll be hard. But it'll be even harder the longer we wait."

"We need to train our people. And don't forget that caravan is coming in two sun jumps."

She stifled a groan. "You're right. We need to get back to headquarters right away and figure it out."

Jayden glanced at the sand clock. "It's angle one-sixty. We'll be spotted leaving the city."

"Then we'll just have to be clever. I'm not waiting another angle. I'll go tell Wazir and his family to get ready." She hurried off.

* * *

345

Disguised as two rich merchants, Wazir and Jayden and their four retainers left Zirdai via the north exit around angle one-seventy. Shyla used her magic to influence the guards nearby to see familiar faces.

"Masters Pramod and Fath, so good to see you again," the one guard called to Wazir and Jayden. "What brings you out so close to darkness?"

"I want to check on Fath's velblouds that are for sale. Make sure it's a healthy flock before I purchase it." Wazir waved to the guard. "You know I can't trust Fath. He might have tied sun cloaks onto sand demons."

The two Arch Deacons that had been edging closer turned away at the friendly banter, no longer interested in the group. Shyla relaxed.

Once they were out of sight, they headed toward their headquarters. Shyla soon discovered that using a cane in sand was difficult. Every step soon became an effort. Jayden walked beside her, helping to support her weak leg. He also erased their tracks.

"Are you going to be able to meet up with the caravan? Or should Ximen and I go?" he asked when they reached the temple.

She considered their strategy to purchase the platinum. Surely her leg would be better by then. And then it hit her. "We can't follow our original plan with the caravan."

"Why not?"

"Because there's a good chance the priestess knows about it."

"Not this again. Shyla, your logic is flawed. Banqui—"

"That's enough." She'd reached her limit and was finished with being nice. "Let's go settle this right now." She limped to the ladder.

"Wait!" Jayden caught up to her. "What are you going to do?"

"You know what I'm going to do. It's time everyone takes the oath."

* * *

Everyone gathered in the common room. Fifty people crammed together. A few had been in the middle of work and full buckets of sand sat by their feet. Gurice and Mojag stood in the front with Ximen. Some had been woken up and they peered at her with tired and grumpy expressions. Too bad.

Jayden helped her to step up onto a low table to address them. "We've gained a number of new members and we've learned some critical information. Danger is approaching and we must be able to counter it as a unified organization. I've heard people talking about being an acolyte, or an original member, or a vagrant. That needs to stop. You're *all* Invisible Swords." She paused and met each of their gazes.

"And you will *all* take the oath and pledge your loyalty to the organization and to each other. You'll all stand as witnesses. As part of the ceremony, I will draw our symbol on your upper arms." There was a rumble of dismay. "You won't see the symbol unless you can wield magic, nor will blood be shed." Shyla drew the glyph on the wall with a piece of chalk. "This is what it will look like."

She let her words sink in before continuing. "As your leader, I will go first." She handed her stylus to Jayden.

He stared at the writing instrument in alarm. "What am I supposed to do with this?"

Explaining how she'd pushed her magic through the instrument when she'd practiced on Gurice, Shyla rolled up her left sleeve, exposing her shoulder.

"I don't think—"

"At least she didn't ask you to cut out her eyeballs," Ximen said, interrupting Jayden. "Like she did to me."

He shot Ximen a horrified glare.

"Ready?" she asked.

"No." Jayden sighed. "I'll try."

Shyla addressed everyone. "As a member of the Invisible Sword, I swear that I will embrace the beliefs and tenets of the organization and fully support its efforts to help those in need."

Jayden traced the crossed blades on her shoulder with the stylus. A tingle pricked her skin.

"As a member of the Invisible Sword, I swear I will not betray the location of our headquarters or the identities of our members to our enemies and would give my life to keep its secrets."

He guided the flattened tip, following the two curved lines of the symbol.

"As a member of the Invisible Sword, I swear not to harm or kill another unless it is absolutely necessary or in self-defense."

He drew a big circle in the oval shape.

"As a member of the Invisible Sword, I swear allegiance to my fellow Invisible Swords."

Coloring in the "pupil," Jayden completed the symbol. An intense heat burned on her skin as if the killing sun shone directly on that small section. No wonder Gurice had thought Shyla stabbed her. Magic snapped and the pain disappeared.

"It worked." Surprise laced Jayden's voice. He then stepped back, allowing the other wielders to see the new glyph.

Shyla thought it was unfair that not everyone could see it. Perhaps she could show them. In order not to upset anyone, she explained what she planned to do. Using her magic, Shyla sent the image of her symbol to the others.

Invisible Sword.

A little over half the room gasped. It seemed that almost fifty people was too many for her to influence at once. She repeated it for the remaining members.

Invisible Sword.

Unable to hold it long, she stopped the command. After waiting a few moments to allow them to recover—and her as well—she pulled her sleeve down and took the stylus from Jayden. "You're next."

He shook his head sadly. "I can't."

Confused, she peered at him. "Why not?"

"Sorry," he said to everyone, but he was staring at Mojag.

Sand exploded from all the buckets. The columns spread out and formed a curtain that swirled in furious circles. Cries pierced the roar of sand. Everyone scrambled to cover their faces, turning their backs to the assault.

CHAPTER

16

It took a moment for Shyla to grasp the significance of the sand attack. Jayden was the traitor! A mix of emotions boiled—surprise, anger, and pain—but she ignored them. For now. Instead, she fought to calm the storm, but Jayden had years of practice in manipulating sand. And all he needed was a fraction of an angle to make his escape. Once he reached the surface, he'd be able to hide. Son of a sand demon!

Then all the sand grains stopped and dropped to the ground. Mojag held out his arms. He'd been the one to stop the attack. He also blocked the exit, standing in Jayden's way. Shyla would never forget the look of hurt betrayal on Mojag's face. Or the fury.

Jayden put his hands up as if placating a wild gamelu. "Moj—"

"No! *You* don't get to talk to *me*," Mojag said.

Shyla sensed a magical struggle between the two. Although impressed by Mojag's strength, she knew Jayden had more experience so she helped the boy.

Sleep.

Jayden glanced at her then at Gurice and Ximen who stepped up beside her. *That's right, you're outnumbered, traitor.*

His shoulders sagged in defeat and he stopped fighting. *Sleep.*

This time he crumpled to the ground. She stared at his prone form, allowing the emotions to roll through her. Perhaps she shouldn't be so surprised. He'd been fighting her ever since they rescued him from the Heliacal Priestess, his resentment coloring all their exchanges. But for him to betray the Invisible Sword? And Mojag? That was a concept just too hard to grasp. What had happened to him? She hoped they'd find out.

Time to focus on the rest of the Invisible Swords. Shyla turned to them. "We'll proceed with the oath."

"Are you crazy?" Ximen asked. "We need to evacuate right now."

"And go where?" she asked.

"The city. We can hide with the vagrants."

Not a bad idea.

"What if they're in on it?" Gurice asked. "Jayden was our liaison with them. We need to know the extent of his betrayal before we go anywhere."

"Should we interrogate him now?" Ximen asked.

"Not yet. We will find out *everything*," Shyla promised. She was finished with being nice. "But not right now. Between the four of us, we shouldn't have any trouble keeping him asleep." Then she addressed the rest of the group. "This betrayal proves that we need to stand united. In order to do that, we need to trust each other completely." She scanned the faces in the room. "Taking this oath is vital and you cannot lie or it will not work. Is there anyone else who wishes to refuse?"

Silence.

"Good, let's get started. Ximen, you're next." She held her breath. Did she have the strength to learn of another traitor?

He pulled up his sleeve. "Let's go."

It took about thirty angles for everyone to pledge their loyalty. They encountered no other nasty surprises and a few good ones—of the people who had come with the ex-deacons, three of them had potential to wield magic. The mood in the room had changed significantly. A sense of purpose and determination filled the air, but also an undercurrent of fear. That was to be expected because they could be attacked at any time except when the sun was in the danger zone.

As the members dispersed to return to work or to rest, Shyla consulted Ximen, Mojag, and Gurice about what to do with Jayden. They sat in a circle around him. Poor Mojag hunched over his crossed legs in utter misery. The others were equally dejected—they'd been friends with him for a long time. No one tried to speculate as to why or how or when he decided to betray them. They knew Shyla would discover the answers.

"I've extra velbloud tethers," Gurice said. "We can secure him."

"It's going to take all of our magic to keep him from escaping," Ximen said, glancing at Shyla.

Between using her magic to keep Jayden unconscious and doing the vows, she'd drained most of her energy. "After I interrogate him, we'll need somewhere to keep him." There wasn't any place in their headquarters. "Somewhere that we don't need a guard or else he'll use his magic to escape. Somewhere where no one will accidentally find him. We'll have to— Oh!"

"Think of a good place?" Ximen asked.

"Oh yes."

* * *

Shyla rested while the others took turns keeping Jayden asleep. When the sun started its jump, she sent out a few members to keep watch on the city. At least they'd have some warning if the priestess attacked. Yes, the priestess. While trying to sleep, her mind had reeled and spun with the implications of Jayden's betrayal. Three things had stood out—the deacons had ambushed the original headquarters, they'd captured Jayden, and they knew how to block magic.

Elek and a few other strong Invisible Swords helped her to relocate Jayden and carry the supplies he'd need to survive. Ximen and Mojag also accompanied them. Gurice remained at headquarters.

After Jayden was secured, Elek and the others left. Shyla, Mojag, and Ximen stood just out of reach. One druk glowed with a yellow light. It cast long shadows from its place on the floor.

"Ready?" she asked them.

Mojag pressed against her and she wrapped an arm around his bony shoulders, squeezing him in encouragement.

"You don't have to be here," she said to the boy.

"I know. I *need* to be here."

Another squeeze. "I know."

"Let's do this," Ximen said grimly.

They stopped commanding Jayden to sleep. It didn't take long for him to wake. He opened his eyes and spotted them. They braced for a magical attack, but he sighed and pushed to a sitting position. He froze when the rasp of metal over stone sounded. His gaze followed the chain from his ankle to the anchor in the middle of the small cavern.

"Is this revenge?" he asked Shyla, referring to when she'd spent twelve sun jumps chained in here as they tested her for magic. He had called it a testing chamber, but to her it'd always be a prison. There was one way out, but there could have been four for all the good it had done her.

"No. It's practical." And maybe there was a little bit of revenge in her decision to bring him here, but she wouldn't admit to being petty. Not now. "Are you going to tell us what we need to know about why you sold us out to the priestess or am I going to have to read your soul?" She'd taken her shield down just in case he attacked with his magic.

"The priestess?" Mojag asked.

"Yeah, I figured it wasn't the prince, too," Ximen said. "Jayden hates the prince."

"He hates the priestess, too." Mojag frowned. "Probably a lie, like everything else."

Jayden flinched. "I hate the prince more. Hated him enough to be willing to stab him with my knife. But *she* ruined that."

Oh no, he didn't get to blame her or anyone else. "By saving your worthless life. Your plan was flawed."

"Not this again. It's definitely not the time," Ximen said. "Is that why you ran to the priestess? Thought she'd help you kill the prince?" He didn't wait for an answer. "In exchange for killing…" His voice hitched. "Bazia, Payatt…our friends…the Invisible Swords."

"No." Jayden shot to his feet. "I didn't tell her the location of our headquarters. Banqui did that."

She groaned. Not this again!

"The idiot snuck out," Jayden said. "Banqui had forgotten about one of his caches when we let him get his personal items. He said there were priceless artifacts inside, but we wouldn't let him leave our hideout. It was too dangerous." He huffed in disgust. "Normally opening those almost invisible doors is just about impossible to figure out, but the Water Prince's personal archeologist certainly knew how to operate them. So smart until he came back. He'd no idea that he was being followed. The deacons showed up in force soon after he returned with his stolen treasures. Don't give me that look, Shyla, he was stealing from the prince just like all the other archeologists before him, saving up for the perfect time to leave the city."

It was difficult to believe Banqui's carelessness was the reason for the attack. He'd spent quite a bit of time in the prince's black cells—an experience, she was sure, that no one *ever* wanted to repeat. "But after we rescued you, I asked you if Banqui was involved. You said you didn't know."

"You asked if he betrayed us. And I didn't know. He could have purposely led the deacons to our hideout."

"Do you know where he is?"

"The priestess has him."

"Why didn't you tell me—oh."

"Yeah, oh. I needed there to be doubt about his involvement."

"Is he alive?" She held her breath.

"As far as I know."

At least there was some good news from all this.

"Speaking of involvement, when and why did you get involved?" Ximen asked.

"Wait," Mojag said. "How can we believe anything he says?"

Ximen and Jayden glanced at Shyla.

"I can tell when he's lying," she said.

Mojag scrunched up his nose. "But he's lied to you a million times. How come you didn't know then?"

Good question. "I wasn't…monitoring him then. I trusted him." Big mistake.

"Monitoring?"

"Right now, I'm using my magic to tap into his surface emotions. If he lies, I'll know. And if he won't answer our questions, I'll go deeper and find the answers." The last part was more for Jayden than Mojag.

"So when and why?" Ximen demanded.

Jayden scrubbed a hand over his face. "When they attacked us, I found the leader and begged him to stop killing our people. Promised him I'd arrange for the Heliacal Priestess to get The Eyes if he stopped." Then he looked at Shyla. "Promised to hand the sun-kissed over."

Ah, so it was an ambush and not very bad luck Shyla had run into those Arch Deacons in Tamburah's judgment room. So much for Jayden not wanting to hurt her.

"My people were dying. I had to do *something*," Jayden said.

"Only ten of us escaped," Ximen whispered.

"They would have killed *everyone*, Ximen. The rest were arrested."

Ximen perked up. "The commanders?"

Jayden shook his head sadly. "They wanted to kill the leaders and those that could wield magic. Good thing you and Gurice weren't with them."

"Oh, so I should thank you for not ratting us out?" Ximen demanded.

No response.

"The exchange with the Heliacal Priestess," Shyla said. "You for The Eyes. Your idea?"

"Yes. I knew the prince had the fake Eyes so the Invisible Swords would have to give the priestess the real ones. I'd no idea *you* had woken them." He glared at her. "They told me you died."

She glared right on back. "Not sorry to disappoint you."

"But we rescued you, Jay. Why keep working for the priestess?" Ximen asked.

"We have *no chance* against the Water Prince. You're all fooling yourselves. I want him dead! And I don't care if I have to work with the priestess to do it."

"What did you tell her?" Ximen asked.

A hushed silence. Would he reveal the depth of his betrayal or would Shyla have to force it from him?

"Not much. I didn't want you or Gurice or Mojag hurt. She doesn't know the location of your headquarters or about Tamburah's second vault. In fact, she stopped assigning deacons to watch our old headquarters. Actually, the priestess doesn't care if you're hiding out in the desert playing at a rebellion. We both figured the new organization would eventually stall and break up." He growled in frustration. "How in the seven hells did you get twenty more people?"

"*We're* asking the questions," Shyla said coldly. "What did you tell her?"

"I recognized the significance of the torque around her neck. She'd no idea. It's an heirloom handed down—or taken—from one priestess or priest to the next. Must have been a gift from the Invisible Sword founders. Despite the rumors, the torques weren't lost. They were entrusted and passed down to the leaders of the Invisible Sword. I found them in my father's things after he died. I hid them, but told the priestess where to find them to protect her pet Arch Deacons." His shoulders drooped. "I wouldn't have told her, except she needed a show of good faith from me before we did the exchange."

"And you were going to let her own The Eyes?" Ximen asked in shock. "So the prince is dead. So what? We'd still have to deal with the Heliacal Priestess who'd have the power of The Eyes at her disposal."

"She never would have woken them," Jayden said. He scowled at Shyla. "Nor would I have told her how."

"Why tell her about the deacons having magical potential? How did she open them up?" Shyla asked.

"Again, so she can defeat the prince. And she didn't open them…I did."

Jayden must have been spying on her and Gurice when she'd worked with Mojag. That meant— "I thought it was from the power of The Eyes."

"Despite what you think, you're not that special. All you need is just regular old magic and someone to teach them."

Ximen shook his head. "So the priestess kills the prince and takes over control of the city. How does that help you?"

Jayden looked at Mojag, and the emotion associated with that gaze touched Shyla's heart. For the first time since all this started, she didn't hate Jayden.

"He did it for the vagrants," she said. "The priestess must have promised him that she would leave the communes alone." He was the Vagrant Prince after all.

"Is she right?" Mojag asked. He'd been quiet up to this point.

"Yes. The priestess will also release our people from the black cells. And no more deaths in the prince's special rooms."

"But you forgot about the deacons torturing people to confess their sins," Shyla said. "Or did you negotiate with her to stop that as well?"

The muscles in his neck tightened. "The deacons don't kill those people."

"So you're okay with torture?" she asked.

"She won't need to torture anyone when…"

Oh, this should be good. "When what?"

"When she has you."

Ah. She shouldn't be surprised. The Water Prince wanted the same thing. And Jayden had set the Arch Deacons on her before. "And when is that going to happen?"

Jayden's posture stiffened but he didn't say anything. His magic flared. Shyla braced for an attack. Nothing happened. It took her a moment to realize that he was preparing to fend off her efforts to read his soul.

"Are you sure you want to do it this way?" she asked.

No answer.

She deepened her connection into his mind.

Jayden commanded, "Stop!" with a full blast of his magic.

Scorching sand rats, the man was powerful. More than she'd thought. Her body locked tight. She was unable to move. And from the unnatural stillness beside her, she guessed Mojag and Ximen had been caught as well.

But that was the thing—while she could counteract his magic with probably a great deal of energy, it was unneeded. The power of The Eyes could not be stopped by magic. And she'd already established a link to his soul. There was no need for her body to move in order for her to explore his mind with hers.

She was curious what Jayden planned to do next. His thoughts raced with possibilities as a grim satisfaction over trapping the three of them flowed through him. Perhaps he could command them to give him the key to the cuff.

Shyla sank lower into the core of his emotions. A red-hot hatred burned for the prince. Why? She sought out the source. An image of a lovely young woman with dark hair and amber eyes. A fierce love and adoration surrounded her...Jayden's older sister. The image flipped, turned upside down and now she was naked, covered in cuts, and bleeding to death in one of the prince's special rooms. Jayden huddled below, watching her die through the metal grate. Listening as her blood dripped into the black river next to him. Shyla felt his horror and fear twisting into hatred and fury as intense as the sun. All directed toward the new Water Prince. A ruthless man who attacked the vagrants soon after he'd won the throne. He claimed they soiled his city and he would exterminate them all.

His anger was certainly justified. But she couldn't sanction what he was willing to do to reach his goal.

Jayden must have sensed her presence. "No, wait. Stop."

Too late. She continued. His feelings toward her were more complex. Jealousy, anger, frustration, admiration, exasperation, and hatred for stealing The Eyes from him, for preventing him from assassinating the prince.

Then she sank to the darkest levels of his mind. There lurked his guilt for not being fast enough to save his sister, for being away from the commune when the guards attacked, for not protecting his people, the self-loathing of working with the priestess. In his mind, he was not a traitor. He did not betray his friends, he was saving them all. He was a hero. There was nothing he wouldn't do to keep them safe and alive. Even tell the priestess when and where to capture the sun-kissed.

Shyla sifted through his memories of the conversations he'd had with the priestess, the exchanges of information, and the plans they made. It was an ugly, unpleasant task. One she didn't relish. One that would take her a long time to recover from. But before leaving his soul, Shyla found a place where Jayden was at peace, where love and not hate resided. His emotions toward Mojag were pure. The fierce protection and brotherly love clear. Shyla paused and absorbed the goodness. This was what she wanted to remember when she thought of Jayden. Not the hate and pain of betrayal.

When she withdrew from his soul, Shyla became aware of her physical body. No longer frozen in place, she filled her lungs.

Ximen had his hand on her arm. "Are you all right?"

"Not really, but I will be."

He nodded his understanding. Ximen wasn't all right either. Mojag stared at Jayden, who was now curled in a ball on the floor. Tears welled from his amber eyes—the same color and shape as his sister's.

"Did you…" Ximen twirled his hand. "You know…"

"Yes, I learned what we needed to know."

"Do we have to evacuate?"

"No. Everything he told us was true." She faced Mojag, putting her hands on his bony shoulders. "He loves you. All your interactions with him were genuine. He never lied to you."

"But he lied to everyone else."

"He believed he was doing the right thing for everyone."

"Except you," Ximen said.

True. "Let's go. We've lots to do to prepare." But she turned toward Jayden.

He'd uncurled and sat up, wiping his face with the back of his hand.

Shyla pushed the druk closer to him with the tip of her boot. "Being locked in total darkness is cruel, so you can have the druk."

"You can't leave me here," he said.

"Why not?" she asked then pointed to the back of the chamber. "You've plenty of supplies for the next thirty sun jumps."

Jayden spun. Water skins and rolls of jerky rested on the low stone table. A cushion sat next to it along with a small pile of scrolls—because they weren't heartless. Collection buckets lined the far wall with a jar of cleanser.

"No," he said with dawning horror. "No. You can't."

"We can. And now that you have lots of time to think, consider this: if we're defeated by the priestess, will we tell her where to find you or not? That is, *if* we live through the battle." She paused to let her words sink in. "I guess if no one shows up after thirty sun jumps, you'll have your answer."

She tilted her head toward the exit and the three of them turned to go.

"Stop," Jayden called, once again using his magic.

But Shyla was ready for him and deflected it. They strode from the chamber, turning right at the first intersection.

"No!" Jayden's last anguished yell echoed off the walls, thudded with their heartbeats, and followed them all the way back home.

* * *

So. Much. To. Do. With only limited time. Before they entered their headquarters, Shyla explained to Ximen what she'd learned and what she was planning.

"Wait. The priestess knows we're going to buy the platinum from Zimraan and you still want to go ahead with the purchase?" Ximen asked with plenty of skepticism.

"Yes."

"And that's where they expect to capture you."

"Yes."

He shook his head. "You're the boss."

And she had the most to lose. When she entered the common room, she noted the quiet conversations and morose expressions, the sense of defeat and fatigue in the air. Time to change that.

"Listen up," she said, projecting her voice. "We've work to do."

They fetched the rest of the Invisible Swords and she issued assignments. Handing a bunch of torques to Ximen, she said, "Figure them out. I want to know exactly what they can do and how to counteract them."

He raised an eyebrow. "Is that all?"

She ignored his sarcasm. "Have Titus help you. Gurice!"

The woman snapped to attention.

"You're in charge of training the new wielders. Start with Mojag. He's quick and from the way he stopped Jayden's sand attack, powerful. Concentrate on manipulation; we'll teach them the other techniques later."

"Them?" Gurice asked.

"Yes, I'll be sending you more soon." She glanced at the two women and the man who'd been cracked. They'd sat together, looking overwhelmed and uncertain.

Then Shyla gestured to Elek and Jaft. "Gather all the warriors," she instructed. "Ask the new members who can fight and see what they can do. I want a status report on readiness in a sun jump."

They nodded and, for once, Jaft didn't have a smart-ass reply. Shyla watched them move among the others. Before they could approach Rae, she pulled the woman aside.

"Rae, it's your choice. Open your magic or join the fighters."

While petite, Rae knew how to use her size to her advantage and was fierce in a fight.

"What do you need more? Wielders or fighters?" Rae asked.

An easy question to answer. "Wielders who can fight."

"Figures." She drew in a breath and straightened her shoulders. "All right. Let's do it now before I change my mind." She gave Shyla a tentative smile.

"Meet me in my room," Shyla said. "I need to talk to the others." She found Yoria, Lamar, and the three ex-deacons and their three friends. Explaining the process of opening their magic, Shyla gave them all the choice. "No one is forcing you to do anything you're uncomfortable with. If you decide to become wielders, then wait outside my room for your turn."

As she headed there, Aphra approached her. "What's my job?"

"That tunnel is very important. Take who's left and keep working on it."

"All right."

Rae waited for her inside her small chamber. She sat next to the bucket of sand, staring at it. "I never thought of sand as a weapon before Jayden attacked us. It was always just a nuisance to me." She met Shyla's gaze. "The Ways of the Yarin are all about defense, and I can think of many instances where sand would make an effective shield."

"I see you're getting used to the idea of wielding magic."

"I'm an Invisible Sword. We don't back down from a challenge."

"Ah, that's my girl. Are you ready?" At Rae's nod, Shyla asked her to concentrate on the sand, willing it to move.

When her magic glowed, Shyla pulled on the edges, opening it up. Rae's fear of abandonment poured out. Not a surprise, but the fact Rae had been three circuits old at the time shocked Shyla to her core. Most parents left their sun-kissed children when they were mere sun jumps old. Rae's hid her from the deacons. Until they changed their minds.

Stay here, her mother says. We're going to play a game.

Rae claps her hands in excitement, but why does Mommy look so sad? The glare of the hot sun makes it hard to see, but tears shine in Mommy's eyes.

Close your eyes and turn around, her mother says.

She doesn't understand this new game or why there are people dressed in green with her and Mommy. Where's Daddy? But she does as she's told. 'Cause it's Mommy. When nothing happens for a long time, she opens her eyes. The heat sears her lungs as she looks behind her. She's alone. Terror strikes her like a blow. Crying out for her mommy, she runs, following the tracks, but they're confusing and she's soon lost. She keeps running even though the sun presses fire down onto her. Her skin turns bright red. The soles of her feet burn.

When she can no longer run, she collapses on the scorching sand. Needles of agony dig into her skin. Then a shadow provides a tiny bit of relief and a man dressed in red looms over her. He scoops her up in his arms.

The trauma of being left in the desert had remained with her all these circuits. Unable to get close to anyone, Rae kept herself emotionally apart. Not anymore. Rae sagged against Shyla, exhausted.

She pulled Rae into her arms. "The deacons forced your parents to abandon you."

"I know. I've known. I just…"

"Couldn't help wondering if they decided to leave you and asked the deacons for help," Shyla said softly.

"Yes." A sigh.

"Now you see the truth."

"I do."

"And the best part—"

Rae jerked away. "There's nothing *best* about it."

"There is. Your parents might still be alive and living in Zirdai. I'm sure they'd be ecstatic to see you again."

The woman stared at her as if Shyla had just told her she could fly.

"Get some sleep, Rae." Shyla pointed. "You're welcome to use my mat."

A small smile tugged at Rae's lips. "No offense, but the piles of sand in level eleven are more comfortable."

"Go, then," she shooed good-naturedly. Then she took a few moments to center her thoughts and emotions before calling in the next person to open.

After the last of the potentials left, Shyla crawled to her mat. Uncomfortable or not, she needed the balm of oblivion. The emotional release of the traumas from nine people had bombarded her. Every bit of her body felt raw as if she'd just walked naked through a sand-storm. She longed for Rendor, and imagined curling up in his embrace, borrowing his strength. With the memory of his scent in her mind, she fell asleep.

* * *

From her vantage point on the edge of the dune, Shyla watched Zimraan's caravan through the holes in her camouflage. Pulled by teams of gamelus, the line of twelve wagons trundled through the sand. Each wagon had two drivers. Guards wearing sun cloaks and swords strode on each side of the line. The sun hovered in the sky at angle thirty-one.

She'd been hidden under a blanket of sand since before the sun started its jump. Ximen and Gurice were also concealed at other key locations nearby. They'd been fighting the magical command not to look to the west since angle twenty—when the Arch Deacons and deacons had arrived to intercept the caravan. Others hid behind dunes. Shyla guessed the extra personnel were there in case they were ambushed. Overall the priestess's people were being careful not to be spotted by anyone.

Shyla counted sixteen Arch Deacons and six deacons—four of them able to wield magic—plus ten more hiding. A total of thirty-two opponents. The priestess certainly had big plans for this encounter. Shyla guessed she should be flattered.

As the caravan approached, the deacons stopped the magical command. To Zimraan's eyes, it would look like a wall of Arch Deacons had suddenly appeared. They wore green tunics and pants, black dillo leather boots, and green turbans. Their faces were covered with veils.

Zimraan cried out in alarm. He raised a hand and the wagoners halted the gamelus. His guards rushed to the front, ready to protect the merchandise. But the deacons remained in place. After a few tense moments, one Arch Deacon strode to Zimraan as the caravan master dismounted.

Shyla strained to listen to their conversation.

"We're here to purchase all the platinum you carry. Also there are agitators in Zirdai who plan to do the same thing. We would like your help in trapping them," the man said.

"I'm sorry, but I already sold all my platinum," Zimraan said.

"Who did you sell the platinum to?" the Arch Deacon shouted, drawing his knife.

Zimraan backed away, his hands up. "The monks."

This answer caused the Arch Deacon to pause. His grip on his weapon relaxed. "The Monks of Parzival?"

"No, the Monks of Arinna."

Shyla smiled. That had been her idea.

"I've never heard of them."

Zimraan lowered his arms. "They're new. They're building a monastery outside the city of Marib."

"We still need your caravan in order to surprise and capture the insurgents," the Arch Deacon said. When Zimraan hesitated, he added, "You'll be compensated and everything will be returned to you."

The caravan master had no real choice. His eight guards were no match for sixteen Arch Deacons. Shyla watched as the Arch Deacons and six deacons exchanged clothing with the wagoners. And then the ones in hiding appeared. Eight of them swapped with the caravan's guards, while two donned the tunics of the men from the last wagon.

The priestess had sent the exact number of people to cover all the caravan's personnel except Zimraan of course. There would be no gaps to warn Shyla or her people that a swap had taken place. Smart. Too bad for the priestess, Shyla already thought of doing that exact same thing.

The people now dressed as deacons moved away from the caravan—her cue to start. Shyla aimed her magic at the sand below the disguised deacons' feet, moving it away. Ximen and Gurice helped her. Cries rang out as they sank and struggled and failed to find firm ground. The priestess's wielders were unable to aid their colleagues. Jayden only had time to teach them how to influence people. A handy skill until the ground dissolved underneath them. She couldn't suppress a snicker.

Not everyone was caught. But she wasn't worried as Elek, Jaft, Lian, and the other fighters—who were now dressed like deacons—took care of them. The priestess's wielders tried to interfere with Shyla's people, but their efforts had no effect. The Invisible Swords all wore rings of platinum on their fingers. Engraved into all the platinum jewelry was the old Invisible Sword symbol. Ximen's experimentation with the torques had revealed that it didn't have to be worn around the neck. As long as it touched skin and had the symbol, it worked.

The goddess had smiled on them because Wazir was a metalsmith. He'd been able to make the rings quickly. His occupation was also the reason he and his family had ended up in the chapel. Wazir had refused to hand over his inventory of platinum to the Heliacal Priestess so she had tortured his family.

When everyone was secured, Shyla removed her camouflage. Her injured leg had stiffened with the inactivity and she was unable to stand. Ximen, who was nearby, rushed over to help her to her feet. So much for her grand entrance.

Grins and whoops sounded from the Invisible Swords when she joined them. She congratulated them on their success. But they couldn't relax yet. The sun climbed closer to apex and the deacons needed to be taken to the monastery where Zimraan's people waited. The monks had agreed to hold on to the captured deacons for a few sun jumps.

To her, the very best part of the plan was that she now had thirty-two Invisible Swords disguised as Arch Deacons and deacons.

* * *

They raced the sun. Zimraan's caravan arrived at the entrances to Zirdai around angle sixty-five. The porters waiting for the merchant sprang into action, unloading the goods, unharnessing the gamelus, and cursing under their breath at the unexpected delay. Zimraan shrugged, claimed traveling in the desert was a dangerous undertaking then proceeded to bark orders.

Zimraan had played his part well. At first he'd been against the idea of deceiving the Heliacal Priestess's deacons, but a large pouch of osees had changed his mind.

Four more Arch Deacons waited as well. They demanded to know what had happened. Shyla's people had ensured their faces were hidden behind the veils. They parted and revealed their prizes—Shyla, Gurice, and Ximen with their hands tied behind their backs. She glared at them all, playing her part.

"The mission was a complete success," Elek said.

"What about the other renegades?" one Arch Deacon asked.

"Dead," Elek said in a flat tone. Muscling past the man, he gestured for the others to go inside.

"That wasn't part of the mission," the man said, trailing them. "The Blessed One will be upset."

"They fought back." Elek shrugged. "Not much else we could do." Picking up the pace, he led them down to level six.

Once they were safe from the killing sun, Elek slowed. The four from the entrance had followed, obviously intent on accompanying them. Elek headed to a less populated fringe of the city.

"Hey, wait, you're not going the right way," an Arch Deacon said.

"I think this is a good place," Elek said.

"For what?"

"For this." He snapped his fingers. Elek's warriors attacked.

The four had no chance. They were unarmed and forced to their knees in a fraction of an angle. Jaft removed their torques and Shyla used her magic to erase their memories. She then went deeper, finding their reasons for becoming Arch Deacons. Her magic wouldn't be able to change their personality or beliefs, but she questioned why they served the Heliacal Priestess knowing they were no longer saving souls, but hurting them.

The priestess does not speak for the Sun Goddess. I do and she is not happy with your behavior.

Her efforts probably wouldn't work for all of them, but two showed promise. They left the Arch Deacons and continued on their journey.

"Are we going to do this for all the deacons?" Jaft asked.

"Eventually. I'd like to do it for all those who are loyal to the priestess. However, for now, only the ones who try to stop us," Shyla said. "Our mission is to get to the priestess. Once we have her neutralized, we can go from there."

"With so many of us, we're bound to draw attention," Jaft said.

"Our numbers will scare most people off," Elek said. "Besides, if we move quickly, they won't have time to gather forces if they suspect we're not legit."

"Are you going to be able to go down ninety more levels?" Ximen asked Shyla.

With her hands mock tied, walking was difficult.

"We've got her," Daksh said, indicating Nard who stood on the other side of Shyla. "If she has trouble, we'll help her out."

"How?" Ximen asked.

Shyla was also very interested in the answer. The two men each cupped one of her elbows and lifted her off her feet. It was strange, but with her feet only a few centimeters off the floor, they could carry her.

"Everyone ready?" Elek asked.

When they confirmed, he set off at a brisk pace. Shyla managed to keep up for ten levels, but after that Daksh and Nard carried her. The big men didn't slow even with the extra weight. Must be nice to be so strong. That thought led to her wondering about Rendor. Would he spot her with the deacons and try to rescue her? No. It was a silly thought. Even Rendor couldn't take on thirty-two deacons.

As expected, no one dared get in their way. Elek took a route that avoided all the crowded areas of Zirdai but wasn't on the edges. Deacons didn't worry about being noticed so if they appeared too furtive, it would trigger suspicion.

They traveled unheeded all the way down to level ninety. There they entered one of the larger caverns that tended to be a gathering place for the residents in the area. There were many of them throughout Zirdai. Due to the wealth of the citizens at this level, this one was extravagantly decorated with oversized cushions, tables, plush rugs, and trol lanterns.

It was also empty.

The Invisible Swords had a moment to exchange a warning before the other side of the cavern filled with a similarly sized group.

The good news—they weren't from the priestess's holy army. The bad—they were the Water Prince's well-armed guards.

CHAPTER

17

The two groups sized each other up. All had drawn their weapons. Invisible Swords disguised as Arch Deacons faced the Water Prince's guards. Rendor had told her the two factions avoided conflicts. Except, apparently, when it came to The Eyes. This was the second encounter. And informing the guards they weren't deacons would just make things worse—although she really couldn't think of how things could get worse.

Captain Yates entered the cavern and proved she hadn't been thinking hard enough. His people parted, allowing him to walk to the front. Yates scanned them. His gaze paused on Shyla. It burned with deadly intent—a pledge just for her. She tried to read him but was blocked. He had gotten another torque. Fear burned up her throat. How many of his guards were also protected?

"Who's in charge?" Yates asked.

"I am," Elek said, stepping forward. "You are interfering with the Blessed One's wishes. Move aside."

"No." Yates looked at Shyla. "The Heliacal Priestess will kill you. The Water Prince won't. His promise." Then he turned to Elek. "Give me the sun-kissed, and you can walk out of here."

His confidence was based on the guess that Shyla would choose the prince over the priestess and not attack the guards with her magic. If she was truly the priestess's prisoner, then he would have been right. Shyla scrutinized the guards, sensing if any of them blocked her. She found four, which she considered a lucky break.

"No," Elek said.

With nothing else left to say the two groups engaged. Yates and Elek crossed swords. Shyla worried for Elek—he wielded one of the stolen swords, but fighting with a weapon wasn't his strongest skill. Unlike Yates, who was much better. Avoiding the fighting, she, Ximen, and Gurice backed up to the far wall.

"Target the guards," Shyla said, aiming her magic at one of them.

"Any special requests?" Ximen asked. "Confuse them, stop them, or put them to sleep?"

"All of them. Just watch where the bodies fall," Shyla said. "We don't want our people tripping over them."

A contained chaos filled the room. Bodies collided, slumped over, and cried out in pain. The hot metallic odor of spilled blood and the sour aroma of sweat polluted the air.

Elek kept up with Yates for a while. Then the captain turned on the speed and Elek was soon unarmed. With his training in the Ways of the Yarin, he was able to dodge Yates' sword. Eventually the captain wore Elek down. Shyla sucked in a breath, but instead of killing Elek, Yates shoved him toward them. Elek slammed into Ximen and Gurice, knocking both down.

Then Yates was in front of her. She glanced up as he reached for her neck. The memory of him choking the life out of Rendor flashed. Yates had said the prince promised not to kill her, but Yates never said *he* wouldn't.

Instead of fingers wrapping around her throat, cold metal pressed on her skin. She yanked her hands free but was too late to stop the cold from ringing her neck.

As the metal tightened, Yates leaned closer. "The torque works both ways. To protect and to prevent."

Seven hells. He'd put a torque on her! A click sounded and her magical connection to everyone was broken.

She clawed at it but it wouldn't budge. Yates reached for her. Remembering her training, she blocked his arm. Then she countered with a strike with the edge of her hand to his throat. He didn't even flinch. Instead he crouched down and did a left hook into the back of her right thigh—where he'd stabbed her. His aim was dead on and the intense pain shattered her concentration.

The next thing she knew, she was dangling over his shoulder as he left the cavern. Her hands were free, but he'd hooked his arm over her legs, anchoring her in place. And his fingers dug deeper into her injury every time she squirmed, trying to get free.

It didn't take long to descend to level ninety-seven. Yates carried her past the guards to the main entrance. The entire level was the Water Prince's. He brought her to an unfamiliar room—not that she'd seen more than a few the couple times she'd been here. Then he dumped her on the floor.

The impact forced the breath from her lungs with a loud *whoosh*. Between the pain from her leg and the inability to draw a breath, she expected to pass out—hoped to once she spotted the prince's black boots standing next to her. But she just wasn't that lucky. Eventually she recovered and looked up at the prince.

"Knees," he said.

Yates yanked her up onto her knees.

"Get used to that position," the prince said to her. "While you serve me, you'll be on your knees."

Serve him? Not a comforting thought. Nothing about this was comforting. Except maybe his promise not to kill her.

He glanced at Yates. "Well done, Captain. You've redeemed yourself." Then he met Shyla's gaze. "I was not pleased with the captain after you escaped. He's proven quite resourceful since, discovering those protective torques the priestess was using. I hope you like your new necklace. It's like my sigil, except once it's clicked into place, there's no way to open it without a key." He leaned closer. "It's thicker, too. No worries that the deacons will cut it off with a pair of metal cutters. And my jeweler added an extra feature. Let me show you. Yates, get the mirror."

Fear pulsed in her heart. Cut off from her magic, she had no defenses. Yates handed the prince a small rectangular mirror and he angled it so she stared at her reflection.

It wasn't a necklace. Not even close. It was a collar. Four centimeters wide and engraved with the Invisible Sword's symbol. On the very front hung a metal ring. That must be the extra feature, but what did it do?

The prince handed the mirror back to Yates, then he pulled out a short chain from his pocket. Before she could react, he snapped one end onto the ring. Then he yanked her forward by the chain so they were almost nose to nose.

"You're going to regret every problem you ever caused me. And you're going to use those pretty blue eyes for my benefit only. Understand?"

All ability to speak fled as terror gripped her.

"No? Don't worry, you will. And don't think that when I take that necklace off you'll have a chance to attack me. I'll be protected and I have a very good imagination when it comes to punishments." He handed the chain to Yates. "Show her to her new room."

Yates hauled her to her feet. Unable to resist, she followed two steps behind him. He led her to an almost empty room. In the middle of the floor was a metal anchor, very similar to the one Jayden was currently chained to. If her situation wasn't so dire, she might have acknowledged the irony. Yates pulled her down and snapped the end of her chain to the anchor.

Before leaving he said, "If you had agreed to work with the prince when he asked you, your accommodations would have been opulent." He left, sliding the door closed. A thin ribbon of light shone underneath so she wasn't in complete darkness.

After a few moments to adjust to the rapid change in her fate, Shyla ran her fingers over the collar, down the chain, and over the anchor, seeking weaknesses. The chain was only one meter long, limiting her range and preventing her from standing up straight. But if she knelt it was the perfect length. Instead she sat cross-legged, close to the anchor.

The link that connected to the anchor and the one attached to her collar were the same design. They had a hinge and a small keyhole. Perhaps she had something in her—

Pack! Yates hadn't taken it from her. It was under her sun cloak, which she also wore. She dug into it. Water skin, pouch of osees, her wrap, a few rolls of jerky, a spider kit, but nothing slender and hooked. She wished she'd brought her cane, although she doubted the tip of the blade would work. For such a tiny lock, the key was probably a simple L-shape.

Once she explored every centimeter of her cell, she'd nothing left to do but think. She used her wrap as a makeshift pillow and stretched out on the hard floor. Her leg throbbed with painful pulses. She considered her chances of being rescued. That was an easy one— zero percent. Moving on, she searched her memories of the fight. She hoped that once Yates left with her, the rest had retreated. A few of the Invisible Swords had been injured, but from what she'd seen, the guards weren't aiming to kill, which probably meant the prince wasn't ready to take on the priestess.

She had been ready. They had enough people and, with the disguises, they could have reached the Heliacal Priestess and taken over. Hopefully, Elek had continued with the plan. From level ninety-six, the Invisible Swords would have better access to this level. Maybe there was a slight probability of being rescued. Ten percent? Fifteen? Better than zero.

Despair tried to creep into her thoughts, but she refused to let it in. She'd figure a way out of this eventually. For now, she'd cooperate until the opportunity arrived. Then she'd take it.

* * *

They kept her locked in that room for a long time. At least she had some water and food, but other bodily functions needed to be tended to. A mild discomfort turned into a painful pressure. A part of her recognized the effectiveness of this torture. She thought of Jayden living in luxury with plenty of buckets in reach. If he knew about her situation, he'd feel vindicated. He'd plotted with the priestess because he didn't have faith in the Invisible Sword's ability to stop the Water Prince. And here she was, his prisoner. Soon to be a wet and smelly one if—

The door slid open. Yates gave her a dispassionate once-over, then unhooked her, yanking her to her feet. Her leg protested and she almost collapsed, but she caught her balance before he towed her from the room.

She touched his arm. "I need to use the collection station."

He sighed. "I advised the prince to lock you in a black cell, but he wants you close by."

Remembering the hole in the floor of the cell, the stench, and the cries from the other prisoners, Shyla was glad she avoided that fate. Although that could change at any time.

Yates allowed her to use the servants' station and then marched her double time to the prince's throne room. Just like all the leaders from the past, the prince sat on an elaborate marble throne on an elevated dais. Trol lanterns ringed the room, an expensive rug ran from the throne to the entrance, and four water fountains—the most decadent feature—splashed merrily in the corners, the sound incongruous with the tense atmosphere. Colorful tile mosaics decorated the walls around the fountains. It was all very...effective.

She was pushed into a kneeling position on the hard ground next to the throne. Her injury ached its displeasure.

The prince leaned over and met her gaze. "I'm seeing petitioners this sun jump. You will tell me when they're lying or if they have any harmful intentions. Yates will be right behind you. He's been looking for an excuse to hurt you, so I'd suggest you don't give him one."

Yates unlocked the collar and took it off. The relief at being able to access her magic was similar to the relief she felt in the collection station. It was gross but accurate. Of course, the prince and Yates were protected along with the guards. She wondered where the prince had gotten the platinum. Then remembered, with the amount of wealth he stockpiled, he probably already had plenty.

When the first supplicant entered, Yates pressed the tip of his knife into her shoulder, reminding her of his presence. Shyla did her job, scanning the man's thoughts and intentions. She considered planting doubts into his mind about the Water Prince's rule, but she didn't want the man to try something stupid and get arrested. She could use one to send a message to her people. But what would she tell them?

Time slowed as one after another entered the throne room and either pleaded their case or asked for something—Shyla didn't pay attention to the details. They all noted her presence, wondering why a sun-kissed was kneeling next to the prince and what it meant for them. Their reactions to her ranged from unease to fear. A few lied and Shyla signaled to the prince with a shake of her head.

One young man's sharp fear stabbed through her misery. By this time, her legs, back, and knees blazed with pain. The man was being accused of selling water to the vagrants. Shyla read his thoughts and learned he was a vagrant and had been buying water for his commune when he was caught.

"I'm innocent," he pleaded. "I was just at the wrong place at the wrong time. Honest."

The prince glanced at her. Here was her chance to do some good.

"He's telling the truth," she said.

"Captain, please show our sun-kissed what happens when she lies."

She caught movement out of the corner of her eye before Yates' fist slammed into the side of her face. Her cheek and jaw exploded in agony as the force of the impact sent her flying. Crashing onto the ground, she tasted blood as her vision flashed from dark to light.

Yanked up by her short hair, Yates set her on her knees then snapped the collar around her throat. She was half dragged back to her room and secured.

"The prince is disappointed," Yates said. "You won't be getting any food or water until he's happier with your performance."

She huddled on the floor for a long time. The young man had been a test and she hadn't passed. The problem was she'd probably do it again. The Sun Goddess had instructed Shyla to stop her people's suffering, not be the cause of it. Not everyone would be a test.

* * *

The next few sun jumps blurred into one long session of misery. The prince was not happy with her performance. Not at all. She grew weaker and more crippled as the pain in her body spread.

After one such session, she lay bloody and broken on the floor of her room. Even though ninety-six levels separated her from the sunlight, she sensed the distant heat and the pulse of disappointment from the Sun Goddess, no doubt regretting her choice of champion. She'd failed the goddess and failed the Invisible Swords who trusted her to lead them. Failed the entire city, which squatted above her like a velbloud too fat to fly.

Her body ached with the need for Rendor's touch. For him to wrap her in his strong arms. She longed to curl up next to him, safe and warm for just a couple angles. And she worried about her parents. Were they suffering as well? Would the King send his emissary to demand their release?

To pull her thoughts away from her painful—and impossible—wishes, Shyla traced the Invisible Sword's symbol on her collar with a fingernail, remembering when she first saw it. That sun jump with Banqui when he'd shown her Tamburah's vault where The Eyes had been found and soon lost. It'd been the beginning of a grand scheme to assassinate the Water Prince. Devised by the Invisible Sword's predecessors, it too failed. She'd hoped this new archive would prove to be more successful. The words "new archive" stirred a familiar feeling. Why? She chased that fleeting grain of understanding. And—

Yates arrived and once again dragged her to the throne room where she endured another session. Despite the consequences, she was unwilling to cause harm. When the prince told Yates, "This isn't working," she feared for her life. But a strange thing happened. Timin, the prince's personal physician, arrived and muttered over her injuries as he tended to her wounds. Food and water appeared with some regularity along with a few comfort items. This scared her more than the beatings. Pain she understood. Kindness from the Water Prince came with a price.

And she was right to worry. Six…eight?…sun jumps later, Yates led her into the throne room. Not again. But instead of being forced to kneel, she stood in front of the prince.

"Since you refuse to use the power of The Eyes for my benefit, I've no choice but to take them from you," the prince said.

She stepped back without thought but was shoved forward by Yates. His meaty hand remained clapped on her shoulder. Hate didn't begin to describe the depth of her feelings for the beast.

"I've figured out that I need to remove your eyeballs, but I'm uncertain of the next steps. Teach me to wield the power and I'll allow you to live," the prince said.

Dying wasn't the problem. No. It was the prince's utter lack of compassion and empathy and his extreme despotism. He'd turn into another Tamburah within a circuit. Shyla didn't think this conversation was going to end well for her.

"So you'd rather die than give this power to me?"

"Yes."

"I'm not fond of you either." The prince sighed. "Captain."

She braced for a punch or kick or the cold steel of a blade entering her back, but he released his hold and strode to the door. He called to his men and returned to his position behind her.

Four guards entered and they dragged two prisoners with them. Their clothing was torn and covered with filth. They stank of the black cells. With greasy hair and sunken cheeks, they stared at her with alarmed dismay. Recognition caused her to gasp.

Hanif and Kaveri.

Dread coiled in her stomach. This wasn't going to end well.

"Let's try again," the prince said. "Tell me how to wake The Eyes or I'll kill them."

"Don't," Hanif rasped. "He's bluffing. He can't kill us or the King—"

"Will do what?" the prince demanded.

"Send his troops to overthrow you," Hanif said.

"Unlikely. The most I'll get is a reprimand for arresting you. It's not my fault if you died during an escape attempt."

Hanif turned to her. "You know what we do for the King. Let the prince kill us. The King *will* send his troops."

"Yes, do it," Kaveri said.

"I'm not scared of the King," the prince said. He motioned to Yates. "Captain."

Yates pushed her aside and advanced on her mother with his knife drawn. Kaveri straightened and glared at the captain in defiance. No fear lurked in her gaze.

Shyla's heart twisted with anguish. "No. Stop!" She was being selfish, and she didn't care. They weren't going to die because of her.

Yates glanced at the prince, who nodded.

"Tell me," he ordered.

"You're right, you have to remove my eyes. I assume they'll turn back into gemstones, but I've no idea."

"Then what."

She was going to enjoy this next bit. "Then you have to sacrifice your own eyes. Once they're gone, you place the gemstones into your empty eye sockets."

The prince paled. "You're lying."

"No," Hanif said. "She's not. I was there. I placed The Eyes into her empty sockets." He shuddered.

Shyla didn't blame him. The memory of the pain haunted her dreams.

"A sacrifice is required," Shyla said. "And a leap of faith."

"What leap of faith?" the prince demanded.

"That it will work for you. That you will be able to wake the power." That last statement resonated. Had The Eyes woken because of her magic or because of who she was?

"They won't work for him," Hanif said. "He has no magical abilities."

The prince rounded on her. "You were able to use magic before stealing The Eyes from me?"

Hanif had seeded the doubt and now it was Shyla's turn to water it. "Yes."

"How? I thought you said magic didn't exist. Did you lie to me?"

"No. I believed magic was a myth. But I was mistaken. I was...shown proof that it existed and was told of my own potential to use it."

"What about me? Do I have potential?"

"I don't know. You would have to remove my collar and your torque for me to see if you have it."

"So you can take over my mind? Nice try."

She shrugged. "Then you'll just have to have faith."

* * *

The Water Prince sent her back to her room while he considered everything he'd learned. She hoped it would take him a long while to work up the nerve. No way the prince would allow anyone else in his organization to attempt to wake The Eyes. He trusted no one and was too power hungry. The priestess could assign an underling to make the sacrifice because her people were fanatics and worshipped her.

It only took a couple sun jumps before the prince called for her. The doubt had grown and he wanted to know if he had magical potential.

Two guards held Kaveri tight—the prince's insurance that Shyla wouldn't double-cross him. Her mother no longer reeked and her torn monk's robe had been replaced with a clean tunic.

The prince noticed the direction of Shyla's gaze. "I'm keeping your parents close. They're being well treated and will continue to be as long as you cooperate."

She wondered if that was the entire reason or if the threat about the King had him worried. Either way, her mother appeared healthier. And, by the gleam in her eyes, ready for action. Kaveri was a trained monk. Two guards, even armed, were no match for her.

Too bad Yates remained in the room and he wore his torque. Plus the prince was trained to fight as well. She'd seen the hard lines of his muscles under his form-fitting tunic.

So she behaved and instructed the prince to gather his will. She sought the glow of potential as he tried to move the sand inside a clock. There was nothing inside him but blackness.

"You don't have potential," she told him.

"You lie." He backhanded her.

She spun with the blow and lost her balance, ending up on the floor. Yates clamped the hated collar around her neck before she could reach the prince with her magic.

"I am the Water Prince. Of course I have magic." He stared at her with such venom, she expected him to order Yates to kill her. "I will have the power of The Eyes. Captain, send a man to fetch Timin. Have him bring his sharpest scalpel." Then he grabbed Shyla's chain and yanked her up to face him. "After I remove your eyes, I will kill you." He shoved her back.

She landed hard on the ground but barely registered the pain. The Water Prince had meant what he said.

* * *

Timin arrived along with a few more guards. Kaveri was taken back to her quarters. She'd raised a blond eyebrow in inquiry at Shyla before leaving. But Shyla shook her head. Too many guards for the two of them to handle.

The physician was horrified by the prince's request. He sounded just like Zhek. And he raised all the same concerns as Zhek. Shyla would have smiled, but she knew Timin was loyal and would do as commanded. And, sure enough, he agreed.

"We'll see if they turn back into gemstones before I sacrifice my eyes," the prince said. He snapped his fingers at his guards. "Keep her still."

Four guards rushed her and held her down on the floor. Yates' huge hands clamped around her head. The fear that had been simmering deep inside her chest boiled over, sending out searing darts of terror. Yates smiled down at her. Ice clutched her skin. She'd never seen him smile. One good thing about dying was she would never have to see it again.

Timin knelt next to her. His normally kind face creased in sympathy and sorrow as if he'd already pronounced her dead. The physician spread her right eyelid open. The small, curved, and oh-so-very-sharp blade descended toward her eye. She gripped one of the guards' hands, blindly seeking comfort. He kindly squeezed back. Her thoughts spun with desperation. Need. To. Stop. This. Now.

"Wait!" she cried. "I'm still wearing the collar! The Eyes won't turn back without magic." She'd no idea if it was true or not.

Timin paused. The prince cursed. She was granted a few more moments as they discussed what to do. Time to think of a brilliant escape plan. Eventually, torques were brought in for everyone, including Timin. All she'd managed to do was delay the inevitable. And here she was, once again immobilized on the floor without any sudden epiphanies.

Then it was Timin, eyelid, blade, squeezing hands—two this time—and torques. The platinum gleamed in the trol light. She focused on the Invisible Sword symbol etched into the metal, hoping for some comfort. Instead that desperately needed epiphany sprang to life. Gathering all her magic in one giant scoop, she released it in one huge explosion of power.

Stop! Stop! Stop! Stop!

They froze. She silently thanked the Sun Goddess as relief rushed through her.

Release me.

They did.

Back away.

They scooted back. She sat up, panting and shaking from her close call. Her magic still held them, even Yates—although he strained mightily so she needed to move fast. The prince's expression was priceless—a combination of utter shock, fury, and murderous intention.

Their torques hadn't protected them because they had been engraved with the *old* symbol of the Invisible Sword. Shyla had retaken the oath with the *new* symbol.

The one with her extra embellishments. It had been her own conviction that she couldn't get past those torques that kept her from doing it. Once she figured it out, she just needed a leap of faith.

She pushed to her feet, turned and— Seven hells!

A dozen guards charged into the throne room. She lost her concentration and Yates surged to his feet, aiming straight for her.

Gone. Gone. Gone. Gone.

Yates paused. "Where's the sun-kissed?" he roared.

"There!" one guard said, pointing.

She didn't have enough power to reach them all. And with the knot of people blocking the entrance, she had nowhere to go. Bedlam ensued for a short—too short— time. Shyla ducked and dodged and fought those closest to her, using her magical commands at every opportunity, but eventually Yates caught her.

"Don't try anything," he said as the cold steel of his knife touched her throat.

Stop.

He applied a slight pressure. A line of fire crossed her neck.

"I'm not going to stop," he said. "And you don't need to be alive in order for us to remove your eyes."

Damn thick-headed man.

The prince's voice cut through the cries and everyone stilled, including Yates.

"What in the seven hells is going on?" he demanded. "While I'm glad you've arrived, why are you all here?"

One of the guards straightened. "We brought you a prize, sire." He gestured and the people near the door moved further inside—the throne room almost filled to capacity. But then, through the midst of them, a man was shoved forward to the middle of the room.

Rendor.

Beaten, bruised, and bloody, Rendor stood before the prince, who eyed him with mild surprise and amusement. Shyla sagged against Yates. Rendor had tried to rescue her and now…now they were both in trouble. Unless she could gather enough magic to freeze everyone.

"Where did you find him?" the prince asked.

"He's been trying to recruit your guards to switch their loyalties to the sun-kissed, sire," one of the guards said.

Really? Shyla strained to catch Rendor's gaze, but his hard stare was aimed at Yates behind her.

"Did he have any success?" the prince asked.

Uneasy chuckling. "No, sire. We caught him before he could do any damage."

"Good work, Lieutenant. Rendor, you should have left Zirdai when you had the chance. We'll deal with you in a bit." The prince turned to Yates. "Captain—"

"He's not your captain," Rendor said. "Not while *I'm* still alive."

Yates tensed. And Shyla inwardly groaned at his bold statement. The big brute was going to get himself killed.

"We can settle this right now," Yates said. He handed Shyla and his knife to the closest guard. "I'll know if you try to influence me with your magic," he said to her, then to the guard, "Watch me. If I signal you, slit her throat."

"Yes, sir."

From her point of view, her situation had improved. The man holding her was no Yates. His mind was easily influenced. She wondered if that had been Rendor's plan all along.

Rendor was given a sword and Yates drew his. The guards cleared a space for the combatants, moving to the sides of the room. Rendor was in no condition to fight. This was suicide. She counted the people in the throne room. The prince, Yates, Timin, and fifteen guards—nineteen total. She'd influenced over twenty-five at one time, but then she hadn't spent some of her energy. And they'd also have to escape this level afterwards. She suppressed those negative thoughts. Instead, she focused on the belief and faith that she could do it. Shyla had to gain control of this situation.

Except Rendor was holding his own. In fact, he looked rather nimble for someone who'd been beaten. The fight resembled the last one—brutal, intense, with minimal flourish. Yates also realized his opponent wasn't as injured as he appeared. The captain changed his strategy, once again targeting Rendor's old injuries.

Shyla drew in her strength. She had to stop everyone, then they'd find her parents, and she'd use the *look away* command to get them all free or she'd die trying.

Except Rendor grinned and countered Yates as if not bothered by the change in tactics. The momentum swung in Rendor's favor. He snaked past Yates' guard, sidestepped lunges, and was quicker overall. The number of cuts grew on Yates' arms, torso, and thighs. And then Rendor increased the intensity of his attack. Within heartbeats he'd unarmed Yates and sent the captain to the ground with a massive blow to his temple. The crack reverberated in the dead silent room.

Shyla half expected the captain to get up. He had an extra thick skull after all, but the man remained unconscious on the floor.

The Water Prince frowned down at Yates for a moment. "Well, Rendor, you proved you're still the best. However, you're still a traitor." He swept an arm out, gesturing to his guards. "Even you can't overcome so many opponents. And one false move, the sun-kissed is dead."

Yet the guards in the room didn't appear to be upset by the defeat of their captain. The man holding

Shyla no longer pressed the knife to her throat. She sensed—

Son of a sand demon!

"I'm still a captain," Rendor said to the prince. "And these are *my* soldiers. They agree with the Invisible Sword that you're not the right person for the job."

Shyla glanced at the four who'd helped to hold her down. One gave her a sheepish look. No wonder he'd squeezed her hand back!

The prince pulled his sword and charged at Rendor. The big man twisted. The blade missed his torso by a hair. Rendor didn't waste any time. Within a few moves, Rendor struck the prince on the back of his head. He crumpled and joined Yates on the floor. A cheer went up.

Dazed by the turn of events, Shyla remained in place as Rendor barked orders to his men. A bunch left and a new batch arrived. How many did he convince? Was that what he'd been doing all this time?

Soon, though, he stood in front of her. "Are you all right?"

From this distance, she noted his bruises had been faked. Probably part of the plan to lure Yates into a false sense of security. She wondered if Rendor had thrown their prior fight. However, she didn't need all the details yet. Right now the fact he'd come when she was most desperate was all the answer she needed.

"Shyla?"

"Are you here to stay?"

Rendor wiped Yates' blood off his sword. He bowed and laid the weapon at her feet. Straightening, he said, "I'm *your* captain for as long as you'll have me."

His words hit her with the intensity of a magical vow, cleansing away the doubt and heartache that had lived in her soul since he'd left.

She jumped into his arms.

He caught her easily. A huge grin spread on his face as he hugged her tight.

"You're hired," she whispered in his ear and was rewarded with a deep rumbling laugh—the best sound in all of Zirdai.

Rendor squeezed her once more then set her back on her feet. His gaze snagged on her neck. "You're bleeding. Timin," he called.

Timin jerked then hurried over to them. Fear and uncertainty swirled in his eyes. "Uh, yes, sire."

"I'm not the new Water Prince," Rendor snapped.

"Why not?"

"I'm the captain of the Invisible Sword."

They both looked at her.

"Oh no, not me. I'm already in charge of one organization."

"You can't leave the position open—there will be civil war," Timin said. "Who, then?"

Good question. She rejected the first name that came to mind and considered the Invisible Swords, then the vagrants. Orla would make a good leader. But that first name was truly the best choice.

Rendor met her gaze.

"Jayden," they both said.

"But he's not…" She couldn't find the words.

"Not what?"

She sighed. "You've missed a lot." But she had as well. "You've been recruiting for the Invisible Sword?"

"Yes. I had to prove to the Invisible Swords that my intentions were honest. I had to make amends before I could return."

"You…" She was going to say he didn't have to prove himself, but he did. Not to her, but to the rest of the Invisible Swords.

"Me?"

"Why didn't you tell me what you were doing?" she asked instead.

He stiffened and the familiar stubbornness crept into his expression. "I had my reasons."

Oh no, she needed a better answer than that. He could have avoided hurting her. Then why— Scorching sand rats. Why didn't she think of this sooner?

"You suspected there was a traitor in the Invisible Sword," she said.

"Someone had betrayed them to the priestess, and I didn't think it was Banqui. But I wasn't sure who it was, so I kept my plans a secret."

While upset he didn't trust her with his plans, she recognized that he'd been right not to. She would have told Jayden right away. The name stabbed into her and the exhaustion from…everything…caught up to her.

"Timin," Rendor snapped. "See to her wound."

The man had been standing there politely waiting as they talked, but he sprang into action.

Shyla waved him off. "I'm fine. It's shallow."

But Rendor was determined and there was no force that could counter a determined Captain Rendor. So she settled on a cushion and allowed Timin to clean and bandage the cut on her neck. Rendor ordered his men to carry Yates and the Water Prince to the black cells. And, she had to admit, that improved her mood greatly.

Hanif and Kaveri were fetched and updated.

Hanif slapped Rendor on the back and beamed at him when he learned of Rendor's actions. It was a huge reversal of Hanif's opinion of the man from when this all started and Shyla had gone to the First Room of Knowledge to find information about the Invisible Sword.

His reaction to the news about Jayden's betrayal wasn't as happy. "Jayden? Are you sure?" he asked in stunned disbelief.

"I'm sure."

Rendor, though, didn't say a word, just gazed at her in concern. She wondered if he'd suspected Jayden all along.

"You still need someone to rule," Timin said. He'd been hovering nearby as if uncertain what to do.

The person would need leadership abilities, be able to organize the various tasks that were needed to run a city, and be incorruptible. Not many people had those qualifications.

She looked at her father. "You have lots of experience with—"

"Not interested," Hanif said. "Besides, I'm a sworn monk. Jayden is the true leader of this city."

"But—"

"I know what you said about him, and I know you read his soul. But did you look deep enough? Or did you just search for the answers you needed?"

Shyla opened her mouth to reply that of course she had, but then reconsidered.

"You should have learned by now that people are capable of changing." Hanif glanced at Rendor, making his point. "Whether or not they choose to exercise that capability is up to them." He smiled at her. "Perhaps you should look again."

She huffed at her father in exasperation.

Unaffected, he said, "In the meantime, *we're* willing to step into the leadership role until then." He took Kaveri's hand in his.

Kaveri gave him an unreadable look. "We are? That's presumptuous, old man."

He waited.

She sighed dramatically. "It better not take too long to find someone else, or I might get used to living like this. Do you know there are collection stations down here called water closets?" she asked Shyla in amazement.

Shyla laughed. The release of tension soothed her. One problem solved…at least temporarily. There was still the issue with the Heliacal Priestess and her holy army.

"Do you know what happened to the Invisible Swords after we were attacked by the guards?" she asked Rendor.

"They retreated to Orla's commune. Zhek checked them over and they're all fine."

"I was hoping they continued with the plan."

"Without you they had no way to get to the priestess." True.

"There are rumors that the priestess is preparing to attack the Water Prince," Rendor said. "She knows you're here and will not tolerate him having The Eyes. Her only strategy is to strike before he does and hope to catch him off guard."

"Except she doesn't know we've taken over so—"

"The advantage is ours." Rendor grinned.

Hanif and Kaveri wanted to get started on familiarizing themselves with the job of running the city. They enlisted Timin's help to show them the ex-prince's main office.

Shyla stood to follow them. They needed to start planning their strategy for countering the priestess, but

Rendor put a big hand on her shoulder, stopping her. "You're exhausted."

Not a question but a statement of fact. And she couldn't argue as just standing up had been a colossal effort—not that she'd admit it.

"All right. But I want a big comfortable sleeping cushion," she said, shuffling out of the throne room. If she never returned to this place, it would be too soon.

Rendor took her hand and led her to his old office. "Yates never used it, and all my stuff is still here." He gestured to the sleeping cushion.

Remembering waking up here once before, she smiled. Rendor had been so upset with her. One of the many times since she'd known him. She collapsed onto it, sinking into the softness.

"Get some sleep," he said, covering her with a fur.

She tugged on his arm. "Join me."

"To sleep?"

"Eventually."

His surprise lasted a mere heartbeat before his expression softened. "You're exhausted."

"But—"

He brushed his lips over hers. "We'll have plenty of time later." But he settled in next to her. "I'll stay until you fall asleep."

Resting her head on his shoulder, she pressed against him, fighting off the inevitable. The strong scent of Rendor filled her senses. And that reminded her.

"How did you beat Yates? The last time your injuries slowed you down. Or were you faking it?"

"No." His grip tightened for a moment. "Not pretending at all. It was Zhek. He did…something…to my injuries. The monks did a great job saving my life, but Zhek tsked over my shoulder and hip and readjusted something. All I know is they were hurting pretty bad after that first fight with Yates, and Zhek made it all go away."

Another reason to test Zhek for magic. "You didn't say anything."

He shrugged. "You'd been stabbed. My pain could wait."

Typical. She snuggled in closer. "I missed you."

"Being apart was torture."

"Good," she said.

He looked at her. "Good?"

"Yes. That ensures you won't do it again."

"I won't."

* * *

When she woke, Rendor was gone. Not that she was surprised, but it still caused a brief moment of panic despite his promise. She understood why he'd left before and, without his efforts to recruit the guards, she'd be dead right now and not just feeling as if she'd died.

Standing required extra effort. She wobbled as her legs adjusted to bearing weight. Good thing no one witnessed her ungainly extrication from the fur and sleeping cushion. When she was steady, she went looking for Rendor.

The servants and guards that she passed eyed her with curiosity and not animosity. Still, she braced for someone to call out in alarm. Each intersection she fully expected to be tackled and arrested. She kept her distance from everyone out of habit, but it soon became clear she'd no idea where Rendor might be in the vast complex.

Shyla asked a passing servant, who escorted her to a conference room. Rendor sat around a low stone table with Ximen, Mojag, and Gurice. A number of torques and deacon robes were piled on the table. A sense of urgency rumbled through the low intense tones of their discussion. Mojag spotted her first. He sprang to his feet and almost knocked her over with his strong, enthusiastic hug. The rest smiled at her with hugs in their gazes.

"I'm glad you're okay," he said. His voice sounded young and vulnerable. But then he pulled away and with clear annoyance asked, "Can you tell them that I know the city better than anyone else?"

"I'll agree you know the city well," she said. "But I won't go so far as to say better than anyone."

He made a disgusted noise and flopped back to his cushion.

"Strategy session?" she asked.

"Yes," Ximen said.

Gurice gestured to the empty seat. "Sit down before you fall down. Mojag, go tell someone to fetch her something to eat and drink."

"Hey. I'm a magic wielder now, and—"

"Are still the youngest and the fastest. Go now so you don't miss anything."

Shyla hid her smile as Mojag rushed from the room. Folding her legs under her, she sank gratefully into the square of softness. The short walk from Rendor's office had drained most of her strength. He shot her a concerned look, but she gave him an *I'm fine* shake of her head. No doubt food and water would revive her. She hoped.

"How long was I asleep?" she asked. She had lost all track of time since her capture.

Rendor frowned. "About three hundred angles. Zhek ordered that no one disturb you."

No wonder she was starving. "He's here?"

"Everyone's here," Gurice said. "Good thing we have the entire level at our disposal to house everyone. We have recovering prisoners, Invisible Swords, and *all* the guards. Once they learned that nothing is going to change with the new regime, well besides no more torture, killings, and corruption, they were happy to work for us."

"Not all are here," Rendor corrected. "About four dozen are in the city on patrol. And those that relished carrying out the prince's bloody orders have been arrested."

Ah. "And how is the prince enjoying his new accommodations?"

"He's not."

She shared a smirk with Rendor. Then she considered Gurice's report. "Did you release all the prisoners?"

"No. We freed the Invisible Swords and the vagrants, but we need to go through the prince's records about the rest. We don't want to free a dangerous criminal by mistake."

Smart. "How many Invisible Swords survived?"

"Twenty-three!" Then she grudgingly admitted, "I guess Jayden did save lives."

"Where are they?"

"In the empty rooms of the guards' quarters," Rendor said. "Timin's been taking care of them."

"Where are the guards' quarters?" she asked.

"They're in the southwestern section of the prince's level right above the prince's special rooms."

"What else did I miss?"

"Mojag just reported that the rumors about the priestess preparing for an attack are *hot*. His words not mine," Ximen said. "We might not have as much time to get ready as we'd thought."

"How soon?"

"Four, maybe five sun jumps at most." Ximen picked up one of the torques and waved it in the air. "What we really need to know is how you countered this.

Assuming that's what happened. Timin was sketchy on the details. Did you wield magic?"

She explained what happened. "Once I realized the symbol on their torques didn't match our new symbol, it no longer blocked my magic."

"All you need is faith that it'll work?" Gurice asked. "That seems, no offense, too easy."

"At first, it did seem too easy. But think about it. When we swore our loyalty to the Invisible Sword, we sketched the symbol onto our bodies with magic. They're connected. And even though the torques no longer worked when we swore with the new symbol, we thought they did and didn't even try to use our magic. It was only when I was utterly desperate that I realized this." She shuddered at the memory. Glancing at Rendor, she asked, "Did you know what was going on in the throne room when you arrived or was that an amazing coincidence?"

"A bit of both," he said. "I had intel that the prince was going to try to wake The Eyes during that sun jump, but I didn't know the exact time. I had to guess based on the activity around the throne room."

Mojag returned with a servant in tow. The woman placed a tray down in front of her. Shyla stared at the meal in wonder until the spicy ginger aroma of roasted gamelu meat caused her stomach to roar. It was the first time she'd had real food in sun jumps. A glass of that pure clear water accompanied the feast. She'd groan in pleasure, but her mouth was full.

Ximen tapped his finger on the torque. "The good news is we can all bypass the protection."

"We can?" Mojag asked.

Gurice updated her brother on what he'd missed. "As long as the symbol remains the same. If they find out the new symbol, we're screwed."

"Good thing we uncovered Jayden's treachery before this discovery," Ximen said.

A heavy silence filled the room. Shyla glanced at Mojag. The boy wrapped his arms around his chest. Hanif's words about a person's ability to change repeated in her mind. Perhaps it was worth the effort to revisit Jayden's soul. And that reminded her.

"How long has it been since he…" She gestured with her fork, unable to say it.

"Sixteen sun jumps since we locked him up," Ximen said.

He had plenty of supplies left. That also meant she'd been taken prisoner fourteen sun jumps ago.

"We do need to worry about the deacons who can wield magic." Gurice picked up one of the platinum necklaces. "These can protect our people and some of the guards, but not all. Do we have any intel on how many deacons have power?"

"I originally thought there weren't that many," Shyla said. "But they've had time to find more." She considered the new wielders in the Invisible Sword and if they were ready to fight. "How do you think the priestess is going to attack?" she asked Rendor.

"If I was going to target her people, I'd send small units to ambush all the clusters of deacons in the city at the same time. Also, at that time, I'd lead a bigger unit to her level and fight my way in."

"You've given this some thought," Ximen said.

"The prince hated her and we brainstormed different strategies. That one had the biggest chance of success with the least amount of expected losses. I expect the priestess will use a very similar plan. If she strikes with surprise, speed, and intensity, it will be hard for us to counter and she'll have the advantage."

"That means the guards throughout the city might be attacked at any time," Gurice said. "Do we need to double them?"

Good question. If they did, that would alert the priestess. "We can assign Invisible Swords to guard the guards. They can blend in with the citizens and not tip the priestess off."

"That's a good idea," Rendor said.

"And I think we should do what Rendor suggested and put together small units and attack at the same time," Shyla said.

Everyone nodded in agreement. Shyla assigned them each tasks.

Mojag hopped to his feet. "I'll keep watch on the deacons. If they so much as twitch in our direction, I'll let you know."

"All right. Be careful."

Mojag scoffed. "It was easy before, but now that I can wield magic, it's—"

"Don't boast," Rendor said. "You'll tempt the Sun Goddess to teach you a lesson."

Shyla waited for Mojag to make a snarky comment. Instead, he nodded thoughtfully before dashing away.

Shyla lumbered to her feet. Rendor grabbed her elbow to steady her. How did the big man move so fast?

"Perhaps you should—"

"Introduce myself to the guards and staff? Good idea," she said. Shyla wanted to ensure everyone was loyal so there wouldn't be any traitors surprising them later.

A grumpy rumble rolled from his throat.

"When's the last time *you* slept?" she asked.

No answer.

"That's what I thought. How about we make a deal? I won't exhaust myself if you don't. We can meet back in your office to rest together."

"Rest?"

"Eventually."

He laughed.

* * *

Shyla walked around the prince's complex, stopping everyone she encountered to say hello and to thank them. Only a small amount of her energy was needed to assess their intentions. A few remained anxious about the prince's capture, but she sensed it was more fear of the unknown than any hostility toward her and the Invisible Swords. Two of the guards tried to hide their anger, which stirred suspicion. For them, she used extra power to dig for the reason. Both were loyal to Yates and hoped for an opportunity to rescue him. Shyla noted their names to give to Rendor.

When the air around her seemed to thicken and drag on her body, she figured she'd reached her limit. She returned to Rendor's office. Disappointed that the sleeping cushion was empty, she kicked off her boots and crawled under the fur.

Sometime later, warmth invaded her uneasy dreams and a solid presence pulled her close. She sighed and melted against him. Her worries soothed.

She woke wrapped in his arms with her head on his bare chest. Taking a moment to breathe in his scent and listen to the steady rhythm of his heart, she kept still. Then she ran a hand over the muscles of his stomach. His heartbeat increased its pace. So did hers as she explored the hard planes, her fingers dipping toward his waist.

Shyla lifted her head and met his gaze.

"I hope we never stop meeting like *this*," he said, then he kissed her.

Heat spread throughout her body as she deepened it, drinking in the taste of him. He groaned and his hands snaked underneath her tunic, resting on her back. His touch burned her skin. They kissed until breathless.

When they broke apart, Shyla sat up and plucked at her tunic. It chafed on her overly sensitive skin. She wanted it off.

Rendor took her hands in his, stilling them. His expression was a combination of desire and concern. "We can take it slow."

"Remember when you said I didn't know everything? Before you kissed me that first time?"

Confusion flashed on his face, but he nodded.

"Then afterwards you said that kiss was just the beginning."

"You have a very good memory."

"I do."

"Do you also have a point?" he teased.

"I do." She smiled. "You were right. I don't know everything and I want to learn what comes after a kiss like that."

Fire ignited in his gaze as he pulled her close and kissed her again, sending pulses of desire straight to her core.

"I think..." he breathed. "That your education...will be extensive." His lips brushed her neck. "And require... multiple sessions." Rendor nibbled on her earlobe.

She gasped, surprised by the intense spike of passion that speared her.

"You've much to...learn." He pulled off her tunic and drew her close.

Shyla's breasts brushed against his chest. Shivers raced along her skin. "Teach me."

Rendor taught her how a touch could make her heart race and her body tremble. But most of all, with his words and actions, he showed her why the joining together of two people was called making love.

* * *

Much later, Shyla lay entangled with Rendor. She watched his chest expand and contract with each breath as he slept. The powerful and stubborn man had shown incredible gentleness. She suppressed the desire to wake him up for another lesson. He needed to rest. So did she, but her body hummed with the aftereffects of pleasure. Eventually, she drifted into a light sleep.

A loud roar woke them as a rumbling vibration shook the floor. Rendor and Shyla exchanged a horrified look.

Everyone living in an underground city knew and dreaded that combination of sounds.

It meant a gas explosion, followed by a cave-in.

19

She and Rendor dressed quickly as another boom rattled hard enough to knock over the lantern. A third roar rocked the furniture and she staggered as the sand clock crashed to the floor. It had read angle three-twenty-five.

"The explosions are not an accident but an attack," Rendor said, strapping on his sword.

It took her a moment to comprehend his words. "Do you really think the Heliacal Priestess would blow holes in her floor to get down to us? It's—"

"Effective. Come on." Rendor headed out into the hall.

A cloud of dust swirled in the trol light. Shyla's boots crunched on grit. She scanned the ceiling, searching for cracks and possible falling debris. The priestess never liked being one level above the Water Prince. In this case, it was a tactical advantage.

Another rumble shook the floor, this one louder than the others. The vibrations shot up her legs and she stumbled.

Scorching hells. If she wasn't so terrified, she'd be impressed. One way to live on the lowest level of Zirdai was to collapse the levels beneath you. "The explosions are coming from below us!"

Rendor increased his pace.

"Where are you going?" she asked.

"The priestess wants you. She probably thinks you're near the Water Prince's main living quarters."

"So?" She sucked in a mouthful of dust as a fifth deafening boom sounded close—too close. The resultant energy wave knocked her to the floor.

Before she could react, Rendor yanked her up. "So she won't destroy *that* area."

"Oh."

"Let's go." He grabbed her hand.

They ran through the tunnels. Two more explosions shook their world and the floor seemed to be crumpling underneath her feet. A thick fog of dust dimmed the lights. Her eyes stung and teared. Breathing without coughing was impossible.

A shock wave slammed into her, ripping her from Rendor, surrounding her with a cacophony of noise. Firm ground disappeared. Her stomach filled with the sickening sensation of falling. She dropped along with the chunks of the floor.

Landing, she thought, *is going to hurt.*

When she hit bottom, the darkness was instant.

* * *

Consciousness came and went. Sensations pounded and dulled. Sounds echoed and died. Eventually, she woke fully. And, for a brief moment, she believed the solid presence beside her was Rendor.

Then she remembered.

Then she cursed her good memory as pain stabbed into every part of her body.

She groaned. The noise bounced off hard surfaces, which seemed to surround her. Grit and the metallic taste of blood filled her mouth. After a moment to gather her energy, she assessed the damage to her body.

Shyla was lying on her side. Rolling over to her back with another groan, she moved each body part from her toes up to her head. None of her bones were broken. A miracle. She explored with her fingers and found bleeding cuts, including a gash on the side of her head. Each discovery caused more pain.

There was a ribbon of dim light shining through a crack above her on the left. As her vision adjusted to the semi-darkness, Shyla realized she was surrounded by large chunks of debris. Another miracle that she hadn't been crushed. Although, if she was trapped, she would have exchanged a quick death for a slower one. Could she hope for a third miracle?

She focused on the crack. That was probably the best direction for freedom. But what if she pushed on that hunk of rock and it caused the rest to collapse on her? Another unwelcome thought—that the entire area around her could settle further at any time—occurred to her. The mound of debris creaked and groaned as if in warning. She needed to move. Now.

Shyla reached and grabbed the edge of the triangle-shaped piece of sandstone. Pushing it slowly, she slid it to the side, but was ready to stop if anything started to avalanche. The muscles in her arms ached as she increased the pressure. The crack widened bit by bit. She halted when the sound of tumbling rocks reached her.

When nothing else happened, she continued. Eventually, she supported the stone's weight as it cleared the surrounding debris. Nothing else fell to cover that space. Not yet. By the time she pushed it all the way to the side, her tunic was soaked with sweat and a horrible headache throbbed.

Carefully, she sat up and peeked out. She was at the top of a large pile of rubble. Thank the Sun Goddess. It appeared as if parts of level ninety-seven had collapsed down into level ninety-eight where the black cells and special rooms were located.

Scanning the destruction, she spotted a number of trol lanterns that had survived, bits of broken furniture, shattered pieces of colorful tiles, twisted and mangled pipes spraying water, and—

A body.

It felt as if the entire city of Zirdai had just collapsed on top of her. She couldn't breathe, couldn't move, couldn't think as she stared at the unmoving and broken form. And from her jumbled thoughts, Gurice's words sounded crystal clear: *Everyone's here...we have recovering prisoners, Invisible Swords, and all the guards.* And Rendor, Hanif, Kaveri, Gurice, Mojag, and Ximen. They were all dead!

A harsh cry escaped her lips and she dropped back into her hole. Curling into a tight ball of misery, she shook as the enormity of what had happened rolled through her. Shyla's thoughts stuck on *how could she? how could she? how could she? how could she?*

How could the priestess kill so many? How could she destroy an entire level? That thought stopped Shyla. A memory crept up from the turmoil—Rendor claiming the priestess would preserve certain areas. Then others sprang to life: Hanif and Kaveri had been in those areas, not all the guards were down here, and Invisible Swords had been sent into the city to provide backup.

Shyla pulled in a deep breath. Not all was lost. There had to be survivors. And she was wasting time. Straightening, she carefully climbed from the space, keeping her weight as spread out as possible. Once she reached the top, she searched for a safe path through the rubble. Perhaps there was a way to get to a higher level.

Her progress was slow and painful, but it was progress until the Heliacal Priestess's voice sounded behind her. She froze.

"Find her body," the priestess ordered. "I want The Eyes."

Shyla glanced over her shoulder. Green-clad figures moved over the debris. They poked long poles in between the gaps. She ducked out of sight. It appeared they were close to where she had landed. Did that mean Rendor survived? Had he told the priestess where to find her? Did she dare hope?

Pushing those thoughts aside, she focused on her immediate predicament. She needed to stay hidden, but she had to keep moving. At least the deacons searching for her made enough noise to cover her own. She altered her route to keep the piles between her and the deacons, then picked up the pace.

She skirted holes that exposed the level below. Zirdai had ninety-seven residential levels, but the black cells and the prince's special rooms were located on level ninety-eight, and a forgotten drainage tunnel was underneath. Not completely forgotten as the vagrants knew about it. She paused. The priestess had to know about it as well. Had Jayden told her? And was there another way down there than that abandoned stairway?

The metal grates in the floors of the special rooms would provide access to level ninety-eight from the tunnel, which connected to the prince's level. In fact, Shyla had considered using them to sneak into the Water Prince's complex. The priestess must have utilized them for her explosions. If that had been the case, then the black cells might be intact, which would be good news. That meant half the level was undamaged. Except, the guards' quarters were located above the special rooms. Nausea churned as she realized the priestess must have targeted them.

Up ahead, Shyla noticed an intact wall—a good sign for more survivors, but bad for her as it blocked her escape. She considered her options, then backtracked to the last hole. Peering into the darkness, she couldn't judge the distance to the ground. She scanned the debris. A weak violet-hued light shone through a gap. It was a buried druk.

Moving pieces of rock, tiles, and a shattered table, Shyla quietly uncovered the druk without alerting the deacons, who still worked diligently.

She crept back to the hole and shone the light down. It was too far to jump. She'd need to climb down. She tied the druk to her tunic and opened it wider. The light illuminated plenty of footholds. However, the entire column could collapse when she added her weight onto it.

No choice. She wasn't going to stay here and be caught. At least if she was crushed by the pile, the priestess would never find her body. Somehow that wasn't a comforting thought.

It wasn't a long climb, but it was harrowing. Each creak of stone, puff of dust, and rumble caused her heart to race. Her shaky legs just about gave out as she stepped onto firm ground on the bottom level of Zirdai. She shone the druk around and blew out a breath in relief. She knew where she was.

Shyla hurried through the tunnel. Dirty water leaked from cracks in the ceiling, creating puddles in the middle. The sound of her boots on the floor echoed overly loud. She soon found the entrance to the corkscrew stairwell that went up to level seventy-eight. Not stopping to rest, she ascended.

As she looped around the main support shaft, Shyla puffed with the effort. At least the thin wedges of steps wouldn't collapse under her weight. When she reached the gap where an entire level of stairs was missing, she paused to catch her breath. She longed for her pack. It contained a full water skin and a few rolls of jerky, but she'd left it in Rendor's office in her haste to escape. And while she was wishing for unattainable things, she included a spider kit. It would make climbing the round shaft in her current physical condition easier.

Ignoring the multitude of aches and pains coursing through her body, she found a few toeholds and fingerholds and started up. Her arms and legs soon shook with fatigue and, when she was about halfway, her grip slipped and she slid back to the bottom. She rested her sweaty forehead on the cool column. It was a minor setback. The second time it happened, she cursed. After a moment, she tried again. This time she imagined what the Heliacal Priestess might be doing to her prisoners. It gave her the energy to reach the stairs.

She sat on the steps, gasping and shaking with fatigue. Her fingertips were bleeding and she'd broken all her fingernails. However, that pain just blended in with all the other hurts clamoring for her attention.

The rest of the trip to level seventy-eight was simple in comparison. She staggered out of the stairwell in triumph only to realize that she didn't know where the guards were patrolling. And in her current blood-stained and bedraggled condition, she would attract unwanted attention. No choice but to go to Orla's. A groan escaped her lips at the prospect of ascending another thirty-nine levels.

It took forever. A long, painful slog, willing her legs to keep going. Repeating the consequences if she didn't return to rescue everyone in her mind, she kept to the shadows and the abandoned tunnels. Even through her fatigue, she noted the sound of the city. It had changed. A buzz of tension, sharp voices, and a hum of fear vibrated through the air. The citizens had felt the explosions and were understandably worried.

Once she reached the commune, she was rewarded for her efforts. Every drop of sweat and trickle of blood to get there was worth it because Mojag appeared as if by magic, followed by Gurice, and Zhek. She blinked at them, sensing a trick. All three here and safe was too good to be true. Were they real?

"Son of a sand demon," Gurice said. "You look like you've crawled through all the seven caverns of hell."

"What happened?" Mojag asked.

Zhek waved them off. "Not now. Fetch her some water. Meet me in the examination room."

No doubt they were real.

* * *

"Scorching sand rats, child. I will not help you re-injure yourself. You should be resting." Zhek thrust a cup of his healing tea at her again.

Gurice entered Shyla's room with Mojag right behind her. "Problem?"

"Yes," Zhek said. "I've patched her up, stitched her up, cleaned her up, and she wants to run off and undo everything!"

"Zhek, there might be survivors." Hopefully Rendor was one of them. "I *have* to lead a rescue attempt. I *need* your restorative, but I'll go without it if I have to."

He strode from the room, grumbling and muttering under his breath.

"I guess that's a no," Gurice said.

"What's the gossip?" Shyla asked Mojag.

"I'm sorry. So sorry," he just about sobbed.

"For what?"

"The explosions! I didn't know what the priestess was planning. I missed it! I—"

"It's not your fault," she said. "She surprised us all. No one expected such an attack. Such disregard for life. Such destruction."

"The priestess was smart to keep her real plans under tight wraps," Gurice said to her brother. "And it's done. Nothing to do about it now. What you *can* do is stop blaming yourself and *help*. What have you learned?"

Mojag straightened and wiped his eyes. "Not much. The guards have told everyone to remain calm, which, of course, no one is. Everyone's convinced there's a major gas leak under the city. The focus is on the Water Prince—no one's talking about the priestess being involved. A few of the wealthy citizens have tried to talk to the prince but were turned away by his guards."

"His guards?" Gurice asked.

A shrug. "Probably deacons dressed in their uniforms."

"Do you know how many?" Shyla asked.

"Twice as many as normally guard the entrance, although now I'm sure the gossip is saying there were dozens of guards. Rumors tend to grow with time. It'll be hundreds by darkness."

So roughly twelve instead of six guards. "What about the Invisible Swords? How many are in the city?" she asked Gurice.

"Two for each of the guard units—a total of twenty-four."

Almost half her people. The tight bands around her chest eased a fraction. "How many wielders?"

"Twelve, except most of them are new. But the other twelve all have protective rings."

Still, it was good news. She had forty-eight guards, and twenty-six Invisible Swords. "Mojag, can you spread rumors as well?"

He perked up. "Yeah. That's easy. I can recruit a bunch of the vagrant kids and it'll be all over the city within fifteen angles."

"Good. I want them telling everyone about the Heliacal Priestess. How she killed so many people to gain power. If the citizens are looking for verification, just have them mention the destruction of the guards' quarters."

Gurice looked at her. "For what purpose?"

"It's time the citizens become more proactive. There's still plenty of deacons in the city."

"Nice."

"I also need you to send runners to the guard units throughout the city."

"What should they tell them?"

"To meet me in the common lounge on level ninety at angle ninety."

"Angle ninety so no one can escape the city?" Gurice half teased.

"No. It's when the Sun Goddess is at her strongest."

"I didn't think you were the religious type."

"I survived an explosion, wasn't crushed into a Shyla puddle, and escaped without major injury. I've gotten the hint."

Gurice laughed. "Just don't rely on it. You're not indestructible."

"I'm not?" Shyla pressed a hand to her chest in mock surprise.

Another bark of laughter.

* * *

Zhek woke Shyla at angle sixty. He stood next to her sleep cushion with his arms crossed and watched as she struggled to move. Every single muscle in her body— even her fingers!—was so stiff they were close to being inflexible. Pain pulsed with every movement. She hurt. Bad. And she'd only managed to sit up. Perhaps she should have added an extra fifteen angles to their timeline.

Zhek raised his bushy white eyebrows.

"Yes, you're right. And if I didn't have so many people in danger, I would drink your tea, crawl under the fur, and embrace your healing sleep."

He huffed, somewhat mollified, and left.

At least he spared her his lecture. The colossal effort to stand left her weak and on the edge of tears. So much for being the powerful sun-kissed.

Zhek returned holding a large glass of orange-tinted water. "Drink this." He handed it to her.

Not sure she trusted him, she said, "It's orange."

"That's what happens when you mix a restorative with pain medicine."

"Thanks." She gulped it. Her relief was as cool as the liquid sliding down her throat.

He grunted. "They're my people, too. I'm coming with you."

She choked. "But—"

"The survivors will need to be tended to. And you know that dolt Timin isn't as good as me."

If Timin had survived, but she quickly stopped those thoughts because she knew they'd lead to her wondering about a certain other person and whether he'd survived or not.

By the time she joined Mojag and Gurice, her pain had eased. She glanced at Zhek.

"It'll wear off in about eighty angles."

Good to know.

They followed Mojag down to the rendezvous point. He took them on an odd route, zigzagging through the edges of Zirdai, but they encountered no one. And no one else was in the lounge on level ninety. They'd arrived early. Shyla wanted to ensure another ambush wasn't waiting for them. She checked all the nearby tunnels and used her magic to sense if Arch Deacons were hiding inside the apartments on this level. All was quiet and rather empty. She wondered if they'd been spooked by the explosions and had gone to the higher levels just in case.

Soon after she returned, the guards and Invisible Swords started arriving. As familiar faces filled the room, she hugged each one tight. Rae, Jaft, Lamar, Yoria, and many others. Not Elek, Lian, or Ximen. Or Rendor. Didn't mean they were dead. Everyone was equally glad to see her as well.

Shyla pushed her fears and doubts to the back of her mind and focused on the task at hand. She explained what they were going to do.

"You've one job. Incapacitate the enemy. Wielders, team up with a fighter. You can freeze your opponent with the stop command long enough for your partner to knock him out. For the rest of you, do whatever it takes to get through. Question any thoughts that are not your own. If something appears impossible, it's an illusion. If they disappear, attack the spot they were just at—they're still there! Don't stop. Understand?"

A chorus of yes.

"Good. I need a volunteer to be my partner." She held up a hand. "I need someone who's quick. I'll be stopping multiple opponents at once." Zhek's fantastic potion had given her a great deal of energy.

"Did you really need to ask?" Jaft asked with an insulted tone.

"As long as you can pace yourself." Did he remember their race to Tamburah's temple?

"I wasn't the rotten velbloud egg," he said dryly. "No worries. There's no sand down here."

That reminded her. "But there's rubble and debris and holes. Prepare yourselves, it's not pretty and there are...bodies buried. There will be unpleasant odors."

Grim nods.

"Jaft and I will take point. Let's go."

They weren't subtle or quiet and they didn't care. There were seventy-six of them and they slammed into the twenty people defending the only entrance into the prince's complex. Shyla almost felt sorry for them. Almost.

She reached the doors first. They were closed. But they were warped and couldn't be locked—one good thing from the explosions. Three dozen Arch Deacons armed with long knives waited on the other side. They all wore torques. Shyla didn't slow down. Freezing a handful, she barreled between them as Jaft flitted around, delivering precise palm-heel strikes to their temples.

However, she needed information, so she made eye contact with the next Arch Deacon that tried to stop her.

"Where is the priestess?" she asked her.

The woman said, "Surrender and I'll take you to her." But she thought, *In the throne room.*

Shyla groaned. Not the throne room. Why couldn't *that* place be a pile of rubble? Shyla froze the woman and continued. She fought her way toward the throne room with single-minded determination.

When she reached it, she had the presence of mind to pause and seek the number of souls on the other side of the ornate glass doors.

"Fifteen people are inside," she said to Jaft.

He inclined his head to the corridor behind them. The two of them had outpaced the rest. A clump of her people fought with the deacons at the end of the corridor. "Better wait for backup."

"Good idea."

Except the doors to the throne room suddenly opened. Two Arch Deacons grabbed Shyla's arms and yanked her into the room. She flew forward and fell onto the floor. The doors slammed shut, blocking Jaft.

Shyla gathered her magic as a ring of people surrounded her. She was about to freeze them when magic grabbed her, forcing her to be still.

They were all wielders. All focused on her.

She was trapped.

CHAPTER

20

"When one of my deacons came running in here with the news that you had arrived with a tiny army, I didn't believe him," the Heliacal Priestess said, stepping through the ring of ten people. "But my holy seers"— she swept a hand out, indicating the people who had snared Shyla with their magic—"insisted it was true, so I ordered my army to allow *you* to reach me but not your pathetic soldiers."

It was awfully quiet on the other side of the glass doors. What happened to Jaft? No wonder it'd seemed easy for her to get to the throne room. From Shyla's prone position on the floor, the priestess loomed over her, beautiful, tall, and regal. Except Shyla made eye contact with the holy despot and, if she could move, would have recoiled at the black rot inside the woman.

Being able to read her soul was due to The Eyes, but Shyla needed her magic to physically influence the woman.

"I'm astounded by your ability to survive and by your incredible stupidity. Why did you return? Why not cut your losses and take your powerful eyes to another city?" the priestess asked with genuine curiosity.

Even though she was frozen in place, Shyla could still speak. "Why? Because you need to be stopped. You just murdered a bunch of people. You say you speak for the Sun Goddess. Do you really believe she would have wanted you to kill hundreds of innocent people so you can gain power?"

"She *directed* me to this course of action. She's upset with how this city is being run. She wants *me* to have control of The Eyes and the city." The priestess's gaze lit with an inner fervor.

The woman believed all the nonsense she'd just spouted. Her faith was rooted deep in her soul. Shyla would get nowhere appealing to the priestess's morality or sense of decency. Instead, she focused on the seers. The ten of them concentrated on keeping Shyla locked down. She fought to deflect their magical commands, but their combined power overwhelmed hers.

"And you are all mindlessly following this woman?" Shyla asked them. "Did you not see the bodies? Feel the vibrations? She risked the entire city with that attack. Your Blessed One is insane."

"Do not listen to the sun-cursed. She lies."

"I've woken the power of The Eyes. I see your soul, Bakula."

The priestess jolted at the mention of her given name. Her hand flew to the torque around her neck. "You can't—"

"I can. *You* do not speak for the Sun Goddess. *You* earned your position by poisoning the previous leader, the Heliacal Priest Uri. A very kind man who trusted you. And you got away with his murder. When you add in all the bodies under the rubble, how many more people have you murdered, Bakula?"

"Stop." She backed up a few steps. "Timin!"

An Arch Deacon pushed the physician into the circle. That made thirteen people. Where were the last two?

"Cut her eyes out," the priestess ordered Timin.

Although haggard and disheveled, he appeared to be uninjured. Blood and dirt stained his ripped tunic, but Shyla suspected the blood wasn't his own.

"I can't. You confiscated my tools."

She growled and sent the Arch Deacon to fetch them. He hurried through another doorway. Thuds and curses abruptly sounded from outside the main entrance, which gave Shyla a surge of hope. But the glass doors seemed to be thick enough to keep her rescuers from breaking through. Unless the noise was from the fighting. Had more deacons joined the fray? Did anyone know about the Water Prince's special access?

While they waited, Shyla didn't waste the opportunity. Appealing to the seers, she said, "Imagine how many more people will die if the priestess wakes the power of The Eyes. Think about how she will rule. Before her term, going to confession meant seeking forgiveness. Now, it means torture and—"

"That's enough. Someone shut her up," the priestess said.

"She wants to silence me because she knows I'm right. I—" A force clamped on her throat, preventing speech. Scorching hells.

When the Arch Deacon returned with Timin's bag, Shyla knew she couldn't count on being rescued. She focused on the closest seer, making eye contact with the young man. His power glowed inside him. It wasn't a crack, but it wasn't wide open either. Odd. Obviously, the seer could wield magic, but did that mean Jayden hadn't had enough magic to complete the process? Would the man be stronger if he had been opened all the way?

"I won't do it," Timin said. "Shyla's right, giving you more power is insane. You should be locked up for the rest of your life."

The word *locked* triggered a faint memory. It danced at the edge of her thoughts. Something with Mojag and—

"I'll be happy to do it," a terrifying and all too familiar voice said.

Yates stepped into Shyla's view. He dragged the Water Prince with him—they were the last two people she had sensed in the room. The prince's hands were tied behind his back. And he'd been gagged. Blood dripped from his nose. His fine clothes were ripped and stained. Hatred lit his gaze. Yates forced him to kneel beside the priestess. The reek of the black cells emanated from him. Now Shyla understood why Yates had a torque and the prince didn't when they had all been in the professor's room. He'd been working for the priestess.

The woman grabbed the prince's hair and yanked his head back so he looked up at her. "You're about to witness a historic occasion, whelp," she said. "When I become both priestess and princess of Zirdai." Then she turned to Yates, gesturing to Shyla. "Be careful. Don't damage The Eyes."

"I won't, Mother."

Son of a sand demon! Or, in this case, son of an *insane* demon. If she wasn't in massive trouble, Shyla would have laughed. Instead, tiny barbs of fear dug into her skin. Yates took the scalpel from Timin and approached.

If only she could move or break the magical hold or shut the seers out! Then it hit her. Not shut them out, but close them like a druk! When Mojag had gotten upset as she opened his magic, she had started to reverse the process before he stopped her. In theory, she could close them, but she didn't have any magic to do it.

442

Yates knelt next to her—an all too familiar and horrific situation. So much for The Eyes being so powerful; the seers just had to trap her in a bubble of magic
and—

Seven hells.

There *was* magic. All. Around. Her.

She glanced at the seer, reached with the man's magic
and closed his power with a mighty slam. The man cried
out and crumpled to the ground. Yates paused, glancing
about in confusion. Shyla did three more before the rest
lost their concentration. She could move!

Knocking the scalpel out of Yates' hand, she sat up.

Yates grabbed her. "You're not going anywhere."

She twisted from his grasp and hopped to her feet.
Before he could straighten, she kicked, aiming for the
dark bruise on his temple from Rendor's strike. The heel
of her boot connected with his skull. The force sent her
back a few steps while he only wobbled. She focused all
her magic on him in one powerful blast.

Sleep.

He swayed but fought the command.

Cursing his thick head yet again, she sent another
blast.

Sleep!

Finally, he slumped to the ground. Then she turned
to the rest of the seers.

They held out their hands. "Don't, please. We—"

"You had your chance. You didn't take it. So I will take *your* magic." Or rather, close it. However she called it, it was still harder to do without using their power.

Once she finished, she looked around for the priestess, but the woman was gone and the prince lay on the floor in a pool of his blood. The priestess had sliced his throat open. He stared at her with wide-eyed horror, but Shyla remained in place until he died, bearing witness. No grief touched her over the prince's death. Instead outrage that his demise was too easy gripped her. He should have been stripped naked and hung upside down for a few sun jumps to pay for his crimes.

An insistent banging on the door spurred her into motion. She opened the glass doors. Jaft, Rae, and a bunch of Invisible Swords practically tumbled into the room.

Jaft gaped at the prone forms. "Did you kill them all?"

"No. The priestess killed the prince, the rest are recovering. Come on, everyone, I need backup." She raced to the other entrance.

"For what?" he asked, almost on her heels.

"To hunt down the priestess."

At each intersection, she sent teams of two to each side while she kept straight with the rest. Something pulled her in that direction. This area of the complex was intact, but soon they reached rooms with collapsed walls or holes in the floor.

They rounded a corner and spotted the priestess. She stood on a small pile of debris. In front of her was a large gap where there used to be a floor. The destruction she had caused prevented her from escaping. Shyla took a moment to appreciate the irony.

The priestess turned and stared at Shyla. The fury in her gaze was mild compared to the evil thoughts in her head.

"You will not touch me," the priestess said to Shyla. "You are sun-cursed. *I* am a child of the Sun Goddess and she *will* protect me." She leaped across the gap.

Or rather, she tried. The Sun Goddess did not grant her wings. The priestess fell without a sound. Although, when she hit the bottom, there was a loud thud. Shyla and Jaft rushed to the edge. Perhaps the priestess survived the fall.

The unnatural angle of the woman's neck meant there hadn't been a miracle.

* * *

Shyla returned to the throne room and sent her people to search the entire level and deal with any remaining deacons or Arch Deacons. "Take a couple of wielders with you in case you find seers."

"Seers?" Jaft asked.

"That's what the priestess called her magic wielders."

"Figures. Come along, Seer Rae."

"Stop that right now or I'll make you *believe* sand rats are crawling up your pant leg."

Jaft gulped. "Understood."

Shyla questioned Timin about the survivors. "What did the priestess do to them?"

"She had them all taken to the black cells," he said.

"Do you know if…" She was afraid to ask about Rendor. Because right now she had hope he lived. If she found out otherwise… No. She was not going to imagine a world without Rendor. "How many people were locked up?"

"I don't know who survived. After the explosions, I stumbled from my room and found a couple injured guards and got to work. When the deacons showed up, they dragged me away from my patients and presumably rounded everyone up."

"Are the black cells intact?"

"I've heard there was some damage and deaths. The priestess was very upset to discover Yates had been incarcerated. Now we know why." He shook his head. "Hard to believe that woman had a child. Yates has been working for the prince a long time. She must have had all this planned out before then."

It made sense for the priestess to have spies in the prince's organization. And he probably had people in hers. No organization was safe from traitors. With that thought, Shyla eyed Timin. "Why didn't the priestess lock you up?" she asked him.

"She wanted me close to harvest your eyes when they found your body. She was livid that you were blown up."

He told the truth.

Timin peered at her with curiosity. "How *did* you survive?"

"I'm sun-kissed. The goddess looks out for me."

"Uh-huh." Timin failed to appear convinced of the divine intervention.

Before she could explain what happened, Jaft and the others returned.

"We got them all," Jaft reported. "This level is secure."

"Good job." Shyla called for Mojag.

The boy raced over to her. "Yes?"

"Go to Orla's and get her grandson, Ilan, and his rats."

"His rats?" Confusion creased his face.

"Yes. We need them for a very important game of hide and seek."

"Oh! Got it." He dashed away.

"Now let's go free our people." Shyla rounded up a few guards to carry Yates to the black cells. "Timin, Gurice, Jaft, and Zhek, you're with us."

Timin brought his bag.

Zhek tutted at him. "*I'm* in charge of the injured. You may assist *me*."

The physician didn't react. Probably too tired to argue.

Each member of the group grabbed a trol lantern as they crossed through the various grottos. Cracked tiles now decorated the big spaces. The water fountains either dribbled water, sprayed it, or were completely broken. A number of the stone benches had fragmented into pieces.

They soon descended to level ninety-eight. Half-collapsed walls and a thick layer of grit covered the stone tables that the guards used while on duty. Many of the druks had shattered, but a number glowed with a purple light. However, the trol light they'd brought along was bright enough to show the dried bloodstains, green mold, and black grime that had built up over the circuits.

Shyla's eyes stung with the sharp odor of urine mixed with feces—all part of the punishment.

"It reeks in here," Gurice said, covering her nose.

The deacons who had been guarding the prisoners lay unconscious on the ground. Two of her guards watched over them.

One of them pointed to a pile of rubble on the right. "That wing contained the prince's special rooms and was crushed during the attack. It's underneath our quarters, which collapsed. None of the guards survived." He clenched his fists as anger and sorrow shone in his eyes.

"I'm sorry for your loss." She'd hoped for better news. Then she remembered that the freed prisoners had been recovering in the guards' quarters. She met Gurice's gaze.

Gurice understood her silent question and pressed her lips together, shaking her head sadly. Grief twisted around her stomach and squeezed.

"Can you please unlock the doors to the other wing?" she asked the guard.

The man and his partner moved to open the main metal doors. Two guards from her group joined them to help.

"Dim your lanterns," she ordered everyone. "Those inside have been in complete blackness for at least a sun jump. Some much longer."

The guards formed two units. Each took a tunnel and began unlocking the individual cells. Once the doors were open, the others streamed in, checking for colleagues and loved ones.

Shyla hung back, afraid of what she might find and what she might not find. Her heart pumped extra hard when Titus limped from a cell. Then she spotted Nard, Daksh, and a few more Invisible Swords. All sported cuts and bruises. All disheveled and weak. All stank.

Wazir survived, but he shook his head sadly when she asked about his three family members. "Wrong place. Wrong time."

By this point, each beat of her heart was a painful spasm. Who else had they lost?

"Shyla, I need you," Zhek yelled from a cell way down at the end of the hallway.

She ran on numb feet, the pressure inside her about to burst. Most of the putrid cells were empty. Stopping when she spotted white hair, she paused in the doorway as her heart exploded.

Rendor lay on the ground. His shirt was soaked with blood. His eyes were squeezed shut in pain. And he pressed his hands over his stomach. Blood leaked from between his fingers.

"Hurry, child, and tell this big stubborn fool that you are alive and well," Zhek ordered.

"He doesn't believe you?" she said, joining Zhek.

Rendor opened his eyes and stared at her. But his gaze was unfocused and his brows were smashed together in confusion. "You're…"

"I'm fine." She caressed his cheek. His skin was hot and dry. Too hot.

"No." He shook his head. "You died. I saw…I saw… you fall… The rubble… Gone… I don't…want to live…without you."

"I'm alive, Rendor. I'm here. *We're* here. Let Zhek take care of you."

He stared at her. "I saw… I saw…"

"The wound is infected. No surprise given the conditions in here. Tell him to let me examine it," Zhek said.

Instead, she laced her fingers through his and pulled his hand away. Then she leaned over so they were almost nose to nose. "I'm here. I'm alive." She kept repeating those two phrases as Zhek worked his magic. She desperately hoped they'd gotten here in time.

Rendor passed out during Zhek's administrations.

"It's for the best," Zhek assured her. "He's been stabbed. It's deep, but the blade just missed his stomach."

"Will he live?"

"He's young and strong and stubborn. But if he doesn't want to, then I've no cure for that. You must stay with him and talk to him once we get him to a better and cleaner location."

She recruited a bunch of strong men to help carry Rendor to another room. Zhek led the way and she was about to follow when she noticed Jaft and Rae clinging to each other as if they were fighting a strong wind. Oh no.

"I'll catch up," she said. She approached them. Both had tears in their eyes. Rae sobbed with little hiccups. It could only mean bad news. "Lian? Elek?"

"Both gone," Jaft said. "Crushed in the explosion."

If the priestess wasn't already dead, she'd murder the woman with her bare hands. No, that was too quick a death. She'd leave her on the surface for the Sun Goddess to cook.

* * *

Shyla stayed by Rendor's side, talking to him and including him in the organization of the cleanup and search for survivors. Shyla learned that Yates had challenged Rendor again. They had fought, but Rendor's heart hadn't been in it and Yates stabbed him, winning the match. Yates tossed him into a black cell to either bleed to death or die of infection.

When Zhek's potion wore off, all her aches and pains returned with such force that slamming into a wall would have been softer. All she could do was crawl under the fur with Rendor and pass out. They were in the room that she'd woken in when the Water Prince's guards had captured her the very first time—a lifetime ago.

When she woke, she learned Ximen, Hanif, and Kaveri were still among the missing. Ilan had arrived with his rats to find bodies. They had good news almost right away as Cat Toy found two guards who'd been trapped under the rubble but were still alive. The rescue sent a pulse of energy and hope through the search crews.

The people had rallied and stormed the chapels, freeing the "sinners" and securing the deacons. Shyla would visit each one and assess them all when she had time. But there was one person she made time for—her friend Banqui.

He'd been captured by the Arch Deacons when they'd ambushed the Invisible Sword and forced to work in the chapel on level seventy-one, melting platinum for the torques. While exhausted and malnourished, he was still in better shape than after spending time in the black cells.

Banqui leaned on Timin's arm as the physician escorted him to Shyla's office and sleeping quarters. Banqui grinned when he spotted her, spreading his thin arms wide for a hug. Shyla obliged, hugging her friend and ignoring the sharpness of his bones under her arms. Timin retreated to give them some privacy.

"I knew you'd come for me," he said.

"I knew you had to be in trouble because you promised you wouldn't leave Zirdai without saying goodbye," she reminded him. But the one thing she wouldn't do was tell him that he'd accidentally led the Arch Deacons back to the Invisible Sword's hideout. The man had suffered enough.

"Ah, yes. Your exceptional memory has saved me again." He pulled back to look at her. His good humor faded. His fingers dug into her upper arms. "You... Your... You..."

She pried his hands off before he could draw blood. "Yes, Banqui. Me."

"How... Why... But you...you...*scoffed* at the notion of magic!" The words burst from him.

"I did. I'm sorry I doubted you."

"What changed your mind?"

She gave him a wry smile. "I did my research and was shown irrefutable proof."

He snorted. "Typical." Then he placed a hand on her shoulder. "After all that, The Eyes of Tamburah found the right person to save the city of Zirdai."

"I had help." She gestured to Rendor's prone form. "Lots of help from people willing to give their lives."

"All great leaders do. Thank you."

* * *

After Banqui left, Shyla worked on writing a list of the guards who'd died. A commotion outside her room interrupted her. She was halfway to the door when

453

Hanif and Kaveri burst in followed by a handful of dusty and sweaty people. All celebrating. She was squeezed between the two as tears of joy blurred her vision.

"Where—"

"Trapped in the prince's main office!" Hanif said. "The entrances were blocked. We couldn't get out. No one heard us yelling."

"Or the deacons were ignoring us," Kaveri added grimly.

"Then the rats came and we thought we were done. That we'd die of thirst and become rat food," Hanif said.

Ilan cradled Cat Toy and beamed.

"I can't wait to feel the sun on my face again," Kaveri said, shivering.

"You're going to have to fill in as the interim Heliacal Priestess. That means you'll have a sun ceremony every angle zero," Hanif said.

She brightened until Gurice and Mojag arrived with bad news.

"They found Ximen's body," Gurice said.

Shyla sucked in a breath as pain dug its claws into her stomach and twisted. Hard. Mojag hung his head. The boy looked exhausted. He'd seen too much death in his short life.

"He's the last of the Invisible Swords," Gurice said. "We lost fifteen members plus the twenty-three who'd been captured."

That was too many. There were only thirty-four surviving members. She glanced at Rendor. Would he be number thirty-five?

After everyone left, she continued working on the list of deceased guards. At one hundred and seventy-five, it was considerably longer than the Invisible Swords. And they hadn't dug through all the rubble yet. Twenty-two guards were still unaccounted for and were presumed dead. That left one hundred and three survivors. Seventeen prisoners died, along with a dozen servants. If she included the missing, the total equaled two hundred and sixty-four.

Fatigue and overwhelming grief pressed on her. For Ximen, Elek, Lian, and the others. Its crushing weight made every breath a colossal effort. Heartsick, Shyla hunched over the desk, staring at the names. The Invisible Sword had won. They'd overthrown the Water Prince and Heliacal Priestess and stopped the horrors. So why didn't it feel like they'd won?

Angles later, she dragged her battered and bruised body from the desk to the sleeping cushion. She pulled back the fur and froze.

Rendor stared at her. His gaze was clear and focused. "We have to stop meeting like this."

And just like that, her energy returned in one blazing rush. "I agree." She hugged him. Hard. He grunted in pain but squeezed her back with equal fervor.

"I thought you were a dream," he whispered in her ear. "The floor swallowed you like a mythical sand beast. No one could live through that." He slid his hands along her back as if reassuring himself of her presence. "You're alive."

"I am equally surprised."

"What happened? How—"

Shyla silenced him with a kiss. "I'll tell you the entire saga later. For now, I want to just *be* in this moment. With you."

"I'm all yours."

* * *

They buried the fallen in batches of roughly forty people at a time. Family members gathered, tears were shed, hugs were exchanged, stories told, and festivities were thrown to bid the deceased a fond farewell and best wishes for their next lives with the Sun Goddess. Kaveri officiated the seven mass burials.

Shyla, Rendor, and Hanif attended all the ceremonies. Hanif was anxious for a replacement Water Prince and wished to return to his duties at the monastery. Unlike Kaveri, who had embraced her new role and went from "filling in" to becoming the new Heliacal Priestess.

When all the people had been buried, Shyla focused on her next task. She gathered with Gurice and Jaft— her new seconds—and Rendor.

They sat in a conference room on level ninety-seven. Cleanup and repairs of the water pipes was ongoing, but it would take a few circuits for the complex to be fully restored.

"We need a new Water Prince or Water Princess," Shyla said. "Hanif doesn't want the job. Do you think Orla would be a good choice? Her commune is not only the biggest but the most organized."

No one said anything. They all stared at her. Their gazes rested heavily on her.

Finally Rendor broke the silence. "Shyla, you know who Zirdai needs. Stop procrastinating."

"I've been busy."

"Yes, we know," Gurice said. "Busy procrastinating."

She crossed her arms and pouted. Her own people had turned against her. Well, that was a bit of an exaggeration. And they might have a small point.

The last thing Shyla wanted to do was talk to Jayden, but it appeared she'd run out of options.

CHAPTER

21

It had been thirty-two sun jumps since they'd locked Jayden in the testing chamber in the lower levels of Tamburah's temple. Shyla went alone. An unpleasant odor greeted her first, one that reminded her of the black cells but not nearly as strong. Then she spotted Jayden. He sat with his back leaning on the wall and his forehead resting on his bent knees.

"Are you here to gloat?" He didn't raise his head or attack her with his magic.

She scanned his supplies. A pile of empty water skins rested next to the low table. It had been overturned at some point—perhaps kicked over in anger. Two full skins and a couple rolls of jerky sat on the scrolls, which were as far away from the collection buckets as the chain attached to Jayden's ankle would allow. He'd rationed his supplies. Smart.

The silence stretched. Eventually Jayden glanced at her. His golden-brown hair was lackluster and a straggly beard covered his face. But it was the apathy in his gaze that alarmed her the most. She scanned his thoughts and emotions, reading his soul. He'd given up hope. He'd lost everything. Everyone he'd loved. No one would forgive him.

"I'm not here to gloat," she said.

"But you won, didn't you?"

"At a high cost. Too high to really call it a win."

He shot to his feet. "Mojag?"

Ah, there it was. He still cared about something. "Annoying as ever."

Jayden sagged against the wall. "Gurice?"

"Promoted to one of my seconds."

"Ximen?"

No matter how she worded it, it wouldn't change the fact. "He died."

He straightened as grief and anger blazed to life inside him. "The Water Prince killed him."

Not quite a question. "No, the Heliacal Priestess."

Jayden jerked as if slapped. His mind reeled and guilt twisted. *My fault.*

"Not your fault." She explained about the explosions. "The priestess collected the toxic gases and released clouds of it underneath the prince's complex. All it needed was a spark. We're still not sure how she managed it. And I'm not sure we really want to know the details—it might be tempting for someone else to copy it."

He was horrified.

"Regardless, two hundred and sixty-four people died. All because of her. The priestess who you conspired with."

"I…" He scrubbed a hand through his hair. "I… didn't think she'd do something like *that*."

"No one did."

His shoulders dropped. "Did any other Invisible Sword members die?"

She found it interesting that he didn't ask if the Water Prince or the priestess lived or died. Listing the names, she felt his pain through her magical connection and suffered through her own welling of grief. By the time she finished, he'd returned to his huddled position on the floor.

"I'm sorry," he said finally. "I made so many mistakes."

His emotions matched his words, but Shyla decided to test him. "If given the chance, would you kill the Water Prince?"

His head snapped up. "He's alive?"

"Why are you surprised?"

"The priestess hated him more than I did. I thought she would kill him with her explosions."

And since he didn't know the full story, that would make sense. "No, he still lives."

Jayden's thoughts spun, but that inner fury, which had fueled him to betray her and the Invisible Sword, had died. "No, I wouldn't kill him. Not anymore. For him, living is a punishment. Dying would be too easy." He told the truth. "What happened? I sense you're not telling me the entire story."

"I'm not. Get comfortable, this is going to take a while." She told him what had happened, including all the gritty and terrible details. Keeping her connection to him, she monitored his reactions. They shared a wry grin when she reached the part about her being chained to the floor.

"Wait," he interrupted at one point. "Why did you tell me the prince was alive?"

She kept quiet and let him figure it out.

"To see my reaction? Because..." He pulled at his beard. "Because of what I did. My desire to kill him clouded all reason, and you wanted to see if I still had the same blind desire."

"Yes. And I can tell even the news of his death has not given you the sense of satisfaction that you sought. Nor the peace you hoped for."

"My sister's still dead. And, like I said, being locked in a black cell would have been a really good punishment for him."

She agreed. "Well, he did spend some time in there." Shyla continued her tale. "And now we're looking for a new Water Prince or Princess," she concluded.

Jayden sat there, absorbing all the information. "Why not you?"

"I have a job."

"Then I'd say Orla would be best."

"We thought she'd be second best. We've another candidate in mind."

"Who?"

"Mojag."

"Mojag? Are you serious?"

"No. I'm kidding."

He smiled—the first genuine smile since his betrayal was exposed. "Can you imagine Mojag in charge?"

"I can. It would be—"

"Fun?"

"I was going to say chaotic, but there certainly would be an element of fun. However, we're considering you for the position."

Jayden opened his mouth and closed it several times. "Wait. Did you say *me*?"

"Yes."

Stunned silence. "Are you insane?"

She huffed. "Why does everyone keep asking me that?"

"Because you tend to do things that are not—"

"Careful," she warned.

"Conventional. And I'm…"

"You're?"

"Damaged, broken, untrustworthy. I betrayed you to the priestess, even knowing that she would kill you. How can you ever forgive me?"

"Do you want forgiveness?"

He paused as he did some soul searching. She waited.

"Yes," he said. It was the truth. "I do. But it's too much to ask of you. Of anyone." His thoughts turned to Mojag.

"As for me, Hanif reminded me that people are capable of changing should they choose to make the effort. And I'd be a hypocrite if I could forgive Rendor's past and not yours. He does have the genuine desire to make amends, and I've been reading your soul this entire time so—"

"You have? I didn't feel it."

"My skills have improved. Desperation is a great teacher, although I wouldn't recommend it." She shuddered at her two close calls. "Regardless, do you wish to make amends?"

"Of course I do." He was surprised by his own vehemence.

"Before we offer you the job, you have to agree to some conditions."

"What are they?"

"First, no more black cells. We're going to rebuild the prison, but it'll have light, and collection stations, and the inmates will help with the city's maintenance unless the prisoner is really dangerous."

"That's a good idea. I agree."

"Second, no more vagrants. They will become a legitimate part of the city. For those who can't afford the taxes or tithes, there will be a system in place to help them find a better job. And children under two circuits old will be exempt from both." They'd finally located the mother of the baby the Arch Deacons had used as bait. As Orla had predicted, the woman couldn't afford to raise a child, but she'd believed the baby was going to be raised in one of the chapels.

"I'm all for that."

No surprise—he was the Vagrant Prince after all. And a part of the bargain he'd made with the priestess included helping them.

"Third, the guards are there to protect the people, not police them. They're to be called protectors."

"All right."

"Fourth, all the artifacts and treasures that the Water Prince collected are to be put on public display and made accessible to the historians. Banqui has officially retired, so you might want to consider hiring Aphra as your chief archeologist, but that's just a recommendation, not a condition."

"I agree to the museum. And she's hired." He swallowed. *If she wants to work for me.*

"You're going to have to get over that," Shyla said.

"Over what?"

"That internal cringing and worrying about whether people will forgive you or not. Just sincerely apologize once and show them by your actions that your intentions are genuine. It's up to them to forgive you. If they don't, then move on. You can't force it."

"In some cases, moving on will be hard." Again his thoughts lingered on Mojag.

"No doubt, but nothing about your situation is going to be easy. In fact, this last condition might be a deal breaker."

"Go on."

"Because you're a magic wielder, you have an unfair advantage over the citizens of Zirdai."

"You don't want me to use my magic?" His confusion was clear.

"Yes."

"But I don't think I can stop…it's a part of me. And I'll need it to defend myself—not everyone is going to be happy I'm the new prince. Plus, I think my magic will make me a better leader."

"We don't. And you'll have protectors to defend you."

He grappled with the implications. "But I can't just… turn it off."

"You can't. But I can."

He stared at her with a growing horror. "You can do *what* exactly?"

She explained about closing the power in the seers.

"But you haven't done it for someone like me! I wasn't cracked and pulled open like the others."

"True. You'll be my first attempt."

"Your first attempt!" His voice was shrill. Jayden took a few deep breaths. "What if you can't do it?"

"Then you'll still have your magic. But you can't be the Water Prince. You have to decide if you want me to close your magic or not."

"And if I choose my magic? Then what happens to me?"

"You can return to the Invisible Sword. We plan to operate separately from the city like the monks do. Helping out if needed and keeping a close eye on the new Water Prince and Heliacal Priestess so we don't have this problem again. Aphra also plans to consult with me on future dig sites." Shyla was looking forward to that collaboration—to be lost in her maps and research again would be a slice of bliss.

"If I rejoin the Invisible Sword, you'd be able to keep a close eye on me, too."

"That's the idea. It'll take some time for everyone to trust you again. As you know from Rendor's reception, my word isn't good enough. You have to prove yourself to them."

"Can I have some time to think it over?"

"Yes, but not much. We need to fill the position or risk one of the wealthy citizens taking it. I'll be back in a sun jump."

"No, please don't leave me here."

Shyla remembered when she'd been trapped down here and it was for twelve sun jumps, not thirty-two like Jayden.

"You've read my soul, you know I've nowhere else to go."

True, and if he saw the destruction the Heliacal Priestess caused, it might help him with his decision. She pulled the key to the cuff around Jayden's ankle from her pocket.

"Don't try anything, or I won't pull my punches this time," she said as she moved closer to him.

"Of all your skills, your fists are the least of my worries," he said with a grin. "Don't forget, I've a hard head."

"I didn't forget. My elbow still hurts," she mock-grumbled as she freed him from the chain. Shyla braced for his reaction, but he only rubbed the raw flesh around his ankle.

Then he straightened and said, "Where to?"

"Where else? Level ninety-seven."

She led him through the city. Keeping to the edges out of habit, she wondered when she'd be comfortable in crowded, public places. Perhaps never, or perhaps when the people embraced their new sun-kissed priestess.

Only two guards watched the entrance to the complex.

"Any trouble?" she asked them.

"A contingent of elders from the wealthy families has demanded to speak to the person in charge," the man on the left reported.

That didn't take long. "What did you do?"

"We reported it to Captain Rendor, and he escorted them to Hanif."

"How long ago?"

"Ten, maybe twelve angles."

"Thanks."

She hurried through the door with Jayden right behind her. The meeting would not go well and she needed to be there to help Hanif. But where should she take Jayden? Perhaps Gurice was in their conference room. Shyla spotted Mojag instead.

"Mojag," she called.

He turned and froze when he spotted Jayden.

"Hi, Mojag," Jayden said.

Ignoring Jayden, Mojag gazed at her, his expression as hard as stone. "Do you need something, Shyla?" His words were clipped with anger. Mojag had been the only one who disagreed about Jayden.

Oh boy. "Can you take Jayden to one of the empty guest suites? I need to rescue Hanif from a bunch of entitled elitists."

"That traitor is dead. Excuse me, but my darling sister has assigned me to rubble cleanup duty." He left without glancing at Jayden.

Wow. She didn't need to read Jayden's soul to know that Mojag's comment had to hurt him like a knife thrust into his heart.

"That's—"

"All my fault," Jayden said, staring at Mojag's retreating form. "And something I'm going to have to get used to." He turned to her. "Do you have someplace I can get cleaned up? I'm going to join that meeting."

"Does this mean you've made your decision?"

"Yes. I'll sacrifice my magic to become the Water Prince of Zirdai."

"I thought you needed time to think about it."

"I'm doing it for Mojag."

"He might never forgive you."

"I know, but if I do my very best as the prince, then maybe in the future I can forgive myself."

"All right." She led him to one of the empty guest suites. "There's a water closet you can use. They just fixed the pipes."

He nodded. And Shyla took note of his bedraggled clothing. That wouldn't do for a prince. She flagged down one of the staff—they were no longer called servants—and asked about clean clothes for Jayden. The young woman said she knew just the thing and dashed off.

By the time Jayden had shaved and scrubbed the grime from his body, the lady returned with a red tunic and black pants made from expensive silk. The pants were a little big, but overall the clothing fit well.

"They were the prince's," she said before leaving.

Jayden and Shyla glanced at each other.

"That's a very good sign," Shyla said.

He laughed. "Since when do you believe in signs?"

"Since I survived an explosion. Come on."

They reached Hanif's temporary office, which had been the prince's main place to do business. Two piles of rubble framed the entrance, which was just big enough for one person to cross. Jayden paused, peering at them.

"This is nothing in comparison to the rest," she said. "No one died here."

He smoothed his tunic. "Two hundred and sixty-four."

"They should never be forgotten."

"They won't be."

Inside the room an angry male voice rose. "Which is *why* we can't leave the running of *our* city in the hands of an amateur."

"That's my cue." Jayden straightened his shoulders and entered the room. "I can assure you the city won't be run by an amateur," he said.

Shyla slipped in. About twenty unhappy people sat around the large conference table. Hanif sat on the far end—literally cross-legged on the tabletop with a serene expression on his face, which no doubt infuriated the elders. Rendor stood along the wall with a couple armed protectors. Something about his posture worried Shyla. Did he think these people would riot?

"Who in the seven hells are you?" the same querulous voice asked.

"I am the new Water Prince."

Jayden's declaration caused an immediate reaction. And, for a moment, Shyla thought being in the middle of a cave-in was quieter. Hanif grinned at Shyla and left the room, leaving Jayden in charge. Shyla stood next to Rendor in case Jayden used magic to defuse the situation.

However, using the skills he learned over the years with the communes and the Invisible Sword, the Vagrant Prince transformed into the Water Prince. Hanif was bound to gloat the next time they were together. While Jayden took control of the meeting, Shyla scanned the "guests" with her magic. No one said *she* couldn't.

Anger, confusion, frustration, greed, and disbelief rolled through them, but nothing dangerous. At least, not yet. Jayden would have to watch his back. Two faces seemed familiar—a young man and his father, their resemblance unmistakable. When the young man glanced at Rendor for the third time, she remembered.

Hastin! Rendor's older brother. No wonder Rendor was so tense. She laced her fingers with his and gave him an encouraging squeeze. He glanced at her and then visibly relaxed before giving her a squeeze back and releasing her hand. She wasn't offended—she knew he needed to be ready just in case violence broke out. It didn't, but a number of poisonous looks were aimed at Jayden as the elders left. Rendor and his men escorted them out.

"You still have a long way to go," she said to Jayden.

"No kidding." He looked at her as if in pain. "Are you going to take my magic now?"

"No. I think that should be done in front of everyone."

Alarmed, he asked, "The entire city?"

"No, just the Invisible Swords, Hanif, Kaveri, and the protectors."

"Do all the protectors know about wielders?"

"Yes. When Rendor recruited them to our side, he told them. When he was the captain of the Water Prince's guards, he always told them what was going on if he could. That's why they trusted him more than Yates."

"Isn't Rendor still the captain?"

"He's *my* captain, not yours. You'll have to find your own."

Jayden was thoughtful. "Perhaps he'll have some recommendations for me."

"I'm sure he will."

* * *

After a time was set for Jayden's unofficial coronation—the official one would be when the King's emissary arrived—Shyla returned to her room. Rendor was already there. He worked at the desk, assigning shifts. Another thing Jayden would need to do was recruit more protectors.

She told him about the plans for Jayden and mentioned that he would be asking for recommendations, but Rendor was distracted and closed off, reminding her of when she'd first met him. And she didn't need to read his emotions to know something was bothering him. She only needed one guess to figure out what.

"Time for a break," she said.

"I need to get this done," he said, writing team names.

"It wasn't a suggestion." This time her voice was firm.

"Huh?" Rendor barely glanced at her. "Just a couple more—"

"*Captain*, take a break."

She had his full attention. Fun. However, his scowl wasn't as fun. Shyla took his hands in hers. "Do you really care what they think?"

"What are you talking about?"

"Your family. Is it important to you that they change their opinions about you?"

He studied her for a few moments. "Are you offering to use your magic?"

"No, but I'm offering you my support if you want to talk to them."

"They're not my family. They disowned me." The words came out flat and emotionless as if he'd repeated this to himself so many times it no longer hurt to say it.

"There's been a lot of changes. You've changed the most. Plus it's a new era. And you're no longer working for the prince, but for me."

He laughed without humor. "I doubt they'd think that was an improvement."

"Insult aside, let me ask you again. Do you really care what they think?"

He bent his head and stared at their clasped hands. Shyla waited as he sorted through his emotions. But before he could reply, Mojag and Gurice poked their heads into the room.

"Are you ready, Rendor?" Gurice asked. "This little sand rat's driving me crazy."

"Sand rat? You're just mad I disarmed you in five moves," Mojag said.

"Disarmed?" Shyla asked Gurice.

"Yeah, we're both learning how to fight with a sword."

"And some of us are quicker to learn," Mojag added with a smirk.

Shyla glanced at Rendor. He peered at the pair as if seeing them for the first time.

"Uh, Rendor, are you coming? Can't have a lesson without the instructor," Gurice said.

"I'll meet you there in a couple angles. Try not to settle any sibling rivalries with the practice swords before I get there."

"No promises. Come on, rat." Gurice pulled Mojag from the room.

Shyla crossed her arms. "You have to answer my question about your family before you can leave."

"They're not my family."

"You said that."

"Yes, but this time I believe it. Why would I care what they think? They're not my family." He pulled her closer. "My family is you and the Invisible Swords."

She leaned forward so her nose almost touched his. "What a coincidence, they're my family, too."

"And me?"

"You're just mine."

* * *

They assembled in the training room. It was the only space big enough for the one hundred and three protectors, thirty-five Invisible Swords, one monk, the Heliacal Priestess, and the interim Water Prince. If this didn't work, they'd need to find another interim prince or princess.

Jayden stood in the front with Shyla. There was a bucket of sand between them. She'd explained to the crowd that Jayden had voluntarily agreed to give up his magic. And then added the disclaimer that this might not work. Gurice gave them both an encouraging thumbs-up. She was sitting in the front with Rendor and a number of the Invisible Swords who knew Jayden. Mojag was as far away as physically possible and his back was turned toward them. If Shyla hadn't ordered him, he wouldn't be here at all.

"Ready?" she asked Jayden.

"No, but I doubt I'll ever be ready." He took a deep breath. "Please continue."

"Use your magic to move the sand."

Jayden stared at the bucket. Grains of sand rose into the air. They converged and formed a young woman around Shyla's age made of sand. Murmurs raced through the crowd at the display. Most of the protectors hadn't seen magic in action. The sound piqued Mojag's interest and he glanced over his shoulder. The sand woman smiled at the boy.

"Is that your sister?" Shyla asked Jayden.

"Yes. Beautiful, isn't she?"

"She is."

"This is how I'll always remember her. I thought she'd be perfect for my last sculpture."

"She is." Shyla focused on him.

Jayden's entire body glowed with magic. Not like an open druk lantern at all. Head to toe, he was filled. When she tried to close it, the power found a way to escape; it was like trying to put too much water into a skin. She needed to switch tactics. If she couldn't squash it, perhaps she could drain it. Shyla tugged on his magic, pulling it from him like unraveling a ball of yarn.

He hunched over with a grunt of pain. The sculpture began losing shape as the grains fell back into the bucket. Then he cried out and went down on his knees as Shyla collected more and more of his power. While she had access to his mind, she erased his memories of the location of the Invisible Sword's headquarters and the tunnel they were building to connect it to Zirdai. If Jayden turned into another despot—doubtful, but better to be safe—she didn't want him knowing where to find them.

When she ripped the last thread from his soul, he screamed and the ball of magic in her hands exploded. The invisible blast sent her flying across the room while Jayden was pushed in the opposite direction.

She had no memory of hitting the floor.

* * *

Rendor was next to her when she woke. Everyone was on their feet and glancing between her and Jayden.

"How is he?" she asked.

"Like you, knocked out." He helped her sit up. "Zhek says he should be fine."

"Did it work?" Gurice asked.

"Give her some time," Rendor snapped.

"It's okay." She stood but grabbed Rendor's arm for support. Thankfully, he kept quiet as he assisted her over to Jayden.

Jayden was still sitting on the floor. He rubbed his chest absently. "I feel empty."

"Can you move the sand?" she asked.

He stared at the bucket. Nothing happened. No glow inside him. Shyla thought she was going to be sick. How could she do that to another person? Turning away to avoid his reaction, she said, "It worked."

477

As Rendor guided her from the room, they passed Mojag. He was staring at Jayden as if he'd never seen him before. It was better than anger. They didn't get far before Shyla sagged against Rendor.

"Should I find Zhek?" he asked, scooping her up.

"It's not something he can cure." She snuggled against his warm, broad chest. "Take me home please."

* * *

The King's emissary arrived two hundred sun jumps after the defeat. Shyla decided that "defeat" was the best way to describe the events leading up to the deaths of the Water Prince and Heliacal Priestess. By then, Jayden was working hard to enact all the conditions he'd promised. And Kaveri had fully embraced her new role. She'd banned the green robes because the people no longer trusted the green anymore. Too many bad memories. They all wore yellow tunics and pants instead.

Hanif was back at the monastery, but he frequently visited the priestess. And the Invisible Swords had returned to the Temple of Arinna. They'd made progress in cleaning out the temple and finished the hidden tunnel into Zirdai. Best of all, in her and Rendor's new room was the biggest, thickest, softest sleeping cushion she could buy.

The emissary interviewed almost everyone involved with the defeat. He spent half a dozen sun jumps inspecting the destruction and visiting all the chapels in Zirdai. Gurice said he even talked to the university's professors.

However, he didn't question Shyla. In fact, he actively avoided her, which was odd. Did he think she'd lie to him? Or was he one of those people who believed sunkisseds should be sacrificed to the Sun Goddess? His strange behavior caused worry to simmer in her guts.

Everyone agreed they wouldn't mention magic or that The Eyes were anything but priceless artifacts that caused the prince and priestess to go to war. They did inform him about the role of the Invisible Swords in the defeat. History was on their side. Yet the King was known to be alarmed by groups like theirs. He feared being overthrown, which was why he had amassed such a large and well-trained army.

Would he consider Shyla dangerous to his rule? He shouldn't. She'd refused to become Zirdai's Water Princess. But Jayden had told her the emissary didn't seem to believe him when he explained why Shyla turned down the role. Did the emissary think she had her sights on the King's job? Why not just ask her?

Everyone released a huge sigh of relief once the emissary concluded that all the events they had reported to the King had been truthful and necessary. He officially approved the appointment of the new Water Prince and Heliacal Priestess. There would be a ceremony and citywide celebration the next sun jump.

A few angles before the event, Shyla dressed in a new tunic and pants. She decided to leave her wrap behind. Rendor looked…damn fine in his clothes. Too fine.

She yanked on his shirt. "We really don't need to go. I think we should stay here and…snuggle."

He stilled her hands. "We have all the time to snuggle. This is an important occasion. One we worked very hard to bring about."

Rendor was right. And it was a lovely ceremony. Jayden looked handsome and regal and quite smitten with Aphra, his new archeologist. Kaveri shone almost as bright as the sun.

During the party afterward, someone tapped on her shoulder. Shyla turned to face the King's emissary.

"Are you Shyla Sun-Kissed?" he asked as if he hadn't been avoiding her all this time.

Strange. No one had used that name in a long time. "Yes."

He handed her a thin scroll sealed with wax.

"What's this?"

"You've been summoned to appear before the King of Koraha."

*Don't miss the final instalment in the
Archives of the Invisible Sword series*

THE KING OF KORAHA

Coming December 2021

ACKNOWLEDGMENTS

In the acknowledgments of my last book, *Chasing the Shadows*, I wondered if any of my readers read the acknowledgments of books. The answer was a resounding yes! And many of my readers appreciated my Acknowledgment Quiz. So in that same spirit, I give you an Acknowledgment Word Search! You will find all the names of those who have helped me make this story better, and those that provided love, support, and wine. A gigantic THANK YOU to all of you!!

```
E  H  G  Y  M  E  M  A  Q  E  S  Z  L  S  K
L  A  A  H  V  I  I  V  N  A  L  U  Q  R  R
O  R  N  T  T  L  C  N  M  N  R  L  I  E  M
I  Y  U  A  C  A  H  S  M  V  A  S  E  L  X
S  M  D  K  W  T  E  A  O  R  T  H  E  E  D
E  K  B  N  A  A  L  S  L  I  O  A  O  C  J
O  X  C  N  I  N  L  P  A  T  H  D  O  J  E
M  O  N  Z  Y  M  E  N  U  C  N  T  N  E  F
R  E  E  M  A  B  N  I  A  A  K  W  Y  E  F
J  B  M  Y  U  H  V  R  M  G  I  R  O  G  Y
R  Q  A  E  F  N  I  E  T  I  N  E  U  R  O
F  O  C  L  F  S  S  K  L  V  K  Z  V  K  O
Y  M  I  C  A  E  L  A  A  I  L  U  J  Z  G
L  G  M  X  N  I  P  T  N  U  A  C  T  N  V
D  T  U  P  I  Z  L  E  B  A  N  N  A  Y  X
```

NAMES:

ANNABEL	JOHANNA	MICHELLE	RODNEY
ELLE	JULIA	MINDY	SAM
ELOISE	KATHY	NATALIE	
JEFF	KRISTIAN	RACHAEL	
JENNA	MICAELA	REEMA	

Turn over for a sneak peek.

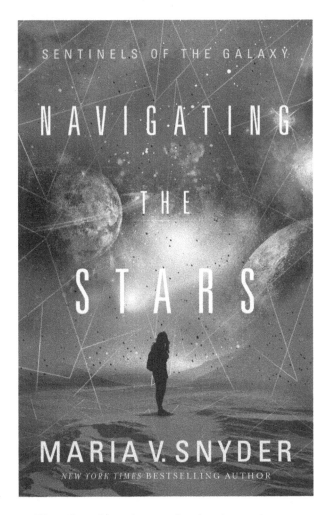

The first instalment in the brand new
science fiction series
Sentinels of the Galaxy

CHAPTER

1

2471:333

"The answer is no, Lyra." My mother utters her favorite—I swear—phrase.

"But—"

"End of discussion."

Arguing is usually futile. But I'm not about to give up. Not this time.

We are having dinner in our housing unit. I'm picking at my reconstituted mashed potatoes, wilted broccoli and mystery protein…er…meat…while my dad scans his list of packing supplies on his portable, only half-listening to my mother's efforts to convince me that traveling to the new planet will be a grand adventure.

"Besides," Mom says, almost breathless. "We'll be the *first* archaeologists to assess the discovery. This new site on Planet Yulin has the potential to explain *who* transported the Terracotta Warriors to twenty-two different planets. We're getting close to an answer."

I gotta admit, my parents are the experts with a capital E on the life-sized Warriors. It's why they've been asked to relocate to the new planet. As for finding an answer to one of the Galaxy's great mysteries, I'm not as confident.

"Think about it, Lyra," Mom continues. "Over two million Warriors were custom-made on Earth by ancient Chinese craftsmen and transported by an unknown alien race to other worlds. We're bound to find evidence of who they were—or are—and why they used Earth's clay and people to create the Warriors. Why not make their own?"

Dad looks up. "The clay's from Earth, but there's no evidence they were made *on* Earth."

"The Chinese calligraphy on them is all the evidence you need," Mom retorts and they launch into an all-too-familiar debate.

I tune them out. Too bad the archaeologists don't know why the aliens needed all those Warriors through-out the Galaxy. Since we've yet to discover any other alien artifacts or sentient beings, we don't have anyone to ask.

And this recent discovery is all the way out on the edge of Explored Space. Yeah, you gotta say it with those capital letters since it's such a big deal that we've traveled so far from Earth. But what really boggles the mind is we're still in the Milky Way Galaxy. Space is big. Really big.

When my parents finish, it's my turn. I ensure they are both paying attention by clearing my throat. Loudly.

In a reasonable tone, I say, "It's exciting that you have a new site to research. You'll have all the top scientists eager to explore with you so you don't need me. I can remain here while you travel to Yulin. After all, I'm seventeen Actual years old—only a mere A-year until I'm of legal age."

Mom bangs her fork on the table. "I said end—"

I keep right on going. "Staying on planet Xinji, I'll be closer to the university—onsite learning is much more effective than distance. Dr. Wendland's research on learning strategies has proven it. And Lan's parents have already agreed to let me stay with them."

Mom and Dad exchange a look, which means they are doing that silent communication thing that parents do. I study them while I wait, sitting on the edge of my seat and resisting the urge to jiggle my leg with nervous energy.

My dad runs a big hand through his short sandy-brown hair, making it stick up at various angles. He normally appears younger than his forty-six A-years, but a sadness pulls on his face, aging him. "We're going to lose her in a couple A-years anyway, maybe we should consider her—"

"Absolutely not." Mom's brown-eyed gaze focuses on my father with such intensity, I'm surprised he doesn't burst into flames. Even though she is younger than my father by two A-years, my mother is in charge of our family. "I can't…not so soon after…Phoenix."

Before you ask, yes, my parents named me and my brother after constellations. Kinda funny considering we can't see either of those constellations unless we're on Earth, which, by the way, neither of us was born on. My parents have some really strange ideas at times.

The mention of Phoenix effectively kills any support I might have gotten from my father. He ducks his head and I wilt.

"Don't ask again," Mom says in the I've-decided-and-nothing-will-change-my-mind tone.

It's not fair, but arguing is pointless and will result in me cataloging thousands of broken Warrior shards as punishment. Appetite ruined, I push my now cold food away and head to my bedroom.

"Li—" my father calls after me.

I keep going. Our unit is small and narrow with a kitchen, common room, two bedrooms and the washroom. Not much space is allocated for housing in the base. The majority of the place is occupied by the scientists' labs, which is where most of the people living here spend all of their time anyway. We aren't a colony, but a research facility charged with assessing the entire planet. The base is filled with chemists, biologists, geologists, physicists, astrophysicists, meteorologists… Pick any "ologist" you can think of and they're probably here, including archaeologists like my parents.

And those ologists have been drooling happy since the announcement of the New Discovery. As for me? Not so much. While they've been talking in excited, high-pitched voices and making plans for the trip, I've been dreading launch day. Don't get me wrong, I'm glad for my parents. They've dedicated their lives to puzzling out this great Warrior mystery and I've no doubt that they'll eventually solve it.

Well…maybe a little doubt.

However, I'm tired of leaving my friends behind and I need to find my own passion. Not sure what that is yet, but I'm pretty sure it doesn't include researching ancient artifacts.

* * *

My room consists of a narrow bed, a few drawers, a desk, a chair, a screen and a terminal to access the Quantum net…well, a fraction of it—it's like being confined to the shallow end of the pool—very frustrating.

When the Quantum net—Q-net—was invented back in 2066, it changed everything. Earth's technology advanced at a sizzling pace, and inventions like the Crinkler engine, which allows us to travel through space super fast, were designed using the Q-net. Now it's used to keep track of…well, everything, but it's most important for knowing the precise location (and time) of all the space ships. Oh, and all the information collected from all the planets is stored within its amazing vastness.

But admittance to this scientific wonder is limited. Since I'm underage, I'm allowed to access the school programs, game programs, entertainment, and communications. At least the Q-net is able to send text-based communications between planets in Actual time. Can you imagine waiting decades for a reply?

I flop onto my bed and stare at the images of my friends from the other planets my parents dragged me to before Xinji. They fill the screen. The reality of space travel—the dreaded time dilation—stares back at me. Many of my friends have died of old age by now, and my two friends from our last assignment on Planet Wu'an are now in their fifties. Thanks, Einstein.

A musical ping sounds. The images fade into the background as the screen displays an incoming communication from a Miss Lan Maddrey.

"Accept," I say.

The words disappear and my best friend's face appears.

"What did they say?" Lan asks, but she notices my morose expression. "Oh, sorry, Li-Li!"

Only my father and closest of close friends call me that. I used to love pandas, okay? My father thought it was cute and that's how I got the nickname.

Her eyebrows smash together and furrow her brow. "Did you tell them about Dr. Wendland's research? I can send them the Q-cluster location to the paper. And my parents—"

"Won't matter," I say.

"Did your mother utter the three dreaded words?" she asks.

"Yes."

We share a moment of silence. Lan's blue eyes shine more than normal as she nibbles on the blond hair at the end of her French braid. She's fifteen, but soon to be sixteen—a little over a year younger than me, but we bonded over our mutual love of Diamond Rockler—the greatest singer in the Galaxy. Our only disagreement was over who he was going to marry, me or Lan, and that was three A-years ago. I wouldn't have gotten so close to her except my parents assured me that this was their last assignment. Sigh.

"My brother works for the port," Lan says. "You can sneak off the shuttle and he'll hide you until it takes off. By the time they discover you're missing, they can't return."

An interesting idea. My heart races with the possibilities. I could start my own life. I hope to attend Brighton University on Planet Rho, a mere four Earth-years away. We measure distance between planets by how much E-time passes while you're traveling, not by how many

Actual years pass. Which means if I stay here, I'll be fifty A-years older when my parents arrive at Yulin, but they'll only be ninety days older. Crazy right?

Regardless, I'd never see my parents again, which is why they won't leave me behind. Not yet anyway. They're still grieving over Phoenix and hoping I'll catch the science bug and stay with them, but I am tired of hanging around ancient things that have been buried for thousands of E-years. My excitement over running away fades.

"Thanks, Lan, but I can't do that to my parents."

She nods and gives me a watery smile. "I understand." She heaves a sigh, then lowers her voice. "When should we plan your..." Lan hesitates. "You-know-what."

I glance at my door. It's closed, but I sit at my desk and insert the entanglers into my ears—they resemble little round plugs, but they allow me to link directly to the Q-net through the terminal. Then I engage the privacy mode. If my parents walk into my room, they'd see a blank screen, but I can still see and hear Lan—another super cool invention courtesy of the Q-net.

How about at my last required soch-time? Do you think Jarren can fool the snoops? I think.

Of course. Who do you think created the dead zone in the back corner of the supply bay?

I laugh. *You mean the kissing zone? I heard Jarren took Belle there for a smooch fest.*

He did not! Lan's cheeks turn pink.

Oh? Do you have better intel?

Shut up.

A knock at my door prevents me from replying. Lan says good-bye and I disconnect and return to my flopped position on the bed. I might be resigned to leaving, but that doesn't mean I'll let my parents off easy. "Display wall art," I say to the screen. Only when it once again shows images of my old friends, do I say, "Come in."

Dad pokes his head inside as if expecting to be ambushed. "Is it safe?"

I huff. My temper isn't that bad. Well…not since I was seven A-years. "Only if you brought something sweet."

He holds his hand out, revealing a plate of chocolate chip cookies. A warm sugary scent wafts off them— fresh baked! My empty stomach groans in appreciation.

"Then it's safe." I'm not above bribery.

He enters and sets the plate down on my desk. He has a box tucked under his right arm. "You okay?"

"I'm gonna have to be. Right? Unless you're here to tell me you changed your mind?" I sit up at the thought.

"Sorry, Li-Li. We're not ready to lose you." My father hunches over slightly as grief flares in his brown eyes.

My older brother decided to leave for Earth two years ago when he turned eighteen A-years. Earth is about ninety-five E-years away. So by the time Phoenix arrives on Earth, we will all be dead and Phoenix will still be eighteen.

Guilt over my earlier snit burns in my stomach.

"You just have to go on one more assignment with us, then you can decide what you want to do," Dad says.

"It's all right." I gesture to the box. "What's in there?"

He sets it down on my desk. "A puzzle."

I've fallen for that before. "Are you sure it isn't a bunch of random rubble?"

"No. We think we have all the pieces, but my assistant swears no one can possibly put it back together." He raises a slender eyebrow.

Appealing to my ego, he knows me so well. "Let's see."

Dad opens the box and pours out what appears to be shards of pottery—all terracotta, ranging in sizes from a thumbnail to six centimeters. I scan the pieces. They'd once formed a specific shape, and I can already see it has edges. Could be a piece of armor. Or a shield. Intrigued, I sort through the fragments, flipping them over and matching colors.

My father hands me the adhesive. "I'll let you prove Gavin wrong." He pulls my straight black hair back behind my shoulders and plants a kiss on my temple. "Thanks, Li-Li."

"Uh huh." The air pulses as he leaves. I arrange the pieces—about a thousand or so. There are markings on most of them. Odd. I group the ones that appear similar together. Reconstructing artifacts is actually fun. Not I-want-to-do-this-for-the-rest-of-my-life fun, but challenging and satisfying to make something whole again.

No one was more surprised than I. Trust me. I was roped into helping my parents a few years ago when they noticed that, after attending my required socialization time, or rather soch-time, and doing my school lessons, I had plenty of free time. I argued there was a reason it was called "free." It went over as well as my bid to stay on Xinji.

I was assigned all the chores no one else wanted to do, like sweeping and running the 3D digitizers—each of the thousands of Warriors has to be scanned and cataloged. But one night I found a half-finished reconstruction of a face and, well, I finished it in a couple hours. My parents made a big deal about it and now when there's a jumble of fragments that is declared "impossible" by the team, it comes to me. Not that I'm that great. There have been plenty of boxes filled with bits that I couldn't get to go together. A 3D digitizer could do it in minutes, but we only have four so using them for repairing broken pottery is not the priority.

This piece is tricky. Usually once I connect the edges, the rest is easier to match. But the shape is…octangular? Strange. Lan messages me while I'm working.

"It's all set," she says. "All our friends have been informed." Her voice is heavy with dismay.

I glance at her. "Thanks."

There's an awkward silence.

"What's that?" she asks.

"At this point, I've no idea."

"No. The markings on it."

I peer at the symbols etched into it. Silver lines the grooves so they stand out from the reddish orange clay. Lan should recognize them. Her parents are the base's language experts and cryptologists. While life-sized and made of terracotta, the extraterrestrial Warriors have quite a few differences from those discovered in China. One is they are covered with alien symbols that no one has been able to translate.

"Uh…it's Chinese calligraphy. Probably the name of the craftsman who built it."

"That's not Chinese."

"Are you sure?"

"Lyra." Her flat tone indicates she's insulted.

"Okay, okay. So it's one of those other alien symbols." She shrugs. "I haven't seen markings like those before."

"Well consider two million Warriors with what… sixty some markings per Warrior, makes that…" Ugh, I suck at math.

"The symbols are not all unique. And they still haven't cataloged them all."

"Don't give my mother any ideas," I say, pressing my hand to my chest in mock horror. But the reality is that with limited funds, personnel and equipment, the Warrior Project is a slow-moving beast.

Lan laughs. I'm gonna miss that light trill.

"Seriously, Li-Li. It's different. It might be important."

"Important enough to keep my parents on Xinji?" Hope bubbles up my throat.

Lan straightens with enthusiasm. "Maybe. When you finish it, bring it to my mom."

"Will do."

It takes me the rest of the night to complete the piece. I'm not exaggerating. The faint smell of coffee wafts under my door as my parents get ready for their day. I stare at the…shield—for lack of a better word—because it's a meter wide and a meter long, three centimeters thick and octagonal (of course—the aliens have a serious addiction to the shape…maybe they are sentient octagons? Hmmm).

The shield has a spiderweb of fine cracks and a few fragments missing here and there—standard for reconstructed objects, but the eight rows of markings are clear. Each row has eight different symbols, but they appear to be similar—like they're siblings, with similar swoops or curls. Then another row also has eight unique glyphs that complement each other—sorry, it's hard to explain. But one row looks like Chinese calligraphy, but I'm not sure.

What I'm certain of is, I've been living on Warrior planets all my life, but I've never seen anything like this before. Excited, I rush out to get my dad. He's sitting at the table, sipping coffee and reading from his portable. My mother is at the counter.

Dad spots me. "You're up early."

"Come on." I tug on his hand. "You have to see this!"

He follows me to my room.

Mom trails after us. "Lyra, did you stay up all night?"

Her tone is disapproving so I don't answer her. Instead, I sweep my hands toward the octagon with a flourish. "Ta da!"

Both my parents gape at it in stunned silence for a solid minute. My father reaches toward it, but I stop him.

"It's not dry."

He snatches his arm back as if he's been burned. When my parents still don't say anything, I say, "This is important. Right? Something different?"

The silence stretches. Now it's getting weird.

"Yes," my mother says finally. "Different."

"Lan said her mom, Dr. Maddrey, would want to see it."

"Oh, yes," my dad says. His voice is rough. "I expect there will be *lots* of people who would want to see this."

* * *

There is a great deal of excitement from the scientists in our base over the strange object with the rows of markings. Theories about them fly faster than a Crinkler engine through space. The one that generates the most gossip is the possibility that the octagon is an alien Rosetta Stone even though it's made of the same baked clay as the Warriors. Lan's parents are put in charge of figuring out the mystery.

"I hardly see them," Lan complains one night.

She's lying on her bed and I'm sitting on her chair as we listen to Diamond Rockler. His voice is like honey—smooth with a thick sweetness. Rockler's heart-melting lyrics fill the small room as a video of him plays on her screen. He's talented and gorgeous and intelligent—that's just not fair. Some people don't even get one of those qualities.

"If anyone's going to figure out what it means, it's them," I say. Frankly, I wouldn't mind seeing less of my parents. They've been asking me to join the crews of people searching through the million fragment piles in hope of finding more octagons. *More data, more data*, my mom's always saying. They're drowning in data, but no one's made any connections. I think they have too much data, but that's me.

"Messages were sent to the other active Warrior planets," Lan says. "The other language experts might have some ideas on how to translate it and they're all looking for their own Rosetta Octagon."

"As long as it keeps everyone busy," I say, smiling.

Lan sits up. "Lyra Daniels, you're not thinking—"

"I am." I insert my tangs into my ears and access the Q-net via the two sensors that were implanted in my brain when I turned ten A-years old. Staying entangled in the Q-net for long periods of time is flirting with insanity. So everyone must be able to completely disentangle. It's the reason terminals are needed to interact with the Q-net. It's funny, to me anyway, that the terminal is a bland plate built into the desk. It's some type of rare metal, but otherwise it's boring in appearance.

Lan's terminal has the same limits as mine, but I've learned how to mask my identity and bypass a few security barriers.

"You're going to get into trouble,' Lan says. But it doesn't stop her from inserting her own tangs to trail me.

"Don't you want to find out who Belle's been hanging out with?" I don't listen to her answer. Instead I concentrate. I view the Q-net as a sphere with a zillion layers, like a universe-sized ball of yarn. And, while I'm blocked from most of the layers, I can find…holes…in the security, almost by feel—it's a strange sensation— and wriggle into an area that I'm not "technically" supposed to be able to access. We call it *worming*.

Video feeds from the cameras around the base pop up.

"Oh my stars, Lyra! You're going to end up in detention if security discovers you."

"Big if. Look, Mom, no ripples."

"How did you…" She sighs. "Jarren, right? He taught you? You're getting better at worming."

I scan the images. People bustle through the hallways. Some stop to talk. The labs techs are busy doing whatever they do. No sound. That would be too creepy. And no cameras in private units. That's an invasion of privacy.

"Found Belle." I hone in on the camera in the canteen. "She's flirting with that chemistry tech— what's-his-name."

"Trevor, but he's too old for her. He's like twenty-three A-years," Lan says. "How do you know she's flirting?"

"She's flipping her hair and eyeing him as if she wants to eat him for dessert."

"For dessert? Really? That's gross."

"Ah youth. So innocent."

She smacks me on the arm with her pillow. "And you shouldn't be spying on your friends."

"Oh? Should I spy on someone else?"

"No." She pulls out her tangs. "We should be planning Jarren's surprise sixteenth birthday party."

I groan. "That's not for another hundred and eighty days."

"Planning," she says with authority, "will be the key to success."

I disentangle from the Q-net and we brainstorm a few ideas. "I think we should have it in a spot he'd never suspect," I say. "Like the middle of a hallway. Or outside the base!"

Just then, Dr. Maddrey pokes her head into Lan's room. "Have you finished your school work?" she presumably asks Lan, but she gives me a pointed look when Lan shakes her head no. Dr. Maddrey leaves the door ajar when she retreats.

My cue to leave. "Better get going, I've a physics test tomorrow that I need to ace now that I'm applying to Brighton University."

"It's two years until the next Interstellar Class ship, what are you going to do for that extra year?" Lan asks.

"I think I'll intern in a bunch of the labs and see if anything catches my interest. Chemistry and biology might be fun. Dr. Nese says he always needs help with keeping the weather instruments clean." And any chance to go outside is always taken. "I'm sure I'll find plenty to do." Even if I have to spend the year reconstructing damaged Warriors. It'll be worth it. And once I get my degree, I could be assigned to a colony planet and interact with normal people.

Lan bounces on her bed. "And my parents already agreed that we can attend the university together even though I won't be eighteen yet!"

The best part. We share a grin. Then I wave a goodbye to the Maddreys and return to my housing unit. The place is empty. Not a surprise, my parents have been busy with the new find.

I settle next to the terminal and access the physics lectures. After two hours, I'm doing head bobs and my stomach growls. However, my parents are still not back. I check their work schedules—yes, they've given me permission—to see if I should wait to have dinner with them or just go to the canteen. Scientists tend to get engrossed in their work so the base has a cafeteria for those too busy to cook a meal. I've seen techs carrying trays back to labs for their bosses.

They both have late meetings and a few "evening" appointments. It doesn't matter that Xinji's sun is still high in the sky, every single colony planet and Warrior planet, as well as the people traveling in space ships, all follow Earth's clock. Days have twenty-four hours. Years have three hundred and sixty-five days (yes, we do the leap years as well). The base's lights and window shutters are programmed to keep Earth time. However, we stopped using the names of the months and days—that would be silly. Instead, we track the year and day. Today is the three hundredth and fortieth day of the year 2471, otherwise referred to as 2471:340.

I was born on 2337:314, and I'm seventeen Actual years old, which means I've lived seventeen of Earth's years. But since I've traveled to two different planets and made two time jumps, one hundred and thirty-four E-years have passed during those seventeen years I've been alive. Boggles the mind, doesn't it?

I scan my parents' agendas idly, noting it'll be a couple days before we have another family meal. Odd that they should be *that* busy. And why are they meeting with Dr. Gage and Dr. Jeffries tomorrow, they don't normally interact. I straighten as my heart sinks. My guts churn as I study their itineraries, trying to dismiss my suspicions. When I reach 2471:360, I'm on my feet. I yank my tangs out and sprint from my room.

talk about it

Let's talk about books.

Join the conversation:

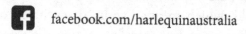 facebook.com/harlequinaustralia

 @harlequinaus

 @harlequinaus

harpercollins.com.au/hq

If you love reading and want to know about our
authors and titles, then let's talk about it.